"GLAMOUR ... SEX ... AND MURDER.
I LOVED IT."
—*Jackie Collins*

Devin Yorke had been married to Paul Bradshaw for four years now. Four years of mega-deals and mistresses, bliss and betrayals, ornate opulence and aching inner need. Four years of getting more than she had bargained for—and less.

Four years to come to the crossroads realization that having everything was not enough if you wanted to find out all you could be as a woman—not just a

TROPHY WIFE

"Generous doses of romance, intrigue and suspense ... perfect reading!" —*Library Journal*

"Sexy and sophisticated ... with a decidedly '90s beat!" —*Literary Guild Bulletin*

"A glamorous world ... great fun to read." —*Chattanooga Times*

"An engrossing first novel."—*American Woman*

"Entertaining ... full of beautiful women, beautiful men, beautiful cars, beautiful clothes, beautiful houses ... greed, ambition, power, and passion in a tale of murder and revenge." —*Pinella Park Press*

…d by the Penguin Group

Books USA Inc., 375 Hudson Street,
…rk, New York 10014, U.S.A.
Books Ltd, 27 Wrights Lane,
W8 5TZ, England
Books Australia Ltd, Ringwood,
…, Australia
Books Canada Ltd, 10 Alcorn Avenue,
…o, Ontario, Canada M4V 3B2
…n Books (N.Z.) Ltd, 182–190 Wairau Road,
…nd 10, New Zealand

…in Books Ltd, Registered Offices:
…ondsworth, Middlesex, England

…shed by Signet, an imprint of Dutton Signet, a division of Penguin Books
… Inc. This is an authorized reprint of a hardcover edition published by
…n & Schuster Inc.
…nformation address Simon & Schuster Inc., Rockefeller Center, 1230 Avenue
…e Americas, New York, N.Y. 10020.

Signet Printing, June, 1996
9 8 7 6 5 4 3 2 1

…yright © 1995 by Kelly Lange
rights reserved

…inted in the United States of America

…UBLISHER'S NOTE
…is is a work of fiction. Names, characters, places, and incidents either are the
…duct of the author's imagination or are used fictitiously, and any resemblance
…ctual persons, living or dead, events, or locales is entirely coincidental.

TROPHY WIFE

⚶

Kelly Lange

SIGNET
Publishe
Penguin
New Y
Penguin
London
Pengui
Victor
Pengu
Toron
Pengu
Auck

Peng
Harm

Publ
USA
Sim

Ⓢ
A SIGNET BOOK

TO MY STURDY BOOKENDS:
Alice — *my mother*
and
Kelly — *my daughter*

ACKNOWLEDGMENTS

Because *Trophy Wife* is my first novel, the people I leaned on for help are legion. Both Devin and I are enormously indebted to the following professionals and good friends of ours:

Fabulous fashion designer **Carole Little,** who provided a wealth of information about the garment industry, and whose Carole Little, Inc. factory in South-Central Los Angeles was the model for Pulled Together; Beverly Hills interior designer **Bette Leon,** who furnished Devin's houses and office complex; brilliant Los Angeles attorney **Hugh John Gibson,** who handled Devin's legal affairs; business maven **Leonard Rabinowitz,** owner of Beverly Hills Jet, who got Devin's private jets airborne; UCLA Medical Center nursing supervisor **Jean James,** who charted Devin's injuries; and the fanciful folks at **Tropical Imports** in Glendale who gleefully choreographed Devin's ill-fated aquatics centerpieces.

Friends who were crowded in my corner handing me cold towels and first aid were my agent **Owen Laster,** who kept whispering sweet words of encouragement; his associate, gorgeous and resolute story editor **Helen Breitwieser,** who insisted that it all make sense; Sergeant **Rey Verdugo** of L.A. Sheriff's Homicide, who kept me honest with police procedure; Captain **Jack Coburn,** paramedic **Joe Kovacie** and the crew of L.A. City Fire's stalwart Engine 97 on Mulholland Drive, who most generously put up with me and my interminable questioning at the firehouse; my editor **Laurie Bernstein,** who worked so hard on *Trophy Wife* that I forgive her constant nagging; her wonderful assistant **Annie Hughes; J. P. Jones,** senior copy supervisor at Simon & Schuster who is, quite simply, a champ; **Verna Harrah,** Co-Chair of Cinema Line Films, who kept shouting, "Story! Story! Story!" in my ear; my business manager **Duncan Smith,** the only numbers-cruncher I know who happens to be a plot wizard; copy editor **Paul Skolnick,** my own personal nit-picker; television news editor **Bart Cannistra,** my computer guru; film producer **Barry Krost,** my cheerleader and super-reader; novelist **Gail Parent,** who's been there, done this, so kept warning me what to expect next; and locksmith **Steve Burger,** who taught me how to pick a lock.

Then there's my pal **Phyllis Marlow,** who actually lived Devin's "fish" story; my jogging partner **Emily Marshall,** whose tale (tail?) I stole about the day she left bandleader **Doc Severinsen** after he softly uttered "I love you sooooooo much!"—but when she looked up he was nose to nose with their dog Arlo. (N.B.: Doc learned his lesson, won Emily back, and they are now living happily ever after on a ranch in San Ysidro, California.) **Karen** and **George Rosenthal,** who put the Pulled Together models on one of their magnificent white Andalusians; and NBC studio makeup artist **Deborah DeAngelis,** whose lovely name I appropriated for a good friend of Devin's, and who makes me up for the news every day, so has to listen and help me work out plot points while I sit in her chair.

THANK YOU, ALL!

BOOK ONE

—◦◦◦—

DECEMBER 1992

1

"*Corinne, I specifically told you seven sharp—you knew how important today is, and it's twenty to eight!*" Devin Bradshaw hissed at her manicurist. A ferocious tension headache was making the left side of Devin's head feel like someone was using a hammer to pound a spike through her skull.

"I'm sorry, Mrs. Bradshaw, but traffic was dreadful in this rain," the woman said, toting her heavy case up the broad curving staircase to the master bedroom suite.

A fierce December storm was dumping water in sheets onto streets and freeways, turning the morning commute into snarling gridlock punctuated by scores of accidents, ranging from fender benders to multivehicle pile-ups. Southern Californians do not know how to drive in the rain.

It was the unexpected downpour that gave Devin the headache, she figured—lately they'd been more frequent and more intense. She'd awakened in the dark at five this morning to the low-volume beep of her digital alarm, the one they'd finally settled on after several trial clocks because it roused *her* without waking Paul. She had set it for an hour earlier than usual so she could get in her workout before the day's wall-to-wall activities began. The dismaying sound of rain pounding on the glass skylights overhead had propelled her onto her feet. Not a word about this deluge on the news last night, she'd groused to herself as she quietly moved across the floor to her dressing room, careful not to disturb her very powerful, very handsome, enormously self-absorbed, rhythmically snoring husband.

She was giving a dinner party in his honor tonight for more than two hundred luminaries here at the eighteen-room mansion they called home. It was to celebrate Paul Bradshaw's receipt of a major government award, which was featured prominently in the national news this week, and the party would double as a presidential fund-raiser.

An homage to her sixty-year-old husband, some hefty
checks to replenish the Democratic campaign chest, and a
huge dose of hard work for the mistress of the manse, the
beautiful thirty-four-year-old socialite Devin Yorke Bradshaw. That's the way she was usually referred to in the
press, Devin pondered, wrinkling up her nose. And now it
was raining!

Even though it was December, this was Southern California, after all, and the weather had been typically mild, so
she'd planned to have champagne and hors d'oeuvres
served outside in the gardens. The trees had been strung
with thousands of tiny Italian lights woven into their
branches. Higham & Johns was to deliver and install two
dozen discreet outdoor heaters that would emit warm flo-
ral-scented air. Several festive bars and food stations were
to be set up this afternoon, and a string quartet in black
tie was scheduled to play show tunes by the pool.

Now what? she thought as she shot a glance through the
French doors to the terrace outside her bedroom. Delicate
ficus trees in earthenware pots were being tossed about,
bent and broken in the angry wind and rain.

The two women had moved into the sitting room of the
master suite, where the manicurist was nervously setting
out her tools, solvents, powders, and polishes on the marble
vanity top. Devin knew she shouldn't blame Corinne for
running late in this storm. Still, she couldn't make herself
ease up on the woman. Corinne should have left home
earlier when she saw that it was pouring, when she knew
that traffic would be impossible. Had Devin been in her
place, that's what she would have done. Now Corinne had
put her nearly an hour behind schedule.

Her skin specialist from Vera Brown's prestigious salon
was due at eight o'clock for waxing, a facial, and a massage.
Since party prepping would have to wait until her nails
were completely dry, Devin had intended to get some personal needs out of the way in the meantime. Her makeup
and hair people would get there in late afternoon, and Tina
Blackwell, the couture manager at Neiman's, was bringing
her dress over at two o'clock—pray God it would be right.
Tina had promised that the alterations would be finished
two days ago, but no! Devin was constantly amazed at how
people just didn't seem to care. Sometimes she felt like the
only good little girl left on earth. And that was lonely.

As Devin sat with her hands outstretched to Corinne's ministerings, her eyes wandered to the graceful peach-and-ivory striped silk chaise longue, and next to it the black glass and brass inlaid table from Didier Aaron in Paris, on which lay a copy of this week's *Time* magazine. Her husband's steel blue-gray eyes gazed back at her from the red-bordered cover. On Monday he had been presented with the distinguished Malcolm Baldridge Award for Humanitarianism in Business by the U.S. Department of Commerce. The President himself, the outgoing Republican to whose campaigns Paul Bradshaw had also been a notable contributor, had been driven over to Commerce from the White House to personally place the medal around her husband's neck.

Paul Bradshaw was the founder and owner of L.A. Garb, the largest manufacturer of sports clothes and accessories in the country. After the city's disastrous riots in the aftermath of the Rodney King beating verdicts last April, Bradshaw had presented a plan to Peter Ueberroth, head of "Rebuild L.A.," to train, employ, and educate a thousand residents of South-Central Los Angeles. His company subsequently rebuilt and refurbished 147,000 square feet of contiguous space on Florence Avenue in the heart of the riot-torn area. There he'd created a huge factory operation, where designers, pattern makers, cutters, office staff, and other employees from his Santa Monica plant started a new L.A. Garb division called Pulled Together, and trained local workers to run it.

Stories in the *L.A. Times,* the *Wall Street Journal,* on local television news, in *Time, Newsweek, People, Forbes, Fortune,* and elsewhere told how Paul Bradshaw had *pulled together* his own competent troops to help displaced workers in South-Central Los Angeles pull themselves and their community together through a new and already thriving business.

Pulled Together put out several lines of casual work clothes, sportswear, sweats, and running shoes, and the label had taken off from the minute it came to market. Each garment bore a hangtag stating that 5 percent of the retail cost of that item would go directly to a special fund to provide social programs and educate students in South-Central Los Angeles. American consumers, appalled by the rioting, looting, and devastation they saw on television and

fearing for their own inner cities, responded to the nationwide publicity attending the launch of the new PT clothing
lines. They got a good feeling when they purchased an item
with the Pulled Together label on it, a feeling that they
were doing something to help. And the President of the
United States gave Paul Bradshaw a medal.

The Secretary of Commerce and his wife, Robert and
Georgette Mosbacher, albeit Republicans, would be in attendance at Devin's party for Paul this evening. They were
friends. And the very popular Democratic President-elect
was in town—Paul Bradshaw had also contributed hefty
amounts to his campaign. Bill Clinton was speaking at a
dinner at the Century Plaza Hotel tonight to honor the new
women senators from California, but a contact from the
Arkansas governor's office had assured Devin that he and
Hillary would make every effort to stop by for cocktails in
the Bradshaw gardens between seven and eight. Perfect,
Devin thought. Hope they wear slickers and rubber boots!

Whether or not the Clintons showed, the attendant circus
was mandatory. Devin was told that, by virtue of their mere
tentative acceptance, several Secret Service agents with
dogs, and a SWAT team, would be coming to the house
this afternoon to inspect the premises and sweep it down
from top to bottom. They never disclosed times of arrival
in advance, she was warned, but they would be here. Telephone technicians would also be coming by to install two
phone lines in the tennis pavilion, and two more lines in a
room that was to be designated for the sole use of the
President-elect. A pair of agents would be left in place, and
no one would be allowed inside that room from the time
the phone installers were finished until the Clintons had
departed the property.

If, in fact, the First Couple–elect did put in an appearance at the Bradshaw home tonight, Devin was instructed,
Secret Service agents (two men and two women) would be
with them at all times. Eight or ten other agents with dogs
would be stationed on the grounds, along with the SWAT
team that earlier cased the place. Also, there would be
officers from the California Highway Patrol, the LAPD,
the Beverly Hills Police Department, and the Los Angeles
County Sheriff's Department stationed along the periphery
of the property. A pair of FBI agents could possibly be in

the mix as well. And, she should know, there would be helicopters from various agencies flying overhead.

Since it would be the dinner hour, the Bradshaws would be expected to provide meals for all of them, whether or not they wanted food. And they should be prepared to feed about twenty to thirty press as well—and she was advised that members of the press corps never turned down food. Devin, with the Clinton people, worked out a plan whereby this whole gang would be offered buffet service in the tennis pavilion. The two land lines to be installed out there were to accommodate the press. The Secret Service, of course, used cell phones, she was told. It had occurred to Devin to ask who would be responsible for the phone bills that a couple of dozen news correspondents would be running up calling Washington, Little Rock, and God knows where, but she let it go. Heaven forbid they should get uppity on her and say never mind, they're not coming. Paul would never forgive her.

Devin was also asked to fax to Washington a complete list of the names, dates of birth, addresses, and phone numbers of everyone who would be at the house tonight, including residents, staff, and guests. Also, she was to inform each person that such a list was being submitted to presidential transition team headquarters. She got all the information to them except the birth dates of her guests. Clinton aides would have to run down those statistics on their own, Devin decided. If she had insisted that each of her guests supply her with the dates on their birth certificates and passports, she knew that only about half the men—and none of the women—would come at all.

As Corinne worked the acrylic paste on one hand to form long, perfectly shaped, simulated fingernails over her own, Devin used her other hand to buzz downstairs. She asked Gussie to bring up fresh-squeezed grapefruit juice, coffee, and one slice of dry whole wheat toast with a little sugarless jelly on the side. Then she spread her computer printout of the day's schedule in front of her and studied it to make sure nothing had been overlooked.

Cocktails at seven; dinner at eight-thirty. The caterers would arrive at four, the bartenders at five-thirty. The twenty-two tables for ten had been set up yesterday and spread with forest green linen. It was three weeks before Christmas—she would acknowledge the spirit of the season with green, without suggesting that this was a Christmas party. It wasn't. It was to curry political favor and to honor her husband for having received the Commerce medal. And it had been her husband's idea.

Maria and Laguya would set the tables this morning with china, crystal, silver, and candles. The florists were due in the early afternoon to arrange flowers for the tables and throughout the house. Mark Janssen, the florist whom Beverly Hills society fought over this season, told her he had an idea for centerpieces that was absolutely dynamite and unique, something her guests had most probably never seen before. And the musicians would be here at six o'clock to get themselves situated and tune up.

Devin had already worked out in her head how to handle the rained-out garden reception. It would have to be moved indoors to the entryway and spill over into the library. Thank God the marble entry rotunda was immense. Most of her living room and dining room furniture had been moved out of the house into temporary storage for tonight's gala dinner, replaced by eighteen of the large round dining tables now set up in those two massive rooms. The other four tables had been placed in the library, but now they would have to be moved out of there to make room for the cocktail service.

The library! One of her favorite rooms in the house now, but only after an enormous outlay of time and money. What a travesty it had been. Before they'd even started building, she'd hired Bailey Senn, one of the premier interior decorators in the country, to do the entire house. And she'd carefully gone over every square inch of the mansion in blueprints with him for endless hours and days, weeks and months, to be sure that each last detail would be exactly right. And still the library had turned out to be a disaster. Not once but twice. Twice Devin had to have the whole room torn out. After the second time, and after she'd gotten a handle on her rage, she took Bailey firmly in hand and told him she was going to *personally show him the meaning of "detail!"*

That week she'd chartered a Falcon 900 from Beverly Hills Jet for a round trip, Los Angeles to Paris. Without saying where they were going, she told Bailey to pack a bag for a few days, and she picked him up in a limousine and took him to Garrett Aviation, the private-jet concourse at LAX.

Fourteen hours later a car and driver met them at Le Bourget just outside Paris and ferried them into the city to the Plaza Athénée on the rue Montaigne, where Devin had booked two deluxe suites. As the bellman showed them to their rooms, she instructed Bailey to get some sleep, freshen up, then meet her in the dining room at one o'clock sharp for lunch.

Devin had preordered. They started with a small *salade,* served with a wine the French call a big white—a crisp dry vintage Corton Charlemagne. And still, Devin wouldn't tell Bailey what they were doing there. Next, with great flourish, their waiter brought the Plaza Athénée's world-famous lobster soufflé for two. After lunch, Devin had arranged for a very special bottle of Château d'Yquem, to be served with assorted fresh fruits and madeleines. Then, after signing the check, Devin steered Bailey out of the dining room and through the magnificent lobby to the front entrance, where their driver was waiting.

The chauffeur whisked them outside the city to the magnificent palace of Versailles. That afternoon, and over the next two days, Devin pointed out sections of floors and ceilings, opulent window treatments, fixtures, fireplaces, and furniture—bits and pieces and areas of the splendid decor at Versailles—to show the celebrated decorator Bailey Senn the meaning of *"detail."* She then gave Bailey the mandate, while keeping the meaning of detail uppermost in his mind, to go ahead and do in her library what Marie Antoinette would have done if she'd had taste.

And now the library was right. The inset bookshelves were right; the stained-glass windows were right. The draperies that were hung at the twenty-four-foot ceiling level and dusted the floors were right. The cherry-wood flooring inlaid with decorative old brass pieces was right; the silk Aubusson rugs were right. The welting on the club chairs was now right.

Even the books were right, most of them bound in rich leather and embossed with gold-leaf lettering. The library was now exactly right, but it had taken the better part of a year and close to half a million dollars to make it so.

She would have those four dining tables moved out of the library to create space for the cocktail hour. They'd

have to be crowded into the living room. There was nowhere else. She'd thought about having them set up in the
massive media game room downstairs, but the forty guests
who would be seated down there might feel they'd been
slighted, relegated to the bottom of the pecking order.
She'd considered doing the cocktails down there, but it
would be awkward ushering everyone downstairs immediately upon arrival. Not right. So she'd just have to jam the
tables together. There was no other way. Damn this rain!

She began looking over her seating charts. They would
have to be revised, but perhaps not drastically, she hoped.
Still, there were some people who simply could not be put
in proximity with other people, not even in the same room.
She'd have to carefully review the entire seating plan now.

At least she hadn't put the place cards out yet—her
schedule indicated that she would do that in late morning
after the tables were set. And of course she would have to
do that chore herself. She always did, to avoid mistakes.
Even then, it could get botched. At her last dinner, one of
their guests, the blowzy third wife of a business associate
of Paul's, had brazenly taken it upon herself to move several place cards around in order to secure more prestigious
seating for herself and her husband. This time Devin intended to put a little dab of Super Glue under each marker
in order to fix it to the tablecloth. Not that Mrs. No-Class
would be here or would ever be on her guest list again.
But one never knew—tonight's crowd would be quite large,
and therefore not completely manageable, so having the
place cards literally *glued* to the linen would give her one
less thing to worry about.

And in case Devin had to change any seating at the last
minute, she could do that: the place indicators were ivory-
colored molded ceramic pieces on which the names of the
guests had been drawn with multicolored art markers; they
could be wiped clean if necessary and new names applied.
She'd hired a Chinese calligrapher to paint the names and
embellish them with flowers. He would stop by at six to
make any last-minute changes.

Corinne was finished, and Lorna was ready and waiting
to do her waxing and facial. She would have to skip the
massage now. Too bad—it might have helped ease her
headache. Devin had hoped she could relax during this
hour, but now she'd have to hurry the session along.

"You've got exactly forty-five minutes to get all of it done," she informed the facialist, more harshly than she'd intended, but her head was throbbing, and her mood was as black as the thundering skies.

Lorna looked distressed but said nothing. She started applying hot wax to her client's legs with deliberately rapid strokes. Meantime, Devin picked up the phone and quick-dialed the private line in Paul's office.

"Good morning, Mr. Bradshaw's office," his assistant Alexandra chirped.

"Alex, it's Devin," she said, skipping the preliminaries. "Please have a couple of workers sent over to the house right away, would you? Tell Paul I need them to break down and move all the tables out of the library, and then rearrange the rest of them."

"Certainly, Mrs. Bradshaw," Alexandra returned, with the coolness that marked all of her dealings with Paul Bradshaw's wife. Maybe Alexandra's frigid manner with her was the reason why Devin never made an effort to be pleasant back.

God, she was tired. She and Paul had come back from Washington on Tuesday, and she'd been working nonstop on this dinner from the minute they'd stepped over the threshold. She'd managed to get only about four hours sleep a night for the last week. Three of Paul's children were coming tonight. And his brother, Sam, with his wife, Lizbeth. All of the Bradshaws hated Devin. They treated her as if she were one of Paul's low-tiered hired help. But on the few occasions when she'd attempted to discuss that with her husband, he'd dismissed her, said she was imagining things.

Devin had met Paul Bradshaw at a dinner party four years ago, when he was still married to Rosemary. In a telephone chat a few days before, their hostess and mutual friend, Muriel Greene, had told Devin she had a feeling that the handsome, dashing, megarich Paul Bradshaw was ready to move out of an old, stale marriage and into a new relationship. "I'm seating you next to him," she'd said. "Just check him out."

These older wealthy businessmen didn't usually break with their longtime first wives until they spotted the prize they wanted next, Muriel had observed. They didn't like to "date around"; that didn't suit their social styles. But if indeed he *was* ready to succumb to the old "thirty-year itch," she told Devin, Paul Bradshaw would be one hell of a catch. Muriel had speculated that it couldn't hurt to present her good friend, the beautiful, talented, icy blonde Devin Yorke, for his appraisal. High-powered hostesses routinely spotted their dinner parties with these kinds of *situations*—it was part of the sport. At cocktails, Muriel had made it a point to introduce Devin to Mr. and Mrs. Bradshaw, and of course Devin had made it a point to more or less ignore the handsome Mr. B. and turn most of her attention to Rosemary. They had a mutual interest, it turned out—they were both auxiliary members of the L.A. County Arts Council.

Paul was tall, trim, and tanned, fifty-six then, with piercing eyes, a smile like lightning, a strong cleft chin, and lavish, wavy white hair. His wife, Rosemary, was also fifty-six, a short, plump, graying, pleasant matron who seemed friendly and eager to please. In her navy blue crepe suit and white shoes, she was a woman whose sense of style had gone into arrested development long before Paul Bradshaw had made serious money, when most of her attention had been diverted to the job of bearing and raising their four children. Rosemary Bradshaw had learned early to ignore her handsome husband's roving eye and roving cock, and as the years went by it seemed the more money he made, the easier that got. After all, he always came home.

Devin Yorke was thirty then, five foot eight, pencil thin and classically beautiful, with sleek luxuriant blond hair that was cropped short at the back of her neck and angled longer in front to just beneath her chin. After graduating from Otis-Parsons School of Design and working as a junior designer at three different fashion houses in L.A.'s sprawling garment district, she'd taken off with her own label, a young, stylish, affordable line of mix-and-match womenswear called Pieces. The garments were designed to be layered on or off, to take a woman through her workday, then out to dinner or to an elegant party. Devin didn't own her company; she had financial backers. But she took home a healthy salary, and she was acknowledged as a fast-rising star in the industry. Devin didn't date a lot of men, and she certainly didn't sleep with any. She had no time for serious relationships; the threat of AIDS ruled out casual sex. And besides, she'd found that too few of the nineties crop of L.A. studs were worth the effort.

Paul Bradshaw had his fill of the young delicious models who posed for the ultrasexy black-and-white ads that had been his creative invention and had captivated the advertising world as well as the buying public. Those women were a dime a dozen, or more precisely, their modeling fees were upwards of five hundred dollars an hour, which price was relative for a man of Paul Bradshaw's means. Off the job they were free, of course, to have lunch with the boss, and maybe "lunch" with him after lunch as well. Paul Bradshaw was one of the most interesting and attractive men in town, certainly, and these "lunches" didn't hurt their potential to be cast for L.A. Garb commercials and print ads. But for Paul Bradshaw, these "lunches" were like Chinese food— an hour later he was hungry again.

That night, seated beside Devin Yorke at dinner, he'd sensed in her a whole other menu item. This goddess in the floor-length sleeveless white silk tunic, her only jewelry the diamond studs in her ears and a sinewy golden snake bracelet wound around the slender upper part of her right arm, which from time to time brushed against his—this vision who was not only beautiful, charming, and poised, and a clever businesswoman besides, but who was actually saying intelligent things to him—was looking very much to Paul Bradshaw like a full-course meal.

He invited her to come to lunch one day soon and tour his huge L.A. Garb operation out in Santa Monica. She did, the following week. And now, four years later, Devin and Paul Bradshaw were married and living in their new 28,000-square-foot, multilevel Mediterranean-style mansion in Beverly Hills with seven in help, and Rosemary Bradshaw was alone in the ramshackle old Tudor house she'd shared with Paul and their children for nearly three decades.

Neither Paul nor Devin had intended it to happen that way. Or maybe they did. This was the way of the nineties. Devin Yorke was a gleaming trophy, and Paul Bradshaw had earned her. And Devin deserved him and the lifestyle that came with him. She'd managed her life with discipline and focus, applying her considerable energy to her education and goals, taking care of her health, her body, and her lustrous good looks, conscientiously tending to her business and her relationships, and resolutely fashioning herself from less than modest beginnings into an undeniably spectacular woman.

Paul was wealthy and generous and crazy about Devin in the beginning, and he was able and willing to take fabulous care of her. And she, in the beginning, was wild about him. Also, she had to admit, she loved being gifted with furs and jewels, being pampered with the best in services and personal care, and flying to exotic vacation spots on the company jet. Paul would beam when he had Devin on his arm; he would show her off with palpable pride. She made him look young and virile. She also made him *feel* young and virile, in the beginning—he'd become a tiger in the marital bed again.

After they'd taken on the outsized task of planning and building the elaborate Benedict Canyon villa, Devin had reached a point where she no longer had time for her career, so she resigned as president of Pieces. Her marriage was her job now, and it was a choice she'd gladly made. And she'd had to work harder at this than she ever had worked before. That was fine—Devin never shrank from hard work. The problem was that this particular work had begun to feel increasingly meaningless.

Today the house was bedlam. By afternoon the storm had worsened, and Devin noticed with annoyance that the army of workers trekking through were dripping water and leaving muddy footprints everywhere. She would have to get Maria and Laguya to go over the floors thoroughly after the heavy foot traffic cleared out. The tables had been rearranged and beautifully set. Yes, they looked a little crowded to her, but it couldn't be helped, and everyone else thought the setting was glorious. She was the first to admit that she was hypercritical—of everything, and especially of herself.

The seating had been an ongoing saga. Her phones hadn't stopped all day, secretaries calling to check directions or dress requirements, then dropping unsubtle hints that their boss had mentioned that he and his wife would love to be seated with so-and-so. One high-powered CEO had actually called in person and confided to Devin that he and his wife were separating, and he asked if it would be all right if he came alone. Fifteen minutes later the man's wife called and asked Devin the same thing. Other guests were maddeningly unresponsive. Regina Montand had not called with the name of her escort—with Regina you never knew. Devin had left blank the place marker to Regina's left, with just the flowers colored in. Hopefully she would catch the name of La Montand's *stud du jour* at the door and have Sun Tang fill it in during cocktails.

Mark Janssen had indeed outdone himself. The house was ablaze with gorgeous floral arrangements, and the centerpieces were going to be outstanding. He'd had three large tanks of exotic tropical fish delivered—vivid red Flame Gourami with metallic blue fins; Siamese fighting fish in a variety of vibrant reds, purples, blues, greens, and pinks; Haplochromas, or Electric Blues, that looked like blue gas-jet flames darting about in the water. Mark had explained to her that the Blues were all female, because if you put two males of this species together they would kill each other. And there were red Discus with turquoise faces and Boesmani Rainbows with streaks of yellows, blues, and greens, looking like saucy Spanish dancers in multicolored ruffled skirts. Mark was going to drop three of these beauties, color-coordinated and compatible, into the flared bottoms of thirty-inch-high gallon-sized crystal vases, with arrangements of white cymbidium orchids, forsythia, and blazing red-flowering tropical heliconia high at the tops to allow the diners to see each other across the tables. Brilliant!

The exotic fish were quite valuable. Mark had paid the Tropical Emporium on La Cienega Boulevard a rental fee to have them "perform" at the Bradshaw dinner. Tomorrow morning he would come over at nine o'clock to transfer them back to their tanks and return them to the store.

Thank God her dress was right. Well, nearly right. It was absolutely elegant, a Christian Lacroix with black puffed sleeves and a tight-fitting bodice of white satin encrusted with seed pearls over a huge skirt done in wide horizontal strips of satin in alternating black and white. She had ordered the skirt to hit precisely at the instep. Unfortunately, it was about an inch longer than it should have been and broke over the tops of her white satin pumps, but she'd have to live with that. If Tina had had the damn thing ready by Tuesday as she was supposed to, the hem could have been taken care of, but it was too late now. She'd have it shortened after the party. There'd be no hurry then because it was a signature dress, so notable that she couldn't be seen in it again for at least a year.

Devin was taking a final walk-through to see that everything was in place and proceeding properly before she retired to shower, be made up, and have her hair styled. It was a little after three. Still early, but she liked to be dressed and ready at least an hour in advance of arrivals to deal with any last-minute glitches, and there were always those. And that's when she'd have to field questions from the world—caterers, valet-parking attendants, bartenders, musicians—and last-minute calls from guests wanting God knows what and expecting to speak to the hostess, of course, as if she had nothing better to do.

That's when she saw the tablecloths. Four of them, in the living room. Presumably on the four tables that had been in the library. The workers from Paul's office had evidently dumped the linen in a heap when they'd broken down those tables to move them, and now the green cloths had been replaced on the tables, each a wrinkled mess. Or so they looked to Devin. That's what happened if she didn't stand over people, she fumed inwardly. She called for Maria and Laguya, who appeared from different directions within seconds.

"Remove everything from these tables!" she addressed them both sharply, pointing out the four with the offending linen. "How in the world could you set these tables with the tablecloths so wrinkled?" she demanded of the two anxious women. "Please put everything—napkins, china, silver, crystal, place markers—over on one of the sideboards until I can press these damned tablecloths."

"I'll iron the tablecloths, Mrs. Bradshaw," sweet Laguya immediately offered, but Devin insisted she would do it herself. She knew that she would be quicker and she would do it right, and time was running out. She didn't want to risk having something amiss again when she came back downstairs after dressing.

As fast as the two women could clear the tabletops, Devin scooped up the linens in her arms and hustled toward the stairway that led to the ironing room. Halfway down the stairs she heard laughing and noise coming from the laundry area, and she remembered that the florist had set up his workers down there. They were using the sinks and the long counters to create the flower arrangements

and centerpieces, since the caterers had the kitchens and
butler's pantry entirely tied up.

She spun around and started back up the stairs, intending
to run up to the master suite and use the iron and wall
board in her room-sized closet. She wasn't watching her
footing over the mound of heavy tablecloths, and she didn't
see the puddle of water in the middle of one of the steps.
Somehow she'd managed to safely skim over it on the way
down, but when going back up onto that same tread, the
ball of her right leather sandal skidded backward over the
water and landed behind her on the step below, throwing
her completely off balance and bringing her crashing down
on the stairs with a reverberant howl, a cascade of wrinkled
tablecloths landing in a heap on top of her.

Laguya, Maria, the florists, and her secretary Peggy all
rushed to the stairwell. Devin, tears in her eyes, was
sprawled on the stairs, clutching her wrist. The pain was
excruciating. She knew it was broken.

2

"**Y**our wife wants us to send two workers to the house
to move some tables," Alex said to her boss, dripping icicles with the words. She was standing in the inner
office suite facing Paul Bradshaw, who sat behind his huge
mahogany desk with the black slate inlaid top, a blend of
the old and the new, the decorative and the functional. It
matched his personality and his persona.

"So send them," he told her, hardly looking up, dismissing her with a wave of the hand.

"Send whom?" Alex persisted. "What employees are so
nonessential that they can take the afternoon off to move
furniture?"

Paul Bradshaw put down the papers he was reviewing,
removed his glasses, and looked up at her. "Alex," he said
with exaggerated control, "I don't give a good goddamn
whom you send. Send a couple of the factory help, send

some drivers, send temps, send my brother, for chrissake! Just do it, and don't bother me with nonsense like this— you know better."

Alex turned on her heel and left his office, closing the door with a bit more of a slam than she'd intended. Lately she was finding it increasingly difficult to curb her antagonism toward her boss. She had worked for L.A. Garb for eight years, since the summer of her graduation from UCLA.

She'd come in as an assistant in the accounting department, until Paul Bradshaw, the company's founder, owner, chairman, and CEO, spotted her and groomed her to be his personal assistant. And his lover.

From the first, she did everything for him, perfectly and just the way he liked it, both in the office and in bed. For two reasons. One, Alexandra Anson was goal oriented, a prototype of the young, upwardly mobile professionals, the Yuppies, of the eighties. The other, she had long since fallen in love with the handsome and dynamic Bradshaw. Her goal, on both counts, was to be Mrs. Paul Bradshaw. And the years went on. Then Paul met Ms. Designer Bitch, finally dumped Rosemary—and married *her*! Devin Yorke! Alex was looking at the big *three-oh* coming up next month. And she was back at square one, exactly nowhere.

Before Devin, Alex had always taken care of the planning, invitations, RSVPs, and preparations whenever Paul and Rosemary entertained. Oh, it was never on the grand scale that Devin's bashes were, but Paul had never liked elaborate parties. Devin, with her at-home secretary and megastaff, was turning him into some kind of society-sucking Ken doll.

Her phone rang. It was Wendy Harris, producer for Maxi Poole, the high-profile newswoman at Channel Six, asking for an interview with Mr. Bradshaw. Alex took the information and said she'd get back to her. She called over to the factory and told Marge, the assistant manager in shipping, to send two day laborers to the Bradshaw home in Bel Air to move some dinner tables. Then she opened her top drawer, pulled out a hand mirror, and stared at her reflection.

A very pretty young woman gazed back at her. Small, delicate features, big brown eyes with thick lashes, full lips, straight, perfect teeth, a wide, sunny smile, and a wealth of dark curly hair. She was five foot four, weighed a hundred and six pounds, had a lithe but curvy body and an engaging, quirky style. She was wearing a charcoal pin-striped Giorgio Armani suit, all business, with a hint of naughty black lace teddy showing at the cleavage. And fun. She was fun; everybody said so. And everybody in the business knew that Alex Anson was Paul Bradshaw's girl in every way, until the chilly blond designer snob came on the scene.

Her confrontation with Paul about furniture movers wasn't about moving furniture, of course. It was about her disgust that Devin Yorke led him around by the dick, or so she perceived. Oh, Alex wasn't blind. She didn't miss the fact that Paul Bradshaw still slept around. But that was the nature of this beast, she knew. He'd slept around on Rosemary, he'd slept around on her, and he was sleeping around on Devin. That didn't change the fact that when Devin said jump, the man leaped through hoops like a dumb teenager. Or that he acted like what had gone on between Alex and him for years never happened at all. In fact, since he and Devin had gotten together, Paul treated Alex more and more like a lackey in the office. Like a slightly sluttish lackey, to be precise. Like she was just a little bit dirty, and he disapproved.

She freshened her lipstick, fluffed up her hair a bit, and replaced the mirror in her drawer, then punched up the intercom and asked if she could come in. At Paul's brusque assent she rose, smoothed her skirt, and went through the door into the inner sanctum.

"Yes?" Paul asked, looking up at her.

"Channel Six would like to interview you tomorrow. Maxi Poole, the anchorwoman. Do you want me to clear your schedule and set it up?" she asked. "Or would you prefer I don't bother you with this kind of nonsense?"

He looked at her long and hard. "Are you on your period?" he finally asked. "Is this PMS? What the hell is wrong with you, Alex? Can we talk about it?"

"There's nothing to talk about," she shot back. "Do you want to do the interview or not?"

Her comment had the effect of a sharp slap across the face. Nobody spoke to Paul Bradshaw like that. Alex seemed to be growing increasingly more hostile. Paul did know why, of course. One day she was his lady-in-waiting— and although he probably should have, he had never discouraged her from thinking so. And the next day she wasn't. One day they'd shared private secrets, and the next she was out of the loop. It was for that reason that Paul put up with her insolence.

He did feel for her, but he'd always figured that at some point she'd get over it. Get over him or whatever it was she'd expected of him. She was cute, sure, and she was funny, and they'd had some good times, but certainly she was never really wife material for him. Hadn't she known that?

And hadn't he taken good care of her? The lynx coat one Christmas, the company car she didn't pay a dime on, the completely paid vacations that he wrote off as business, and more than twice the going salary for her position? Now she was punishing him for Devin, and he didn't like it. She was a damn good personal assistant, that was true, and hot stuff in bed—they'd had a few romps in the hay since Devin. But they'd stopped being regular lovers four years ago, for God's sake, and Alex wasn't getting over it—she was getting worse.

Studying her brazenly insolent expression now, he made a decision he'd been wrestling with. A decision that "the report," which was hidden in his top-secret file, secret even from her, strongly recommended he make.

"Yes, Alex, I'll do the interview," he said then in measured tones. "Set it up, and let me know what time." She said nothing, and went back out the door.

There was a message on her voice mail. She punched in her code and heard Paul's ex-wife's voice: *"Hi, Alex, it's Rosemary. Give me a call, will you?"* Click. Odd, she thought, how her former nemesis was now her pal. Two rejected women, rejected by the same man. A very exclusive club. Rosemary had to know about her ongoing affair with Paul when she was married to him—women always do—but she'd lived with it. Most probably she'd felt that living with it was better than being divorced from him. But Alex and Rosemary had never talked about that. She dialed her number.

"Hi, Rosemary—how are you?" she asked.

"So he's having a big party tonight, huh?" was Rosemary's reply.

"Very big. The President-elect and his wife are coming," Alex confided.

"Well, so are Josh and the girls," Rosemary sighed, referring to three of her four children with Paul Bradshaw. "Will you be there?"

"Don't be silly," Alex replied. "Why would I be there?" In the old days, she always *had* been at the parties Paul and Rosemary gave. Rosemary used to think it was so Alex could help; actually it was so Paul could have his little fun, make eyes at her across the room or cop a feel if they passed in a deserted hallway. Or maybe Rosemary knew exactly why Alex was always on their guest list. It didn't matter now.

"Is there something I can do for you?" she asked the older woman.

"Yes . . . I wonder if we could have lunch?" Rosemary asked. "There's something I'd like to talk to you about."

"Sure. Say when."

They made a date for the following day, leaving the hour and place to be decided in the morning. It would depend on what time the television shoot was set for and how the rest of Paul Bradshaw's day fell into place. Alex always took her lunch when Mr. B. was at lunch.

She spent the remainder of the afternoon setting up the Channel Six interview, juggling her boss's schedule, and fending off people who weren't important, or whom he didn't want to see, or for whom he didn't yet have an answer on something. Between calls, she caught up on his correspondence. She was surprised that he hadn't buzzed her for any reason for a good two hours. Nor had he emerged from his office.

His private line had rung three separate times. Had to be Devin. Only she and his kids had that number. Once Alex had picked up, then pretended it was a mistake and clicked off right away. But she'd heard Devin's voice, whining about something. Alex caught her saying, ". . . the pain is awful!"

Spoiled brat. She probably had a hangnail. And Paul would likely send out the head surgeon from Cedars to treat it. And God forbid the doctor should damage Devin's manicure in the process, or his medical career would be finished among the rich and famous in this town. Alex begrudged Devin Yorke Bradshaw every waking minute of every day. But truth to tell, she would swap places with her in a heartbeat.

She checked the big mottled-copper clock on the wall opposite her desk. It was after six. Everyone else on the floor had left for the day. She had been certain that Paul would leave the office early, to get home to prepare for his big-deal party. She picked up the intercom.

"Can we go over your schedule for tomorrow?" she asked. "I'm leaving soon."

"Yes, Alexandra. Come in," he said. He never called her Alexandra. Maybe she'd been too peevish with him, she thought. She'd make it a point to try harder to tone that down. The party tonight, the medal in Washington, the cover of *Time* magazine, all the other press, the attention he and Devin always got was making her more and more resentful. But as hurt, disappointed, and infuriated as she was with him, she was very much aware that she had what was probably the best executive assistant's job in town. Maybe in the country. Besides, she was in love with her boss, and being around Paul Bradshaw was as essential to her as breathing.

She entered the executive suite, walked around to Paul's side of the desk, and spread his Day Runner out in front of him. Indicating each appointment with her pen, she talked him through his upcoming day. At nine o'clock he had Terry Kenley, his vice president of merchandising, to discuss what they should do about their top knitwear designer. Her last collection hadn't sold well. They would determine tomorrow whether to dump her or keep her, and if they decided to keep her, Paul would listen to whatever suggestions Kenley had to turn the woman's spring line around.

The television interview was set for eleven at the Pulled Together facility in South-Central L.A., so he'd have to leave the Santa Monica plant by 10:15 A.M., she told him. Alex had rescheduled several appointments to free up drive time, plus an hour and a half for the interview and camera walk-through of the factory.

An appointment that he'd told her absolutely could not wait had been moved to the next afternoon; she had reset another for the following week. At one o'clock he had lunch at his mother's house in Mulholland Estates. It was a family gathering that Paul had called, which included his brother, Sam, who was L.A. Garb's chief financial officer, both their wives, and several of their children. Paul had not discussed with Alex the agenda of this family luncheon meeting, but he called them periodically, always at his mother's home, and L.A. Garb being a family-owned corporation, usually they involved family business. Alex suspected that often they simply served for Paul Bradshaw to remind his extended brood whom they should thank for the lush lifestyles they enjoyed.

"Alexandra," he said when she'd finished going over his schedule, "sit down. I want to talk to you."

"Shouldn't you be getting home?" she asked. "For the party?"

"Please sit down," he said again, indicating one of the chairs in front of his desk. Her heart did a little nosedive. He was going to give her a lecture; she could feel it coming.

"Alex," he began, getting right to the point as he always did, "you and I have run our course. It's not working for us anymore. Today is your last day here. In lieu of notice I'm giving you three months' pay plus two weeks' severance pay for each of the eight years you've been with L.A. Garb, based on your current salary."

He was using a tone she was very familiar with—that tone of finality she'd heard so often in business dealings when there was only one side in a given conversation, his side, and he held all the cards.

"I'll be happy to provide you with excellent references," he continued. "I've drawn up a letter of resignation for you to sign." He handed her a letter on company letterhead that she could see he had pounded out at the computer terminal on his desk and printed out himself.

"Unless," he went on, "you would rather be terminated and collect unemployment insurance. You'll still get the benefits I outlined, which amount to seven months' pay at your current wage. It's up to you."

Alex's mouth dropped open in disbelief. "You . . . you can't do this!" she blurted.

"I just did," he pronounced abruptly, as if he'd anticipated histrionics and intended to cut them off cold. He got up and walked over to the closet, removed his umbrella, and headed for the door.

"I'm leaving now," he threw back at her. "Please clean out your office, turn in your keys and parking pass at security, and don't come in tomorrow. Anything of yours that's

left behind will be sent to you. And leave that letter on my
desk, signed—or not, whichever you prefer."

Alex jumped out of her chair and headed him off, throwing both hands flat against his chest to stop him. *"You owe
me!"* she shrieked. "You owe me another chance! We can
work this out!" Angry tears were streaming down her
cheeks.

"No, we can't," he said. "You've been beating up on me
for Devin every fucking day for four years, Alex, and you
know it. I've had it."

"What about me?" Alex shouted. "What about all the
years I've given you . . . everything. . . ?" she stammered.

Paul looked down at her stonily. "Get out of my way,"
he said, brushing her to one side with his umbrella. She
was sobbing now. He strode out the door, through her office, and out into the corridor without looking back.

Alex followed him, in shock. Suddenly she screamed at
his retreating back: *"You'll be sorry, Paul Bradshaw. I
swear to God, I'll make you wish you'd never met me!"*

3

"Why do I have to go, Sam? Tell them I'm not feeling
well. Go without me," Lizbeth Bradshaw argued.
She couldn't stand Devin Yorke, she had never much liked
her husband's brother, and she was uncomfortable around
their crowd of rich and powerful men with their ridiculously
skinny, snobby women.

"For God's sake, spare me," Sam Bradshaw implored.
"You pull this same song and dance every time. You know
we have to go, so please, can we skip the whole hoo-ha
this once? I'm tired, Beth, and I'm not thrilled about going
to their damn dinner either."

Samuel Bradshaw III was sixty-two, a year and a half
older than his brother, Paul. And he'd worked for him for
thirty-one years as his main money man, the CFO at L.A.
Garb. Sam was a very good accountant, but as the company

and its divisions had mushroomed to better than a billion-dollar business over the years, Sam often had the feeling that his department had grown beyond his control, and the demands of many of its complex dealings were almost beyond his expertise. More and more often in these last years, while dealing with young Turks in the world of high finance, Sam had tap-danced as fast as he could and found that he could barely keep up. But he kept that to himself, and his brother kept him in the job.

Paul had also bought and paid for his spacious contemporary house in Trousdale, a tony development in the northernmost corridor of Beverly Hills, inhabited largely by the movie industry's *nouveaux riches*. And the company provided Sam with a good salary, generous yearly stock options, and trust funds for both his children. Paul gave his brother a new car of his choice every year—Sam liked Cadillacs. Technically, it was a company car, but Sam had exclusive use of it, and the company paid all the bills, including insurance, tax and license, service and maintenance, gas and oil.

And Paul had already sent over an early Christmas present—Sony's very latest theater-sized TV monitor for his outsized den, complete with a giant satellite dish that he'd had workmen install on the hill behind Sam's house. Paul knew that he loved the college bowl games during the holiday season. His card read: "Hey, big brother—now you can watch your guys kick 'em through the uprights LIFE SIZE! Merry, merry to you, Beth, and the kids, from Santa."

Santa! Sam resented his brother, Paul, enormously. It wasn't just the money. He resented the fact that Paul was younger, taller, trimmer, better-looking, wittier, more charming, polished, successful, and, yes, wealthier. Much wealthier. He resented that Paul owned what Lizbeth called a truly vulgar mansion in Beverly Hills, a compound on the beach at Malibu, an apartment at the Pierre Hotel on Fifth Avenue in New York, and a ski chalet on Red Mountain in Aspen. And a Gulfstream-4 private jet, a triple-engine, high-performance Scarab offshore racing boat with a crew of three on staff, and a silver-gray stretch Mercedes limousine with his own personal chauffeur. He resented that Paul usually let his driver sit in the lobby of the Santa Monica plant doing nothing all day while he tooled around in his red-hot Ferrari Testarosa, and that he happened to look great in it. And although he would never admit it, even in the deepest recesses of his soul, Sam resented the fact that Paul had the beautiful Devin Yorke and he had Lizbeth.

"I have nothing to wear," Beth was complaining now.

"You should have thought about that sooner, hon," Sam said wearily. "It's after six, and I don't want to be late again, so you'd better get ready."

He noticed that she'd had her hair done. Her silver-gray hair was tortured into such a tight, heavily lacquered 'do that he was sure it wouldn't move in a stiff wind. He wondered why she would spend all afternoon in a beauty salon and pay good money to get her hair to look like that.

Sam was not a happy man. Something Paul had told him today—almost in passing, it seemed at the time—was weighing heavily on his mind. He knew his younger brother well, and despite Paul's breezy style, he knew that his brother never said anything he wasn't deadly serious about.

Sam Bradshaw had a great deal of respect for money. That's why he had become an accountant. But with his brother, Paul, it was never the money. With Paul it was the challenge, the competition, the rush that came with making the deal, the satisfaction of opening markets in new countries, of creating casual, comfortable clothes he could see people wearing everywhere in the world. Paul Bradshaw had never cared about the money, never even thought about it, but it kept rolling in and multiplying. "That's why I have you, Sammy," he'd tell his brother. "To take care of the money."

Tonight, while waiting in the dusky half-light for his cheerless wife to dress for dinner, Sam was feeling that his life was over, that he had a date with the hangman tomorrow at one. His brother had taken him to lunch today, expressly to tell him about "the report." Sam had known that something was up over the last few months, of course, but in answer to his inquiries, Paul had given him nondescript responses that didn't make a lot of sense but didn't have to, because his message to Sam in the subtext was always loud and clear: *This is none of your business.*

Sam was used to that kind of condescension from his younger brother—when Paul had conducted his market research with bankers and had decided to go ahead with the Pulled Together division, Sam Bradshaw, his own chief financial officer, was one of the last to know about it. And just today Sam had found out about "the report." Paul had received the finished report last week, he told his brother, just before he and Devin had left for Washington.

"Christ, Sammy," he said, "it's shades of your old stomping grounds, Price Waterhouse—the damn report is like the Oscar envelopes, top secret. Nobody's seen the thing but me!"

Although he'd been busy with the quick cross-country trip to receive the Commerce medal, the big dinner party tonight, and this and that, Paul told him, the stuff of that report was never far from his mind. He was now ready to act on it, he'd said, and he'd taken his brother to lunch today to tell him about it first. The rest of the family would learn his plans at the meeting tomorrow at their mother's house, away from prying ears at the firm.

Paul had already talked to Regina, he told Sam. He hadn't told their mother what the meeting was about, but she was accustomed to Paul calling these family meetings on a day's notice from time to time. Sam was to be there, and he was to make sure his son, Myles, was there too. Myles ran the company-owned Bradshaw Automotive, a full-service auto shop near the Santa Monica plant that took care of the company's fleet of vehicles, plus all of the family cars, Paul's limousine included, and outside work as well.

Myles Benton Bradshaw, Sam's firstborn, had turned up dyslexic as a child. He'd been slow to learn, had flunked out of Cal State Northridge, but he had a natural aptitude for mechanics, and he'd made it through L.A. Trade-Tech. Sam had his brother to thank for setting up Bradshaw Automotive for Myles. It had been the ideal solution. Myles was perfect to run the shop, and the shop was a perfect place for him. At thirty-six, Myles lived in his parents' guest house. He had no taste for social life, he was happiest on a motorcycle, and he was devoted to his father.

Paul had also told him that Alex would be inviting Sam's daughter to the luncheon meeting tomorrow, if she was in town and available. Allena, Myles's younger sister, was an attorney specializing in the high-stakes music industry, and her work took her all over the world. Devin would be there, he said, and three of Paul and Rosemary's kids. Paul had visibly winced a bit when he said that. Because what he didn't say, didn't have to say, was that his youngest son,

Pauly, *wouldn't* be there. Nobody in the family knew where Paul Bradshaw Junior was.

Paul's chauffeur had driven Sam and his brother, in the torrential rainstorm, over to Michael's in Santa Monica. They'd talked about everything at lunch—the new summer parachute-cloth group for Pulled Together, the big dinner party tonight, their mother's arthritis, who was going to win the Super Bowl. Then, while they were waiting for the check, Paul brought up "the report," and spelled it out for him.

Sam was speechless. The check came. Paul signed it and seemingly forgot about the subject as they made their way through the downpour back to the waiting limousine. In the car, he told Sam that Bill and Hillary Clinton might stop by tonight for cocktails, then he launched into a discussion of the problems the President-elect was facing with the nation's economy. There was no more talk about the Bradshaw brothers' economy, and Sam didn't pursue it. But he knew Paul, and he knew he had heard the death knell of his future. Then, as they pulled up in front of the company's corporate office building in the rain, Paul shifted gears again.

"So, Sammy, tomorrow at one, huh?" he repeated. "Kippie's doing Mexican—your favorite, *chiles rellenos*. You tell Myles I gotta have him there. Alex will get ahold of the rest of the clan."

Paul started chatting about the report again. Sam must have looked crestfallen, because his brother went on about how it was nothing personal against him. Sam wasn't comfortable discussing sensitive matters in front of Julius, Paul's longtime driver, even though Paul had always seemed oblivious to the man's presence in the car. Paul would babble on about anything—problems in the family, high-level business dealings, even his extracurricular women, and all the while Julius would keep his head straight ahead and his eyes on the road.

Sam put a hand on his brother's arm. "Let's talk about this later, okay?" he asked.

"No problem, it's finished," Paul shrugged. "Tomorrow at one, and we'll go from there. And it's gonna be okay, Sammy—it's gonna be fine, and we'll all just get richer." Then Paul gave his brother a bear hug before they both climbed out of the limousine, and that was the end of the discussion this afternoon. The discussion that presaged the end of Sam's life as he knew it.

As he sat in his massive living room now, he focused on what tomorrow held. Not fair, Sam thought. But Paul had all the power. He could do exactly what he wanted to do, and he'd made it quite clear that he meant to do this.

Sam thought back to the exact moment when the balance of power had shifted in his family from him to his brother, Paul. It was when he was fifteen, on the day his thirteen-year-old brother beat him in the regional Contra Costa County swim-meet finals. It was a first. His kid brother had never bested him in a competitive event of any kind, and everyone, even Pauly, had laughed at the time and called it a fluke.

Even now, though, Sam vividly remembered how it felt swimming those last two laps, pushing himself so furiously that he thought his heart was going to explode, and still he couldn't overtake his little brother in the next lane. He kept seeing Pauly's blond head bobbing and splashing, to his right and just slightly ahead.

Later, when they were at home in their room, Pauly told him he shouldn't have kept checking on the other racers; he should swim with mental blinders on, keeping his eyes and mind, his total focus, on nothing but the finish line. That's what Pauly did. And from that day forward, Paul Bradshaw always finished first.

Early in his senior year at Stanford, Sammy was dating beautiful brilliant Cathy Carroll, a prelaw student. Until he brought her home for Thanksgiving and she met his younger brother. Paul was a junior at Berkeley, a track-and-field star and a campus leader who always managed close to a 4.0 grade point average. Sam would never forget the day his brother said he needed to talk to him, man to man. Paul took him totally by surprise when he told him that he and Cathy had been seeing each other and they were in love. By early spring each had lost interest in the other and had moved on to new relationships, but not before together the two had ripped out Sammy's heart.

Sam had been kept out of the service because he had flat feet. Paul served for two years in Korea as an Army lieutenant and had come home a hero to Martinez, California, with a bullet wound that had decimated his left clavicle

and the Distinguished Service Cross for leading his platoon
out of a firefight in the freezing hills of Inchon.

By then Sam had gone to work as a junior executive for
the accounting firm of Price Waterhouse in San Francisco.
After the war, Paul came home and started a business with
a pal of his from Berkeley, the son of Eugene Ziffren, a
prominent and well-to-do womenswear manufacturer in the
Bay Area. The partners had been staked with a $20,000
loan from Ziffren Senior, and they rented a full floor of
factory space south of Market Street in San Francisco's
seedy Mission district.

The new company manufactured trim for the garment
industry—hooks and eyes, zippers, cloth flowers and appli-
qués, studs and sequins, buttons and bows. It was an industry that Paul Bradshaw had known nothing about but made
it his business to learn from top to bottom. Within five
years, Z&B Trim was selling product nationwide, and the
company was worth close to a million dollars.

Paul Bradshaw sold out to his partner and moved his
young wife, Rosemary, and their new baby girl to Southern
California, where the Los Angeles garment industry was
second in volume only to that of New York's Seventh Avenue. It was 1960. Jan and Dean, Roni Spector and the Ro-
nettes, and the Beach Boys were telling young Americans
that L.A. was the place, that La-La Land was where all the
fun was, and Paul Bradshaw, would-be surfer, sailor, and
beach lover, was drawn southward to find his place in the
sun. He was twenty-eight years old.

He invested his money in a struggling young company
that was making baggies—funky oversized tropical-print
swim trunks for men—in a two-story brick building near
the beach in Santa Monica. Less than a year later, Paul
Bradshaw owned the company outright. That small line was
the beginning of the now world-famous, extremely profit-
able California sportswear company L.A. Garb.

That's when Paul had asked his older brother to move
down from the Bay Area and come to work for him. Tonight,
thirty-one years later, Sam Bradshaw was regretting that decision. Yes, he was comfortable. More than comfortable. Yes,
he and his family had the best of everything. But somewhere
along the way he'd lost his own identity. Lost it to his kid
brother, the guy who took care of their parents all through
their father's illness. The guy who, after the elder Samuel

Bradshaw died, had moved their mother down here, bought her a house, and now was paying all her bills. His younger brother, who took care of Sam's own family, of Sam's own kids, and who made Sam feel impotent. Somewhere in the course of the last three decades, Sam had lost himself. And after lunch tomorrow, Lizbeth, the kids, and the whole damn family would also know that Sam Bradshaw should never have left Price Waterhouse, should never have moved here from San Francisco, and had managed to fail, at this late date, as a businessman, a husband, and a father.

Oh, he loved his brother. They were blood. But he hated him too. He hated him because his whole life had become a reflection and repetition of that day at the Martinez Civic Pool, when the coach pinned the regional finals first-place ribbon on Paul Bradshaw's T-shirt. Sammy was supposed to step up and receive the second-place ribbon that day. Instead, he ran to his mother's station wagon, crawled into the back seat, and waited there until his family got in and they all went home.

Funny, Sam remembered now, his brother had just wanted to win the swim meet, but young Sammy wanted the hundred-dollar prize, an enormous amount of money back then for the middle-class Bradshaw family. Even now he had to admit that as callously nasty, as facilely corrupt, as his brother could be, greed had never been one of his seven deadlies. That's because money had always come easily to Paul, Sam reasoned—his brother had simply never much concerned himself with it. Power was Paul's aphrodisiac. Sam was the one obsessed with money. Which, of course, was what had led him into money handling as a profession.

If there had never been a kid brother, Paul, Sam Bradshaw was convinced his life would have been entirely different and a whole lot better. That's the way he saw it when he contemplated these larger issues, usually in the dark night of the soul after four or five martinis.

Beth was ready to go now, and in fact she looked very nice in her ankle-length black silk skirt and silver-beaded top. She was a handsome woman, really, and Sam knew he should be proud of her. She was tall and large-boned and always maintained a regal bearing. She was one of the San Francisco Allenwoods, an old-money family who'd operated shipping concerns out of the port of San Francisco back in the Roaring Twenties.

But she was sixty-one, and she looked it. She wasn't interested in face-lifts or skin peels, hair dyes or exercise classes. She wanted to grow old gracefully, she always said, and she was doing that. People admired Lizbeth Bradshaw. So why wasn't Sam Bradshaw proud of her, or satisfied?

It was the comparisons, always the comparisons—to his brother's success, his brother's wealth, his brother's life, his brother's wife. And by comparison, on all levels, Sam Bradshaw came in second, and had every day of his life since the regional finals at the Martinez Pool.

Beth held out her black mink jacket to him, and he slipped it around her shoulders. Rain was coming down with a vengeance now, and the wind-chill had turned it into pounding hailstones for a time, a rarity for Beverly Hills. Beth was wearing sensible shoes—she wasn't about to ruin a pair of silk evening slippers in a downpour like this, she said.

He knew she didn't want to go. And he *really* didn't want to go. Neither of them relished facing the inevitable comparisons, on yet another evening at yet another of Sam's brother's wife's dazzling dinner parties. Indeed, a dinner to honor Paul for great humanitarian deeds, for being recognized by the President of the United States, and for being on the fucking cover of fucking *Time* magazine. But he had to go. Because his little brother was his fucking boss.

Sam wished he could shake his black mood. He flipped on the windshield wipers, backed the Cadillac out of his garage, and skidded the big machine around into the driving wind and rain. And his mind flashed on a terrible thought: *A man could have a hell of an accident in weather like this!*

4

Devin stood on the stairs, looking down at her beautifully dressed, perfectly coiffed guests mingling in the entryway. The musicians, seated on the landing just below her, were playing selections from the score of *Phantom*. Tuxedoed waiters were circulating with trays of cold drinks and hot hors d'oeuvres. Everything seemed to be going as well as could be expected.

She was stunning in her black-and-white Lacroix, her sleek blond hair styled high at the crown and swept up at the sides with diamond clips, but the effect was palliated by the bulky plaster cast on her arm. The first gasps she'd heard from most of her guests were not "How divine you look!" but a variation of "My God, what happened to you?" The answer she'd repeated contained no mention of wrinkled tablecloths. She would simply smile and mumble something about a tennis accident and wave it off. Only one had looked askance and blurted out, "Tennis in this rain?"

"A nondisplaced linear hairline fracture of the right distal radius," Doctor Silverman had called it. Devin called it six weeks in a fucking cast. It produced a weird combination of discomfort—it was painful and it itched at the same time. The doctor had prescribed ice packs and elevation. She prescribed vodka and codeine. At the moment, she was feeling no pain.

It was past time to serve dinner, but Devin was delaying, still holding out hope that the Clintons would show. Four Secret Service agents had arrived late this afternoon to check out the premises and the guest list, and now they were mingling, but that didn't ensure that the First Couple–elect would arrive.

Paul had come home from work in a foul mood. No trace of it now, she noticed, as he stood by the fountain, handsome in black tie, chatting up Los Angeles mayor Tom Bradley and his wife, Ethel. Paul would do about three minutes with "Hizonner," Devin predicted, since Bradley was now a lame duck, having announced at a recent press conference that he would not be seeking another term.

The tables looked gorgeous. Mark's tropical fish were a stroke of genius. The seating had been a bear, but creative in the end, she thought. She'd particularly amused herself by putting Céline d'Orsay next to the womenswear designer who everyone knew was having an affair with her husband. The designer's name was Robert. Maybe Céline would get it and extricate herself from that disastrous marriage before she was laughed out of circulation, Devin thought.

It was a quarter to nine. She'd have to start nudging people inside to the tables soon and give Andres the green light to begin the dinner service. Paul had moved on to

Marva Modine, she noticed—the gorgeous leggy manne-
quin who was this season's top model in L.A. Garb's sen-
sual print ads. Marva was barely wearing a clingy gold
metallic shift with spaghetti straps—the dress was about a
foot and a half long in its entirety. She weighed ninety-
something pounds, and her legs were about eight feet long,
Devin noted. Her skin had a tawny glow, and her voluminous mane of streaked blond hair was tousled to distrac-
tion, creating the illusion that she'd just tumbled out of
bed. Or maybe she had.

As Paul backed Marva further into a corner, Devin made
a mental note never to invite this vamp to the house again.
Not that that would make any difference, she sighed. She
watched Marva throw her head back and laugh while putting a hand seductively on Paul Bradshaw's chest. The girl
was no dummy—she knew who was buttering her bread.
Devin turned and continued up the stairs. She needed to
pop another Tylenol with codeine before dinner.

God, she thought, how many more of these do's could
she do! Or even attend? How many more times could she
pack her bags and travel by her husband's side to New
York, to Washington, to the tropics, to the snow. Yes, she'd
known what she was getting into, and she didn't expect
sympathy from anyone—women around the world would
trade places with her in a second, she knew. But for Devin
it had become a total overwhelm. Her nerves were termi-
nally frayed. She was snapping at the help. She didn't like
herself lately. She was ignoring her friends. She was working all the time. But the work was without substance—it
was all frills.

She walked into her enormous peach-and-ivory marble
bathroom—it was larger than the entire studio apartment
near MacArthur Park that she had rented during her years
at Parsons. What had happened to her dream of making
stylish, comfortable, affordable clothes for the working
woman? she lamented to her reflection in the massive mirrors. She had been well on her way, productive with her
growing business, content in her small, tasteful Wilshire
Corridor condo by then, working long hours, seeing good
friends, taking in plays and movies, reading the latest
books, exhausted but satisfied at the end of the day.

The only thing her former life had in common with this
one was the exhaustion. But it was a different brand of

tired. Back then she was often weary but always fulfilled; now she experienced a kind of fatigue that drained her spirit and left her empty. *What's wrong with this picture?* she asked the beautiful woman in the mirror. And when had she stopped having fun and turned into a consummate bitch?

She sometimes wondered if Grace Kelly had ever had these same doubts. A hardworking actress suddenly whisked off to become a princess. A classic Cinderella story. Women all over the world had envied her. But what about the private Grace? Devin was sure she'd had to work even harder as the wife of Monaco's potentate than she ever had as a movie star, but with a totally different set of rewards. Had Princess Grace, Devin wondered, ever looked into her palace mirror and questioned *her* choice? She must have.

Swallowing another pain pill, Devin closed her eyes as she felt it go down, and focused for a minute on the throbbing in her wrist. She'd been thinking a lot about the single-career-woman-versus-major-league-wife dilemma lately, and she had a pretty good idea which side she was leaning toward. But like Princess Grace, she'd made her choice, and along with the cons there were plenty of pros. Just look at this damn bathroom, she smiled sardonically— a family of six could live in it, and it was all hers! Pros and cons. Good and bad. That was *life,* wasn't it? It was the way things were, and she had to accept it. Or not.

In the beginning it *was* a fairy tale for her. Devin Yorke's own personal Cinderella story. She'd fallen passionately in love with the handsome, urbane, witty, rich, powerful, interesting Paul Bradshaw, and it was the stuff of dreams when he'd swept her off her feet and made her his princess. She'd loved every second of it back then. When he walked into a room, her heart would stop. When he touched her hand, a hormonal surge would raise her temperature. Everything about him was thrilling. She was in heaven sitting next to him on an airplane headed for Rome, or walking barefoot with him on Santa Monica beach on a Saturday afternoon.

Back then, she saw only the good things. In the raging wildfire of early love, she reflected, we see what we want to see. Also, she reminded herself grimly, Paul had *shown* her only the good things then. Powerful, intelligent, charming, sociopathic men are brilliant at that, so who could blame her for falling for him? Now, after four years of up close and personal, she saw past all that into the heart and soul of the real Paul Nathan Bradshaw.

So Devin Yorke, working girl turned trophy wife, had learned another of life's hard lessons. It didn't matter who you were—Grace and Rainier, Gable and Lombard, Tristan and Isolde, Cinderella and Prince Charming—the intensity could not endure. The magic *always* evolved into real life. Had they lived, even Romeo and Juliet would have found that out. Happily ever after was only in books and movies, and when reality set in, it had better be a reality you wanted to live with. And just maybe it shouldn't be about giant bathrooms, she ruminated. Maybe all this beveled glass and Italian marble didn't make up for his coldness, his lies, his humiliating cheating. That was what Devin found herself debating lately as she contemplated her fourth year as Mrs. Paul Bradshaw.

The Tylenol and codeine mixture was working—the pain in her wrist had eased back to an ache. God, what a day from hell this had been, every waking second of it, exacerbated by that incredibly stupid fall on the stairs. She'd refused to allow the accident to hold her up for a minute more than necessary. Each person on her staff was working like ten on the dinner-party preparations, and she would not pull one of them off to take her to the doctor. She drove herself, steering with her left hand and holding her useless right below her breasts, close to her body, shielding it from further assault. Peggy had located an orthopedic surgeon just a mile from the house on Roxbury Drive in the flats of Beverly Hills. An X ray, a quick set, a prescription from the pharmacy on the ground floor of the building, and she was out of there. Thankfully, it wasn't a severe break, just a hairline fracture. But it had put her further behind schedule.

Wheeling her Jaguar back up the curved cobblestone driveway to the villa, she was more annoyed with herself than hurting. And in her haste, and in the driving rain, and dealing with the bulky cast, not to mention the effects of the pain pills that she'd downed as soon as she was out of the drugstore, she'd bumped up against the back of Paul's little Ferrari. Her houseman had moved her husband's pride and joy to the end spot in the eight-car garage just to make sure it would be out of harm's way, far from the big refrigerated trucks, the florist vans, the generators, and what have you that were coming and going all day. Devin had stooped over in the rain to examine the back end of the red Ferrari. Luckily, there seemed to be no harm done. Paul cared more about that damn Ferrari than he did about . . . no, she wouldn't even finish that thought.

Nine o'clock. If dinner got any later it would be a social gaffe. Face it, the Clintons weren't coming. She freshened her lipstick, dabbed some powder on her nose, and gave her décolletage a quick spray of Giorgio. She straightened her shoulders and mentally prepared to get on with it. She was the general; her troops were downstairs waiting on her orders.

As she walked back through the master bedroom she flashed on a delicious idea. What if she just got out of her dress, kicked off her shoes, turned up the electric blanket on the down-covered oversized bed, and crawled under the covers? Never to be seen or heard from again tonight. What would happen? The cocktail hour would go on. And on. People would start wondering, getting antsy, commenting to one another. They'd drink too much, they'd be hungry, and they'd get cranky. Then Paul would come looking for her. And she'd be asleep. She chuckled, then picked up the phone on her night table and pressed the intercom number for Andres' station in the kitchen.

"We're going to go ahead with dinner now," she told him. He was aware that she'd been stalling for the possible arrival of the Clintons. "I'll prod them to their tables, Andres," she said. "Prepare to serve the soup tureens in exactly ten minutes."

"Yes, Mrs. Bradshaw," Andres returned. He'd been through this drill with her many times.

Devin swept down the stairs then, pausing on the landing to speak to the musicians. "Pick up the pace, now, would you?" she instructed. "We're about to serve dinner, and I need some marching music to get people into their seats."

She descended the rest of the staircase to the final strains of the theme from *Miss Saigon,* then smiled with satisfaction as the quartet launched into a rousing rendition of "On the Barricades" from *Les Miserables* as she moved from group to group, urging her guests toward the elegant dining tables.

*   *   *

Devin surveyed the room. She'd placed herself at a table in the living room, and Paul with a group in the dining room. They would swap places between the entrée and dessert. Funny, she thought, it was impossible for her to stop working for a damn minute. She was the producer, director, choreographer, set designer, musical director, head chef and bottle washer. And ironer, she noted with chagrin, glancing down at her injured wrist. Somebody had to do it—how come it was never the guy? The hostess's job was to do it all; the host's job was to be charming and have a wonderful time.

She'd seated Paul at a table with the Mosbachers and three heavy-duty industrialists and their wives, couples who could be counted on for checks for the Democratic coffers. And for the Republican war chest, Bob Mosbacher knew, if called for at the next society fund-raiser they graced. Devin had put a good friend of hers with them: sexy, off-the-wall actress Debra DeAngeles, who'd come alone. Debra would liven up that group, give them something pretty to look at, and balance the table. Paul always got a kick out of Debra, and Debra, at the moment, was between men.

At the far end of the living room, at a table near the French doors to the patio, she'd put the gold-clad, leggy supermodel Marva Modine on the immediate left of Paul's brother, Sam. Just to make the uppity Lizbeth uncomfortable. Paul would never get it. Sam wouldn't get it. But old Beth would! And on Sam's other side, she'd put his mother. Regina, the Bradshaw matriarch. Paul was her favorite, and subtlety was not her strong suit. Devin could see the woman's heavily made-up face, arch disapproval etched upon her angular features as she talked into her older son's ear. Possibly nagging Sam that he should exercise, take off twenty pounds, be more like his brother, Paul. Devin loved it!

At the next table was Sam's son, Myles, with another one of his loser dates, a gum-chewing, leather-clad, airhead aerobics teacher from Redondo Beach, in high-heeled boots, with pink-and-orange spiked hair. Actually kind of cute. Devin had to smile. She wondered if Myles did it just to piss off his mother, or if he was really attracted to women like this. Probably a little bit of both, she guessed. Myles was in leather, too, making his usual statement in the black-tie crowd. Devin smiled again. Pouring outside, and the couple had arrived on his Harley, both drenched to the skin, but Myles had bitched to the valet squad that the cycle had to go under cover to protect it from the rain. Wonderful!

Seated at the same table was Myles's sister, Sam and Lizbeth's younger child. Named for her mother's family, the San Francisco Allenwoods, Allena Bradshaw. Such a fascinating girl, Devin thought, watching her now, sitting erect, smiling, chatting, charming, definitely the drawing card at that particular table. But you couldn't miss the other side of Allena, Devin mused, which was probably the linchpin of her appeal—a little smug, superior, certainly bored, and no one knew what really went on in her head. A fascinating *girl*? Devin corrected herself. This was a woman! Thirty-two, Devin knew, just two years younger than herself. And bright and successful, a prominent attorney on the music scene. Devin had always felt that she'd like to know Allena better. What a foil to her brother, the rock 'n' roll listener! Here was a rock 'n' roll lawyer, but dressed in parchment crepe Ungaro, understated and tasteful, beautiful and reserved. No date. Allena seldom had dates. In fact, Allena was rarely in the country. And almost never with her family.

And Devin had seated Alan Cranston, the outgoing senior senator from California, at her own table, which had caused a huge flap between herself and Paul. Cranston had recently left office when his term ended under a cloud stemming from the Lincoln Savings and Loan scandal. Paul hadn't wanted to invite him, but Devin had insisted. Alan Cranston had been a friend of Paul's for decades, and he was now a friend of hers. They both knew Cranston to be an honorable man, she'd argued, and you don't abandon a friend because his image is tainted. Devin had put him on her left, a place of honor, to show the Bradshaws' support for the man.

She did give in to Paul on the salad. She liked to serve greens after the entrée. He contended that this wasn't Europe, that Americans liked their salad before the main course, and serving it after was an affectation and a waste, since nobody wanted it then. Fine. Salad had been served. Andres' staff was now bringing around the steaming individual cachepots of seafood with shiitake mushrooms *au vin* in puff pastry.

Her attention was diverted by a splashing noise in the middle of the table. It was coming from the centerpiece! One of the tropical fish seemed to be flapping uncontrollably at the water's surface. A beautiful red-ochre dazzler with wide yellow stripes. She watched in horror, as did the rest of the guests at her table, as the frantic splashing slowed, then stopped, and the brilliant fish sank like a stone to the bottom of the vase. And lay there, perfectly still. Quite obviously dead.

As the diners paused and digested this occurrence with ill-disguised dismay, one of them with a fork full of *seafood* suspended between dinner plate and mouth, the late tropical centerpiece pièce de résistance, its tiny body already permeated with gasses emitted by the decaying process, slowly rose toward the surface of the water in the vase, bubbles emanating from its epidermis, as ten sets of astonished eyes followed its progress until it lodged among the stems of the floral arrangement at the top.

Just her luck! Devin thought. They gave her one with a bad heart! She cleared her throat and flashed a wan smile around the table, attempting to break the tension.

"Guess it was, uh, just his time," she sort of tittered. Jay Savage, Paul's urbane president at L.A. Garb, jumped in to help her put the table at ease.

"Tough break, Devin, but he's in heaven now, swimming around at the big presidential dinner in the sky," he grinned, eliciting semiembarrassed laughter. Slowly the guests resumed eating, trying valiantly to ignore the tail of the brilliant red dead fish undulating in the water being stirred up by the other two fish swimming in the vase. The survivors. But not for long.

Moments later, just as the diners at her table thought it was safe to dive back into their seafood compote, tropical fish number two, a neon green number with navy blue splotches on its back, went into the same convulsive splashing mode, then dropped like dead weight to the bottom, pausing for a bit before it, too, began rising in a hail of bubbles to a watery grave among the flora, close to its deceased colleague.

Devin looked around in alarm. Her worst fear was instantly realized. Conversation had virtually stopped, and most eyes were riveted to the bottoms of the fourteen centerpieces on the tables around the room. *All the damn fish were dying!*

Suddenly, one of the guests jumped to her feet, knocking her chair over backward. It was Mary Steenborne, a well-known environmental activist with the National Sierra Club.

"They're not getting enough oxygen!" Mary shouted, and she ripped the orchids and companion flowers out of the top of the vase at her table. "Remove the flowers! Remove the flowers!" the woman demanded, waving a dripping bunch of exorbitantly expensive blooms in her fist, hell-bent on saving the lives of the extant fish.

Most of the dinner guests were paralyzed. Devin threw down her napkin and rose just as Paul emerged from the dining room, a set smile on his face and murder in his eyes. Devin leaped into the hall and bounded through the double doors of the main kitchen, with Paul at her heels. She called out for Maria and Laguya. They were both in the butler's pantry, helping Andres with dessert.

"Run immediately, get the waiters to pick up all the centerpieces off the tables!" she fairly screamed at the astonished women. "And pull the flowers out of the vases! The fish are dying!"

While the two women tried to assimilate that startling piece of information, Devin looked down at the desserts they'd been assembling on serving trays: two hundred and twenty delicate crèmes brûlées baked in small white French dishes that were shaped like—fish! Devin had chosen them to carry out Mark's tropical fish theme.

Someone behind her was tugging on one of her giant puffed sleeves. She whipped around, annoyed. It was Bruno, their French butler and house-man.

"Excuse, please, Mrs. Bradshaw," he stammered, obviously flustered, while outside the mansion's massive front doors, several dozen members of the Washington press corps were sloshing in the mud and trampling the flower beds.

"Please, Madame," the hapless Bruno persisted, "the Monsieur and Madame Clinton—*they are arrived!*"

5

Marva leaped up in bed. She thought she'd heard a noise at her window, extraneous to the pounding rain. She was alone in her ground-floor apartment. It was probably her imagination, she decided, or perhaps some woodsy creature snapping twigs outside, darting for a dry place to wait out the downpour. She lay back down, closed her eyes, and smiled as she thought again about the hilarious debacle at the Bradshaws' dinner party that evening. She was just beginning to doze when she heard the sound again.

This time there was no mistaking—something was actually striking the windowpane of her corner bedroom. Marva froze. She reached into the top drawer in the nightstand next to her bed and removed an ebony-handled .22-caliber snub-nosed pistol, a gift from an aging actor she sometimes dated. The stylized gun had the look of an antique, but in fact it was new, it was in perfect working order, it was loaded, and Marva was an expert shot.

She leaned on her elbows, holding the poised pistol in her left hand, and cocked it. Then listened. And heard it again. Someone seemed to be tossing handfuls of dirt, or pebbles, hard against her bedroom window. Then she thought she heard her name being called, softly. A reflexive chill gripped her body. She'd always feared that some pervert would spot her, follow her home, case her habits. And now, since she'd become highly recognizable because of her sexy, glitzy L.A. Garb print ads, she felt even more vulnerable. Maybe it was time to move to one of those heavy-security high-rise buildings on Wilshire Boulevard in Westwood. She could certainly afford her own condominium now.

"Maaaar-va," she heard the whispered call again, and this time the voice sounded vaguely familiar. She got up, clutched her short creamy-silk nightshirt close with her free hand, and noiselessly moved to the side of the window, keeping the .22 pointed toward the street. She peered out through the slim opening between the black pine shutters and the window casing, and was astonished at what she saw. On the soggy grass directly below her window stood Paul Bradshaw, still in his tux, his bow tie undone and hanging loose, his ruffled dress shirt open at the neck. Rain drenched his hair and drained in rivulets down his face. Marva lowered her shooting arm and opened the shutters.

"What the hell are you doing here?" she mouthed, keeping the gun below the sill and out of sight.

"I want to see you. Can I come in?" he called, grinning a little sheepishly.

"Wait a sec," she said, holding her index finger up, then closed the shutters again. She went over to the nightstand to the right of her queen-sized bed, slipped the gun back into the top drawer, then bent down to the shelf below and turned off the volume on her answering machine. She would probably get a call in the wee hours—she usually did—and she didn't want Paul Bradshaw hearing the sweet nothings that would be meant for her.

She darted into the black marble bathroom off her bedroom and ran the hot water tap. After patting some moisturizer on her face, she reached into a drawer, took out a sponge and a tub of MAC, and quickly smoothed the bronzing makeup over her forehead, cheeks, chin, and throat. She dipped her little finger into a pot of color and dabbed it on her lips. With a brush, she fluffed and tousled her hair, giving it that "just tumbled out of bed" look that no woman gets by just tumbling out of bed. She gave it a quick spray to hold it, but loosely.

Then she ran a washcloth under the steaming faucet and sponged under her arms and beneath her crotch. She was not big on the appeal of the natural, earthy, sweaty scent of a woman. She believed in enhancing her pheromones with expensive oils, musks, body creams, and perfumes. She picked up a bottle of Gale Hayman's ultrasensuous Delicious and spritzed it in her hair, on her neck, down the front of her body, and between her legs. The whole regimen took less than two minutes. Satisfied with the result, she moved slowly to the front door and opened it.

Paul Bradshaw had a bottle of champagne in one hand and two stemmed glasses in the other. He'd apparently gone to his car to get them. Beyond the low hedge that surrounded the apartment complex, Marva could see the top of his red Ferrari, lit by a streetlight and glistening in the rain. This should be interesting, she thought. She opened the door wider and he lumbered over the threshold, dripping puddles onto the bleached pine floor.

"Wait here," she said, putting a hand up to stop his progress into the living room. "You're drenched. *Don't move,*" she exhorted in her sultry cadence, taking the chilled champagne and glasses out of his hands. His eyes followed her long languid body as she set the wine and flutes on a low coffee table and moved out of the room, while he obediently remained rooted to the spot. She reappeared in a minute with a wooden hanger, some towels, and an oversized white terrycloth robe.

"Take off your clothes. All of them," she said, offering the hanger.

"Right here?"

"Right here," she echoed. "What's the big deal? There's nobody here but me, you're soaked, and I don't want you tracking water all over my place. I'll hang up your tux to dry."

Marva set the robe and towels on the black granite credenza in the entryway. Then she went over and sat on the edge of the couch and deftly twisted the wire off the champagne bottle. She popped the cork and poured herself a glass, raised it toward him in toast, then sank back into the overstuffed down sofa cushions. She lifted her long legs up onto the smoky glass coffee table and crossed her bare feet at the ankles, wiggling her red-painted toenails. After indulging sensuously in a long, appreciative sip of the champagne, she looked up at him expectantly and watched.

"Well?" she threw out after a long moment. Paul still stood just inside the front door, still holding the hanger, still dripping.

"Well, what?" he rejoined.

"Well, take off your clothes," she challenged. Paul Bradshaw was of another generation, twice removed from hers, and clearly not comfortable with stripping in a living room he'd never been in, in front of a woman he'd never been intimate with. She guessed that he belonged to the soft-music, candlelight, champagne, get-a-little-drunk-and-ease-into-it school of romance, even around the women he cheated with.

Marva was patently enjoying his discomfort. She was an upper-hand kind of woman. Maybe it was because she came from money and was unimpressed by it. Maybe it was because she was so stunningly beautiful. Or maybe it was because she was so inaccessible. Even in the act of having her, men got the feeling that they couldn't have her. Not really, not completely. Everything about Marva Modine, including her flirty, flaunty, come-on moves, set up a need in men that made them crazy with desire.

Always she toyed with them, and if she deigned ultimately to make their lustful dreams come true, if it suited her, still they never felt they had her. Though she was true to what she advertised—aggressive, bawdy, down-and-dirty between the sheets—her chosen were always aware that, on some level, something in her was holding back, even laughing at them. Except for one lover who came and went, and who had that selfsame effect on Marva.

She was aware that Paul Bradshaw had desired her since the day her agency had sent her to the Santa Monica plant to audition for her first L.A. Garb shoot. But Paul Bradshaw could have lots of women, and he was married to the ultimate woman, so he wasn't as weak-kneed and obsessive about Marva as most of the men who wandered into her web. He no doubt knew that he would have her in time, and they both had been enjoying the game. He was probably here tonight only because of the fiasco at their dinner, with the Clintons there, no less. He must have been furious.

"Come on, take 'em off," she was taunting him now, pouring herself more Dom Pérignon.

He set the hanger down on top of the entry cabinet, threw his tuxedo jacket on top of it, and began slowly releasing his onyx studs. Reaching behind him, he unhooked his black satin cummerbund and tossed it on the table. He took off his dress shirt, revealing a cotton tank top beneath. Chippendale's this wasn't, Marva chuckled to herself; men his age wear undershirts. The phone rang.

"Who the hell would be calling you at two in the morning?" he asked, looking annoyed.

"Lots of people," she smiled, ignoring the ringing. It stopped, and they both heard the machine click on. He started to unzip his fly.

"Aren't you going to help me?" he queried, taking a couple of steps toward her.

"Uh-uh-uh-uh!" She raised her eyebrows and pointed a finger at him, like a mother reprimanding a wayward boy. "You're all wet. Take everything off, including your shoes and socks, dry yourself with those towels, put on that robe, and *then* you may come over here and have some champagne."

Marva watched him do exactly as he was told, and he reminded her not of a little boy, but of her father. Her father who'd tried so hard to understand her but never could, just as he could never understand her mother, his second wife. Her mother was sixteen years younger than her dad, of aristocratic French parentage, and exotically beautiful. And obdurate. She had to have the handsome and wealthy American businessman Marvin Modine—until she got him. After two years and one child, she left him, and left her toddler with him, and moved back to Europe.

Marva had seen her mother only once in the ensuing years, and that was four years ago when she was doing a shoot for Paris *Vogue*. She'd stayed on after the job was finished to track down her mother. It wasn't difficult; Magritte de Batiste had been written about often over the years. She was on her fourth marriage, to an expatriate Austrian count, and living in Provence. Marva managed to reach her by phone, and Magritte arranged to drive in to Paris and meet her only child for lunch at the Ritz.

When the woman walked into the posh dining room, there was no mistaking her identity. Marva was looking at a more mature, more graceful, more sophisticated, even more beautiful version of herself. Her tall, perfect body was richly draped in a chic ecru silk Chanel suit; her gloved hands had reached out to embrace her daughter. Marva's mother was thrilled to see her, she'd said. And absolutely overwhelmed by how beautiful she was.

Her mother knew both the maître d' and their waiter by name, and she ordered for them both. Her mother was gracious, warm, witty, charming, endearing. She asked about her father, her half sister Gabrielle, and her own life, hopes, and dreams. After lunch she signed the check, kissed her daughter warmly, and reiterated how wonderful it was to see her. And excused herself, saying she had weekend guests at home. Acknowledging people at several tables on the way, she rushed out the door. And Marva went into the restroom and threw up.

Paul Bradshaw stood before her completely naked now and asked for permission to move.

"First," she said, "take one of those towels and wipe up the muddy water you've drizzled on my floor. Wipe it properly—you missed a spot," she admonished, brandishing her glass.

He scoured the pine boards. Even with the most powerful of men, Marva Modine had all the power. For as long as she wanted it. Which usually wasn't long.

Marva had informed him that nothing at all would happen unless he put on the condom she provided—this was the nineties, after all, and safe sex was de rigueur. Paul Bradshaw did as he was told. Their lovemaking had been efficient, mechanical, perfunctory. In midstroke, Marva's bedside telephone had rung again. Paul had barely noticed; Marva had smiled. Afterward, she'd feigned a contented sleepiness and rolled over, pulling the black satin jacquard duvet cover up beneath her chin, leaving him alone to wriggle into his damp clothes and find his way out. Now he was gone, and she lifted the gun out of the drawer and idly toyed with it as she picked up the phone receiver, tucked it between her ear and her shoulder, and dialed.

"Hello, darling," she breathed after a moment, propping herself up against the pillows. "How are you?"

After a moment, she launched into entertaining patter about the Bradshaws' calamitous dinner party, the arrival of the President-elect and his wife in the very middle of this high farce, and how Paul Bradshaw had shown up outside her window in the rain. She laughed raucously as she described the paces she'd put him through. Yes, she said, she was looking into her crystal ball and could see a little Alpha Romeo Spider in her next L.A. Garb contract.

Then she listened. And smiled, and purred. Settling back into the pillows, with her free hand she began fondling her swollen nipples, gently, slowly. Then she moved the other hand, still holding the pistol, over her stomach and down between her legs. Tenderly, she stroked her creamy wet clitoris with the pistol's ebony handle. She closed her eyes and emitted little moans.

"Yes, darling," she whispered. "Oh tell me. Tell me." Her hand worked deftly, quickening the rhythm, working the smooth, gleaming black wood around the lips of her vagina until she threw her head back and screamed aloud with pleasure.

Then she was quiet. She murmured responses into the phone. Finally she whispered dreamily, *"Oui,* my love. Until tomorrow. *Adieu."*

6

Inhale ... "Shhhhhhh-it!" Inhale ... "Shhhhhhhhhhhhhhh-it!" Devin Bradshaw intoned rhythmically as she pulled up seventy pounds, doing sitting leg lifts on a Nautilus machine in the Bradshaws' well-equipped gym. She easily hauled more than half her own weight, but John Tanner, her personal trainer, wouldn't increase the amount because he wanted her toned, not bulky. They would have to avoid upper-body training today, until he could design some maneuvers that wouldn't aggravate her fractured wrist.

"Shhhhhhhhhhhh-it," she grunted with each exhalation, and Tanner, who was exercising the same muscle groups on a facing twin machine using a hundred fifty pounds of weight, started chortling. The more she cursed, the harder he laughed, and it was breaking his stride, messing up his breathing. He barely finished the twenty-five reps along with her, then he threw his head back and broke up in a paroxysm of laughter.

"What is this?" he gasped, reaching for a water bottle. "Why are you swearing like a sailor at six-twenty in the morning? Is the rain getting to you? Does your arm hurt? Is this workout that tough? Are you hung over?"

"No, no, no, and no," she responded petulantly, wiping her face with a towel, not sharing his amusement. After a beat she offered, "My posh dinner party last night turned into a giant train wreck!"

"That bad, huh? How giant?" he managed to sputter before he started laughing again. Then he noticed that she was close to tears.

Devin had been referred to John Tanner two years before by a woman she'd met at a gallery showing of Roaring Twenties American art. They'd stood next to each other for a long time in front of an early abstraction in oils by the poet e. e. cummings. Something about that colorful canvas had held the two women. At some point they'd struck up a conversation.

"It actually looks like his poetry, doesn't it?" the Titian-haired woman remarked quietly to Devin, without taking her eyes off the painting.

"I love it," Devin had replied. "I didn't even know he painted."

"Oh, all his life. I'm Gabrielle," she'd said then, turning to Devin for the first time and extending her hand.

"How do you know so much about e. e. cummings?" Devin had asked, wanting to know more about the work and the artist. The young woman told her that she worked for Sotheby's in decorative arts—it was her business to know. They chatted about the piece, turning their attention back to its bold swirls and boxes and circles, its myriad brightly colored geometric shapes.

"What does it say to you?" Devin had asked.

"Um ... I see a pear, I see a banana, a round basket of tomatoes, an orange Popsicle, and that brown and yellow blob in the upper right corner is a hamburger. But that's just me," she chuckled. "I see food everywhere!"

She was outgoing and pleasant, close to her own age, Devin guessed, with fresh skin and a huge untamed mane of red curls, maybe fifteen pounds overweight, but stylishly dressed and very pretty. She asked Devin what *she* saw in the painting.

"As a matter of fact, I see high-tech exercise equipment, and the aura of bright colors I imagine your body puts out when you're going full tilt in a vigorous workout session."

Both women laughed. Gabrielle, or Gabby as she said she was called, commented that any explanation of abstract art always said more about the observer than about the piece. Devin confirmed that her daily workout was almost as important to her as breathing, and for the first time in her life she no longer had to go to a public gym, because now she had the luxury of a state-of-the-art gym right in her new home. It had two of everything, Devin told the woman, because it was designed for her and her husband to exercise together, but he was a workaholic and he rarely set foot in the place, she laughed, except to plant a kiss on her head on his way out the door. Working out was probably on her mind because she was currently looking for a personal trainer to come to their house every morning, Devin said.

"Wow, I've got just the guy for you!" Gabby had exclaimed, and Devin got the feeling that this gregarious woman probably had just the right person for absolutely everything.

She'd gone on to explain that a client of hers was moving to Dallas, and she'd been complaining to Gabby that what she was going to miss most about L.A. was her daily exercise partner. He was a man who'd put himself through college by working as a personal trainer, and now that he had a "real" job, he still trained one lucky client just to help himself keep rigidly to his own workout routine. It had to be at some ungodly hour of the morning before he went to his office, Gabby had said, but maybe that would work for Devin. No, she didn't know what he did for a living, and no, she didn't remember his name.

"But trust me," she'd confided, "I saw him once and he's drop-dead gorgeous, with sandy brown hair and a body to die for. And my client, by the way, is totally buff!" Gabby took Devin's number and promised to check with her customer to find out if this stud was looking for a new client to train.

On the following day she'd left his name and number on Devin's answering machine, along with another litany of praises that had come from Gabby's customer. Devin was intrigued and called the man. John Tanner. They'd met in her home gym and talked about the equipment and her workout needs.

Six A.M. was fine with Devin; she thrived on discipline, and she liked the idea of having that kind of pressure to make her get up early every morning. And the twin his-and-her machines suited Tanner perfectly because, as he'd explained, he would be working the program right along with her. And since they were both exercise fanatics, they would have a session every morning. Nowhere could she find another trainer willing to work seven days a week, she knew.

She'd bought the e. e. cummings abstract, and she bought John Tanner for the time between six and seven-thirty every morning. He was a lawyer, but he rarely talked about the law. He'd made it clear that he didn't want to talk about his cases or his clients, and Devin didn't push.

Now she was near tears, and Tanner's brow furrowed. "What could be so terrible about a simple dinner party?" he asked.

"There was nothing simple about this one," Devin said weakly, and she went on to recount the whole gruesome story, until he could no longer maintain his demeanor of concern and burst out laughing again.

"I'm sorry," he muttered, making a valiant attempt to stifle a smile, because it was apparent that Devin was devastated.

When she got to the part about the Sasheen Littlefeather–type animal activist running amuck, carrying huge sloshing bowls of fish, dead and alive, trailing water and expensive cut lilies and orchids on the tables and the rugs, he lost it.

"I've seen that movie," he laughed hysterically. "Jamie Lee Curtis in *A Fish Called Wanda.*" Tanner's taut six-foot-three frame was doubled over on the exercise bench.

"Then the Clintons came ..." Devin continued soberly.

"The *who?*" he screamed. "The Bill Clintons, as in our next President and his wife?" he gulped, and dissolved into fits again.

Devin smiled weakly. Then she began to laugh. Then she roared right along with him as she recounted how she was lying to Mrs. Clinton about the way she'd fractured her wrist, while all hell was breaking loose around them, and both Clintons just stood there looking uncomfortable, like they had inadvertently wandered into a loony bin and were casting about for a graceful way to escape.

"So there I am with one good hand, trying to run these dying fish to the kitchen sinks in a six-thousand-dollar Christian Lacroix that's too long, so I keep tripping on it. My guests are horrified and can't eat the seafood, of course. And my husband is furious," she recited forlornly, intermittently howling in spite of herself as Tanner choked with laughter.

"It's probably in the paper this morning," she gasped now. "In the 'Stupid' section—Liz Smith or something. I have to meet Paul for lunch at his mother's today. Now *there's* another great laugh, his *mother,* oh God ..." and she was racked with laughter again. She caught her breath and babbled on, "Just pray none of the family mentions the fucking fish . . ."

Suddenly they heard a door upstairs slam shut with ferocity. The front door, Devin realized. Tanner quieted down and looked at her quizzically.

"That would be my husband," she said, her frivolity vanishing instantly. It was the first time in their marriage that Paul had left for work in the morning without kissing her good-bye.

7

Billy Hilgarde sat in a scarred, torn, caramel-colored vinyl chair in front of Paul Bradshaw's desk. It was a rare occurrence when the big boss came down to South-Central, and Billy was determined to get through to him today. He didn't have an appointment, but he'd sweet-talked his way past his friend Ruby Johnson, the production manager's assistant who assisted Mr. Bradshaw when he was here. He'd flashed Ruby one of his big engaging grins and promised he'd take just five minutes of the man's time, ten minutes max—it was important, he'd told her; it was for the workers.

Billy had celebrated his thirtieth birthday the night before. A bunch of the gang at Pulled Together had surprised him with dinner and some crazy birthday presents at his favorite restaurant, Maurice's Snack 'n Chat on Pico Boulevard, where Maurice Prince, the woman who owned the place, made the greatest pan-fried chicken and spoon bread on earth. And forget about her fresh banana pudding and cream!

He smiled now, thinking about last night. He hadn't a clue in advance about the surprise party. Henry Lewis, who ran the shipping department, had steered him to Maurice's for an early supper, and he was bowled over when about thirty of his pals at the factory jumped out of Maurice's kitchen yelling *"Happy Birthday!"*

Billy was six foot six, a strapping young black man with an outgoing personality and a broad, Magic Johnson smile. He was serious about his career in the garment industry. His mother wondered when he was going to get serious about meeting the right woman, getting married, and starting a family. He had a naturally sweet nature that came from her, a hard-work ethic that came from his father, who'd been a sound technician at CBS Television City on Fairfax for twenty-five years, and he had a deep concern for social justice that came from both of them. His infectious, offbeat sense of humor was entirely his own.

Everyone at Pulled Together knew that Billy Hilgarde was trying to unionize the shop. He'd brought organizers in from the ACTWU—the Amalgamated Clothing and Textile Workers Union—to speak to the workers in the employees lounge and explain the benefits of belonging to the union. Now he needed to get Mr. Bradshaw's ear. He'd been trying to nail down an appointment with the man for a couple of months, but Alex Anson, Bradshaw's eyes, ears, and right hand in Santa Monica, kept putting him off. "He's too busy this week," she'd say. "We'll get back to you." But she never did. So he'd planted himself in this chair for a half hour before the CEO was even due to show up, and he wasn't going to leave until he'd said what he needed to say.

Paul Bradshaw was on the phone. He was doing a good job of ignoring Billy, though he hadn't actually thrown him out of the office. But inwardly he was furious with Ruby for letting Hilgarde in. The last thing Bradshaw needed in his company was the unions. First the ACTWU would come in, then the ILGWU, the Teamsters, and the rest of them. Unions were firmly entrenched in New York's sprawling garment district, but they hadn't been able to get a solid toehold in Los Angeles beyond a few of the older, smaller companies, and he sure as hell didn't want them in his operations, either here or at the Santa Monica plant.

He'd come to the Pulled Together factory in the pouring rain this morning because Maxi Poole, the anchorwoman from Channel Six, was going to interview him here about the new, already enormously successful division he'd started in South-Central L.A. after the April riots. His policy to employ mostly blacks, and kick back 5 percent of the retail price of each garment to fund community programs for inner-city kids, continued to attract media attention. They were to do a thirty-minute interview about the business, then he would take the newswoman on a walk-through of the site while her camera crew recorded.

It was after eleven, and Ruby had buzzed ten minutes ago to tell him that the television people were in the outer office, waiting to set up. It wouldn't do to get caught by the press tossing this young, idealistic labor organizer out the door. Bradshaw finished up his call, put down the phone, and squared off to face Billy Hilgarde.

"Okay, now we'll grab the five minutes you asked for, Mr. Hilgarde," he said, forcing a smile, checking his watch. "But you don't have an appointment, and I've got people waiting, so we've gotta be fast. What's up?"

"I think you know I want your assurance that you won't oppose attempts to make Pulled Together a union shop, Mr. Bradshaw," the young man said.

Paul had done his research on Billy Hilgarde when he'd first been informed of his union-organizing activities. Tom Brandt, his vice president of production, had recruited Hilgarde from GUESS? to start up and run PT's marking department, and the guy was doing a remarkable, truly innovative job. Most garment manufacturers still did their marking by laying out the separate sections of a pattern in each size on blueprint paper, then twisting, turning, and fitting them together until they'd arranged the most possible pieces on a given cut of cloth. Next, they traced the outline of the pattern sections on the paper. Then a copy of the marked blueprint was set up on top of several layers of fabric, and the garment was cut according to the pattern tracings. Billy Hilgarde was a computer whiz, and he'd programmed the young company's entire marking operation on computer. Now the parent plant was looking at Hilgarde's technique for possible adaptation by the marking department at the giant L.A. Garb factory in Santa Monica as well.

"Billy," Paul Bradshaw said to him now, "you've got a great future with this company. You're making top dollar, and you are very valuable to us. I have big plans for you. Tom told you I'm considering elevating your job to a management position—then you wouldn't even be eligible to belong to a union. Why are you so intent on bringing the unions in here?"

"It's not for me, Mr. Bradshaw," Billy responded. "It's for the troops. The rank and file. They came in, they trained, they learned, they're working a lot of extra hours, and they're turning out a hell of a product for you. They deserve fair treatment and decent benefits, don't you think? I'm sure you can see that this company can only be helped by keeping the workers happy."

"GUESS? is putting out terrific product," the chairman rejoined. "Its people are happy, I assume. That's where we got you—you were doing well there. GUESS? doesn't have unions. You never made any attempt to organize while you were there. Why us?"

"It's simple," Billy returned evenly. "There isn't a job at GUESS? that pays only minimum wage. And their benefits are top of the line. Health coverage. An excellent dental plan. They give maternity leave, they run a day-care center, they have a retirement plan. We have none of that at PT."

"Well, we'll get it. We're new. Our start-up costs are astronomical, and we're not proven yet," Bradshaw protested. "Give it time, Billy."

"Mr. Bradshaw," Billy asked him then, "do you have any idea what it's like to try to live on the minimum wage today? On about a hundred-and-forty dollars a week after taxes? To support a family on that?"

"Yes I do, Billy," Bradshaw said. "That's how I started—"

"I don't think so, sir," Billy cut him off. "You had the benefit of a college education. And a loan to start your first business. I appreciate what you're doing here for my people, Mr. Bradshaw, but they need a living wage, and dignity, or you'll lose them."

"Oh yeah?" Bradshaw snapped. "Where are they gonna go?"

"I don't know," Billy said thoughtfully. "They have skills. They can get other jobs."

"In this economy? Are you so sure?"

"No," Billy responded, "but the sad fact is they can actually do better on welfare. You'll rob them of incentive if they can bring home more money by not working at all," he went on. "This company is young, everybody has high hopes, and now is the time to get off on the right foot."

Paul Bradshaw had had enough of this. There was no way that Hilgarde was going to convince him to support union organizing at Pulled Together. He had thought that if he talked to him a bit, dangled hope of a promotion, he could appease him, put him off, satisfy him that the company was going to take care of him and would come through for the workers without the unions if he'd wait. But this guy just kept on coming. He was a black Jimmy Stewart, for chrissakes! Only he didn't understand that this wasn't the movies. This was business.

"Look, we'll talk again," Bradshaw said firmly. "I have a television interview to do, and they're waiting out there. Let's have lunch one day next week out in Santa Monica, and we'll continue this. Call my office and we'll schedule a day."

"No you won't," Billy said quietly. "I've tried that route with Alex Anson. That's why I sat in here today without an appointment. When I found out the TV news people would be here."

"What the hell do you want?" Bradshaw asked, bordering on angry now.

"I can't negotiate with you for adequate wages and benefits for your workers," Billy answered, "so I want to bring the unions in here to do it. I want your promise that you won't oppose garment-industry unions at Pulled Together. Then we can have an easy transition, and you'll be able to negotiate with the company's elected union leaders, to their satisfaction and yours."

"Or what?" Bradshaw asked, fury glinting now in his steel-gray eyes.

"Or I'll tell Maxi Poole what really goes on here," Billy intoned. "I'll tell her that despite the cover stories, and the hero worship, and the medals they're pinning on you, this place is no better than a sweat shop, and the black workers that you purport to be *pulling together* and helping are actually being exploited by you for profit."

The two men regarded each other in silence for a moment. This kid had giant balls, Bradshaw thought. "Is this a threat?" he asked finally.

"No, it's a strategy," Billy said. "I've read a lot about

you, Mr. Bradshaw, and I know that you've always used strategy to your advantage in business."

"Billy," Bradshaw said then, "this is a white-owned but black-run operation. That's what I intended from its inception, and that's the way I set it up. You're young, you're bright, you're educated, skilled and ambitious. Most of the workers here are green, most never saw the inside of a factory like this until we opened up and trained them. You, on the other hand, have invaluable experience in the garment industry. You're one of my key players. It's conceivable that you can one day be president of Pulled Together. Why are you so willing to toss that away, risk pissing me off, for something I won't give you and that wouldn't do you a damn bit of good anyway?"

"First of all," Billy answered without skipping a beat, "because I'm giving you credit for being the humanitarian your press notices say you are. And second, because I have to do it for my brothers. They're not as strong as I am. You're right, most didn't have the advantages I had. If I don't help them, then I lose what my dad taught me is the most important thing I have. And that's not money, or things, or the potential presidency of this division. It's my self-respect."

Billy Hilgarde was either very good at playing hardball, Bradshaw mused, or he was actually sincere. Touching, but totally unrealistic. "So if I don't sign this, do you intend to make some kind of a scene out there?" he asked, cocking his head toward the outer office where the television news crew was waiting for him.

"I don't make scenes, Mr. Bradshaw," Billy said. "What I'll make is an appointment. For a press conference. Where I'll not only tell Channel Six, but everyone who'll listen, the other side of the story of the prestigious and highly acclaimed Malcolm Baldridge Award Winner for Humanitarianism in Business."

"And what the hell is that supposed to mean?" Bradshaw shot back, his eyes narrowing.

"It means the *big unmentionable* around here," Billy Hilgarde returned, not shifting his eyes from Paul Bradshaw's feral stare. "Laborers getting paid for six hours on the clock and putting in eight or ten."

That struck a nerve with Bradshaw, who put both hands on the edge of his desk and strained his body forward.

"That's bullshit," he roared. "Fucking bullshit! No one here is asked to work any longer than they're clocked."

Billy didn't press the issue. What they were talking about was against the law. It was a dangerous topic, and both men knew it.

"Or we can go forward here at PT with real humanitarian conditions and even greater success," Billy went on quietly. "Then I'll tell *that* to the media, and I'll support you a hundred percent. The choice is yours. I hope you'll do the right thing."

Bradshaw was livid. He almost never lost, and he was losing this one. To a black kid who wouldn't back down, even though by all good business standards Hilgarde had nothing to gain and everything to lose. The man would not go away, and he would not be put on hold. It was nearly eleven-thirty. The television crew was waiting.

"Well?" Billy Hilgarde challenged him. "Do I have your support, sir?"

Bradshaw straightened up and glared at him. "Get the fuck out of here," he hissed. "Get out of my office, Hilgarde, before I break your balls!"

8

"This guy has to be really busy," Reporter Maxi Poole remarked impatiently to her crew.

"This guy has to be really rude," Wendy Harris, her producer, retorted.

"Second that," their cameraman, Pete Garrow, spit out with a disgusted shrug.

The three had been waiting in Paul Bradshaw's anteroom for forty minutes. Time is crucial in the television news business, and this was an especially busy news day, because when it rained in Southern California all hell broke loose on the streets and freeways. Wendy had the six o'clock show to produce back at the station's Burbank studios, Pete was needed on the street to cover breaking news, and Maxi was behind schedule getting this interview on tape and the piece written and edited before she prepped to anchor the Six. With massive cutbacks in the business shaving news personnel to the barest minimum, none of them could afford to waste time waiting on an interview subject for a feature story.

"Come on, Maxi, let's split," Wendy urged.

"Yeah, fuck him, we're doing him a favor and he doesn't have the courtesy to let us know why he's held up or how long he's gonna be," Pete said, making moves to gather his camera gear. Both of them looked to Maxi for a decision.

"The only thing that makes me want to hang in is the chance to put him on the spot about the fish that committed suicide at his dinner party last night," Maxi chuckled.

"Can't wait till you nail him with that," Wendy laughed wickedly. "Better save it till the end, though," she cautioned.

"Oh, of course," Maxi agreed. "If he throws us out, at least we'll have the interview in the can."

"Did you see the A.M. show on Channel Eight this morning?" Wendy asked. "They had this huge tank full of tropical fish labeled *DEAD FISH LOOK-ALIKES,* and Dr. Bruce, their medical editor, explained with a straight face exactly how the Bradshaw fish expired. He put his hands in the tank and pointed out which species would have keeled over first and why—he was showing their gills and stuff!" Wendy howled with laughter.

"Shhh," Maxi warned, glancing up at the closed inner office door behind which Paul Bradshaw, garment industry mogul, noted humanitarian, *Time* magazine cover-story subject, and killer of fish, was ensconced.

"Yeah, and Howard Stern was all over it like a cheap suit on the radio this morning when I was coming in," Pete snickered. "Who the hell leaked it so everybody had it by morning drive time, even in New York?"

"*Everybody* leaked it!" Maxi grinned. "I'm sure half the people at the party couldn't wait to get out of there and phone their favorite news contacts. Debra DeAngeles called me at midnight last night, and she couldn't stop laughing. Evidently Bill and Hillary Clinton, the dinner guests coup-of-the-month, arrived just as the fish were dying at the tables!"

"Oh yeah, the *world* had this dish before the sun came

up," Wendy giggled. "I mean, think about it," she ran on in her rapid-fire staccato. "The overnight producer at Channel Eight had to find a contact who knew a tropical-fish vendor so they could get him to open up the place before the morning show and set up Dr. Bruce with a tank of fish in the studio. We're talking massive, early leak!"

"And we're talking a guy everybody loves to hate," Pete put in. "New York has Donald Trump, and we've got Paul Bradshaw. Why the hell are we doing this piece on him anyway, Maxi?"

"Martin," Maxi shrugged. It hadn't been her idea to do a story on the well-publicized altruistic accomplishments of the socialite chairman of L.A. Garb. Their new news director, Martin Berman, had assigned the three to do a quick piece on Bradshaw to capitalize on all the ink he'd been getting since the President presented him with the Malcolm Baldridge medal this week. Berman was a hardworking, hard-driving import from the CBS-owned station in Chicago, well known in the industry as the market most committed to hard news in the country. Growing up in Southern California, in one of the bedroom communities of the sprawling San Fernando Valley, he was a news junkie even as a kid. He'd worked his way through USC's School of Journalism by gofering at Channel Six in Burbank, then he went off to work at a series of stations after graduation, moving steadily up the news ladder to better jobs in bigger markets. Now he was home, he was the boss, and he had a lot to prove. His mandate from upper management was to reverse the ratings slide that had been going on for a year at Channel Six. Berman felt strongly that the way to do that was to cover the news, Chicago-style.

"Chicago is a *news* town," he'd told the division president at his job interview, "and L.A. has always been a *lifestyle* town. But when the nineties rolled in with horrendous economic chaos, L.A. turned into a news town, but this station didn't get the memo."

That statement and philosophy nailed the job for him. Los Angeles stations had traditionally given their viewers what cynics in the business labeled "rock 'n' roll news"— light on world and national issues, heavy on local crime, racial tension, and car chases on the freeways—starring blond anchorpersons, glib sportscasters, and weather comics, and liberally peppered with show-biz reports and cuddly animal stories. Today's L.A. viewers didn't give a damn anymore about a cat trapped up a tree, Berman told his troops, because its *people* were trapped on the streets of skid row, sleeping in packing crates in the rain.

And actually, his plan for the station reflected his own deep-rooted personal views. His parents were hardworking liberal Jewish professionals, his father a pediatrician and his mother a high school teacher, and they'd instilled in him not only the drive to get ahead but also the responsibility to give back. Although he was a young bright Yuppie firebrand who would first and foremost get the job done, whatever it took, Martin was pleased that the only M.O. in these deep recessionary times was to serve the viewer, to help the people. Had he arrived in La-La Land in the middle of the eighties, the decade of excess, he would not have been above dishing up sex, drugs, and Is-Elvis-Really-Dead stories on his newscasts, if that's what got the station ratings. But he was glad that it wasn't. And as Martin Berman had explained it to Maxi this morning, much as he had no use at all for a fat cat who got a medal from a lame-duck Republican president, if a story on L.A. Garb's Pulled Together operation in South-Central Los Angeles turned even a few of the station's minority viewers on to potential jobs at the man's new factory, he wanted it on his air. It fit into Martin's big picture: he would make Channel Six the station of record for the real news, news you could use because it affected your life, your kids, your health, your wallet. What he hadn't explained, but Maxi understood, was that when he had the station's news operation revamped in that mode, viewers would flock to Channel Six, the ratings would go up, Martin Berman would be a hero, and he'd climb even higher up the corporate ladder. And buy himself a Porsche. Everybody wins.

"Okay, I'll call Martin and see if we can blow this pop stand," Maxi told Pete and Wendy, pulling a small cellular phone out of her oversized tote bag.

Just then they heard a loud voice from inside Bradshaw's office. Moments later a tall, athletic-looking young black man burst out of the door, slamming it shut behind him. Eyes straight ahead, looking at no one, he strode resolutely through the anteroom and left. Maxi dropped the phone back into her bag, and the TV crew turned six expectant eyes toward the closed office door. They spun around in unison when the stylish black woman who'd greeted them on arrival walked into the room. Wendy quickly glanced at the clipboard on her lap, where she'd jotted down the woman's name.

"Hi, Ruby," she said, flashing her trademark ebullient smile. In less than desirable circumstances, Wendy Harris was the most diplomatic of the three. "What's happening?" she asked.

"I'll see if Mr. Bradshaw's ready for you," Ruby responded with a worried look. "Sorry for the delay," she threw over her shoulder as she disappeared through the inner office door.

"This is a crock!" Pete groused. He was accustomed to having doors open and people welcome with enthusiasm the man with a camera on his shoulder. He'd been spoiled by the seductive power of television, which usually rendered even the most unpleasant of persons thoroughly charming in his company.

Ruby came out, still somber, and closed Bradshaw's door behind her. "Come with me, please," she said grimly, and ushered them into an adjacent room. So much for the cheerful, bustling, happy shop portrayed in all the magazine and newspaper articles, Maxi thought. These people seemed downright miserable.

Bradshaw's assistant led them into a shabby conference room. Its furnishings consisted of an oblong brown Formica-topped sectional table with scuffed-up molded plastic chairs in disarray. The only other accessories in the room were a phone on the table, a clock on the wall, and an overflowing trash can in the corner.

"Will this be alright?" Ruby asked. The three looked dubious, and Wendy suggested that they do the interview in Mr. Bradshaw's office.

"Most of his narrative will be over pictures of the factory," she told Ruby, glancing around at the barren walls, "but the few establishing head shots we'll use would look better in an office setting."

"Well, I'll ask him," Ruby said, and motioned them once again to follow her. She led them back to Paul Bradshaw's inner office door and opened it wide.

"Jesus Christ, Ruby, can't you knock?" the man inside barked, and Ruby visibly flinched.

All four stood rooted in the doorway, looking aghast at

a red-faced Paul Bradshaw seated behind his desk in shirt-sleeves. In fact, in the very same red-and-white striped Turnbull & Asser dress shirt they'd all seen on the cover of *Time* magazine. His media shirt.

One of the chairs in front of Bradshaw's desk had been knocked over on its back, and there were papers strewn around it on the floor. Ruby hated it when Paul Bradshaw spent time at the South-Central factory. She usually swallowed half a bottle of Mylanta by the time he finished his business there.

"Uhh ... this is Maxi Poole and her crew," she stammered. "They'd like to do the interview in your office, Mr. Bradshaw."

Bradshaw narrowed his eyes and shot another vexed look at Ruby, then got up and walked around to the front of his desk, where he stooped to pick up the papers and right the tattered, vinyl-covered chair. The four remained huddled in the doorway.

"Come in, come in," Bradshaw motioned irritably. "Let's go, can we? I have a lunch meeting."

Great, Maxi thought. First we waste half the morning, and now we get beat up by this jerk.

9

Scud Joe Jones leaned back against a low board fence near the corner of Florence and Normandie in stormy South-Central Los Angeles, baseball cap on sideways, frayed blue denim shirt collar pulled up under his Laker jacket, his elbows resting on top of the staves, his hands clasped in front of him, his eyes scanning the street, looking at everything and at nothing in particular. A couple of brothers hanging with him crouched under a nearby doorway overhang, but Scud Joe liked the rain; he felt untouchable in the rain.

Joseph Bernard Jones was called Scud Joe because he'd once lobbed what he claimed was a live grenade into the middle of a group of Bloods who were selling crack on Century Boulevard, because they were dealing on his turf. The grenade didn't go off, but it scared the hell out of four Eastlys who were all bigger than him.

Scud Joe turned to watch a sleek new black Pontiac Trans Am pull to the curb and screech to a stop in front of him, splashing water and mud up on the sidewalk. He stooped and peered inside, and saw an old pal behind the wheel—Billy Hilgarde, his best friend all through George Washington Elementary.

"Hey, Joey, ain't got enough sense to get out of the rain?" Billy called out. "C'mon, let's go for a ride!" Scud Joe grinned and jumped in the car.

"What's shakin', bro?" Joe smiled broadly, and gave his pal a high five. He loved Billy Hilgarde, but he didn't get to see him much. Their lives had gone in opposite directions. Billy went on to Jordan High, then to Harbor College to learn computers, and now he was some kind of big mac daddy in the rag business. Scud Joe had dropped out of high school, lived on the streets, cadged money and drugs in whatever creative ways he could, and was a big mac dad in an L.A. street gang called the Crips.

"Same-o!" Billy said, wheeling the dazzling racing sedan into traffic. "So when are you gonna get a job?"

"Hey, don't start in," Scud Joe warned. "What brings you down here? You slummin'? Or just pissed?"

Billy had a habit of cruising the 'hood looking for Scud Joe when he needed to let off steam. It was great therapy. An hour with the guy always whacked things right back into perspective for Billy Hilgarde. He fervently did not want to live the life that Joey did, and he knew how easily he could have fallen into it.

"I'm ticked," Billy told him. "Can't get the boss to see things my way, the workers' way, on bringing in the unions. We just had a blowout in his office. He'll probably fire me."

"So shoot him," Scud Joe grinned.

"Sure, that's good, Joe, that's what I'll do," Billy said, rolling his eyes. "So how's your ma?" he asked.

"Aw, she doin' okay, but I stay away from her. She can't help it, when I go on home she gotta rag on me."

"Yeah, well, who can blame her?" Billy scolded his friend. "You're smart, Joey, you could *do* something with

your life. Get a job. Have your own crib, a family, a life.
It's not too late, you know."

"Get outta my face, willya?" Scud Joe whined. "Ever'
time you come by I gotta put up with ten minutes of nag-
gin' before we can even talk!"

"Okay, so I've still got eight minutes left," Billy laughed,
looking at his watch. "Wouldn't it be nice to get a paycheck, make some money, buddy?"

"You shittin' me?" Scud Joe shrieked. "Man, I see more
money in a week coming down every which way than you
see all year. *You oughta wear the colors, hook up with me!*
Fuck that job you always comin' down here freakin' over.
You meet me every day, stick with this shot caller, I'll make
ya rich. You wanna get rich, Billy?"

"Sure, I want to get rich," Billy said. "But I don't want
to get dead."

"Hah! You see me dead? You been called down to Scud
Joe's funeral? I ain't dead, am I?"

"No, you ain't dead—today," Billy Hilgarde said grimly.
"And that's a damn wonderment, brother. That's a miracle."

"Okay, okay, yer ten minutes is up, ain't they?" Scud
Joe stopped him. "So who's the dude makin' you crazy?
Talk to me."

"Paul Bradshaw, the owner where I work," Billy answered. Joe let out a low whistle. Even he had heard of
Paul Bradshaw.

"Want him wasted?" Scud Joe asked, only half kidding.

"Yeah, right," Billy groaned in exasperation. "Waste him
for me, that'll solve everything." They were heading east
on Florence Avenue toward the Pulled Together factory.

"So you wanna eat lunch?" Scud Joe asked. Usually it
was lunchtime at the plant when Billy came looking for
him, and usually Billy needed to grab a bite.

"No, I'm not hungry—are you?" he asked.

"Hell, I got all day to eat, brother," Scud Joe said. "I'm
not the one has to punch a fuckin' time clock."

Scud Joe was always honored when Billy Hilgarde came by
for him. Scud Joe had never in his life felt as important as he
acted, and though he wouldn't admit it, he had great respect
for what his old school *compa* had made of himself. He was
pleased that some of the gang saw him climbing into the big
black Trans Am and riding around with Billy Hilgarde.

"Tell you what," Billy said. "Let's drop by the plant.

You've never been there. Maybe you'll be turned on to learn a real trade and hire on. Make your ma happy. I'd even stick my neck out and speak for you. What do you say?"

"Hey, Billy, if you want to stop by the place, show me around, show off what a big fuckin' deal you are over there, great, but don't be countin' on me to learn no job, okay? Now I told you, yer ten minutes is up."

They were coming up on the colorful entrance to Pulled Together that fronted on Florence near San Pedro Street. Four of the men in the shipping department were members of Saint Elmo's Village, an old and well-respected center for black art in South-Central, and they'd volunteered to paint a mural on the block wall out front when the plant was new. They'd enlisted the help of other artists from Saint Elmo's, and the troupe spent weeks after work painting a colorful scene of black men and women, all smiles, sketching, cutting, sewing, selling, and strutting in brightly colored garments with oversized Pulled Together hangtags on them.

Paul Bradshaw had okayed the project, then made sure his publicity people in Santa Monica kept the press alerted. The work in progress was documented in newspapers and magazines and on television news and talk shows. And the media was there in force for the grand unveiling ceremony, at which Paul Bradshaw, his jacket slung over his shoulder, in his red-and-white striped shirt with cuff links from Cartier and his red Armani silk rep tie, did interviews explaining how 5 percent of the selling price of every garment made there was going back into social programs for the community.

"Ever see this?" Billy asked Scud Joe, indicating the vibrant mural, shimmering now in the pouring rain.

"'Course I seen it, ever'body's seen it," Scud Joe sneered.

"You don't like it?" Billy raised his eyebrows.

"Hey, lot of us know a lotta brothers 'n' sisters inside," Scud Joe told him. "Or got family works inside. And they ain't got smiles on their faces like these cats in the picture, you hear me? Lookit you, you ain't got no smile on your face when I see you," Scud Joe observed.

"You got a point, Joey," Billy said thoughtfully. "That's because everybody hates the boss."

10

Tanner sped down Benedict Canyon in his brand-new midnight blue six-cylinder BMW 325i electric-ragtop convertible. It was a present he'd bought himself for working about a hundred hours a week since August on the intricate and very nasty La Flame Cosmetica case—and winning. The gift he really wanted to give himself was a few straight nights of more than four hours' sleep.

Right now he was hip deep in product litigation for Kid Kountry, a long-established family-owned Southern California toy manufacturer. The company prided itself on being one of the last holdouts against so-called Saturday morning violence toys, yet still competitive in the high-end world market. Tanner was very confident about this one. Even the judge would probably remember fondly his old KK Teddy bear, which could well be still around with the grandkids, with all its eyes and ears intact.

An interesting personal sidelight for Tanner in the process of working the KK case was that for the first time in his thirty-seven years he had actually given a little thought to being a father. Nothing concrete, of course. He certainly had no plans, but he'd had a specific attack one particular midnight in the very masculine office of his very bachelor apartment in L.A.'s posh Sierra Towers, when his minimal maple and stainless-steel desk was littered with KK Pound Pups—chipper Scotties, endearing basset hounds, lovable Dalmatians, and a big English sheepdog with sad, hug-me eyes. He'd had an interesting albeit fleeting flash, after looking too long at all those glistening noses, floppy ears, and silly tails, that there ought to be a little kid in here. But then he looked around his efficient office at the hard, ivory travertine floors, with no rugs for little pudgy knees to crawl on. And he took stock of his high-tech, state-of-the-art, computerized, digital, multicomponent toys, any one of which could be put out of commission by a spilled cup of milk or jam from sticky fingers. Poor kid, he'd thought. The only child-friendly item in his whole office was the soft mohair throw his mother had insisted on placing over the back of his black leather sofa, knowing about her son's long work nights when he never made it to his bedroom but dropped exhausted onto the office couch fully dressed. Just for a few minutes' rest, of course, because for the moment he couldn't keep his eyes open, but many mornings when the clock radio blared out the five-thirty news headlines he woke up there, clutching his mom's hand-crocheted "blankie" up around his neck.

Nope, he had no place for kids. No time for kids. Or a wife. Women, yes, there were a lot of those, but he would gently nudge them out of his life when they showed dangerous signs of wanting to move in. There were just so many hours in the day, and he needed twice that many, with zero complications.

It was seven-forty-five in the morning, after his workout at the Bradshaw manse, and he was headed home to shower, dress, and get himself in to his Century City office. He was looking at a work day featuring KK corporate lawyers and a major deposition, but he had Devin Bradshaw on his mind.

Tanner had been training Devin almost every morning for two years. At first he'd thought she was pure ice goddess, but over time he wasn't so sure. Lately she seemed to be warming up quite a bit, and he couldn't deny how much he was enjoying the thaw. That's what worried him. And lately she'd been showing him cracks in the dam of her high-profile marriage to clothing czar Paul Bradshaw, and it also bothered him that he found himself enjoying that. This morning he'd been witness to Bradshaw slamming out the front door. And deep down, Tanner liked it.

Get a grip, Counselor, he told himself. Devin Bradshaw was a hands-off proposition, he'd known that from day one. In fact, he'd made that one of his Top Ten Tanner Rules for a Trouble-Free Life, or as trouble-free as you have a right to expect on the fast track in Los Angeles in the nineties.

Devin knew that he was an attorney specializing in corporate law. She knew she was his only workout client, and that by 7:30 A.M. he had to be gone. But his real life had nothing to do with what he and Devin did every morning, which was strictly heavy-duty exercise. When you train one-on-one, nonstop and hard, for ninety minutes, it's grueling. You talk to distract yourself from where you hurt. And Tanner had established early that the talk would be about muscle groups, gym equipment, movies, the weather. Getting personal could lead to chitchat about his cases and his clients, and he didn't want that. Devin Bradshaw was society. So was his last client. These women traveled on the high-dish circuit, and professional ethics forbade that Tanner discuss his work casually with them. Better it just never came up.

There was another reason for his strict adherence to this particular Tanner Tip for Personal Survival. Devin Bradshaw was devastatingly sexy. And Tanner spent more time with her on a regular basis than with anyone else in his life except his secretary, who was fifty-seven years old and ran his office like a Prussian. That, too, worked for him. With Devin Bradshaw, he didn't want to know too much about her. Didn't want to get close, or personal, or intimate. Because he was attracted to her, of course; he'd have to be a castrated Tibetan monk not to be. So he didn't want to risk even a nanochance of succumbing to that impulse, of wanting her, or, worst case, of actually getting into something with her. Something sexual.

Hey, maybe he was flattering himself that there was any danger of that. But it was a known fact that a lot of gorgeous younger women who were married to rich older men had affairs, Beverly Hills–style, with their personal trainers. Or their tennis pros. Younger guys with Southern California surfer looks and hard bodies who could keep it all uncomplicated. But Tanner was not your ordinary trainer.

He'd worked his way through Stanford undergraduate, then law school, as a part-time personal fitness trainer. Friends of his were waiters, waitresses. Some of the guys parked cars, or worked in the library, or drove for limo companies. His roommate was a weekend usher at the old Palace Theater in San Francisco, back when it still had ushers. Tanner had always been athletic, but he wasn't interested in team sports. So he studied anatomy and learned professional fitness and took on regular clients before class in the mornings to earn spending money.

His parents paid his tuition and board, and would have toked him to a hefty allowance had he wanted it that way.

John Junior was an only child, and the Tanners were more than comfortable. But young John had been independent from the day he first walked at ten months old and managed to get himself outside the Tanners' Spanish villa in Brentwood Park, then outside their unlatched gate, and made serious tracks, mostly by crawling, on Bristol Circle toward heavily trafficked Sunset Boulevard. The nanny got fired, but Johnny survived.

After law school he came back to Southern California and clerked for a year while he studied for the bar. Then he went to work in downtown Los Angeles as a public defender. Backbreaking hours for low pay, and more learning while he took graduate courses in corporate law at USC.

His dad let him know that the door was always open for him at Brigant, Hale, Tanner & Lowe. In fact, Tanner Senior had often told his wife that he was mystified as to why their son chose not to come in from the cold. But Tanner didn't want to go into his father's firm until he felt he'd earned it. Until he was good enough. It wasn't just integrity. His dad was a brilliant criminal attorney, and although Tanner had chosen corporate law, he had no intention of setting himself up for comparison before he was ready. He made that move when he was thirty, and by the time he did he was ready and he was good.

He and his father were close. They had dinner together often, talked shop. And in Tanner Senior's opinion, as he liked to put it now, a big part of what made his son so damned good at their profession turned out to be those early years as a court-appointed attorney, when he'd defended every kind of ratty-assed criminal known to man. And he was proud of his son for doing it as he did everything—his way.

Tanner stayed in shape his way, too. It had occurred to him that there probably wasn't another lawyer in the history of the world who busted his buns as a personal trainer every morning for a hundred dollars an hour. But when he looked around at colleagues in the firm, or guys his age whom he'd gone to school with, he was beginning to see a lot of balding heads and flabby middles. He could thank some good genes for his thick head of hair, but for his hard body, that was trickier.

He was brutally busy now. And it was a temptation every day of his life to skip his morning exercise. To stay in bed for that blissful extra hour or two. So he took on just one client, with a specific profile, as a discipline to force himself to do his daily workout. A man or woman, with a gym at home—set up so he could do his own program, too—who wanted to go six or seven days a week and who needed to do it very early. David Geffen had a trainer at five every morning. Cher used Body by Jake at six. And Devin Bradshaw had Tanner, and it worked for both of them.

It wasn't for the money, certainly, but he took it. After all, he was a professional. And he was definitely not Devin Bradshaw kind of wealthy, not even close, so he had no qualms about taking his hourly rate. The way Tanner looked at it, it bought dinner.

But now it threatened to buy him trouble, and that was entirely his own fault. He'd been thinking about Devin too much lately. Like now, when he should have his mind on Kid Kountry business. And instead of it being the usual self-imposed torture that intense morning workouts were, after which the most horrendous of days could only get better, he'd lately found himself actually welcoming the wake-up call from hell, the cold shower, careening around the corner up Benedict Canyon to the Bradshaw gym, and punishing his body. With Devin Bradshaw.

He was beginning to feel fireworks just beneath the surface, waiting to happen. Dangerous. So dangerous that if these intimations persisted, he knew, he was going to have to quit this particular morning gig. He'd have to find a new client to moonlight with in order to keep himself in shape— one who would make him properly hate it again.

11

Rosemary Bradshaw sipped a glass of chablis and idly scanned the lunch crowd at the elegant Bistro Gardens in Beverly Hills, which was packed now despite the rain. For a long time after her divorce, she hadn't been able to go out to her favorite places. She couldn't bear to read "poor Rosemary" in the eyes of friends, hadn't wanted to feel the stares of people who knew that the rich, powerful, charismatic Paul Bradshaw had left her for a much younger woman.

Nor could she have dressed up and come here even now, she knew, if it weren't for Jenny. Miracle worker Dr. Jenny Evans, the therapist she'd been seeing since the day that Paul had left her a note on a Post-it affixed to the bathroom mirror. *"I've moved into the Beverly Wilshire,"* it read. That's all. Rosemary had thought about suicide back then. In fact, she'd seriously considered suicide more often than she cared to admit. The only one who knew exactly how often was Jenny.

She glanced up again toward the crowded restaurant entryway. Uncharacteristically, Alex was fifteen minutes late. Odd, the friendship she'd developed with Alexandra Anson, her ex-husband's longtime lover. But she'd always known that Alex had never posed a real threat, that Alex could never steal her husband. Paul was not the sort of man who would marry his secretary. Jenny had helped her understand that on some peculiar level it had even been a comfort when Paul was with Alex, because that kept him from seeking out and finding a woman who *could* take him away from her. Like Devin Yorke.

Ever since Devin had breezed on the scene and turned all of their lives upside down, Rosemary had found herself actually feeling empathy for Alex. No one knew better than Rosemary how deeply it hurt, after years of being loving and being loyal, to be royally dumped by Paul Nathan Bradshaw.

Maybe she was able to feel for Alex because Rosemary was truly becoming whole again. She'd lost fifty pounds in the last two years. On Mondays, Wednesdays, and Fridays without fail, she exercised in the gym that Paul had had built in their home. On alternate days she walked for miles in the nearby hills above Mandeville Canyon. She worked with a nutritionist who changed her diet. She'd been referred to a color specialist who brought her hair back to just a shade lighter than her original chestnut, with streaks of pale gold woven through it. She kept busy with her charity work, she enjoyed seeing friends again, and she was doing well with the children now—except for Pauly.

Pauly was her youngest, her last born, Paul's namesake,

her secret favorite. Now Paul Junior was breaking her heart. He'd probably been doing drugs as far back as junior high, certainly all through high school, and by the time he was floundering in college he had alienated all his old friends and was running with a crowd he never talked about and never brought home. He stole money from her. From her cache in the kitchen for deliveries and such, from her emergency supply in the bedroom under the lining of a dresser drawer, from her purse. In the beginning he would try to cover it up—he'd take some and leave some. Later he just took it all. He even blatantly violated her checkbook and wrote himself hefty sums, forging her signature. And she had allowed it by looking the other way. Jenny explained that she *enabled* him.

She and Paul couldn't help but be aware that their son was in deep trouble, but he was always too busy to address it seriously, and she was committed to pretending that their life was perfect. So they did nothing back then beyond a few pep talks about late nights and poor grades. They were both in a classic state of denial. By the time Rosemary came to grips with reality, Pauly had slipped away. Now he was living hand to mouth on lower Third Street near downtown Los Angeles, in a slum apartment he shared with whoever was around. Dirty hair straggled to his shoulders, his teeth were decaying, he wore rags, he rarely saw any of his family, and Rosemary lived in terror that he would get AIDS from sharing needles. He was twenty-seven years old, and she feared that he would never see thirty.

Paul Senior was no help. He was emotionally unavailable to his first family. Today Rosemary had a plan to get his attention, and she needed Alex Anson's help.

She looked up to see Austin, the Bistro Gardens captain, escorting Alex to her table. Austin wore his usual patronizing smile, but Alex looked grim. Rosemary could see that something was very wrong.

"I'm sorry I'm late," Alex said, without offering an explanation. As she put down her purse and settled herself at the table, Rosemary sat quietly and scrutinized her. Alex had not dressed appropriately, her makeup was streaked, her eyes were red, and she was obviously distraught.

"What's wrong?" Rosemary finally asked, and that was enough to cause tears to well up and spill over the young woman's cheeks.

"He fired me," she barely managed, her voice breaking. While Alex groped in her purse for tissues, Rosemary pushed her wine glass aside and signaled their waiter.

"Two Stolichnaya martinis, very cold, with olives," she ordered. "Please serve the cruets in a bowl of ice, and use absolutely no vermouth." Alex was wound up tight and ready to break, and the first thing Rosemary wanted to do was calm her down.

"All right, not another word about it until your drink arrives and you've had four sips of it," she counseled. "You really don't want to make a scene at the Bistro Gardens."

She reached across the table and gave Alex's hand a supportive squeeze. Rosemary had an acute sense memory of exactly how the younger woman was feeling. Alex straightened and managed a feeble smile.

"That's better," Rosemary said. "Now, let's make small talk for a bit. Look, two tables over, it's Joan Collins. Now there's a survivor! Like her hat?"

Alex laughed in spite of herself. There was a time when Rosemary Bradshaw would definitely have been the last person on earth from whom she'd have expected support or solace.

"My God, Rosemary," she whispered, "you're a much better person than I am."

"Oh, please!" Rosemary rejoined. "What's that supposed to mean?"

Alex looked squarely at her. "It means if another woman cheated with *my* husband for years, I wouldn't even speak to her, let alone try to help her. The fact is," she added in even tones, "I'd want to kill her."

There, she'd said it. In the three years since they'd become friends, neither woman had ever broached the subject, yet always it hung in the air above them like the sword of Damocles. A lengthy moment passed.

"I have long since forgiven you," Rosemary replied at last. "It took a lot of therapy to make me realize that you were not to blame—he was. If it hadn't been you, it would have been some other woman. God knows I can't blame you for falling in love with him—no one understands better than I do how seductive Paul Bradshaw can be."

"But every time I look at you, I feel guilty, Rosemary. Did you know that most of those nights he was working late, we ended up in a suite at the Sunset Marquis ...?"

"I knew that," Rosemary said quietly.

"Do you remember when you two took the kids skiing at Avoriaz, and Paul had to leave to take care of some business in the city? We spent four days together at the Hôtel Crillon in Paris . . ."

"I *didn't* know that."

"The kids knew, too," Alex went on relentlessly. "Pauly caught us once. He showed up at the beach house and found us in the master suite . . . in bed . . . naked—"

Rosemary winced. "Stop it," she demanded, holding up both hands. "While you're unburdening your soul, Alex, you're hurting me, and I won't allow it."

Tears streamed from the younger woman's eyes, but she broke off her intended litany of perfidy.

"We both have other issues now," Rosemary went on, leaning toward her, softening. "Let's not dredge up the past at this late date."

Alex took both of Rosemary's hands in her own and closed her eyes. "Thank you," she breathed.

Their drinks came, and now that the veil had been lifted from the topic of her illicit relationship with the other woman's former husband, Alex was able to talk freely about what Paul had said to her and done to her. Rosemary listened and was amazed that she actually felt real sympathy. Mentally, she noted her own detachment as Alex poured out words of anger, hurt, betrayal. My God, Rosemary marveled, this woman was talking about the man she'd spent most of her life with, and she didn't feel much of anything. Except healthy. She would discuss these emotions, or lack of them, with Jenny.

Alex had come to a stop in her diatribe and was looking squarely at Rosemary. "You know," she said then, "I actually feel better now that I've got it all out. Maybe there really is something to this therapy business. Or maybe it's the martini," she added, managing a weak smile.

"Either way, it's all about state of mind," Rosemary affirmed. "We've both been through the same thing, Alex, and I'm here to assure you, life goes on."

"You know, Rosemary," Alex blurted, abruptly shifting gears, "you are a stone fox in that gorgeous suit. Escada, isn't it? That pink is to die! Speaking about life going on, I've got a great idea—can I fix you up with my dad?"

That caused Rosemary to throw her head back and laugh

out loud. "That is most definitely the last thing I expected to hear you say," she managed. "Where on earth did that come from?"

"Well, you're beautiful, that's easy to see," Alex said thoughtfully, "but today I see something else. You are one helluva woman, Rosemary. And my dad's a pistol. He's tall, almost trim, he's got plenty of hair and deadly Irish eyes. And funny! If he weren't a big-time agent, he'd have his own talk show."

"He also dates women half his age, you once told me," Rosemary reminded her.

"Yes, but never for long. He needs substance in his life. When he wants to be with someone he can talk to and relax with, he bugs *me* to have dinner with him, for God's sake. I mean, a lot!"

"Okay, okay," Rosemary laughed, holding up her hands. "I see what's going on here now. You're doing a great job of trying to get your mind off Paul."

"Paul *who*?" Alex looked up at her from under still wet eyelashes, lifting her martini to her lips.

"That's the spirit. Now let's talk about why I invited you here today. "

"I'm all ears," Alex offered gamely.

"I need to know . . . is Paul sleeping with anybody?"

"Excuse me . . .?" Alex gulped on her vodka.

"Look, you and I both know that he's a man who sleeps around. I'm guessing he hasn't changed. Has he?"

"No. He hasn't changed," Alex said quietly.

"I want names."

"Well, I can only guess . . ."

"Alex, you're in a position to see, to hear, to know. Tell me names."

"But, why?"

"Because he's forgotten he has a family, and a son who's going to die if he doesn't help . . ."

"Pauly," Alex murmured.

"I've tried to get his attention," Rosemary went on. "I've even tried begging and pleading. Now I'm going to try threatening him."

"*Threatening* him?"

"At his luncheon today. At Regina's house. Three of my kids will be there. I intend to drop by in the middle of it, take him aside, and tell him in private that I happen to know he's sleeping with so-and-so and so-and-so, and unless he personally takes Pauly in hand—finds him, brings him home to his own house, gets him help, and stays with it until Pauly's okay, really okay—I will march into the other room and tell Devin, in front of his mother, his brother, and his children. But I need names."

"You wouldn't!"

"Why wouldn't I? What have I got to lose? And I have my son's life to gain. So who's he jumping into bed with these days, Alex?"

"Janna Best, for one," Alex said tentatively.

"Oh, tell me about Janna," Rosemary urged, smiling a little wickedly.

"She's a model we used for the spring catalog, and—"

The sound of a muffled beep cut off Alex's narrative. She reached into her purse and fished out her beeper and glanced at the number on the LED display. The call was from the South-Central plant. Alex didn't know all the extension numbers there, but somebody at Pulled Together was trying to reach her, and she knew that's where Paul was this morning. She excused herself and headed back toward the pay phones.

"Afternoon, Pulled Together." The voice of Ruby Johnson answered Alex's call.

"Ruby, it's Alex—you paged me?"

"Yes, Alex. Just to keep you posted. Mr. B. has finished with the television people and he just left for the meeting at his mother's. He didn't tell me what was on his agenda from there, but I assume you know."

Evidently, Alex noted, Mr. B. also didn't tell her that she no longer worked for him. She thanked Ruby for the update, hung up the phone, and smiled. Paul obviously hadn't told anyone that she'd been terminated—that news would have circulated fast on the healthy interoffice grapevine. Maybe he had reconsidered. She decided to float one more trial balloon. If anyone knew the score, it would be her friend Geneen Landers, Paul's brother's assistant.

"Hello, Sam Bradshaw's office," Geneen answered on the first ring.

"Hi, Geneen, it's Alex. Ruby called me from PT and said Paul was on his way to that family meeting at their mother's. Is everything all right at the store?"

"Alex, where the hell have you been all morning?" a puzzled Geneen demanded.

Good, Alex thought, she has no idea I've been fired, either. Maybe I haven't been. "Bitching migraine," she lied. "Couldn't lift my head this morning." The lie was probably a prophecy, she knew, because her migraines usually kicked in on the day after excessive stress. By tonight she'd very likely have a killer.

"Are you better now?" Geneen asked.

"A little," Alex said.

"Still, you should have called in, Alex," Geneen chided. "Everybody's been looking for you. You weren't answering at home, but I guess if you were so sick . . ." Alex and Geneen worked closely together managing the Bradshaw brothers' schedules.

"Well, Paul had his morning mapped out for him, so I just stayed in bed with the lights out and the phone turned off until my head stopped pounding," Alex told her. "Why? Are there any fires to put out?"

"No," Geneen responded. "Both of them are on their way to Mulholland Estates now. Paul is coming in from South-Central, as you know."

"Are you going to that meeting?" Alex asked her.

"Nope. Are you?"

That was a relief. Had Geneen been asked to be there but Alex had not, that would be a signal that it really was over for her.

"What's that meeting all about anyway, Geneen, do you know?" she asked.

"No clue," Geneen replied. "Family stuff of some kind. When I asked Sam about it, he actually blustered, said it was nothing that concerned me."

"Well, I know it's not a birthday or anything like that," Alex countered. "I wasn't asked to pick up gifts or send flowers."

"Maybe one of their boys knocked up some woman and she's threatening to have the baby and cash in," Geneen stage-whispered. Alex chuckled. The Bradshaws were a tight bunch, she'd give them that. They stuck together, even though they didn't seem to like each other very much.

"So how are you feeling now?" Geneen asked again.

"A little better, so I thought I'd check in, see if everything was okay—see if there was anything I should know," Alex prodded.

"Everything's fine," Geneen said. "It's quiet. Are you coming in this afternoon?"

"You know, since there's nothing pressing and I'm still kind of wobbly, I think I'll just crawl back into bed. But promise you'll call if anything comes up, okay? If the machine picks up, that means I'm asleep, but I'll get it later."

Geneen assured her she would, and they said their goodbyes. Who knows, Alex told herself, maybe this was just another one of Paul's flareups. It was hard for her to believe the man would fire her, if for no other reason than the practical fact that it would take someone else a very long time to become half as good at her job as she was. She rejoined Rosemary in the dining room.

"Nobody at the office seems to know I've been fired," she told her. "Maybe he's relented."

"More likely he hasn't gotten around to telling anyone yet," Rosemary said dryly. "When have you known Paul to relent?"

"You're right," Alex conceded, turning glum again.

"Listen, Alex, why don't you come with me?" Rosemary suggested. "You can pressure him for your job back."

"You mean . . . I can threaten him too?"

"Why not? You've got more on him than I ever will. And you could back me up."

"Oh Lord, Rosemary, I couldn't."

"Alex, I told you I have nothing to lose. Tell me, what exactly have *you* got to lose?"

"I don't know . . ."

"If you don't give it a shot, where will you be tomorrow? I'll tell you where—still fired."

Alex grinned. "Okay, you're on," she said, picking up her purse. "Let's go."

"Wait, hold it," Rosemary laughed. "Let's have lunch, and we can work out our strategy. That's why I made our date so early. We've got plenty of time."

"No we don't. I have a better idea. Let's head him off before he gets to Mrs. Bradshaw's house. That way maybe we won't have to make the big scene. We'll just threaten to go over there and bust him in front of his whole family if he won't give in."

"Good idea. But how will we know where to find him?"

"Easy—he'll be coming from the South-Central plant, so he'll have to go up over Mulholland to get to his mother's, and he's due there at one o'clock."

Rosemary looked at her watch. "It's twelve thirty-three," she said. "Okay, let's get going."

Reaching into her purse, she dropped a twenty-dollar bill on the table to cover the bar tab, then ushered Alex through the crowded restaurant. She stopped to tell Austin that something had come up and they had to skip lunch, then the two women rushed out the front door into the rain. Rosemary wasted no time handing another twenty, along with her ticket, to the valet parking attendant.

"Rob, we have to leave my friend's car here for a couple of hours," she told him. "And we need my car, fast."

Within a minute, Rosemary's black Mercedes screeched up to the curb, and Rob jumped out and held the door open. Both women ignored the umbrella another attendant was attempting to hold over them as they hurried to the car. Rosemary tossed her purse onto the console and jumped into the driver's seat, while Alex scurried around and got in on the other side. As Rosemary quickly pulled away, her purse tumbled onto its side, spilling some of its contents—including a small, gleaming handgun.

"Jesus!" Alex shrieked. "What the hell is *that* for?"

"Umm ... to help make my point in case Paul doesn't see it," Rosemary muttered, scooping her belongings back into her purse while she steered the big sedan northbound on Canon Drive.

"Rosemary, you can't legally carry a gun!"

"I'm *not* carrying it. I mean, I don't usually carry it—I keep it in the house. It just seemed like a good idea to bring it with me today."

"Is that thing loaded?"

"Of course it's loaded. Now tell me about Janna Best ... and the rest of them."

12

"What a dickhead!" Pete Garrow sneered, gathering up his tripod, lights, cable, and sundry items of camera gear. They had finished the interview with Paul Bradshaw and he'd left the plant, but not before he'd blandished Maxi Poole with unctuous flattery and invitations to tour the main operation and lunch with him in Santa Monica, while acting as if Pete and Wendy were not in the room.

The three had put up with his forty-minute stall while they sat in his outer office, then they endured his cantankerous mood, but once he was seated, miked, and the lights came on, he astonished them by doing a one-eighty. Pete was looking through his camera lens at Mr. Nice Guy all of a sudden. Mr. Concerned Employer, Mr. Equal Opportunity, Mr. Humanitarian Medal Winner.

"What prompted you to create Pulled Together?" Maxi had asked.

"I simply want to give back to the community," Bradshaw had responded. *I simply want to throw up,* Pete had thought at the time, rolling tape.

The Q&A went on in Maxi's usual style, starting soft, then gradually toughening. When she asked what the money from the 5 percent give-back on each garment was specifically earmarked for, Bradshaw flashed a big, sincere-looking grin and said, "I'm glad you asked about that." Then he went on to say that his people here at PT were working with him on a multifaceted program for the South-Central community, it was very exciting, and he would be making an announcement soon.

"A *big* announcement," he'd repeated, smiling broadly, "and I'm promising you today, Maxi Poole, that you will be the first journalist we call." Maxi smiled too, because she knew what her colleagues were thinking. She stole a glance up at Pete behind the camera. He pulled back from the lens just long enough to let her see him roll his eyes.

Bradshaw even batted back the dead-fish question, which Maxi delivered deadpan. "Unfortunate," he responded, managing to look concerned, "but as I'm sure you know, table accessories are not my department. You'll have to ask the florist how that could have happened. Terrible," he added sadly.

That signaled the end of the interview for Paul Bradshaw, as the three journalists had known it would. It was obvious that the questioning would not be going into any territory from there that Bradshaw had any desire to traverse. He smiled again and stood up, unclipping his microphone and dropping it on the chair behind him.

"Maxi, I enjoyed it," he said. "I'll be watching us on the news tonight. But I'm running late and I've really got to leave." Pete shut down the camera and switched off the lights.

"What about our background shots of the factory?" Wendy spoke up. "We can't edit this piece without them."

"Can't do it, honey," Bradshaw said to Wendy. "Ruby can help you get the shots you need." Then his expression changed from condescension toward Wendy to the full-out charm treatment for Maxi, complete with a big come-on wink, and he left the office.

Pete fell into the nearest chair and shook his head. Idly, he looked around the office at the shabby desk, the mismatched chairs, the lime green vinyl-covered couch and the cheap prints on the walls. "This place is a dump," he remarked after a minute. "It sure doesn't look like him, does it?"

"I get the feeling Bradshaw doesn't spend much time here," Maxi observed.

"You gotta know he doesn't love coming down to South-Central, not an uptown dude like him," Pete allowed. "Of course he'd have to come here for interviews, because it looks good, looks like he's involved with the community, doing his part."

Maxi chuckled. "Yup, Paul Bradshaw definitely looks out of place here."

"You mean like a fish out of water," Wendy chortled mischievously.

"Uh-huh," Pete grinned. "Actually, he looks like a twenty-four-carat asshole!"

"Well, we have to get all our B-roll background and cutaway shots without the man's voice," Wendy said, getting back to business. "Let's figure out how to get this done fast." She and Maxi sat down on the cracked vinyl couch to look through Wendy's notes.

"There are some weird vibes in this place, aren't there?" Maxi half-whispered then.

"You're not kidding," Wendy confirmed. "You know, I'm getting the feeling that everybody's scared of this guy Bradshaw. Ruby acts terrified to make a move."

"Well, who could blame her? We watched him nearly take her head off, even in front of *us,*" Pete put in.

"It's not only Ruby," Wendy added. "From the second I started setting up this story, every call I made, every person I talked to, from the security guard in the lot to the woman who directed us to the man's office, acted . . . uptight. Nervous. Have you guys noticed that?"

"Yes, and it's curious," Maxi agreed. "This is an exciting workplace, a young, thriving, successful business that's getting a lot of positive press nationwide. These people should be proud. They should feel very good about themselves and what they're doing here. Even the name implies team spirit—'Pulled Together.' But I don't feel any spirit here."

"It'd be interesting to talk to some of the workers, see what they have to say," Wendy commented.

"Yes, but that's a whole other story," Maxi said. "And probably a much better one."

"What do you think? Does it interest you?" Wendy asked her.

"Could be. Let's make some calls when we get back to the newsroom, see what we dig up. But let's not mention it to Martin until we find out if there's anything to it. At this point, it seems our new boss is a member of the congregation nominating this guy for sainthood."

There was a light knock on the door and Ruby came in. She settled herself carefully on the only available chair, a beat-up bentwood with a dirty, partly sprung cane seat.

"Mr. Bradshaw had to rush off to a meeting," she said to the journalists. "I'm sorry, but would you like to go ahead with your tour of the factory?"

"It's not going to work as well without his narration,"

Wendy said, "but we'll take some specific shots that corre-
spond with some of the things we've got him talking about,
and we'll lay his sound over the pictures."

"I remember every word the man said," Pete chimed in.
"Why don't you two take the tape and split." He handed
Wendy the interview cassettes. "I'll grab a few shots of the
operation for B-roll."

"Sounds good," Maxi agreed. "And Pete, don't shoot
everything that moves, okay? We don't want to make this
an epic. But get plenty of faces of people working, and I'll
button it with the company address and phone number so
any viewers who are interested can contact them for jobs."

Ruby offered to escort Pete around the plant while he
got the footage they needed. The three crew members
hauled the gear back through the outer office, and Wendy
and Maxi prepared to leave.

"I'm sorry it turned out to be so late and so rushed,"
Ruby offered.

"Wasn't your fault," Wendy smiled. "By the way, is it
always so *tense* around here?"

Ruby instinctively looked over her shoulder. "Uhh ... it
was particularly tense today," she managed.

"Yes, who was that fellow who stormed out of Bradshaw's office acting like he wanted to smack somebody?"
Maxi asked her.

Maxi never expected answers to questions like this that
were clearly none of her business, but her reporter's instinct
prompted her to throw them out anyway, and she was always amazed at how often people would actually respond.

And Ruby's instinct as a personal assistant to the CEO
of the parent company told her to sidestep the question,
but she thought about it for a minute. The working conditions at Pulled Together were deplorable, and she was on
Billy Hilgarde's side a hundred percent. The Channel Six
team was the press, this community's local television news
press. Maybe they could help.

"You never heard it from me?" she appealed cautiously.

"We never heard it from you," Maxi and Wendy confirmed in unison.

Ruby then filled them in on Billy Hilgarde and his efforts
to organize the workers and bring the garment industry
unions into the Pulled Together division.

"It's not that the employees want anything more than

they deserve," she told the news crew, "or more than they were promised in the first place. Most of the workers spent weeks in training for no pay, on the assurance that when we got into production with the new line they'd be compensated for that time, and paid decent wages. Now Pulled Together is up and running and cranking out product, and people here aren't even pulling down minimum wage."

"Wait a minute," Maxi put in. "They've got to be getting at least minimum wage. Bradshaw runs a huge corporation. If he weren't paying minimum wage here, the state would shut him down. One complaint—"

"Nobody's going to complain," Ruby cut in. "Where else are they going to work? It's the nineties. Firms are downsizing, not hiring. And a lot of businesses in South-Central were burned out in the riots. There are no jobs out there. The workers know it and Bradshaw knows it, and he's got them right where he wants them."

"The IRS would pick up on it if this company were not paying minimum wage," Wendy persisted.

"Oh, the pay is there on paper," Ruby explained. "He hires workers for part time, pays the minimum wage for five hours, and lets the suggestion seep out that they're expected to put in eight, ten hours a day. For the team, he tells them, until we get on our feet. Those who don't give extra time aren't put on the schedule for the next week."

"Are there a lot of those?" Pete asked.

"There are some," Ruby told him. "But they're just bodies to Bradshaw. If they won't work, there are plenty who will. People are hungry in this community."

"Then there have to be a lot of very angry people on both sides of the factory walls who feel they got lied to and slapped in the teeth," Pete put in.

"Oh yeah," Ruby lamented. "Mr. B. ought to carry a gun when he comes down here. This is dangerous climate for him, tooling around South-Central in his fancy cars and limousines."

"Is Pulled Together making a profit yet?" Maxi asked.

"I wouldn't know," Ruby replied. "I don't see the books. But the orders are coming in faster than we can cut the goods, and his overhead here, unlike the Santa Monica plant, is bare bones. This place is a pigsty, you can see that. And with only part-timers, he doesn't even have to pay benefits. No pensions, no medical, no dental, no day care, no lunchroom, no nothing."

"By the way," Maxi said, "Bradshaw said the company was working with you people here at PT on a big community program to be funded by the 5 percent give-back. What do you know about that?"

Ruby smiled grimly. "Nothing," she said. Maxi and Wendy exchanged glances.

"What's with this guy Billy Hilgarde?" Pete asked her then. "How come he's got the balls to challenge the man?"

"Billy's got skills, and experience. He's good. He came from GUESS? and he can always go back there. The Marciano brothers who own GUESS? are princes. When Billy was promised a management job down the line here at PT, he saw this new operation as a terrific opportunity, and the brothers wished him well and gave him a going-away party. And told him if it didn't work out he was welcome to come back."

"What about you?" Wendy asked.

"Oh, I can always get a job. Billy brought me in here—he and I have been friends for a long time. I was working at Carole Little. And I *will* leave, if things don't change. But for now I'm going to support Billy." She paused, looking hard at the crew. "Listen, do I have your word that if you do something with this information, you'll never reveal me as a source?" she demanded again.

"You can count on it," Maxi vowed. She took Ruby's remark and demeanor as a cue that the conversation was over, at least for now.

"Okay, shall we?" she nudged Wendy.

They said their good-byes and left Pete to get shots of the factory for their piece. As soon as they were out of earshot, Wendy said, "You know, I don't get it. This guy Bradshaw is loaded with money, and he's getting accolades for making jobs available in South-Central from here to Washington, D.C. Wouldn't you think at this point in his life he'd just do the right thing? I mean, he doesn't need to screw these people."

"Maybe he can't help it," Maxi theorized. "Maybe, like the tortoise and the scorpion, it's his nature."

"And maybe it's just stupid," Wendy carped. "And greedy!"

"One thing's for sure," Maxi threw out. "As volatile as it is down here in South-Central, for him to make a factory full of enemies is definitely not healthy."

13

"Guess they pay you big bucks here, you got this bran'
new car," Scud Joe observed as Billy maneuvered
his black Trans Am up to the rain-drenched Pulled Together gates on Florence Avenue.

"When I got the job here and got a raise, I traded in my
old Toyota and put a down payment on this baby," Billy
said. "Treated myself—first new car I ever owned. You still
got the VW?"

"Nah, I can't have wheels no more," Scud Joe said,
frowning. "Just get ripped off. My bug got stole four times,
and the last time it stayed stole. You can't hang on to no
car in the 'hood 'less you stand over it with a gun."

"You have theft insurance?" Billy queried.

"You nuts, man?" Scud Joe exclaimed.

"So what do you drive?"

"Oh, I had four, five nifty rides since the bug," Scud Joe
grinned. "For a while, anyways. I rack some wheels ever'
now 'n' then," he bragged.

"So now you're stealing cars," Billy commented soberly.
"Dammit, Joey, you're going to end up in jail or dead."

"Yeah, well ain't we all?" Scud Joe shot back. "Besides,
I don't mind jail. Three hots and a cot. Last time in, I got
my teeth fixed. Hey, lemme drive this thing, willya?" he
asked, as Billy inserted his card in the slot to open the
parking-lot gate. "I never drove a bran' new car in my life."

"We're here," Billy said.

"On the way back then, okay?"

"Not okay. It's got less than three thousand miles, and
not a scratch on it. I'm not letting you drive it. You don't
even have a license," Billy complained.

"Hey, Billy, I ain't gonna crash it. Okay, just lemme
drive it around the damn parkin' lot," he whined.

"You serious?" Billy asked, looking over at Joe, and for

an instant he saw the face of the eager little boy he was pals with in grade school.

"Just lemme take it around the lot a couple times, okay?" Scud Joe asked again, and Billy hit the brakes and threw the gear shift into *park*. He got out and walked around to the passenger side, opened the door, and scooted Joe over the bucket seats and behind the wheel.

Scud Joe shifted into *drive* and inched the car forward, gingerly at first, a hardened gang-banger looking like a kid at Disneyland. He speeded up till he was doing forty miles an hour up and down the aisles of the big PT parking lot in the pouring rain.

"Whoa, slow down!" Billy yelled at him, but Scud Joe pressed down on the accelerator and made like Mario Andretti skidding around curves, splashing through puddles, clearly having the time of his life.

Suddenly, Billy jabbed him in the ribs. "Jesus, slow down. *Now*! That's him!" he shrieked. Scud Joe jammed on the brakes.

"That's *who*?" he demanded.

"*The boss*, and he looks like he's in one helluva hurry," Billy exclaimed, pointing to a trim, older man in a dark suit with a shock of white hair, who belied his years by sprinting down the rain-slick steps. He was hustling toward a red Ferrari parked in the number-one spot by the side doors to the plant. Scud Joe recognized him from television.

"Paul Bradshaw!" Joe breathed.

"Paul Bradshaw," Billy confirmed. "And I don't need him seeing me tearing ass around his parking lot with a lunatic."

Scud Joe screeched the Trans Am into an empty spot facing the entrance to the factory and turned off the ignition. They watched Bradshaw jump into his sports car and peel out, almost as fast as Scud Joe had been driving. Joe started Billy's car again and backed out of the parking spot. He took a turn around the lot, then drove out the automatic exit gate.

"Hold up! Where the hell you going?" Billy shouted.

"Goin' after him," said Scud Joe, hanging a right onto Florence Avenue.

"You crazy?" Billy hollered. "*Stop the car and get out, Joey, and let me drive!*" he ordered.

"Willya chill?" Scud Joe enjoined. "Let's just see whatcher man's up to, okay?"

Two blocks away, they caught the back end of the red Ferrari disappearing onto the on-ramp to the northbound Harbor Freeway toward downtown Los Angeles. Scud Joe maneuvered into the right-hand lane.

"Goddammit, don't get on the freeway," Billy spit out. "I don't have time for this shit!"

"What are you talkin' you don't have time, you're on your lunch hour, ain'tcha?" Scud Joe threw back. "It's important you know your enemy. Your man might be visitin' a fly houchy for a little noontime meal, in a hurry like that, or goin' out buyin' some guns or somethin'," he said, a wide grin splitting his caramel brown face. "We just gonna find out, can't hurt nothin'," Joe added, as he roared up onto the on-ramp.

Billy groaned. Up ahead they could see the red Ferrari darting in and out of the five freeway traffic lanes in the rain, doing eighty where the speed limit was fifty-five. Scud Joe picked up speed and kept the fire-engine red flash in sight, whooping and laughing and slapping his knee.

Billy looked at him with alarm. "What the fuck are you on, Joey?" he asked him.

"Everythin', as usual," Scud Joe howled with laughter. Billy dropped his head into his hands. He couldn't look.

"You crazy sonofabitch," he wailed. "You're gonna get me fired—or killed."

14

"I'm sorry, Mr. Bradshaw was busy earlier and couldn't return your calls," Ruby Johnson was saying to Devin on the phone, "but he asked me to call you and let you know that—"

"Busy doing what?" Devin broke in.

Actually, Paul Bradshaw had just rushed out of his office after mumbling something to Ruby about a meeting at his

mother's house. When he'd arrived at Pulled Together that
morning, he'd given her strict orders that she was not to
tell his wife a thing, nothing. If Devin phoned, Ruby was
to simply say that he was busy and couldn't take her calls.
Mrs. Bradshaw had called three times. Evidently they'd had
some kind of tiff, more than likely having to do with the
big dinner party last night, Ruby guessed. She'd heard the
morning news anchors joking about dead fish and the new
President, and when she got to work everybody was buzzing about it.

"In fact, I think Mr. Bradshaw has left the building,"
Ruby told his wife.

"You think?" Devin sputtered. "Don't you *know*?"

"All I know is he left this office and he asked me to call
you—"

"Did he take the limo?" Devin interrupted.

"I'm sorry, Mrs. Bradshaw, I just don't know," Ruby
told her. She winced as Devin slammed the phone down in
her ear.

Ruby didn't like covering for Paul Bradshaw. Rumor had
it that he was a notorious player. She'd once witnessed him
coming on blatantly to one of their in-house models, Vanna
Brylock, a stunning young black woman. She'd watched
Vanna put him off delicately but expertly, with a lingering
look from under her long lashes that suggested maybe another time. Ruby recognized it as the *job-security* look
women use when men in power make moves on them.
Later, Vanna confided to her that she wanted nothing to
do with the boss, but she had a child and she needed the
steady work. She'd asked Ruby to warn her when Bradshaw was due at Pulled Together, and now Vanna made it
a point to stay out of the man's way.

Ruby hadn't lied to Devin Bradshaw. She really wasn't
completely sure that Bradshaw had left the building. For
all she knew, he could be holed up in a locked office with
some intimidated young woman who feared for her job.
Nor did she know which car he was using. She hadn't seen
Julius Jackson, his chauffeur, on the premises, so she
guessed he hadn't come in his limousine, but as usual Bradshaw had told her very little. Alex Anson, his assistant in
Santa Monica, handled every detail of his day.

When he was here at PT, he routinely treated Ruby with
faintly discernible disdain, and at times with outright con-

tempt. Prejudice? she wondered. At first she'd felt honored being tapped to act as Paul Bradshaw's personal assistant at the factory, but she soon regretted it. She'd come to dread his visits here, which worked her nerves to the edge of illness. Today he'd humiliated her in front of the television crew, then split without doing the factory tour with them. Ruby would have to decide what to allow the cameraman to shoot. She was sure that Mr. Bradshaw would disapprove in retrospect, then let her know how inept she was. After the shoot she would try to get some work done in the production office, but she was visibly upset and vaguely nauseous.

She knew she had to find another job. And she knew several other employees at Pulled Together who felt the same way. Two things were keeping her there—her loyalty to Billy Hilgarde and the fact that good jobs were scarce. Still, tomorrow she would make some calls and start looking, in case she needed a backup position to jump to in a hurry.

Devin had spent the morning trying to think. Trying to remember the last time she'd been happy with Paul. She couldn't recall the point at which their life together turned that terrible corner. Probably because there hadn't *been* an actual turning point, just a gradual deterioration of their relationship. Now she was most content when he wasn't there.

Still, she kept trying to make things right. She'd called the office several times this morning after he'd stormed off without speaking. He didn't make it easy. His leaving for hours last night without a word of explanation was a deliberate slap. Devin was quite sure that he cheated on her, just as he had cheated on Rosemary. Maybe she was just getting what she deserved, she considered. His excuse with Devin was he hadn't been in love with Rosemary for years, but he'd stayed with her as long as he did for the sake of the children. What was his excuse now? she wondered.

Both Paul and Alex were out of the office this morning. Maybe he was sleeping with Alex Anson again. God knows, Alex wouldn't need any coaxing, Devin thought with chagrin. She'd tried the Pulled Together factory then, and Ruby Johnson confirmed that yes, Paul was there, but he couldn't take her call. Devin wanted to tell him that friends were calling to say that last night's dinner wasn't so bad, that it could happen to anyone.

Right, she thought. Dinner guests making their obligatory morning-after thank-you calls. They probably would have said to Mrs. Lincoln, *Other than that, dear, the play was wonderful!* Paul should be trying to make her feel better about it, not blaming her. She wanted to talk to him, reason with him, make everything all right.

It didn't help that she was exhausted. She couldn't remember when last she'd had a good night's sleep. It was long before the hectic trip to Washington and the rigorous preparation for last night's dinner party. And today she was being ridiculed in the press, pitied by her friends, and repudiated by her husband. She had a tension headache, a fractured wrist, and a broken heart. And for what? What was she accomplishing on any personal or practical level? Nothing she could be really proud of. She longed to start a family, but Paul was adamant about not wanting a second brood.

Certainly she worked hard enough. She'd put this house together, this *hotel*, as it sometimes seemed. But what good was it to her? Here she sat in her lavish private sitting room with its impeccable antique furnishings, its lush Persian rugs, French doors opening onto magnificent gardens, and she was alone except for the staff. She was miserable, empty, and feeling worthless.

She checked her phone directory and dialed the number in Paul's limousine. No answer. Next she tried the car phone in his Ferrari. He picked up.

"Bradshaw!" his voice crackled.

"Paul, this is Devin," she said. For a moment there was silence.

"What do you want?" he asked then.

"Paul, please, stop blaming me for last night," she started. "I feel as bad as you do about it, you have to believe that, but it wasn't my fault."

She heard him sigh. "It was humiliating!" He said it very quietly, and she could feel his controlled fury. "It's my job to work my ass off to pay for everything, and it's your job to just make sure things run smoothly."

"I'm sorry," Devin repeated. "I don't know what else I can say. I'll see you at Regina's."

"Didn't Ruby call you?" he barked.

"Yes, she told me you were on your way to your mother's . . ."

"Didn't she tell you that I said you're not to go over there?"

"Well no, I—"

"Incompetent bitch!" Bradshaw muttered.

"I was just leaving. What are you saying? That you don't want me there?" Devin felt dizzy.

"That's right, I don't," he said.

"But . . . why?"

"Good-bye, Devin."

There was a sharp click at the other end. Devin put down the phone, and tears welled up in her eyes. Not for her ruined relationship with her husband, but for herself. For the good little girl lost, for the late Devin Yorke. How ironic to feel such profound sadness, she thought, amid all this luxury. To be lonely surrounded by so many people, people who were written about in society pages, those who counted in New York, Washington, Los Angeles, Europe— decidedly the A-list. Who would ever suspect that loneliness would pervade the life of a wealthy, privileged, very busy trophy wife?

Trophy wife! The buzzword grated. Face it, she told herself, that's what you've become—*Devin Yorke Bradshaw, Trophy Wife!* The rest of the reasons for her to be a wife to her husband had vanished. She knew what it looked like when they'd first got together, her marrying an extraordinarily wealthy man who was nearly twice her age. But no one dared say a word to her about it, not even her mother, nor would she have listened if they had. How could they know? Back then, she loved him passionately, and forever, period. Back then, the trappings were just incidental. Now they were all there was.

What about all those other women on whom the glitzy media pinned the label "trophy wife"? Was money really what mattered to them? She knew some of them, lunched with them, had been entertained in their homes. And of course she heard the talk, the jokes. That Carolyne Roehm loved her enormous indoor riding ring more than she loved her financier husband, Henry Kravis. The tales about Pat Kluge complaining that after putting up with John for so long, she now had to make do with a lousy twenty million and the house in Virginia. That Peter Brandt was living in the guest house of his Connecticut estate with a gorgeous model, while his trophy wife, Sandy, clung to her "rightful" place in the main house, which she had painstakingly remodeled into an exact replica of Mount Vernon. Georgette Mosbacher had even come out with a best-selling book about her life, stressing that women, above all, must be fiscally self-reliant. The ladies who lunched whispered that in fact Georgette renegotiated her prenuptial agreement with Robert Mosbacher every six months.

Devin would be lying, she admitted to herself now, if she said the money, Paul's money, meant nothing to her. Having every material thing in the world that she could possibly desire was certainly seductive. Hell, it was wonderful. It was every woman's dream. If the well-known "trophy wives" of the nineties put money at the top of their priority lists, that was okay with Devin. It was more than okay, as long as they were also loved and they kept their self-esteem.

Sadly, Devin saw now, in her years with Paul she had lost her self-esteem. She'd always had a healthy sense of her own worth. An overachiever in school, she'd studied diligently—friends used to tease her when she was a cheerleader because she took textbooks on the team bus. An overachiever in business, she'd learned her craft, developed her talents, and honed her skills. She was proud of her accomplishments. Yet here she sat, deflated, defeated, and divested of any shred of the old Devin Yorke dignity.

What happened? When did it happen? While rushing headlong on the society circuit, traveling, decorating, running to charity lunches, playing hostess, checking her computer to see which of her outfits were in the Beverly Hills house (or at the beach, or in the New York apartment or the Aspen chalet), while dressing to within an inch of her life, meticulously maintaining her hair, makeup, skin, nails, her face, her body, working at looking great not just every day but every single hour of the day, because being on display was her job? She simply hadn't noticed that moment in time when her self-respect had vanished.

And there was something else she was missing. Something every young girl grows up believing is her fundamental birthright: love. The love of a wonderful man who puts her feelings, her concerns, above everything else in his life. Sure, maybe she'd seen enough, learned enough, lived enough to know it could never be perfect, fairy-tale-style.

Still, it had to be better than this. It had to be better than having the man you once idolized, deeply loved, and built your life around dismiss you, barely tolerate you, blatantly cheat on you. She deserved to have love in her life, she told herself, and she certainly wasn't getting it from her husband.

Where had the love gone? She could no longer ignore the truth—for Paul Bradshaw, the chase was better than the conquest. The struggle to get his trophy—be it a house, a boat, a car, a deal, a woman—was infinitely more exciting for him than having it. Devin Yorke was a big prize, and he had gone after her big time. And now that he had her, there was something elemental in his psyche that said, "Next case!" And where did that leave her? In a marriage without love.

To some women, to many women she knew, all the money, the homes, the clothes, the jewels, the status, were worth the price. But not to her. Time to ask herself the hard questions. Was she ready and willing to walk away from it all? To go back to doing work she loved and to regain the most valuable thing any woman has, her self-esteem? And to have another chance at finding love?

If she stayed, with the bloom completely off the rose, or off the imported Phalaenopsis orchids as the case may be, would she be a whore? Untrue to herself for material and social gain? A *trophy wife*? If it looks like a duck, if it walks like a duck . . .

Decision time! Suddenly she knew what to do. She no longer needed to weigh the pros and cons, as she'd been doing for months now. Her father had always told her that the big decisions in life made themselves, that eventually you reached a point where you knew, with no more doubts, the right thing to do, and any other course was simply not possible. She had just reached that point. She would leave Paul Bradshaw!

The decision mobilized her into action. The hardest part would be telling him. She knew she had to do it immediately, before she lost her resolve. Paul had a subtle, expert way of trivializing what she had to say. She closed her eyes and visualized his reaction if she waited until he got home tonight. He would put an arm around her, flash that charming grin of his, and say something like, *Darling, it's too much stress, or PMS—let's not overreact to a bunch of fuck-*

ing goldfish. We've both been through too much today. I'll make you some tea, give you a little sleeping pill and tuck you into bed. You need a good night's sleep, and we'll talk about this in the morning. Then the next morning, while he was at work, an exotic flower arrangement in a huge basket would arrive at the house, created by Mark Janssen, of course, who, like her, would be forgiven for being a killer of fish. Attached would be a loving note signed by Paul. And there would be a little blue box from Tiffany containing an expensive bauble that he'd sent Alex to pick out. No, she would tell him *now,* and move out immediately, before he had a chance to dismiss what she had to say. Decision made, leaving him would be easy. Confronting him would be hard.

Ruby had said that he'd just left the South-Central factory. That meant he was probably on the Harbor Freeway, heading north through downtown Los Angeles. Past the downtown interchange he would take the Hollywood Freeway, then on to the Ventura Freeway across the San Fernando Valley to Coldwater Canyon. Then he'd travel Mulholland Drive, westward along the ridge of the hills, to his mother's home in Mulholland Estates.

It was just a ten-minute drive from their villa on Benedict straight up to where it crossed Mulholland, where he would have to pass. Paul was probably about thirty minutes away from that same intersection. She would jump in her car, shoot up through the canyon, and head him off. She would wait there for him on Mulholland Drive, wave him down in his red Ferrari, catch him off guard, say her piece, then leave. Let him announce *that* to the family at lunch!

She leaped into her closet, grabbed a raincoat, and got into it on the run. Scooping up her keys from the dresser, she bolted down the stairs and into the garage, punching the button to activate the garage-door opener as she sped by. She jumped into her Jaguar and fired it up, backed out, turned it around, and gunned it down the drive and out through the massive iron gates of the estate. She refused to break her stride, lest she waver and change her mind.

Careening around the precipitous curves of Benedict Canyon Drive in steady rain, she could feel her heart racing in her throat. Her head was pounding. Her hands were sweating. *Please, God, let me just* do *it,* she prayed. Paul would be completely distracted. His mind would be on the stuff of his meeting. He'd be in a raging hurry to continue on his way. He would be severely annoyed that she'd come out there to detain him. He would not have the inclination or the time to sweet-talk her out of this. It was the perfect opportunity. By the time he came home tonight, she'd be gone. She would throw some things into a couple of bags and take a suite at the Bel Air Hotel, or someplace else convenient and temporary. The first step was the hardest. Plenty of time to figure out the next steps after she took this giant leap.

With a steel grip on the wheel, she powered over rushing water on the perilous canyon road, her mind racing through the short, laconic speech she intended to deliver, repeating it over and over. Three sentences. *Please don't say a word. I just want you to know that I'm leaving you. I'll call you later tonight and let you know where I am.*

She thought about her friend Emily Martin, a beautiful, talented comedy writer who was married to a handsome, charismatic, high-profile television talk-show host. Devin used to jog with her in the mornings and listen to her anguished plaint that her husband of eleven years seemed to put everyone and everything in his world ahead of her, to the point where she felt he was hardly aware that she was there. In a crowd, she said, women would knock her down and walk over her to get to him. She'd agonized for a long time about leaving him. Then finally she made up her mind to do it. She would tell him the next morning at breakfast.

Their cook served orange juice, coffee, oatmeal, and toast, while the two sat facing each other at the table as they did every morning, insulated behind the morning newspapers. Emily told Devin how the print on the page in front of her blurred as she focused on what she was about to say. Then out of the blue, and totally out of character, her husband astounded her by saying in soft, caressing tones, "Do you know how much I love you?" Without removing the newspaper from in front of her face, she closed her eyes. What's wrong with me? she thought. He *does* love me. He gives me everything. Half the women in America would kill to be married to him. I'm a spoiled, selfish, demanding brat. She was torn. "I love you so much," her husband purred again. Emily's heart melted and she put down the newspaper, only to see that he was nose to nose with Woody and Guthrie, talking sweet talk to their two German Rottweilers. She left him that afternoon.

Devin kept repeating her terse mantra aloud, trying to bolster her own resolve. She had reached the stop sign at the top of the hill at the intersection of Benedict and Mulholland. Maneuvering her black Jaguar across the slick, windswept roadway high above the city, she completed the turn and parked on the San Fernando Valley side, on a muddy shoulder overlooking a sheer cliff.

She glanced at her image in the rearview mirror, as if to reassure herself that she was really there, that she was really doing this. Then she got out of the car and stood in the rain, on the edge of the sparsely traveled road, facing east. Paul would be coming by soon; there was no way she could miss him.

She mustered her strength and said a prayer. *Please God, let this be quick and painless and over with.*

15

"Where in the world could your brother be?" Regina Bradshaw inquired of her older son, Sam, not really expecting an answer.

It was ten to two. Paul was nearly an hour late for the family luncheon that he himself had set up the day before, forcing invitees to rearrange their schedules. Now most of the Bradshaws were sitting or milling in the spacious, comfortable family room in Regina's Mediterranean villa. Sam was pouring himself another vodka over ice, ignoring Regina's houseman, Arthur, who was standing at the ready behind the bar.

"I can't imagine," he told his mother. In truth, it would be fine with him if his brother never showed up. Sam Bradshaw had been living in dread of this meeting since Paul had spelled out the agenda for him yesterday at lunch. Indeed, he had been able to think of nothing else since.

He'd been pondering, brooding, coming up with plans,

dismissing those plans, agonizing over his situation, telling himself it was probably for the best, then telling himself that was bullshit, and intently trying to figure out exactly what he was going to do next. He'd come home from Paul's dinner party last night half in the bag, and he'd had himself a few more drinks after Lizbeth went to bed. He got drunker, then he got sober, without sleeping so much as five minutes through the night.

Lizbeth was here, at Paul's insistence. She knew that Sam was in a state, knew he hadn't slept. She'd quizzed him repeatedly about it, but he wasn't about to tell her. His brother was mercurial. Sam knew that Paul could as easily as not surprise the hell out of him today by telling the family something entirely different from what he'd laid out to him at lunch yesterday, with no explanation to his brother apart from a conspiratorial wink.

Paul's three children were speculating on why their father was so late. That in itself was an indication that something big was up, one of them said. Paul Bradshaw was a stickler for punctuality. Sam glanced across the room at Lizbeth, looking very much at ease on one of his mother's silk-covered couches, chatting quietly with their daughter, Allena. Good old Lizbeth, she did always come through. Sam knew she no more wanted to be here than she'd wanted to be at his brother's dinner last night.

And Allena—poised, charming, beautiful Allena. She not only looked at ease, she *was* at ease, anywhere, anytime. Both Sam and Beth had often wondered why Allena seemed to have no interest in a lasting love relationship. But the eighties and nineties were a very different scene from the simple times of Sam's coming of age. Women today were liberated; they had careers; they married in their thirties and had babies in their forties. And Allena Bradshaw, his own daughter, was one of the most liberated women he'd ever known, with one of the most important careers a woman, or anyone, could have.

Then there was Myles. Myles had shown up last night at his uncle's black-tie bash in biker duds, with yet another in a long line of temporary bimbos. Temporary with Myles, that is; she'd be a bimbo forever, Sam noted laconically to himself, downing half his Stoli in a gulp. Myles sat alone on his grandmother's weathered old leather Ruhlmann chair, the one she'd insisted on moving down from San

Francisco, her husband's favorite. Sam could clearly picture his dad relaxing in that very chair. Observing his son, Myles, in it now, his boots up on the ottoman, Sam considered how unlike his father Myles looked, how unlike his father Myles was.

A darkly rugged young man, Myles was tall and thin, verging on gaunt, with a shock of shaggy, dirt brown hair and hooded hazel eyes that seemed to telegraph amusement, even mockery. He dared to be different, but his father, who understood him best, knew that it was just a pose. Myles didn't want to be different; he had trouble fitting in. What others saw as defiance, Sam knew to be diffidence, even fear. He even understood his son's predilection for bimbos. Myles had never had success with what Sam called "uptown" women. At thirty-six, to his mother's chagrin, Myles had never brought home a woman who remotely measured up to her Allenwood family standards. Nor had he ever had a relationship with any woman for very long. The one relationship in his life that did endure was with his father. Myles could certainly afford to be on his own. He made a good living in the company-owned automotive shop. But Myles had no desire to move away from home. He lived alone in the guest house on his parents' property in Trousdale.

Myles had come along too early, just ten months after he and Lizbeth were married, but from the first, Sam had doted on his little guy. After Myles, the young parents were more careful; Allena wasn't born until four years later. But father and son were kindred spirits. On the surface, except for a certain sameness of gesture and speech patterns, the two looked like products of unrelated gene pools. Only Sam was keenly aware that there were more similarities between the two than differences.

Sam had agonized over his son's academic failure all through his school years. It wasn't as if Myles didn't apply himself—the lessons seemed always just one step beyond him. Sam and Beth tried tutors; that didn't help. They'd had him tested for learning disabilities, and yes, he was dyslexic, the technicians said. But there was more. Myles Benton Bradshaw had a slightly substandard IQ, read the ignominious reports. But Sam had never accepted that. Myles just didn't test well, he believed. And back then, Myles stuttered badly, an impediment that became even more severe when he was overly stressed, which he very often was.

His sister had never studied half as diligently, but she'd breezed through high school and USC and went on to get her law degree at Yale. Myles had wanted to be a doctor, but with his poor grades it was out of the question. He'd flunked out of college, then went on to a trade school and learned automotive engineering. Now Allena was practicing at a prestigious L.A. law firm that specialized in the big-moneyed music industry, and her older brother was greasing cars.

Sam had always favored Myles, probably because Allena was her mother's favorite and his son needed him so much more. And Myles deeply touched his heart. No one knew better than Sam Bradshaw how humiliating it felt to be bested at every turn by your younger, only sibling.

Sam's eyes drifted back to his mother, and for just a minute he reflected on the wide range of familial genetic makeup that presented in his two children. Allena was much like the genial, outgoing, charming senior Sam Bradshaw, and Myles was a DNA copy of the stoic Regina. And dropping down a generation, Allena water-skied over the tops of life's crises, large and small, and conquered all—she was all Paul. Myles, her mirror opposite, was introspective, quiet, moody even, like himself, the acorn that fell very close to the tree.

He had to smile as he thought back to yesterday afternoon, to Myles's response when he'd told him what was going to happen at this meeting today. Myles suggested they go away someplace, go down to Cabo, skip the family announcement altogether and chill out. "We'll sail, maybe snare a marlin," he'd said, "and let Uncle Paul have his fun without the two of us there to humiliate."

He'd told Myles no, they had to be at the meeting. Then they could go away on a trip. Because then it would be with Paul's blessing, and with Bradshaw money, he explained. But if they bolted and ran, defied his brother, Paul would cut them off completely. Lizbeth would suffer too, and maybe even Allena.

Sam reflected on other occasions when he'd saved Myles from himself. Myles marched to his own music; he had frequent flights of fancy. Even today, he had his own bizarre thoughts about why his uncle hadn't shown up. Watching him now, isolated from the family chat, once again Sam got the nagging feeling that maybe his son needed professional help.

"Probably Devin is holding him up," Sam's mother remarked archly now. Regina, like the rest of the Bradshaw family, had never approved of Devin Yorke, and she didn't bother to hide it.

"Why don't you make some calls, dear?" she asked him. Sam never would have suggested it. Shrugging, he picked up the phone on the bar and punched in the private number for Paul's office. He could hear his mother, ever forgiving of her favorite son, commenting to the rest of the family that something more important must have come up.

"After all," Regina was saying loftily, "Bill Clinton is in town. I'm sure whatever Paul wanted to tell us can wait. We might as well sit down and eat."

Geneen Landers, Sam's own assistant, answered his ring. He remembered now that Alex hadn't come in this morning. Obviously his brother's calls were being forwarded.

"Geneen, it's Sam. Do you know where Paul is?" he asked.

"Yes, Sam—Ruby Johnson said he was on his way over to your mother's house from PT. He should have been there an hour ago."

"Will you call around, Geneen?" Sam asked. "See if you can track him down?"

"Of course. But where could he be?" Geneen ventured.

"That's the sixty-four-thousand-dollar question—he seems to have fallen off the face of the earth," Sam answered, and with that, he felt his face inadvertently redden. Poor choice of words, he realized.

16

Devin sat on the chaise longue in her private sitting room, the doors locked, dull, rain-washed light filtering through half-closed shutters, oblivious to the rivulets of mud and water dripping from her clothes onto the plush cushions and the silk rug beneath her feet. It had been a disaster. If only she could roll back the clock to late morning, to before she'd made the impulsive dash to the top of Mulholland Drive in the rain to tell her husband she was leaving him. She fervently wished that she could undo what was done.

Maybe she should talk to someone, she reasoned. Her mother? Celia Yorke had moved back to Michigan after her divorce from Devin's father, virtually divorcing eighteen-year-old Devin at the same time. They spoke on the phone infrequently. Her mother would probably get hysterical. She thought Paul Bradshaw was the salt of the earth. In her mother's eyes, rich was synonymous with perfect.

Who else? A friend? Sadly, Devin had let all her close friendships wane during her years with Paul. Maybe Tanner. Tanner had actually made her laugh in the gym this morning, and that had felt good. But even though they worked out together every morning, she really didn't know him well. The person she should talk to, of course, was her lawyer. Or maybe she shouldn't tell any of it to anyone at all. Her injured right arm was aching with reflected pain. There was dried blood between her fingers, running across the back of her hand and into the cuff of her ivory silk blouse. There were small dark spots of blood splattered on her raincoat.

"Stop it—are you trying to kill me?" Paul's furious cry still echoed in her head. Devin squeezed her eyelids closed in an attempt to black out that fleeting moment of fear on his face, but the image etched behind her eyes lost none of its graphic intensity. She had never before seen Paul Bradshaw register fear, in any situation. She'd witnessed bouts of fierce anger. At times she'd watched his features contort to reveal hatred, envy, vanity, lust. Over the years she had seen him arrogant, evil, vicious, vengeful, cruel— but she had never seen him afraid.

She stood up and shrugged out of her sopping raincoat, letting it fall to the floor. Blood was smeared on the front of her ivory wool skirt, where she'd mindlessly wiped the back of her hand. She unclipped her belt. Stepping out of her skirt and kicking off her high heels, she slowly removed the sodden, muddy clothes.

Naked, she walked into the massive master bathroom, and examined her body in the expanse of mirrored walls. She felt as if she were looking at someone else—a tall thin stranger with an impassive face and a short crop of wet blond hair. The other woman looked strong, beautiful, sexy. Devin felt weak, unappealing, and dirty. Curiously, she touched her breasts, then her nipples, as if to ascertain that the body she stroked was alive. Her flesh was cold. She felt nothing.

She stepped into the shower and let the rush of hot water and steam penetrate her shivering body. With a sharp loofa sponge, she dug fiercely at her arms, her legs, her chest, her stomach, and around to her back and down over her buttocks, then back again several times over. Getting out of the shower finally, dripping water on the marble floor, she could feel the blood pulsating angrily beneath her skin, could see the punishing red glow she'd raised over her limbs and torso. She dried off hurriedly and wrapped herself in the fresh, peach-colored terrycloth robe that hung behind the door.

Hurriedly, she scooped up the wet, wrinkled heap of clothes from the sitting-room floor and carried them down the back service staircase, through the kitchen, and out into the garage. There she found the boxes of large green trash bags that Jos used for yard work. Quickly she stuffed the clothes, including her heavy Burberry trench coat, into a plastic bag, then drew the yellow band at the top to close it. She buried the bag deep into one of several trash cans at the far side of the garage, carefully packing it underneath other green bags full of weeds, twigs, and brush.

José hadn't come today because of the rain. Maria and Laguya were busy elsewhere in the huge house. Peggy was working on correspondence in the office. Nobody saw her. The trash would go out on Monday with the regular pickup. She never wanted to see those clothes again.

She hurried back up the rear staircase and into her bedroom suite. Again, she scrubbed her hands and face. Fiercely, she willed that getting rid of the blood and dirt on her body, and the clothes she wore, would erase the rage she felt and the deed she'd done. She had started to dress when the phone rang. For a moment she panicked. Then, allowing the answering machine to get it, she sat on the bed and listened.

"Devin, this is Sam Bradshaw. Do you know where—"
Devin picked up the phone.
"Hello, Sam."

"Where's Paul?"

"Why, I'm fine, Sam. Good of you to ask," she returned icily. She might as well divorce the whole damn unpleasant family, she thought.

Ignoring her sarcasm, Sam told her that Paul was long overdue at their mother's house. "Do you know where he is?" he demanded again.

"I have no idea," she said in measured tones. "I spoke to him in the car sometime after noon, and he said he was on his way to Regina's. I haven't heard from him since."

"Was he supposed to pick you up for the lunch at Mother's?"

"No."

"Well, why didn't you come?"

Devin ignored the question. "Sam," she said, "I don't know where Paul is." With that, she hung up.

Quickly, she dressed in tan slacks and a shirt. Then she stood on a chair and pulled some Louis Vuitton cases down from the upper shelves, opening them out on the long upholstered bench in her dressing room. Her mind kept flashing back to the ugly scene in the rain. Paul staggering, clutching his eye, furious, soaking wet and bleeding; she racing her Jaguar down the wet, treacherous canyon road, feeling the blood running over her hand, seeing his jagged flesh.

She started throwing things in the suitcases, grabbing outfits at random—shoes, scarves, belts, a couple of purses, underthings, jewelry. Workout clothes, though she had no idea where she was going to exercise. She just knew she had to get out of that house, fast.

17

"Probably another fool racing on Mulholland," Fire Captain Jack Croece observed.

"And lost it in the rain," added Joe Gaines, LAFD paramedic.

The two slipped and slid in the muck just off the roadway, attempting to secure a lifeline down the steep, muddy grade from a figure-eight winch aboard their fire engine. About a hundred and fifty feet below, almost at the Valley floor, they could see what looked to be the back end of a small red car. It was hung up in a thick clump of gnarled laurel sumac trees growing sideways out of the jagged terrain. Engine 97 had taken an EMS emergency call directing them to a possible car over the side on the north edge of Mulholland Drive between Benedict Canyon and Beverly Glen. The tip had come in to 911 from a woman who happened to spot the vehicle down below.

Sighting cars over the steep cliffs bordering the highway was part of life for residents of the Mulholland corridor— it happened with regularity in all kinds of weather. Its precipices, shrouded in dense growth, were a favored venue for murders, suicides, dumping bodies and stolen cars, and speed freaks losing it around the treacherous curves. Street gangs ran regular drag races along Mulholland on Saturday nights. Some won, some lost, and some took the long, long plunge.

And Mulholland was the city's most popular movie location for murder, suicide, and accident scenes. Production companies were continually hauling battered vehicles up over the cliff sides, and taking "bodies" away on stretchers. Passersby couldn't always tell what was real and what was not, contributing to the endemic blurring of the lines between reality and fantasy in La-La Land.

Croece and Gaines, with the help of two LAPD blues who'd also responded to the call, had dragged the steep canyon with their eyes, the four of them walking Mulholland in the unrelenting rain from Benedict Canyon west, until Croece spotted the bright red splotch of color down through the tangled overgrowth below. The captain had immediately called for hook-and-ladder backup from the nearest truck company, Station 102 in the San Fernando Valley. Their engine up top had only water pump and hose; this situation called for ladders, tools, rescue equipment, and manpower.

"Christ, I'm too old for this," Croece groused, after losing his footing and sliding several perilous feet down the slick incline before stopping himself on a low-hanging branch.

Captain Jack Croece was a gentleman and almost never

cursed. But even after more than thirty years with the department, the thought that some hapless, helpless driver was very probably inside the wreckage made him tense, sickened him. This accident couldn't be too old, he reasoned, because he could still see traces of the skid marks, deep indents off the edge of the ridge, fast being obliterated by the pouring rain. Instead of waiting for help to arrive, he'd made the decision to immediately effect the climb down into the steep canyon.

"I can take it from here, Captain," Gaines told his superior.

Joe Gaines had great admiration for his boss, who was a soft-spoken, distinguished-looking man in his fifties with white wavy hair and neatly clipped mustache, a man in top physical condition who loved to cook, play softball, and read poetry, and who was not afraid to get dirty. He shot a glance up at the two AIDs, Accident Investigation Division police officers, who were standing together up on the road now, watching as he and Croece struggled with the rope. The cops had their own problems in this era of Rodney King, it was true, and Gaines was sure those guys worked hard, but he was very proud to be a paramedic with the Los Angeles City Fire Department. There were only eight men on regular rotation at the small fire station on Mulholland east of Laurel Canyon, but they were a highly trained, disciplined, close-knit unit, and they saved lives.

Richard Oheata, the squad's second paramedic, had come off the engine and joined them on the ridge. "Holler out what you need, partner," he said, putting an arm around Gaines. Rich would stand by up top, ready to haul down any supplies and equipment Gaines might call for should he find someone inside the car.

"Okay, Cap, I'm ready to go down," Joe Gaines told Croece now, giving the rope a yank to test the rigging on the canvas harness and alert Bill Browne, their engineer up on the truck, that he was ready for him to play out the line.

"Go for it," Captain Croece okayed, and Joe hoisted himself over the side. Deftly, he rappelled down the nearly vertical face, shielding his upper body to keep from being scratched by the dense brush and natural chaparral that lined the canyon. Joe Gaines was twenty-nine years old with bright green eyes and an abundance of dark hair, tall, trim and muscular, and as fit as any professional athlete.

He had a trauma kit fastened to the tubular strapping on his harness, and a radio clipped to his waist. If anyone was inside that car and alive, he'd have the captain radio Air Ops for a pair of choppers out of Van Nuys Airport, one to spot in this marginal weather, the other to get the victim or victims evacuated to the nearest trauma center.

Minutes later he reached the vehicle, a late-model Ferrari Testarosa. The front end was almost completely ripped off. It clung to the frame by just its right front fender—the rest was dangling from the small rocky promontory where the car had landed. Gaines looked inside and saw a man doubled over at the wheel, almost certainly dead, he thought. He tried opening the accordion-pleated door, but it was sealed shut.

"One male, can't tell his age, appears to be the driver, badly crushed, looks like substantial traumatic injuries," he reported on Croece's radio signal. Then he saw the man move.

"My God, he's alive," he barked. "Get me a Physical Rescue Assignment and an air ambulance. We need heli-tac for hoist and rescue. And have the task force load the jaws of life . . ."

Though the driver's door was jammed shut, Gaines could see through the shattered side window that the victim was bleeding profusely. The broken windshield was plastered with bloody fragments of flesh and hair. The roof of the car had collapsed, probably from several rollovers, forcing the driver's face and upper body down against the steering wheel. But the man was breathing, Gaines was sure of it now. He could see the faintly rhythmic heaving of his back and shoulders, and he could hear him gurgling blood.

"Cap," he radioed up to Croece, "send Rich down with a backboard, a cervical collar and neck rolls, ASAP."

He tugged at the driver's door again; it wouldn't budge. Scanning the rain-soaked ground, he picked up a jagged boulder and smashed through the window with it. Reaching inside for leverage, he yanked on the car door with both hands until it finally gave. He managed to force it open wide enough to squeeze through and get to the victim inside the crumpled vehicle.

"Gaines . . . ," Croece's voice squawked from his radio receiver. "Oheata's on his way down. But Van Nuys might not have enough visibility to get the choppers out in this weather. How bad is the victim?"

"Bad," Joe returned. "Barely alive. There's no way he'll make it if we have to haul him up the mountain . . ."

He stopped. He thought he heard the man saying something. "My aah . . . my eyes . . ."

Gaines reached for the injured man's head and gently lifted it from the dashboard. His face was covered with dried blood, through which fresh blood still oozed. On impact, his head had slammed into the windshield and his face was jammed down through the metal steering wheel, opening a massive gash across his forehead and down through his left eye. Gaines popped the trauma kit open.

"Choppers en route in borderline visibility," Croece's voice rasped through the radio. "Should be here in five."

The man looked familiar, Joe thought. In his fifties maybe, good-looking, tanned, well dressed, driving a Ferrari. These hills were full of film directors, producers, movie stars. This guy looked like he was *somebody*.

He quickly swabbed the gaping head wounds with alcohol and applied bandages to stanch the bleeding. Then he took a knife and cut away the blood-soaked, red-striped shirt and red silk tie. The man's upper chest was caved in, his rib cage crushed. Gaines felt for a pulse at the base of his neck. It was weak, but it was there.

At his touch, the man let out a low moan, followed by slurred, barely intelligible words. "No Dev, ahh . . . don't . . . my eye . . ." If by some miracle this poor guy makes it, Joe thought, his left eye will certainly be useless.

"Hang in, buddy," he murmured as he quickly and skillfully cleaned out the bleeding chest wounds. "You're looking good, you're looking good, guy. You're gonna be okay . . ."

He was hastily wrapping a tourniquet around the man's upper body, over his clothes, when he heard the whir of the helicopters through the din of the driving rain.

"You just might be one lucky sonofabitch," Joe breathed at his unconscious patient, then he backed out of the pulverized sports car, peered up through the rain, and waved his arms at the two choppers approaching the crash scene.

Fire-5, a Bell Jet Ranger, stayed topside, its blades whacking the air, the two pilots spotting and providing radio guidance in the near-zero visibility, while from the ground Gaines motioned to the pilots aboard Fire-2, the big Bell 412 carrying the payload: more paramedics and crucial medical equipment. Landing in this precarious terrain was impossible.

From the base of the cliff, Rich Oheata hit the ground running, hauling a backboard and a bundle of supplies. Right behind him on the ropes came four men from the task force hook and ladder, guiding the bulky jaws of life.

Fire-2 was in low and hovering now, and the heli-tacs pushed open a door. They threw out ropes, and the two paramedics on board dropped to the ground. The tacs lowered more medical equipment, then a litter basket to haul the victim up into the chopper.

Gaines had done everything he could at that point, which was clean the wounds and stop the bleeding. Without speaking, the four paramedics and four task force firefighters fired up the jaws and went to work to physically pull the car apart.

"Major hemorrhaging and internal injuries, besides what you see," Gaines briefed the others.

It took eighteen minutes to cut the victim out of his car. He looked bad. They did a full C-spine—tied the man down to a backboard for spinal stabilization, put a cervical collar on him, braced him with neck rolls on both sides, then taped his head to the board to keep his neck rigid.

"You're gonna be okay," Gaines kept encouraging him.

"Yeah, buddy, you're in good hands. Nobody dies with Engine ninety-seven on the case," Rich Oheata joined in.

Carefully the men hoisted the victim into the basket, and the tacs on Fire-2 hauled him aboard. After clearing it with Croece, they took up all four paramedics to continue treatment. Then the tacs pulled the doors shut, and Fire-2 eased up and peeled off toward Holy Cross Hospital in Mission Hills, one of only two trauma centers left to serve the extensive San Fernando Valley since recent cutbacks had shut down the rest of them.

En route they clamped an oxygen mask over the patient's nose and mouth, and maneuvered his torso into a MAST suit, military anti-shock trousers, to force blood up into his vital organs. They hooked up two large-bore IVs for fluid replacement to build up his blood pressure, and intubated him with a tube down his throat to force air into his lungs. Still, his blood pressure was bottoming out.

"Damn, we're losing him," Gaines muttered as the chopper began its descent onto the hospital grounds.

"We've done everything we could," Skip Moessen, the chief paramedic from Fire-2, murmured, largely to reassure himself.

"Jesus!" Skip said then. "Look who this guy is . . ." No one had taken time to check the man's identity.

"Who is he?" Rich and the other med, Ab Moranis, asked at the same time.

"You guys read *Time* magazine?" Skip asked. "He's on the cover!"

Gaines was bent over the patient, monitoring his vital signs. "He's also dead," he said.

18

"*Track him down?*" Alex muttered the words aloud. A message from Paul Bradshaw's brother on her voice mail at the office echoed one he'd left for her at home: "Alex, this is Sam. Geneen says you're feeling better now. We can't locate Paul—I need you to track him down."

"Sure, Sam, I'll track him down," she repeated now to the empty walls. After her mission to the mountaintop with Rosemary, Alex had gone straight home and found Sam's urgent message. She got right back into her car and came in to the office.

Sam had tried his brother's house, he'd said. No, Alex knew, Paul was not at home. Interesting—Ruby Johnson had told her that Devin had been calling the Pulled Together plant all morning and he wouldn't take her calls. Paul and Devin must have had a beaut after last night's dinner debacle. Alex smirked. That story was all over the press today. Paul had been fighting with Devin more and more frequently, and Alex had a ringside seat for the ongoing match. She'd witnessed the progression from their lovey-dovey first year, when Paul was on the phone with Devin constantly, to their second year—married then—

when they spoke several times a day. In their third year
together, the pair connected during business hours now and
then. But their fourth year had been something else again.
The four-year itch—Paul had it, and Alex loved it. Back
during *her* years with him, he had settled into a relationship
with Rosemary that seemed to work for both of them. Alex
had figured that after thirty-three years of marriage, adul-
tery was like the Laundromat—less work for mother. But
Devin Yorke was a whole other breed of lynx.

Ruby had also filled her in on the fight Paul had this
morning with Billy Hilgarde. In normal circumstances, Paul
Bradshaw wouldn't have occasion to speak to some worker
in the marking department, wouldn't even know his name.
But Hilgarde was trying to organize PT into a union shop,
and for months he'd been working his way underneath Paul
Bradshaw's fingernails on the issue. Alex's orders when
Hilgarde called were to shine him on. "Mr. Bradshaw's on
another call." "Mr. Bradshaw's in a meeting." "Mr. Bradshaw's out of the office." "Mr. Bradshaw's out of the country." She'd used them all on Hilgarde, five or six times
over. She'd wanted to tell him, "Mr. Bradshaw is on another planet!"

Track him down? No, she was not about to start calling
around town asking people if they'd seen her boss. She had
her own agenda. She slipped into Bradshaw's inner office.
She debated locking the door so she could count on privacy
to snoop for any evidence that Paul had put her termina-
tion into the pipeline. No, if someone did try to come in,
that would look suspicious. After all, Paul was among the
missing. People were working the phones, searching for
him. They could well be dropping by his office to see if
he'd shown up or if Alex had heard anything.

Sam certainly didn't seem to be aware that his brother
had fired her last night. Maybe Paul hadn't got around to
making it fly. She left the office door closed but not locked,
then did a quick, thorough riffle through Paul's papers and
computer files. Nothing. Just the letter of resignation he'd
punched out yesterday on his computer. Should I? she wondered. Then she did. Delete it. What did she have to lose?

The letter! The *printout* of the letter. She never did sign
it—in a fit of pique, she'd crumpled it up and tossed it in
the trash. Specifically, into the wastepaper basket under
her desk.

Alex scooted out the door and sat down at her own desk. Stooping over, she drew the little wicker basket out and peered inside. Good, the maintenance people hadn't emptied it overnight. They often overlooked this one because it was small and tucked under her desk, while the larger trash can that seemed always overflowing was more visible behind her chair.

The crumpled letter was not on top of the litter where she'd tossed it last night. She shuffled through the shallow basket. Not much in it. She was certain this is where she'd pitched the damn thing. And she was just as certain that it was gone.

"Mr. Sam is wanted on the phone," Kippie announced to the assembled Bradshaws at lunch in Regina's dining room. "It's Mrs. Bradshaw. The *other* Mrs. Bradshaw," she amended, with an apologetic look toward her dowager employer.

"Where is Paul?" Regina demanded of the woman. "Does Devin know?"

"Let me get it, Mother," Sam said, standing and dropping his napkin on the table. He went into Regina's study to take the call.

Quietly, in measured tones, Devin dropped the bombshell. She'd just been informed that Paul had been in an accident on his way to Regina's—he was dead on arrival at Holy Cross Hospital.

Sam's heart did a flip-flop. He listened to Devin spelling out the particulars. Odd, Sam thought, she was not hysterical, not even crying. In shock, maybe, but he doubted that. He had always been convinced that with Devin it was about money from the get-go. When she'd said her piece and hung up, he put down the phone and sank back into his chair, taking a minute to process what he'd been told.

Recovering, he went back into the dining room and took a seat—specifically, the seat at the head of the table that had until now been reserved for Paul. He had everyone's full attention. All Bradshaw eyes in the room were riveted on Sam, waiting for him to speak. He would long remember that moment as his first real taste of power. Quietly, he told them the news: Paul was dead.

He put a protective arm around his mother, who was at his right, gazing at him in disbelief. Regina broke down.

Sam and the rest of the family tried vainly to comfort her, but she was inconsolable. "My Pauly," she moaned, over and over.

Sam helped Kippie take her to her room, then he called for Dr. Aarens. The rest of the Bradshaws remained seated around the dining-room table, ignoring half-eaten lunch dishes, speaking in hushed tones, stunned.

Devin sat alone in her kitchen study. The police had arrived while she was upstairs packing. A man and a woman in uniform. They had something to tell her, they'd said, but first they had insisted that Mrs. Bradshaw be seated on one of the chairs in the entry rotunda. They both continued standing while the woman spoke. Mrs. Bradshaw's husband had had an accident in the rain, she'd said. The paramedics had done everything they could, but Mr. Bradshaw expired en route to the hospital. An investigator from the coroner's office would be coming by very soon to talk to her. Sorry she had to go through that, the woman had said sympathetically, but it was routine.

That was more than two hours ago. Finally, she heard the bell, and Maria ushered two men into the room. They introduced themselves and showed badges and ID cards. They were not from the coroner's office; they were LAPD detectives. Devin asked Maria to bring coffee. They declined. She'd like some tea, she said, while they, too, stood before her uncomfortably. She'd forgotten their names already.

"Please," she said, "sit down." They did—reluctantly, she thought. Nobody spoke for a long minute.

"Did he say anything?" she asked then. One of them, the tall one, reached into the inside pocket of his jacket and produced a notebook.

"Yes," he said, consulting his notes. "According to the paramedics at the scene, he was saying something like . . . ," and he read the text in a monotone: " 'My aah, my eyes, my eye, help me, no Dev,' and 'my eye' again, repeatedly." The officer looked up at Devin. "Does that mean anything to you, Mrs. Bradshaw?" *Oh God,* she thought, *his eye . . .*

"No," she told the detective. Both of them were studying her curiously. "Did you want to ask me anything?" she ventured after a bit. "The policewoman who was here said you'd have some questions ... but you're not from the coroner's office after all ..."

The shorter, Irish-looking one cut in. "Do you know anyone who'd want to kill your husband?"

"Kill him?" Devin repeated.

"Yes, Mrs. Bradshaw," he returned. "It was not an accident. The ER doctors found that your husband was shot in the side of the chest with a .38-caliber hollow-point bullet. There was just one small, clean entry hole. The paramedics missed it because his body was badly mangled from the crash."

The taller officer consulted his notes again and picked up the narrative. "The killer evidently pulled the victim's jacket back, shot him under the arm through the chest, then closed his jacket back over the wound," he read dispassionately. "Then shoved his car over the cliff," he added, snapping the notebook shut.

His partner nodded. "It was murder, Mrs. Bradshaw," he said.

19

Alex pulled into her parking space at work. It was Saturday morning, and she was numb, confused, and frightened. Sam had called the office yesterday afternoon with the news that Paul was dead. Killed in an accident, he'd said perfunctorily, then he dictated a laundry list of things he wanted done.

"Have notices posted at the plant, apprising the workers of Paul's tragic and untimely death, and informing them that on Monday the factory will be closed in Paul Bradshaw's memory. Call Ruby Johnson and have her do the same at Pulled Together," he'd rattled on, obviously reading from notes. Alex was then to call a list of key players from both operations and summon them to a closed-door meeting this morning at Santa Monica headquarters.

When finally she'd escaped from the office and reached

the seclusion of her small apartment north of Sunset, she
locked the door, lowered the blinds, sat on her bed, and
called Rosemary. The two women agreed not to tell anyone
what they'd done yesterday. Then this morning, Alex heard
on the news that the police were calling it murder. Who
would murder the garment czar? was the question investi-
gators wanted answered, the reporter said. From Alex's
vantage, close to the profusion of conflict that pervaded—
even energized—Paul Bradshaw's life, she could think of a
lot of people who might not be unhappy to see Paul Bradshaw dead. Even herself. She loved him and hated him,
still, and the combination had induced a rage of tears
throughout the night.

She had put a lot of effort into getting herself together
this morning, but she hadn't been able to pull it off. Her
usually sparkling brown eyes were red and swollen, her face
was puffy, and no amount of makeup had helped. From
years of experience crying over Paul Bradshaw, she knew
she wouldn't look normal until she'd gone two straight days
without shedding a tear, and the immediate outlook for
that was doubtful.

She made her way through the lobby of the L.A. Garb
complex, and up the stairs to the executive suites. Her office door was open, as was the door into Paul's inner sanctum, now filled with people. It was after nine o'clock; she
was fifteen minutes late. Big mistake. She should have
been early.

Standing at the doorway to Paul's office, Alex felt like
an alien on her own turf. Sam Bradshaw was ensconced
behind Paul's massive desk, while around him sat a somber
group of the company's top lieutenants. Geneen Landers,
in gray flannel business suit and midheels, her makeup
flawless, her auburn hair brushed into a sleek pageboy, sat
at Sam's left taking notes.

"Aah, Alex," Sam said, looking up at her. "Come on in.
We've started. Grab a seat." Alex nodded to several of her
colleagues, most of them sitting on chairs brought in from
the conference room.

"We're in the process of working out a reorganization of
duties," Sam briefed her as she made her way to a spot on
one of the couches. She settled down, her emotions badly
scrambled, and tried to digest what was going on.

"And this involves you, Alex," Sam went on, directing

his remarks to her. "Geneen will continue as my personal assistant, and I'll need you to brief her on Paul's systems for the next couple of weeks, maybe longer, whatever it takes."

"Then what?" Alex heard herself asking.

"I don't know yet," Sam replied, "but I assure you that you are, and will continue to be, a valuable part of the team."

Charlie Fine sat on a lone chair in a far corner of Paul Bradshaw's spacious office, isolated from the rest. He had deliberately stayed on the periphery of the group, turning a chair around from the built-in fax station to face the imposing mahogany desk where Paul's brother Sam was now holding forth. As the second in command at L.A. Garb, Sam's ascension was natural, of course, but Charlie had his doubts. Big doubts. Still, even he knew that Sam Bradshaw had to be given his shot. Who knows, he reasoned, listening to him effectively demote Alexandra Anson from her role as personal assistant to the top executive—maybe, like Harry Truman, he'll rise to the job.

Charles J. Fine was known as an astute, sagacious money manager as well as a longtime friend of Paul Bradshaw. He was in attendance at this meeting for entirely different reasons than most of the others grouped around the new boss. By the terms of Paul Bradshaw's will, 45 percent of the company shares would go to the Bradshaw Foundation, which Fine administered as Paul's chosen trustee. He and Paul had set up the foundation years ago, though they'd never kept any money in it. Now it would be funded, and Charlie would be voting that block of stock, and having been close to Paul Bradshaw and his company's operations for the last twenty years, he had never thought that Sam was much of an asset.

It was in Paul's interest for Charlie to be brutally honest over the years, and he'd never been less than that. He had always made it clear how he felt about Sam—nice enough guy, but a fairly empty suit. Not the best person to have just a heartbeat away from the top. But Paul had never been able to see his brother with the same unmitigatingly objective eyes with which he looked at all other aspects of his giant business holdings. Blood was blood, Charlie knew. Besides, Paul had always told him that he had no intention of dying, that he was going to live forever. "In the year three thousand," Paul would joke, "the only survivors on earth will be me, Dick Clark, and the cockroaches." And until yesterday, Charlie wouldn't have ruled that out.

The Bradshaw Foundation had been created to serve several purposes. It was an ego trip for Paul, of course. It would keep his name in the limelight by doing good deeds, and Paul liked to joke that it would cover his ass in case there really was an afterlife. On a fiscal level, because its objectives were wholly charitable, it would enable the heirs to avoid a substantial amount of estate tax on nearly half the company. From the outset, the practical purpose of the Bradshaw Foundation was to preclude the necessity of breaking up the company or having to sell it upon the owner s death in order to pay the taxes.

Another 45 percent would go to the Bradshaw Family Trust. The income from that block would take care of Paul's mother, his brother, Sam, his wife, all their kids and spouses, and their offspring. Sam Bradshaw was the trustee of the family trust. Sam would be voting that block of stock. And not unexpectedly, with no opposition, Sam had immediately appointed himself the new CEO of L.A. Garb.

Paul's wife stood to inherit the other 10 percent. Her portion would be subject to the marital exclusion on estate taxes. And it meant, of course, that Devin Bradshaw would have the swing vote. That, Charlie knew, could make for a very interesting situation.

Sam Bradshaw sat at his brother's desk observing the assembled troops, *his* troops now, each looking back at him expectantly, some taking notes. At first he had intended to hold this meeting in the considerably larger conference room, but there was something about his brother's private office that he knew would be empowering. Sam was moving, moving, moving, getting on with business. He'd thought long and hard last night, and he admitted to himself that although a very small part of him mourned his dead brother, the rest of him felt liberated, exhilarated, as if his life were just beginning.

He told them now that all the workers had been notified that Monday, the first business day after his brother's death, was to be an official day of mourning for Paul Bradshaw. That the dual American and California Golden Bear flags would be flown at half staff on the Santa Monica grounds, and all operations would be idled at both plants. The company would resume business as usual on Tuesday, he said.

He had spoken with Devin last night. He'd told her he felt the funeral should be held on Thursday, and he would be glad to plan it. She didn't resist. And tonight he would go over to his mother's house to be with her. Regina Bradshaw was in her eighties, and she'd always been strong, but her younger son's death had thrust her into despondency. She'd lost her husband years ago, but always, to her sons, she had seemed invulnerable. She was almost never ill, not even with the commonplace ailments that fell most people from time to time. Sam and Paul used to kid that she was their Rose Kennedy, that she would more than likely outlive the two of them. Now her doctor was keeping her sedated to withstand the shock of losing her son.

Sam told Alex that he would need her and Geneen to stay for a few hours after the meeting, and that the three of them would have to get together tomorrow as well. Alexandra Anson knew more about running L.A. Garb than anyone else in the company, Sam knew, and he needed her to help with his transition. He wanted her to go over current company business with him and Geneen—to take the bulk of the weekend and start bringing them up to speed.

His eyes lingered on the young Irish beauty. She looked like she'd been weeping. Everyone knew that she'd slept with his brother for years. She was probably still in love with him, long after he'd married Devin. For an instant, as Sam Bradshaw sat in his brother's former office, at his brother's former desk, with his brother's former title and power, he lusted after his brother's former mistress.

20

It was Monday morning, the company day of mourning at L.A. Garb for founder and owner Paul Bradshaw. Devin was in her gym at the Benedict Canyon mansion. At close to 6 A.M. she was going through the motions of her warm-up stretches, waiting for Tanner to arrive. He'd called her on Friday night, said he'd heard the news. He was sorry. And did she want to skip her workouts for awhile? No, she'd told him, giving up exercise wouldn't help. In fact, she knew that her daily exercise was part of her salvation.

Her mind was skittering between sadness, fear, grief, relief, shock, guilt, even crazy humor. I should be wearing a black leotard, she flashed, watching herself in the floor-to-ceiling mirrors, reaching over to touch the floor in hot-pink bicycle pants and a halter top. When she straightened up she saw Tanner's reflection in the mirror. He'd been standing in the doorway, watching her.

"Hi," she said, cheerlessly.

"How're you doing?" he asked.

"In what area?"

"I can see you're doing fine physically," he quipped. "How about emotionally?"

She grabbed a towel off the balance bar and sat astride one of the leather-and-chrome exercise benches. Tanner sat at the other end, facing her.

"Emotionally, I'm a mess," she told him, draping the towel around her neck.

"I can't even imagine it," he returned. "I've never been married. Losing your partner this way, *any* way, has to be awful. Want to talk about it?"

Curious question, Devin thought to herself. She'd been doing nothing but talk about it since it happened—to Sam, to the police, to her mother, to friends who called. But could she really *talk* about it?

"I was going to divorce him," she blurted out.

"Oh. Umm ..." Tanner began, clearly having no idea how to respond to that.

"Yes, I told him I was leaving him, just before I ... just before he—"

"Are you sure we should discuss this?" Tanner put in, visibly uncomfortable with the abrupt turn the conversation had taken. "You're under a lot of stress. Maybe we should just get going with the workout."

"You're right," she sighed. "Forget I said that. I'm not in my right mind ... haven't been for a long time."

Tanner let that one go by him. He'd heard the news. He knew it was murder. His advocate instincts told him Devin wanted to talk, and those same instincts told him he didn't want to hear it.

For her part, Devin wasn't sure what made her want to tell all to Tanner. Probably because he was an outsider, neutral, had no bias, no personal stake in her situation. Like an impartial therapist to bounce things off, just to sort them out for herself. They started working through their program, first the slow maneuvers, saying nothing at all. Devin finally broke the silence.

"I don't know how much longer I'll be working out in this gym," she said.

"Oh?" he managed. "It's a great gym." Stupid thing to say, he told himself. Why did he feel this conversation was a minefield?

"Yes, well, it isn't my gym," she returned.

"Oh," he said again.

"The house belongs to the Bradshaw Trust," she went on. "I don't own it. I'll be moving. I don't know where. Don't know if I'll have a gym again, and if I do, it won't be anything like this. Five, four, three, two ...," she resumed her count.

In a conversation with Sam Bradshaw over the weekend, her brother-in-law had made it clear to Devin that her home was owned by the family trust, not by her. The same was true of the beach house in Malibu, the New York apartment, and the ski chalet in Aspen.

"As my brother's executor," Sam had told her, "I've been going over financial records." She'd wanted to throw at him, *What took you so long?* but didn't.

"The house is new, of course"—he'd pointed out the obvious—"and the numbers show that furnished, decorated, and landscaped, and including the extensive art collection, it cost somewhere in the neighborhood of thirty-two million dollars."

"Uh-huh," Devin had said. She'd wanted to say, *Get to the point, Sam,* but didn't.

"I know how hard you worked on the house, Devin," he said. "How much of yourself you put into it."

"Uh-huh."

"Well, there's a way you can keep it," he'd said.

"I don't want it," she'd countered without hesitating. That was the one thing Devin was sure of. She had no desire to stay in the mansion, wouldn't dream of living there. It was too big, too formal, too much. Even more, it represented a phase of her life that she had decided to put behind her even before Paul was killed. She intended to go ahead with the plans she'd made on Friday morning, before the tragedy on Mulholland Drive. She would buy a small house or a condo, or lease a place, and get on with her life.

As if he hadn't heard her, Sam then outlined his plan for her to keep the mansion, to own it outright. She could buy the house from the family trust for a portion of her considerable stock in the company, he'd told her. She now owned 10 percent of L.A. Garb, worth, he estimated, about fifty million.

"You'd still have plenty of shares left, with a comfortable income," he'd pushed.

"No, Sam. I wouldn't be interested in keeping the house if you *gave* it to me," she had insisted.

"You're just upset," he'd said then, in what she detected was a definite *big-smart-men-know-better-than-dumb-little-women* tone of voice. "The memories are too recent."

Right. It's been all of three days! she thought, but didn't say. But she instinctively understood that whatever it was that Sam Bradshaw was selling here, it was certain to be good for him and bad for her.

Tanner's voice broke into her reverie. "That's probably healthy, moving out," he was saying now. "You'd really rattle around, alone in a place this big."

"This kind of palace owns *you,*" she said. "Managing it is a full-time job. The fact is, I don't think I wanted it when I *wanted* it. Four, three, two . . ." Tanner said nothing.

"Say something," she said. "Three, two . . ."

"Devin, I don't have anything to say. None of it is my

business," he told her. Maybe too forcefully, he realized, when he saw her face register hurt.

"Look, if you want to talk, get it out of your system, if that would help," he added, then immediately wished he hadn't. He was breaking his own cardinal noninvolvement rule.

Too late. First she launched into the business of the house, and what Sam had said about her trading stock for it. "So what do you think about that?" she asked him then, not really expecting an informed reply.

He answered her question with a question of his own: "Who owns the rest of the company stock?" She told him. "And who controls the two large blocks?" That one was easy, too. The trustee of the foundation and Sam Bradshaw.

"Okay," Tanner said, "then here's what I think about that. If I were your brother-in-law, I'd be thrilled if you opted to keep the house, in return for which a large chunk of your stock in the company would revert to my control."

"Hmmm. Three, two, one . . ."

"Then, as trustee, I would have the majority vote, which I don't have now. That would give me all of the power behind L.A. Garb."

"What kind of power?" Devin asked him.

"Oh, power to make myself boss for life, power to make all the decisions, to buy airplanes, boats, island retreats or whatever for the company and have some fun, power to pay myself a few million a year in salary, that kind of power."

He was sounding like a lawyer, Devin thought. She suddenly realized how fortuitous it was that she happened to have a personal trainer who was well versed in the law. "And if I *don't* sell back my shares?" she asked, already knowing the answer.

"Then you've got the swing vote. And I *don't* control a majority block. Which means I can appoint myself CEO only if there's no opposition, and for only as long as the fifty-five-percenters want me there."

"Hmmm . . . ," she said. "That's me and Charlie. Three, two . . ."

21

"Today was a designated day of mourning for garment industry legend Paul Bradshaw, founder of the giant Southern California-based clothing company, L.A. Garb," intoned Maxi Poole, reporting the lead story on the Six O'Clock News.

Viewers were shown a montage of pictures—the Santa Monica factory, its empty parking lot, flags in the courtyard flying at half staff, and the Pulled Together plant in South-Central Los Angeles with its colorful mural stretching the length of the nearly block-long wall outside. Significantly, there were no people in any of the shots, no activity stirring at either location.

The anchorwoman went on to detail what was known about owner Paul Bradshaw's murder. Next, over file-taped footage she recapped Bradshaw's life as a garment industry leader and a popular, wealthy international social and philanthropic figure. Viewers saw a photo taken in 1960 of a grinning, twenty-eight-year-old Paul Bradshaw on Santa Monica beach, proudly holding up the fledgling company's first product, a pair of brightly colored men's baggies that retailed for twelve dollars. They saw Bradshaw a few years later, romping in the same Santa Monica surf with his wife, Rosemary, and their four young children. Then there was Paul Bradshaw's society wedding at the Bel Air Hotel to beautiful and talented designer Devin Yorke. And Bradshaw just this past week, in Washington, receiving a medal from the President of the United States. The final shot in the sequence showed Paul Bradshaw's red Ferrari in a mangled heap at the muddy bottom of the cliffs below Mulholland Drive.

Then, over silent footage of Maxi's interview interspersed with some of the scenes Pete Garrow had shot of the workers in the plant, Maxi Poole said that on Friday morning, the day Paul Bradshaw was killed, she and her Channel Six news crew happened to be at the Pulled Together factory. They were there to shoot a profile on Bradshaw, she said, focusing on his significant contribution to the community by investing in the area and providing a thousand jobs for the people of South-Central Los Angeles. Reporter Poole went on to tell of overhearing a very vocal argument between Bradshaw and an employee coming from inside Bradshaw's office, right next to where she and her crew had been waiting.

Next, the tape showed Billy Hilgarde at work, sitting at a computer terminal manipulating a pattern overlay. "Immediately after hearing that argument," the reporter went on, "my colleagues and I observed *this* man, William Hilgarde, head of the Pulled Together marking department, storming out of Bradshaw's office and slamming the door behind him. As he walked through the small room where we waited with our camera gear, Hilgarde appeared to be very agitated."

The tape went to close-up, split-screen pictures of Billy Hilgarde and Paul Bradshaw, as the reporter continued, "A coworker later confirmed that Hilgarde and Bradshaw had been at odds for several months. The reason, we were told, was that Hilgarde had been trying to organize the South-Central Los Angeles factory into a union shop, and Bradshaw was fighting it."

Coming out of the tape, the studio camera had widened to show Maxi Poole, live on the set, with an interview guest beside her.

"This is Reginald Duke. He's a shipping clerk at the Pulled Together plant. Mr. Duke, tell us what you saw out in the factory parking lot at about twelve-thirty P.M. last Friday, after we had finished taping our interview with Paul Bradshaw."

"Mr. Bradshaw came out the building and got in his car," Duke responded. "He revved up and took off like a shot."

"And where was Mr. Hilgarde?" Maxi asked.

"Myself and another guy seen Billy sitting in his car in a spot facing the front doors. When Mr. Bradshaw came out the doors and pulled his car out, Billy followed him."

"And you told me earlier that Mr. Hilgarde was not alone?"

"No, he was with another guy."

"Someone who also works at Pulled Together?"

"No, brother's a gang-banger, big time."

"Can you give us his name?"

"No, I'm not givin' no name, I told you that before," Reginald Duke said with a scowl.

"All right. Then can you tell us, did you see where the two cars went?" she asked.

"Yeah, they were both going real fast, so my friend and me ran to the gates and watched both of 'em head on down Florence, then up the ramp to the freeway."

"Hilgarde was following Mr. Bradshaw," the reporter clarified.

"I don't know what was in the man's head. I'm just sayin' they were goin' in the same direction."

"Did it appear that Mr. Hilgarde had been waiting for Bradshaw to come out of the factory?" the reporter questioned.

"Well, I don't know that," Duke said, "but as soon as the man took off, Billy took off behind him. Actually, Scud . . . ahh, the other guy was the one drivin' the car."

"Do you know whose car it was?" Maxi Poole asked.

"Sure," Duke answered. "Billy Hilgarde's car, brand-new black Trans Am. They hadda be doin' sixty down the road, both of 'em, Billy in his ride and the boss in his red Ferrari."

"Thank you, Mr. Duke," Maxi said, and the camera zoomed in for a close shot on her.

"It was shortly after that encounter that Paul Bradshaw was found in the same red Ferrari, very close to death with a bullet wound in his chest, at the bottom of a steep cliff off Mulholland Drive near Benedict Canyon. Channel Six News has learned tonight that technicians at the LAPD crime lab have identified the transfer of traces of black paint onto the mangled car, presumably from another vehicle.

"No one has yet been charged with the murder of L.A. Garb owner Paul Bradshaw. We'll keep you updated on this breaking story as the details unfold. Meantime, coming up, we'll have more reaction to the industry leader's death from friends and colleagues around the world."

Like all employees at L.A. Garb, Billy Hilgarde didn't go to work on this day of respect for the company's murdered CEO. He was sitting in the living room of his small apartment on Crenshaw Boulevard in South-Central Los Angeles, watching the early news on Channel Six.

When Maxi Poole had finished that part of her report, he zapped off the set and grabbed his leather jacket from a nearby chair. Feeling in the pockets for his keys, he fairly jumped out the front door. He took the stairs two at a time, all three flights of them. Loping through the underground garage, he got into his black Trans Am, started it up, and gunned it onto the street. He turned east on Slauson Avenue and headed for Crips territory in the heart of South-Central. He had to find Scud Joe.

22

Devin was next in the long waiting line at Sweetzer's, a small crowded garment-district eatery in South-Central Los Angeles not far from the Pulled Together plant. She sat down at the next available table, just vacated by three young black men who might well work at PT, she realized. Ruby Johnson had told her that Sweetzer's had the best food in the vicinity of the factory, and many PT employees ate there. The table, covered with red-checked oilcloth, was still cluttered with dirty dishes and lunch remains from the previous patrons. Ruby was meeting her here for lunch, and Devin was early.

Devin hadn't known the place, but she was certainly familiar with the area. She'd worked for years at several firms in L.A.'s sprawling garment district in the downtown environs, and her former company, Pieces, was less than a mile away.

The person Devin had most often dealt with at the plant was Ruby Johnson, Paul's assistant at PT. After hearing what Tanner had to say this morning, Devin had called and asked to see her. The two had never had much of a relationship—in fact, the last time they'd spoken, Devin had ended the conversation by slamming down the phone.

She would apologize today; she was grateful that Ruby had agreed to meet with her.

Devin had formulated the idea this morning in the gym. That ninety minutes seemed to be the time of day when her brain cells were functioning at peak efficiency. Perhaps exercise did for her what meditation did for others. Or maybe it was Tanner.

Devin knew that she had to get back to work, and fast. She didn't know what kind of income she'd get from her stock ownership, but even if it turned out to be enough to live on, she wanted and needed to work. This morning she had tried to assess her personal picture. She was a fashion designer, and a good one. She'd had impressive success with the company she started, but it was now operating smoothly and profitably without her. She was quite sure they wouldn't need her back at this point, and in fact going back to Pieces might be a backward step.

Start another company? Maybe. She could sell some of her stock in L.A. Garb and bankroll it herself. This time she'd own it outright. She'd bounced the idea off Tanner in the middle of her pull-down reps, and he offered a suggestion that had started her thinking. Wouldn't it be logical, he'd asked, for her to go to work for her own company, the one she already owned a piece of?

"I thought of that," she'd told him. "But the new chairman, CEO, and big kahuna is Paul's brother, Sam Bradshaw, and he hates me. It's that simple. I couldn't work with him, and he certainly wouldn't want me around."

"But it's a big company," Tanner said. "Isn't there something you could do where you wouldn't be directly in his path?"

That's when it hit her. Pulled Together! The young, fresh, exciting new line that America was buzzing about, and it was on the other side of town. That new division of the company really hadn't jelled yet. Maybe there *was* a place for her in the South-Central operation. She had no knowledge of how PT was structured, but she decided to investigate.

Devin had met Ruby Johnson twice, at the opening of the South-Central factory and again when the mural was unveiled. Ruby was a tall, handsome woman, thirty-something, with long, upswept black hair, high cheekbones, and a strong cleft chin. She remembered that Ruby had a striking, high-fashion look. She saw her now, in a chic rust-colored suit and matching heels, working her way through the crowd, greeting friends along the way.

"Ruby, over here!" Devin called out, standing up and motioning toward her. Devin suddenly became aware that most of the eyes in the room were trained on her. Ruby spotted her then and couldn't suppress a smile.

"It's not just that you're the only blonde in the joint," she explained, dropping into the chair opposite Devin. "You might be the only white person in here!"

"God, that hadn't occurred to me," Devin rejoined, extending her hand to Ruby. A waitress had cleared off the table and was wiping it down with a sponge.

"Hard to believe you really are that color blind," Ruby said, eyes narrowing. Sobering then, she added, "I'm sorry for your loss, Mrs. Bradshaw."

"Call me Devin, and thank you, Ruby. It's like a nightmare that I haven't fully awakened from yet."

"I'm also sorry I was evasive with you on Friday," Ruby put in, but Devin stopped her.

"I understand," she said, and she did. "And I'm sorry that I hung up on you. I took my frustration with Paul out on you, and that wasn't fair."

"Only four days ago," Ruby remarked pensively. "It seems like weeks, doesn't it?"

"It seems like a lifetime," Devin said. "So much has happened, and so much has changed."

The two were silent for a minute, listening to the clatter and din of the busy lunchtime crowd. The rest of the diners had slowly turned their attention away from Devin Yorke Bradshaw.

"What brings you here?" Ruby asked finally.

Devin didn't want to reveal just yet that she was entertaining thoughts of going to work at Pulled Together. She told Ruby that she was interested in learning more about all facets of her late husband's business, because she now owned a substantial share of it. Ruby looked at her hard.

"Mr. Bradshaw's funeral is Thursday, isn't it?" she asked.

"I know what you're thinking," Devin responded. "That I'm jumping on this awfully fast, not waiting a decent interval— something like that, right?"

"Okay, right," Ruby said quietly, not shifting her eyes from Devin s gaze.

"All right, I'll level with you," Devin returned the woman's candor. "The fact is, I need to go back to work. For my soul. I started thinking about this long before my husband was killed. And now I need it even more, because suddenly I don't belong anywhere."

"And you want to work at Pulled Together?" Ruby couldn't hide her astonishment.

"Why not?" Devin countered.

"Well, for one thing, your ratio of whites to blacks would be about the same as it is in this funky restaurant," Ruby told her.

"So what?" Devin asked. "Really," she went on when she saw that Ruby was speechless, "what are you telling me? That I'd be shunned? Hated? What?"

"No . . . I'm just amazed that you'd want to put yourself in that situation. You'd want to come down here every day? Eat in places like this?"

"You said the food was good," Devin smiled.

"You like ribs?"

"Yes. As a matter of fact, I love ribs."

"Okay, then you don't have to have them," Ruby conceded, smiling back. "The salads are good too. Shall we order?"

Over fresh seafood salad, home-baked pan bread, and iced tea, the two women talked. Devin told Ruby she wanted to be educated, to learn as much as she could about the Pulled Together operation to assess whether she could fit in there in some meaningful way. She fired questions at Ruby, the right questions, because she knew the ins and outs of the garment industry. At the end of an hour, Devin had learned a great deal. And at Ruby's suggestion, she made an appointment to come back to South-Central for a tour of the plant the following afternoon.

"Alright, now let me ask you the obvious one more time," Ruby said, when their rapid give-and-take was winding down. "Why here? Why not Santa Monica, where the executive suites are plush, and you can drive to work without getting carjacked?"

"I can get carjacked in Beverly Hills," Devin said. Ruby didn't respond. She was waiting for an answer to her question.

"Okay, here's why," Devin sighed. "Sam Bradshaw,

that's why. He's not a great fan of mine. More accurately, he loathes me. And the feeling is mutual."

"Now *that* I can relate to," Ruby grinned.

"Really?" Devin asked with a look of uncertainty. "You know, I wasn't sure that you wouldn't run back and report all this to Sam, but I decided to take the chance. I had no idea who else I could talk to, and besides, it's no secret to him that he and I are oil and water."

"Don't worry. I've never even met Sam Bradshaw—but I've heard a lot about him. Rumor is rampant, as you can imagine, now that he's taking over the company."

"Promise you'll keep all this confidential, then?"

"Promise," Ruby said, offering her hand, and Devin astounded her by giving her the triple street handshake.

"Lord, woman," Ruby squealed, "where did you learn that?"

"Ruby," Devin said, "I ran a company on Central Avenue, very near here, for four years. Called Pieces. Half my employees were black. More than half."

"I know Pieces," Ruby assured her. "I have a lot of Pieces outfits in my closet. If I'd known last night that I was having lunch with you today, I'd have worn my Three Shades of Gray group."

That produced a huge smile on Devin's sunny face. "My 1987 fall line," she said. "You made my day!"

Ruby was looking past her now, waving hello to two men who had just come into the restaurant. "They're from the plant," she said. "Henry Lewis and Billy Hilgarde. If you do come to work at PT, you're going to get to know Billy real well. You'll meet him tomorrow when I show you around."

Devin's eyes had darkened. "Isn't he the man I'm hearing about on the news?" she asked. "The one who had a fight with my husband on Friday morning, then followed him—"

Ruby put a hand on her arm to stop her. "Listen to me," she said, and she tightened her grasp on Devin's arm for emphasis. "Whatever happened to Mr. Bradshaw, let me tell you this. Billy Hilgarde never killed anyone.

23

Alex was sitting by her own desk in the outer office of what had been Paul Bradshaw's executive suite, but on the wrong side of it. Geneen Landers was in her chair. It was Wednesday afternoon, five days after Paul was killed, and Alex's world had been turned completely upside down. It did appear that she still had a job, but that was small comfort. She'd been working fourteen hours a day, every day since it happened, and at night she hardly slept at all. Now Geneen was taking over her former office as personal assistant to the CEO, and Alex wasn't sure where she would be assigned when the transition was complete. Her professional prospects were in the hands of Sam Bradshaw, the older brother Paul had loved, had more than tolerated, and privately had considered a little less than competent.

Geneen had always been a friend, and certainly there was no blaming her. Still, it was painful to have Geneen climb above her to the top executive-assistant spot. Alex wondered about their respective wages. She'd never known how much money Geneen made, but she was quite sure her own salary was at least double, maybe triple. Now what? she wondered.

Also unsettling was the many times she'd caught Sam Bradshaw's small, dull blue eyes trained on the curve of her hips or the swell of her breasts. At first she thought she might be imagining it, but now there was no mistaking Sam's predatory looks. Still, she saw little choice for herself but to wait and see how everything shook down. Sam had been juggling personnel around from the minute he'd assumed leadership. In the meantime, Alex had all she could do to make it through the long days and troubled nights.

Today she'd been walking Geneen through Paul Bradshaw's computer files. It was not a big stretch for Geneen, because Sam, as chief financial officer, had always had access to most of the company's programs. Now Alex was showing Geneen Paul's private, coded files and instructing her on the confidential symbols and passwords she'd need to know to get into them.

"By the way," Geneen said to her now, "Sam told me to red-flag anything listed under the heading 'B.S.&S.' What file is that?"

"B.S.&S.?" Alex repeated. "I have no idea."

Behind closed doors, Sam Bradshaw sat in the inner office at the massive slate-topped desk, putting the finishing touches on the eulogy he would deliver at his brother's funeral in the morning.

"He was a loving son, a loving husband, and a loving father to his children. He was a good man, a kind and generous man, a brilliant man. He was my only brother, and I will miss him more than I can ever ... ever ..."

He tapped out the words with two fingers on the keyboard at his brother's computer terminal. He had scheduled the funeral for ten o'clock at St. John's Episcopal Church in the heart of Beverly Hills. The service would be open to the public. And to the press, Sam had decided. Ever practical, it had occurred to him that the publicity could only be good for business. Paul Bradshaw had cut a dashing figure across the local and national landscape, and Sam was sure the church would be filled to overflowing tomorrow.

After the interment, there would be a reception at his brother's Benedict Canyon villa, by invitation only, to be catered by Chasen's. Joan Rivers had used Chasen's to cater her husband Edgar's shiva. Sam remembered the press notices. He instructed the catering manager at the swank restaurant to serve the same dishes. Hot hors d'oeuvres, small finger sandwiches, assorted salads, cheeses and relishes, and Chasen's world-famous chili.

The private reception was turning into a social event, he knew, a tough ticket. Sam had assigned L.A. Garb's in-house public relations department to draw up a long list of family, friends, colleagues, clients, politicos, civic and religious dignitaries, black leaders, and of course, favored members of the media. It was short notice, but each invitee had been personally called or faxed. Now people who were not on the list were calling the office, asking if they might come by to pay their respects. Sam knew that many wanted to come just to see the much-photographed mansion, even if they happened to detest Paul Bradshaw.

Satisfied with the eulogy now, he turned his attention to the task of combining office staffs, Paul's and his. He'd made the decision to convert all of his former financial operations to one of L.A.'s large business and accounting firms that specialized in fiscal management. That would eliminate the need for several staffers, and Sam intended to have each of those who would be terminated notified on Friday. He didn't want it done before the funeral, but he saw no point in letting it drag on needlessly. And he wanted them given their pink slips all on the same day. He didn't want to have to witness an endless series of those dreary, guilt-charged going-away parties, with the interminable office collections for gifts, the touchy-feely cards to sign, and the gooey cakes dished up on paper plates. One party, to include them all, that he could probably avoid.

He shuddered as his mind flashed back several years to Lois Lindberg's pathetic anniversary party. Lois had been a secretary in Sam's department since the day he'd started at his brother's young garment firm more than three decades ago. When her twenty-fifth anniversary with the company was coming up, Geneen had made it a point to remind him that the office should do something special for Lois.

Mrs. Lindberg's anniversary fell on a weekday. Sam had reluctantly decided to take the whole staff to lunch. A special lunch for Lois. Better to keep the bathos and the bad wine and the mess out of the office, he'd thought. And it would be mercifully quicker. He'd given Geneen a budget and told her to handle it.

Geneen chose a less than mediocre restaurant—some German beer and schnitzel parlor off the San Diego Freeway in Culver City. Later, she'd said it was the only place she could find that could handle fourteen people for lunch, drinks, and a festive cake for the amount of money he'd allowed her to spend.

For a gift, he'd gone into the locked closet in his office complex and picked out one of the company gifts left over from several Christmases past. A silver-plated letter opener from the corporate catalog at Tiffany, still in its original blue box. Rather nice, he'd thought. He'd told Geneen to have it engraved with something appropriate and rewrap it for Lois.

Since his department had distributed that particular gift item long before Geneen had come to work at L.A. Garb, she wasn't familiar with it. When Sam had given her the box, she didn't know that it was recycled, or that it wasn't genuine sterling silver. Nor had she known that Lois, along with several of the other financial department office staffers, had received that exact letter opener for Christmas sometime in the seventies. That had crossed Sam's mind, but he figured it was so long ago that Lois would probably have lost it or forgotten about it by then, and besides, this one would be monogrammed. Sam Bradshaw was a money counter; sentimentality was not his long suit.

At the last minute, Sam couldn't attend the lunch. Something had come up. But the rest of the office gang went. And many of them had indeed remembered the twenty-dollar letter opener, and all of them had really hated the restaurant.

That afternoon there was a buzz going around the executive suites about the whole affair, and Sam's brother Paul got wind of it. He'd called Sam into his office and quizzed him about what exactly had been done to honor Lois Lindberg's quarter century of loyal service to his department and to the company. Sam told Paul that he'd sent the whole staff to lunch on him, and he gave her a nice gift from Tiffany.

"What I heard," Paul had hissed at his brother, "is that you sent them to some fucking rathskeller, that you didn't bother to show up yourself, and that you gave her one of your leftover corporate Christmas trinkets from the Year One!" Sam could still remember feeling his face heat up.

Later that afternoon, Paul sent Alex over to Lois's office bearing a huge gold box containing twenty-five exquisite, long-stemmed red roses, one for each of her years of service. Tucked under the box's gold ribbon was an envelope with her name on it, and in it were papers outlining a special pension plan for her that Paul had had Bruce Henning, the company's chief counsel, set up that afternoon. Even though such a duty would normally fall to the company's financial department, Paul obviously had not trusted Sam to take care of it. The company pension drawn in Lois's name would pay the woman half her current salary for life, starting whenever she elected to retire.

Big spender, his brother, Sam groused. Lois Lindberg didn't know it yet, but she would begin collecting on that generous pension fund next week.

24

Billy Hilgarde's eyes traveled up the tone-on-tone textured walls to the twenty-foot-high vaulted ceiling, then down over the dramatic, aubergine silk, gilt-fringed draperies that dusted the polished rosewood floor. He let out a low whistle.

"And this isn't even the main event!" he breathed in hushed tones to Ruby Johnson. "Did you catch that other living room across the hall? It's about five times as big!"

Billy and Ruby had just arrived at the Bradshaw mansion, and Bruno, the butler, had settled them in the small east sitting room. Devin had invited the two for an informal supper tonight, so they could talk in private about the goings-on at Pulled Together.

"What do you think?" Billy went on. "Should we wander around and have a look while we're waiting?"

Ruby, cool and chic in a slim black linen sheath, shot him a stern look. "Sit, Billy," she commanded. "We'll let Devin give us a tour if she wants to."

"Oh, it's *Devin* now?" Billy mocked, raising his eyebrows.

"I told you, she's okay."

"Oh, right," he said, rolling his eyes. "Last I heard, she was the ice queen. One lunch later she's your new best friend?"

"Shush! You're going to like her," Ruby said. "She absolutely doesn't fit the bitch-snob thing I tagged on her. You'll see."

"What makes you say so?"

"For one thing, I had her meet me at Sweetzer's because

I wanted to make her squirm, but she didn't even notice that everyone else in the place was black. Joke was on me! She was ready to order the ribs, for God's sake, until I explained that with Jocko's sauce they had about eight zillion calories."

Bruno came back into the sitting room with a tray of caviar canapés, which he set on the coffee table in front of the two guests.

"Mrs. Bradshaw is on the phone," he said. "She asked me to tell you she'll be with you in two minutes."

Bruno went over to a gleaming, hunter green, marble-topped bar in the corner and came back with a bottle of chablis and three chilled glasses. After uncorking the wine, he ceremoniously poured a small sampling into a glass and handed it to Billy, who accepted it with a half smile and took a sip.

"Uum ... no, I don't think so," he said then, with a solemn look at the butler. "Can you bring us something with a little, ahh, brighter éclat?"

Ruby nudged him hard in the ribs. "I can't take him anywhere!" she groused to the butler. Bruno laughed and filled the glasses.

Devin came into the room then, and offered her hand in greeting. "Thanks for coming tonight," she smiled. "Nice to see you again too, Billy." Then she picked up a glass of the wine and sank into one of the chairs opposite them.

Billy studied Devin Bradshaw. She'd changed clothes since he'd met her earlier today when she was touring the plant. She looked hot, he thought, in a nubby oatmeal-colored cashmere sweater and narrow matching slacks. She also looked incredibly cool for a woman who was going to bury her husband in the morning.

He wondered why Devin Bradshaw would invite him to her home, since that reporter Maxi Poole had all but convicted him on television of murdering her husband. After seeing that report, Billy had chased down Scud Joe and told him to keep his head down and talk to nobody about last Friday. But who knew if it did any good. Joe Jones was a loose cannon.

Now here was Billy, sitting pretty in the mansion of the widow. Even more intriguing, this woman did not look like she was hurting. Right now, exchanging pleasantries with

Ruby, Devin Bradshaw looked nothing but cool, like butter wouldn't melt in her mouth.

"Nice house," Billy offered after a bit.

"Thank you," Devin said, "but I won't be here long. I'll be moving into a much smaller place very soon."

Not sure how to respond to that, Billy figured it was as good a time as any to ask to see the place. "I'd love to look around, see more of it," he said. "Uhh, before you leave, that is." Ruby groaned, but Devin laughed.

"Come on, bring your wine," she told the two of them. "I'll give you the tour. I'm proud of it. I worked hard putting this place together, and I won't get to show it off much longer."

She escorted them out of the sitting room and across the hall to the immense, lush living room, chatting amiably, putting them at ease amid the sumptuous surroundings. She guided them down the broad central hall and into a warm, oak-paneled game room, its glove-leather couches set on Navajo and Anasazi rugs, overlaid in a profusion of color on the terrazzo floor. Eight pairs of French doors looked out onto an expanse of lawn and gardens that rolled down to an Olympic-sized swimming pool, lit like a shimmering midnight blue jewel, with twin tennis courts beyond.

It was obvious to Billy that Mrs. Bradshaw delighted in showing off the house. It was almost as if she didn't live here, he thought—she seemed as much in awe of everything as he was. The tour ended in the kitchen, where a cook was stirring something sizzling in a sauté pan, and the room was filled with the delicious aromas of buttery herbs, lemon, and garlic.

"We're having shrimp scampi, and the best onion soup you've ever had in your life," she told them.

"Smells like I've died and gone to heaven," Billy remarked.

"I am really going to miss Andres' onion soup," Devin said. "And him!" she added, standing on her toes to give the chef a peck on the cheek.

"We're going to have supper in the *little* dining room," she announced then, steering them past a butler's pantry into a magnificent, softly lit room that looked anything but little to Billy. In the center was a stunning dining table that consisted of two broad bone-colored stone columns topped with a polished slab of thick black glass. One side of it was covered with several crystal bowls of chunky, multicolored cabbage roses, interspersed with flickering candles of varying sizes and hues; the other side was set for three.

Bruno materialized and pulled out chairs for Devin and Ruby, then refreshed their glasses with more wine. A woman in a white uniform appeared from the kitchen with a bottle of Evian and set about filling their water glasses. Devin waited until both had left the dining room, then immediately launched into comments about their meeting that morning at Pulled Together. Mentioning several of the people she'd met, she asked questions about them and about their work. Billy was guarded, not sure what her agenda was, but Ruby was candid.

"Henry Lewis?" Ruby responded to Devin's inquiry about the head of PT's shipping department. "Henry's a great guy, and he really knows what he's doing, but his department has the biggest problem with workers faking their hours, because he's got the largest number of employees. I don't know how much longer Henry will put up with it. He's good, he's got a ton of experience, and he can get a job anywhere—"

"Faking their hours?" Devin interrupted.

Ruby looked over at Billy, throwing him a cue to explain. He hesitated, but it occurred to him that for months he'd tried to get a hearing from this woman's late husband, who wouldn't give him the time of day. Now here he was, in the man's dining room, albeit his *little* dining room, with the man s widow, who happened to be a big stockholder in the company. He had no idea if it would do any good, but it certainly couldn't hurt to tell her some of the things he'd been trying to get across to her husband for so long.

"They fake their hours," he began, "on the minus side. It's an unwritten, never-talked-about policy at the plant."

Billy explained how that scam worked at Pulled Together, by tacit pressure on the workers to put in more hours than they were paid for. Ruby joined in, and the two warmed to the subject, unleashing a litany of fraudulent practices and assorted ills that PT workers were expected to tolerate if they hoped to keep their jobs. Devin listened in silence, except for an occasional question, or when she wanted something explained or clarified.

The conversation stopped each time one of the staff came into the room to clear or serve, and again at the end of the meal when Andres put in an appearance and was bathed in compliments by the three of them for his exquisite cuisine.

"This stuff is astounding—I've never seen a dessert on fire before!" Billy raved. It was baked Alaska, pearly white cake with flaming liqueur on the outside and frozen ice cream on the inside.

"Unbelievable!" he repeated, flashing his wide, boyish grin, scooping up the confection. Devin seemed delighted by his enthusiasm.

"Pauline," she called out to the general direction of the kitchen, and Pauline appeared at the table in an instant. "Seconds on the Alaska for Mr. Hilgarde, please. But Ruby, since you saved me from some dangerous ribs yesterday, I'll save you from any more cake and ice cream, okay?"

"That's fair," Ruby smiled.

Pauline arrived with another huge serving of baked Alaska and placed it in front of Billy, who pronounced that he couldn't turn it down, it wouldn't be polite. He had the women laughing while Pauline poured coffee. The Billy Hilgarde charm was infectious.

"Let me ask you something now," he said, suddenly sobering, looking squarely at Devin. "Ruby told me you were looking into the possibility of coming to work at Pulled Together. Are you serious? And have you decided what you'd want to do there?"

"I am, and yes I have," Devin answered thoughtfully. "I sensed some bad vibes at the plant today—tension, low morale, a ragged feeling. You two have confirmed tonight that I didn't misread the climate."

"You weren't at the factory that long," Billy said, "and everyone there was putting on a good face for you. Even so, the mood was that obvious?"

"Oh, yes," Devin confirmed.

"I guess it's pretty blatant. The television crew picked up on it too," Ruby observed.

"Billy," Devin said then, "Ruby is familiar with the company I started up and ran before I married Paul Bradshaw. Do you know Pieces?"

"Of course I know Pieces," Billy replied. "And I know that your name was on the label, but you did much more than design the line."

"That's right," she countered. "And I'd like to do the

same for PT. Turn the place around and make it a happy shop, for one thing. That means right every single one of the wrongs you've outlined."

"Tall order," Billy observed, adopting Ruby's full-out candor now. "Ruby told me the new big chief is not a pal of yours. And I hear he's even tighter with a buck than your husband was, if you'll pardon me for saying so."

"Yes, right on both counts. It won't be easy. I'd really like your support if it comes to that," she told them.

"You've got it," Ruby said.

"Billy?" Devin looked at him.

"Listen, Mrs. Bradshaw," he leveled, "if your blueprint really is to stop the crap like you say, and to put some positive programs in place, sure, you'd have my support. That's all I've ever wanted for the place."

"How do you see your role at PT?" Ruby asked her then.

"Same as my role at Pieces," she responded. "I would oversee all design, bring cohesiveness and integrity to the product, streamline the production process from sketches to completed samples, make shipping more efficient, beef up sales—all of it."

"You mean hands-on the whole operation?" Billy asked. "Make it independent from the Santa Monica management?"

"Yes. My feeling is that the Pulled Together line is too big and too different to fit the mold of the main L.A. Garb product, or at least it should be."

"You'd be taking on a fifteen-hour-a-day commitment," Ruby said. "What about your life?"

"The life I've known since I left the business ended on Friday," Devin said quietly. "I'm going back to work. It's not about money. I've decided where I think I'm needed, where I can make a difference. I want to run Pulled Together."

"And how are you going to get the Man to go for that?" Billy asked, his eyes narrowed.

"I have no idea," she said. "But I'll think of something."

25

Briskly walking the treadmill, Devin tried to keep her mind off her husband's death. And his funeral today. She'd found her emotions colliding crazily since last Friday on Mulholland Drive, and her feelings about Paul's death shifting from one hour to the next.

It helped to focus on the prospect of heading up Pulled Together. Her tour of the plant, then dinner with Ruby Johnson and Billy Hilgarde last night, had convinced her that she was right for it and it was right for her. After they'd left, while idly doodling sketches for the line, she'd been mulling over different schemes to make it happen, though none seemed even remotely feasible. Her biggest obstacle was Sam, of course. But there was no question that Pulled Together needed leadership and that she had the will, the energy, and the credentials to do the job.

She couldn't sleep last night; she was in the gym early this morning, warming up, waiting for Tanner. Paul's funeral was at ten o'clock. That her husband was dead seemed a blurred, discordant dream that she'd soon wake up from. She'd had nothing to do with plans for the church service, the interment, or the reception afterward here at the house. Sam had made it clear that he would take care of everything, that she didn't have to do a thing except show up at the church and be escorted to her seat. Devin had no trouble reading the subtext: her input wasn't welcome. Fine, she thought. Even when she'd been part of the family, they had never made her feel like family. In fact, they'd treated her not just as a family outsider but as a family enemy. Now it seemed as if they hated her even more. Since Paul was killed, all her conversations with Bradshaw family members had been perfunctory, cold.

She knew why. They had always thought she was a classic gold-digger, even though when she married Paul she was madly in love with him. With his death, it was as if their malevolent feelings about her motives had triggered fulfillment of their ignoble prophecy. Now Devin was the first outsider to own a block of the family business. Now she owned a chunk of the Bradshaws, and they didn't like it.

Funny, Devin thought as she punched up the digital speed readout on the treadmill, one thing you could say for Paul, he wasn't greedy. Arrogant, vain, condescending, cruel at times, a womanizer always, Paul Bradshaw was a lot of things, but never greedy. He was profoundly generous. Maybe it was just an extension of his power trip, the heady power of being able to lavish extravagant gifts on people, but Paul was expansive, he did love to give. Not so his brother Sam. For a man who made a lot of money, who had a lot of money, and who had access to anything in life that money could buy, Sam Bradshaw brought new meaning to the concept of cheap. Devin didn't know him well, but she did know *that* about her brother-in-law.

In the many times she and Paul had been in the company of Sam and Lizbeth over the years, often with business associates or with family, Devin never once saw Sam reach for the check. Yet he would actually complain about the check. He'd say to Paul, be it at dinner for four or forty, "You know, I never got my baked potato, so make sure you don't pay for it." And he was serious. Paul would laugh. "That's my money man," he'd say.

Yes, Devin thought, the two brothers were most definitely different. It was like comparing Kennedy and Nixon. You had to be charmed by Paul. Devin had been, certainly. And you had to like Paul, if you weren't in bed with him, so to speak. But Sam was something else entirely. He was closed, calculating, critical, glum. Sam Bradshaw was hard to like.

The faster she moved on her power walk, the more entrenched became her resolve to run the Pulled Together division. It felt exactly right. After four years of the frivolous, albeit rigorous work that went with being a trophy wife, a role Devin had tried on but found didn't fit, she ached for work she could feel was worthwhile. Heading up PT would be a challenge for her, and she would be good for the company. But Sam Bradshaw controlled L.A. Garb now, and she knew that he'd never let her in. She had to figure out a way to make him do it.

*   *   *

Tanner came into the gym and started his warm-up
stretches while Devin was finishing her aerobics on the
treadmill. He knew that her husband's funeral was just a
few hours away. He figured her mood would be somber,
so he purposely said very little. And once again, the woman
threw him a curve.

"Tell me, Tanner," she said, without breaking her stride,
"how do you get a sonofabitch to give you something that
he doesn't want to give you? Something big."

"Okay, I'll bite," he answered. "What is it you want, and
who's the sonofabitch you want it from?"

"I want my husband's brother, who, as you know, is now
in control of the company, to let me run the South-Central
division. And, as we've also discussed, the man hates my
guts."

Tanner scrutinized her face and saw that she was serious.
I know we talked about you working for the company, preferably outside of the dreaded brother-in-law's periphery,"
he said, "but you want to be head of the *division*?"

"That's right."

"Isn't that a bit of a stretch?"

"I can do it," she said. "I've done it before. Granted, on
a smaller scale, but I've done it all, and I've done it success-
fully. And I'm a stockholder. Who would be more conscien-
tious? I'd be protecting my own interests."

"Who would you replace?"

"Nobody," she said. "That's just it. Paul had the division
under his umbrella and ran everything himself from Santa
Monica."

"Then why wouldn't Sam Bradshaw do the same?"

"Sam is not Paul," she countered. "I called Charles Fine
yesterday, after you made me realize that I actually have
the swing vote. Do you remember I told you about
Charles?"

"He controls the Bradshaw Foundation."

"Yes," Devin confirmed. "He's also on the board. He
really knows all the players and how the company works.
And Charlie told me, reluctantly, that he doesn't think Sam
can handle it."

"Then what about the two of you combining your clout
and voting Sam out of there?"

"I'd thought about that, thanks to you, and in fact that's

why I called him. To feel him out. I've known Charlie for years, through Paul, and he's truly a wonderful man.

"He's also very wise," she went on. "He feels that Sam has to be given his chance, and he wishes him well. He said he'll be watching closely, of course, to protect the interests of the foundation, but he would not make a move to oust Sam just now."

"Any speculation about how long he'd give him?" Tanner asked.

"I asked him that."

"And?"

"And he said it was impossible to tell. If the company showed drastic reversals he'd have to take some action, but he said Paul left all the systems so well oiled that the company could probably run itself for years."

"Interesting conversation," Tanner submitted. "I'm sure you started the man thinking."

"Charlie was thinking before he was born," Devin said. "But yes, he is aware, as you've made me, that together we do have a great deal of power. What's so wonderful about Charlie, though, is that he's not about power. Charlie only wants what's right."

Devin switched off the treadmill and went over to the bar to do her cool-down stretches. Tanner assembled the weights they'd each be using, then he handed her a bottle of water. They went to work in silence on parallel benches.

"Any thoughts?" Devin asked after awhile.

"I do have some," Tanner put out, controlling his breathing, speaking when exhaling. "Give me five . . . let my ideas jell . . ." They kept working.

When they'd finished their bench presses, Tanner sat up and wiped his face and neck with a towel. Devin pulled herself up on the opposite bench, and he tossed her a towel. Two-minute break time.

"Okay," he said to her then, "listen while I think out loud, and tell me if I've got anything wrong."

"Shoot," she said, pulling a cotton headband on her forehead to keep the sweat from rolling down into her eyes.

"Here's how it stands," Tanner started. "The way your husband set up the company, his brother, Sam, holds all the power. Barring an ouster by Fine and you, which isn't going to happen, the only way he could be knocked off the mountain is if the company were sold. Since there appears to be plenty of liquidity to pay the estate taxes, the company is in no danger of dissolution. Right so far?"

"I think so," she returned, paying rapt attention.

"Now," he went on, "it requires at least thirty-three and a third percent ownership to force dissolution or sale of a company. But you only own 10 percent of L.A. Garb. So you have no leverage there."

"Hmmm."

"Okay, stay with me now," he urged. "There is one little-used legal loophole in this area. If a minority stockholder who owns less than a third of the company alleges that there is some kind of fraudulent activity going on, that other stockholders are conspiring to defraud, and if that can be proved, then in that instance only, the minority stockholder can sue the wrongdoers and force the sale or dissolution of the company."

"Fraud!" Devin pronounced with a shriek. "I know all about fraud at PT, plenty of it!" She quickly highlighted the workplace atrocities that Billy and Ruby had made her privy to.

"Okay, we've got to get on with the workout," Tanner said, "so here's the short version of what both of us are going to do ..."

Devin followed intently as he sketched out his strategy. After he got to his office this morning, he told her, he would write up a brief outline of a plan he had and fax it to her here at the house. Meantime, she was to do more research. Document what was actually going on at Pulled Together and make a list of witnesses who could potentially give testimony to fraud. After she had studied, thoroughly digested, and memorized the information Tanner faxed, he said, she would be ready to go to Sam Bradshaw and tell him she wants to head up the PT operation. And she must carefully rehearse her presentation, he told her, like a lawyer preparing a case.

First, according to the agenda he painstakingly spelled out, she would remind Sam of her qualifications. Then she would outline her plans to expand the line and make it bigger, better, even more successful. She would tell him that she'd be a hands-on manager, she'd work harder than anyone there. She would take a reasonable salary. She would be a major asset for the company.

She must make this pitch to Sam in good faith, Tanner said. Then if, as expected, Sam turned her down, with the information he is going to fax her this morning, she'll play hardball.

26

Devin stood on the gleaming marble floor in the immense three-story entry of the mansion, murmuring greetings as people arrived, mouthing good-byes as others left. Hundreds had been in and out of the villa since Paul's funeral this morning, most of them people she didn't know.

Solemn in a slim, black silk Krizia suit and pearls, Devin had been exchanging hands and words with guests for what seemed like hours. Strangers stopped and introduced themselves as associates of Paul or friends of the family. Some didn't bother—they simply looked right through her and walked right past her. It was easy to pick out the lookie-loos who were there to see and be seen or to examine the celebrated manse. Devin was too tired to care.

Paul's mother was seated in one of the front sitting rooms, looking ashen, surrounded by family and friends. Sam was in the game room, holding forth in front of the ban Working the crowd, Devin knew. The bartenders were serving drinks, the waiters were circulating with hors d'oeuvres, and the caterers had set up the huge table in the main dining room with a sumptuous buffet. It was just a week ago today, Devin realized, that the house had been filled with guests at the Bradshaws' last glittering party. And Paul Bradshaw had been the host. Now Paul was dead.

She willed her thought processes to skip, cartoonlike, from the moment of her decision to leave him last Friday to today, and the simple fact that he was gone. She tried to keep her mind focused on her life, her future, and how she might carve out her place at Pulled Together. She didn't want to think about the way her husband died.

It wasn't robbery, they said. Nothing had been taken. Paul's cash and credit cards were intact in his wallet. He was still wearing his twenty-five-thousand-dollar solid-gold Cartier Pasha watch. It was some kind of grudge, they said, a hate murder, a crime of passion. Somebody wanted Paul Bradshaw dead. And one of the officers had told her pointedly that most homicides of this nature are committed by family members, by loved ones.

The funeral had been like an extension of the dream she'd been living. The nightmare. A car had been sent to pick her up. Alone at the church, she was escorted by an usher to the second row on the right of the aisle. In front of her, already seated, was Paul's mother, Regina, between Sam and Lizbeth. In the rows behind her were several of Paul's and Sam Bradshaw's children, some with their spouses. Devin sat alone in her pew—a terse metaphor, she knew, a harbinger of the ostracism to come in her dealings with the Bradshaws.

Paul's casket stood inside the low gilded chancel that led to the altar. The church was adorned with flowers of all variety; some, since it was the middle of December, would have had to be flown in from warmer climes. Dozens of tall, yellow tallow candles were ablaze upon the altar. The organ was playing softly. Devin felt light-years removed from the reality of the moment and from the man inside the closed coffin in the center of the sanctuary.

Someone had slipped into the pew and sat down beside her. She turned to see Allena Bradshaw, who reached for her hand and gently squeezed it. Devin squeezed back, grateful. Sam turned around, saw his daughter, and stage-whispered that she was supposed to be sitting in one of the pews behind.

"I'm fine, Dad," Allena had told him quite definitively, not whispering. Sam flashed the two women a sour look, and turned away. Allena squeezed Devin's hand again. Beautiful, mysterious Allena, always seeming to rub just a little bit against the Bradshaw grain. Allena had stopped by the house briefly after the funeral; now she was gone.

Sam Bradshaw had been the first to stand at the pulpit and speak. Pontificate, Devin mused. Faking sincerity, and not quite pulling it off. Paul had been a master at it. Sam, as usual, was not nearly as good. He was followed by a series of eulogizers, some Devin had never met. To her amazement, members of the press had been allowed inside the church. Camera technicians crouched in front of the congregation, taping the succession of dignitaries at the pulpit. Still photographers lit up the church with rapid-fire flashes. Devin felt as if she were watching a movie.

She wasn't aware that it was over until she saw everybody rise and Allena took her arm and led her out of the church. At some point Allena had kissed her on the cheek and disappeared, and a tall, thin man in a black suit—an usher, she guessed—was guiding her back to the limousine that had brought her there. She was driven to Forest Lawn in Glendale, alone again.

The hard rain of the week before had eased to an intermittent drizzle, and the short-mown cemetery grass was spongy beneath her feet. Her high heels sank into the muck. Someone held an umbrella over her head. It was her driver. They followed the black-clad crowd across the rolling lawn to the gravesite. The stately, polished mahogany casket was already in place.

The minister was droning the Twenty-third Psalm. "Yea, though I walk through the valley of the shadow of death, I will fear no evil . . ." Devin squeezed her eyelids shut, trying to block out the image of her husband actually lying dead inside that box. She began deliberately sketching in her mind: a long, slim, loose-cut dress in a small-flowered print. "Street Smarts" by Pulled Together, she'd call it. Mentally she used brush strokes to fill in the black-and-white lines with color.

Eyes still closed, Devin caught the scent of jasmine on the sodden air. Jasmine didn't grow in Glendale. She raised her eyes and followed the musky fragrance. There beside her stood Rosemary Bradshaw. Their eyes met, and the older woman smiled. Actually smiled. At her? Because the man who'd dumped her was being lowered into his grave? Devin had no idea. She smiled back. The wives' club.

Now she dealt with the sea of people traipsing through her house, muddying up her rugs, dropping food on her floors, smoking, chatting, networking, behaving like this was the social event of the season.

Aha, she caught herself, but this was not her house. Not her floors, not her rugs. She, like the rest of the guests, was just a visitor here. She wondered how many of the people milling around actually cared about Paul Bradshaw. She wondered if *she* still cared. She refused to analyze her feelings. It was all surreal. She made the proper motions and said the proper things, all the while purposely focusing on Tanner's fax.

Upon arriving home from the cemetery, she'd gone immediately into her cluttered office. True to his word, there it was, rolled up in the paper catcher suspended beneath her fax machine. She perused it quickly, then read it again slowly. Now, while managing each encounter in the entryway of her house that was not her house, eyes vacant, she kept going over and over the scenario Tanner had outlined.

The single page of typed print danced like a photograph in her mind's eye. If Sam Bradshaw turns down her good-faith request for the position of head of the division, she will hit him with her knowledge of the fraudulent conditions at the PT factory, the fact that she has witnesses who will testify to it, and her plan to therefore bring a derivative action in court to force L.A. Garb's dissolution.

She will explain to Sam that as a major stockholder, owner of 10 percent of the company, who has certain knowledge that fraudulent practices are rampant in the Pulled Together division, she wishes to sue the wrongdoers. However, since the wrongdoers are the people running the company—headed by him, Sam Bradshaw—her position will be to bring suit against the wrongdoers in the name of the company. And if she wins, if fraud is proven, she will point out, a criminal case will be brought, and as the CEO who makes company policy, Sam will likely go to prison if convicted of these fraudulent practices.

Tanner's fax then spelled out the particulars of Section 2000 of the California Corporations Code. It explained that technically, her suit would have to prove that the fraud cited was costing the company, and therefore the stockholder bringing suit, significant amounts of money. But the fraudulent activity that Devin had outlined cost only the workers, and actually *made* money for the company.

Probably, stated Tanner's fax, Sam Bradshaw would not make that distinction. But if he did, or later consulted with lawyers who clarified that point for him, Devin would tell him that she did not want tainted money, and she would think that Sam wouldn't want his children or Paul's children to accept tainted money either, money earned on the backs of South-Central L.A.'s laborers.

Tanner's scenario suggested that Devin present herself as Samson in the temple of the Philistines, willing to pull the temple down around all of their heads rather than allow the corruption within to continue. If Sam Bradshaw tries to call her bluff by reminding her that in the process of trying to destroy the company she will be wiping out her own inheritance, she will tell him that she never had and never needed millions—and by the way, for every million dollars she loses, the Bradshaw Family Trust will lose several million.

If Sam still resists her request for the job as division chief, she should threaten him with widespread, negative publicity, with blaring the loathsome details of fraud at Pulled Together to the world media. No one, she should tell him, will buy the clothes.

She refocused her thoughts to the present as a familiar face approached her. A beautiful face, alight with a broad smile. Her friend Debra DeAngeles, the dazzling, outspoken actress, star of a glitzy nighttime network soap opera. When Devin ran Pieces, her company supplied wardrobe for the show. She'd gotten to know Debra, who, phony as she looked, was as real as you get.

Debra was in red: a short, skin-tight, mandarin red ruched envelope of a dress, with matching red four-inch high heels and a wide-brimmed black straw hat, her only touch of black for mourning, but mitigated by an outrageous curving broad red feather. Very Debra, Devin thought, and it made her smile.

Debra approached her, it seemed to Devin, in slow motion, a bright red flame emerging from a sea of anonymous people shrouded in black with dun-gray faces. Then, still in slow motion, Debra was upon her, all red, gently wrapping her arms around her and drawing her close. Bringing her lush, crimson lips to Devin's ear, she whispered to her. Onlookers might have thought that Debra was mouthing condolences. What she breathed in Devin's ear was: *"You're free now, darling—and you're rich!"*

Sam Bradshaw waved the bartender out of his way and fixed himself another drink. Sam was precise about the way martinis should be mixed, with good Russian vodka out of the freezer, stirred, not shaken, and poured over crushed ice into a chilled glass, with two olives on a toothpick.

The reception was showing the first signs of winding down. It had been a huge success. The world showed up, and Sam had talked to everyone who was anyone at all. Interesting, he found that for the first time in his life he didn't have to make an effort. What a difference a week made. People sought him out. He saw new respect glinting in their eyes as they shook his hand. He was treated with a deference he'd never known before.

Savoring the first sip of his fresh drink, he turned back toward the guests. Devin was walking through the room now, stopping to speak quietly to one group, then another. Sam was surprised to see her. It was as if he and Devin had been observing an unspoken pact today to steer clear of each other, to stay in different rooms and out of the other's space.

He watched her graceful movement through the still-crowded game room. Much as he detested the woman, she was one beautiful broad, Sam thought. But what to do about her? He had to get control of her 10 percent of the company. Or at least knock it down some, so he'd have a clear majority vote. His best hope was to sell her back her own house, but she wasn't going for it. At least not yet. Sam was feeling greatly empowered. He was confident that he could talk her into it. As Devin made her way toward him, it occurred to him that maybe he should warm things up a bit between them, try to soften her a little. Catch this mama bear with honey.

She caught him looking at her now, and he smiled. She smiled back. An icy smile, he considered, but then, the woman had ice water in her veins. She moved in beside him, leaned an elbow on the bar, looked over her shoulder at the bartender and asked for a glass of Evian, then turned back to Sam.

"How are you holding up?" she asked.

"All right, under terrible circumstances," he proclaimed soberly. "I was just going to check on Mother."

"She looks tired," Devin responded. "Perhaps you should get her car. Yet I can't blame her for lingering. When she gets home, away from all the people, it's really going to hit her."

"Beth and I are going to take her home, and we'll stay with her tonight," he said.

This affability between the two of them was new, Sam observed, and Devin seemed as interested in maintaining it as he was.

"Sam," she said then, "I need to speak to you."

That pleased him. Maybe she couldn't bear to part with this place after all. She had created a showplace here. People were strolling about in awe. And Devin certainly could afford it. *Hello, seven percent!* he thought optimistically. That would give the family trust the majority he needed.

"Sure," he said. "Let's go into Paul's study and sit down."

"No, this isn't the time or place. I'll come to your office in the morning, preferably early, like nine o'clock. Will that work for you?"

"Are you sure you wouldn't be more comfortable talking right here?" he countered. "Most of the people will be leaving soon."

"I'm sure," she said. "Nine o'clock?"

"How about breakfast at nine?" he suggested. "At the Polo Lounge." The celebrated Polo Lounge was in the Beverly Hills Hotel, very near the Benedict mansion. The entertainment industry elite regularly did early morning business there over toasted bagels.

"No," she said. "I'll see you in your office. Okay?"

Sam could see in the level gaze of her implacable green eyes that she would accept no other alternative. Well, he could put her in her place later. There was nothing he would like better than to put Devin Yorke in her place. But for now he would condescend to give in to her little power play, or whatever she was doing. He needed to cut a deal with her.

"Okay, sure, if that's what you'd prefer, Devin. Nine o'clock tomorrow, then."

"Good," she said, giving him an impassive smile. She picked up her glass of water and made her way out of the room.

Sam followed through the open double doors a few minutes later, speaking to people as he passed. He negotiated the corridor to the massive living room, catching up with some of the guests he'd missed. Along the way he encountered Alexandra Anson. She was still technically in charge of appointments in the L.A. Garb CEO's office.

"Alex," he stopped her, "clear my morning schedule for a nine o'clock meeting with Devin Bradshaw, would you?" He saw that Alex's brown eyes were devoid of any of the new respect he'd been enjoying. She still looked at him with the same slight edge of disdain that she always had.

"You *have* no schedule, Sam," she said evenly, with a half-smile bordering on a smirk.

Little bitch, he mused. But very cute. The woman had slept with his brother for years. Looking at her stare him down, he wanted her. Just as he wanted his brother's plane, and his brother's limousine and driver, and the big office, and full control of the company.

He glanced around the magnificent Mediterranean mansion, teeming with personal and business friends of Paul's. He wanted his brother's friends. He wanted his brother's social life. Maybe he would even live here in his brother's house, as trustee of the estate, write it off for business somehow. He was giddy with power. He had always wanted everything that Paul had, and now it was all his.

You too, little Alex, he thought, smiling back at her defiant, wild Irish face with the smattering of light freckles brushed across her nose, the curly dark mane of out-of-control hair, the eyes still red from crying over his dead brother. *I'll have you too, in time.*

Who knows? he ventured in his wildest imaginings, catching sight of Devin's sleek blond head above the crowd across the room. *Maybe I'll even have the frosty widow!*

27

"There are few homes in America," declared reporter Maxi Poole on the Six O'clock News, "in which you won't find something with the familiar diamond-shaped L.A. Garb logo on it, be it a piece of clothing, a pair of shoes, a digital watch, a fishing hat, a set of sheets, a bottle of cologne, or a bar of soap. Today, the visionary who created the trendy line of homegrown consumer goods, sixty-year-old Paul Nathan Bradshaw, was buried at Forest Lawn."

At this point, tape of the funeral service came up, showing hundreds of onlookers under a sea of bobbing umbrellas, crowding around the gravesite. The camera zoomed in on the minister, then panned down to the polished wooden coffin gleaming in the drizzle, then cut from face to somber face of celebrities dodging raindrops.

"... California governor Pete Wilson, actress Angie Dickinson, Joanna and Sidney Poitier, U.S. Senator Dianne Feinstein, Laker stars James Worthy and A. C. Green, and there's Magic," intoned the reporter, "and some of the young people from television's *Beverly Hills 90210,* Shannen Doherty, Luke Perry—you see a lot of L.A. Garb clothes on the characters in that show."

From the service at Forest Lawn, the coverage skipped to the gates of the Benedict Canyon mansion. "After leaving the cemetery, friends and family gathered at the Bradshaw home to pay their respects," Maxi Poole went on. Having followed several groups of people streaming past the majestic cantera-stone columns and through the imposing front doors of the mansion, the tape cut to the exterior of St. John's Episcopal Church in Beverly Hills.

"Earlier, Bradshaw was eulogized by many, including the Reverend Cecil Murray, nationally known black minister from the First AME Church in South-Central Los Angeles." The shot switched to Reverend Murray at the podium.

"This man was above all a humanitarian, a giver," the minister said solemnly. "He invested in our community. While others turned their backs, out of the ashes of South-Central Los Angeles Paul Bradshaw built a beautiful factory. He trained our people, and he gave them jobs. And as you know, for every garment purchased, Brother Bradshaw—and he is our brother, O Lord—Brother Paul Bradshaw mandated a percentage of the monies from the sale of his product to set up and fund social programs for the youth of our beleaguered neighborhoods."

At that point the tape ended, and Maxi Poole came on camera in closeup. "But there are questions tonight about that percentage of the gross that Reverend Murray men-

tioned," she said. "I talked with several Pulled Together
employees, all black residents of South-Central Los
Angeles. None was willing to go on camera or be identified,
for obvious reasons—they fear for their jobs. But no one
knew of any such programs being sponsored or paid for by
Pulled Together, or by the L.A. Garb company.

"In a call to Samuel Bradshaw, former chief financial
officer and now head of the company, I asked if he would
give me an interview, and he graciously agreed. But when
I said that I wanted to talk about what specific South-
Central L.A. programs were being funded by the earmarked five percent of the purchase price of garments from
the new division, he was suddenly too busy to talk to me."

At this point more pictures flashed on screen, part of the
footage the Channel Six crew had shot inside the factory
on the day Paul Bradshaw was killed. But the faces of the
workers on the tape were defocused, the pixel scrambled
to conceal their identities. Over scenes of various plant operations, Maxi Poole's voice continued: "There were also
some very serious allegations, made to me by several PT
workers, of fraudulent practices going on at the plant that
amount to flagrantly ripping off the workers. Channel Six
News is investigating these charges, and we'll bring you
specifics as information comes to light. If any of these
charges are founded, it will be a sad final commentary on
the illustrious life of the man who was buried this morning,
Paul Nathan Bradshaw, the founder of Southern California's largest garment-manufacturing enterprise, the world-
renowned L.A. Garb."

Devin was taping the news coverage of the funeral. She
wanted to be able to reflect upon this momentous time in her
life when she had some distance from it. Now she watched
reporter Maxi Poole's piece in astonishment. Fraud allegations had leaked to the press. This woman was a dogged
reporter, Devin knew.

While the images of the ongoing television newscast
flickered across the screen in front of her unseeing gaze,
Devin mulled over the presentation she would make to
Sam Bradshaw in the morning. An aggressive news investigation into fraud at Pulled Together could cripple the company, she knew, but it could also be the catalyst to get
Devin the brass ring.

28

"I can't believe you've come here to threaten me. On the morning after your husband was lowered into the ground!" Sam Bradshaw hissed at Devin, who was sitting in front of Paul's massive slate-topped desk in the CEO's office.

"Call it what you like, Sam," Devin rejoined. "I've given this a lot of thought. I want that position. And if I don't get it, I'm going to sue."

"You've given it a lot of *thought?* Since *Friday?*"

"I think fast, Sam," she said.

Her brother-in-law leaned forward, elbows on the desk, and looked at her hard. "Tell me *why* you want to do this?" he demanded.

"I told you—I want to work, I'm good, and I want to protect my interests as a shareholder in this company."

"You're rich, Devin," he told her then. "Irv Chapman will be calling you this week to set up an appointment. He'll explain exactly what your interests are, and what your income will be."

"That has nothing to do with my heading up Pulled Together," she commented.

"Look," Sam said, softening, trying another tack, "Paul's death is a shock and you're not thinking clearly. What you need is a long vacation. Get away. Ski the season in Aspen, relax at a spa, go to Europe, do some sightseeing, shop. When you come back, you'll be far enough removed from everything that's happened to figure out what you want."

Devin sat back in her chair and paused for a bit, studying her brother-in-law's face, discerning the condescension he was trying to pass off as concern. Finally, she spoke softly.

"Sam, you are probably the last person on earth who would know what it is I need. I know what I need. And you'd better take me seriously, because I will not give you another chance to save this company and yourself from what I intend to do."

Sam's face dissolved from bogus caring to outright fury. "You're pissing up a rope with your fucking lawsuit," he spit out.

"Charming," Devin managed. "But let's for a minute say that my suit has no merit. That I lose, and the sale of the company is *not* forced, and you *don't* go to prison for corruption and fraud. Think of the publicity, Sam."

"You're full of shit, Devin."

"Sam, let's try to have an adult conversation, shall we? The publicity surrounding such a lawsuit would be ugly. People will find out how you're cheating black factory workers at Pulled Together and they'll be outraged, and customers who bought PT garments thinking that a percentage of the money they paid would benefit the South-Central community will know they've been defrauded. They won't buy the line anymore," she went on. "Even if they love the clothes, they won't want to be seen in them. It will become politically incorrect to wear garments by Pulled Together."

"The company you'd be undermining is partly yours," Sam retorted. "You'd be cutting off your nose to spite your face."

The man was a walking cliché, Devin noted silently. "Let's talk about the negative publicity you'll have to wade through if I sue—" she started.

"The publicity would come down on your own head," Sam broke in. "A modern-day Medea. Doesn't wait for her husband to grow cold in the grave before she makes a power play to get control of his company."

"Don't kid yourself, Sam," Devin shot back. "The backlash on my lawsuit will make national news. Business will drop off, the division will fold, and the company will take a tremendous loss. And if you manage to stay out of prison, at the very least you'll lose all credibility as the new CEO of L.A. Garb. You'll look like a colossal failure by comparison to your wunderkind dead brother."

"You must have really hated Paul," Sam breathed malevolently.

"Hated?" Devin weighed the word. "No, never hated. I came to be very disappointed in him."

"Really!" Sam raised his eyebrows. "Disappointed enough to kill him?"

"I won't dignify that with a response," Devin returned.

"And I won't stand for your blackmail."

"Hardly blackmail, Sam," she replied evenly. "If you don't let me in there to clean up the mess you and Paul made, the fallout will ruin you all by itself."

"And exactly how is that going to happen?" Sam demanded, his words iced with derision.

Devin reached into her purse and took out a VHS videotape box. "Don't you watch the news?" she asked, tossing the cassette on the desk, watching it skid across the slate toward him.

"What's that?" he asked, instinctively rearing back from the black plastic case. Devin had labeled it: *SIX O'CLOCK NEWS*.

"A reporter who's asking questions about fraudulent practices at the Pulled Together factory," she told him. "And promising to get to the bottom of it."

"Oh, it's that Poole woman—she tried to talk to me," Sam sneered, snatching up the tape box, turning it over, then dropping it back on the desk as if it were toxic.

"Some of the PT workers are already talking to her."

"She can't prove a thing," he said, but Devin saw him wince.

"Understand this, Sam." She locked on to his gaze. "You have two choices. You can make me head of Pulled Together, and I'll clean up the rats' nest you've created there. And this," she said, picking up the news tape and gesturing with it, "will go away. Or don't," she went on evenly. "Then my lawsuit will get this reporter's investigation off to a rip-roaring start, and every newspaper, magazine, radio and television news organization—not to mention tabloid rag—in the country will jump on the story. It's up to you."

Sam sat perfectly still, staring at her, visibly seething. It occurred to Devin that he looked as if he'd like to kill her.

"What exactly would you do at Pulled Together?" he demanded to know. She told him.

"And what kind of salary are you thinking about?"

"Reasonable," she said.

"And when would you want to start?"

"Immediately."

"After the first of the year . . ."

"Monday," she countered.

"Impossible," Sam snapped. "We would have to define your job description, negotiate your compensation—"

"Sam," Devin cut him off, "either I start work on Monday or I go to my lawyer on Monday. Which will it be?"

Tanner's fax had stressed that she had to give Sam Bradshaw that ultimatum, because if he were allowed to stall, he might figure something out that would derail their plan.

"Fine," he forced out between gritted teeth. "Monday."

"Good," she returned, getting to her feet. "Put out a memo—this morning. Be sure all the managers at PT know they will henceforth be reporting to me, not to you. And fax it to me at home." She turned to leave.

"What about your duties, your salary. . . ?"

"Pick a figure that's appropriate, Sam. Just don't insult me, and it'll be acceptable. As for my duties, I know exactly what I have to do."

"You're making a big mistake—"

"Good-bye, Sam," she said, then wheeled around and strode out of the room. She walked briskly through the outer office, past Geneen Landers and Alexandra Anson seated on opposite sides of the desk. Geneen nodded; Alex ignored her.

Bypassing the elevators, Devin sailed down the two flights of stairs to the street level, mentally congratulating herself. Sam Bradshaw blinked! When she'd reached the lobby and was heading for the big glass front doors, she heard her name called. Turning, she saw Alex Anson coming down the stairwell.

"Mrs. Bradshaw," Alex said as she approached, "Sam wants to see you." Having tossed that out, Alex turned to go back up the stairs.

"Just a minute, dammit," Devin hurled at the woman's back. "Either you be civil, Alex, or I'm leaving, and you can tell Sam why."

Alex stopped abruptly and turned around. Devin took slow strides toward her until they were face to face.

"What do you want?" Alex asked.

"I want you to get yourself a book on basic manners," Devin said in measured tones. "What does Sam want?"

"He wants to have his picture taken with you," Alex returned, her disdain ill concealed. "He's got people from the public relations department coming to his office with cameras."

"Thank you," Devin said, then deliberately turned in the other direction and traversed the polished pine plank floor to the bank of elevators. They must put something in the company water, she thought. Here they're all nasty, and at Pulled Together they're all scared.

Sam still sat behind the enormous desk, drumming his fingers on the hard black surface. His face was dark with anger. He knew that Devin was right about fraudulent practices at the South-Central plant. He also knew that even if she didn't have a legal leg to stand on with the scenario she'd laid out, she was also right about the negative publicity. It would kill Pulled Together and kill him along with it.

Once PT got solidly in the black and was hauling profit, Paul and he had always planned to gradually iron out the legal and fiscal irregularities in the division. But now was not the time. Money was tight. With Paul's death, there would be hefty estate taxes, upwards of $200 million, even with the foundation. The prudent solution would be to take the company public, but with an independent board, Sam knew, he would almost certainly lose control. He was determined not to break up the block of shares he controlled. Now, with the company dangerously cash poor, leaving it open to hostile takeover or even collapse, Devin was putting his heels to the fire. Too bad she wasn't in the Ferrari with her husband, Sam thought, when it soared over the cliff. Ruminating for a few moments on that gratifying image, Sam was almost startled to see the woman, very much alive, walk back into his office.

"You want to take pictures?" Devin smiled.

"I think we should," he said. "Put a good face on it for the press."

A man and woman entered the office then, both carrying camera equipment. Sam introduced them to Devin. Marianne Gibbs and Jonathan Rainey, from L.A. Garb's in-house PR department. They positioned Sam and Devin against a wall, in front of a blown-up print of Paul Bradshaw on the recent cover of *Time* magazine. The photo would send a message: a tightly-knit family, having lost its beloved leader, regrouping and moving forward.

"Shake hands, you two," Jon Rainey instructed. "Now smile."

Both cameras flashed in rapid fire. Between rolls, the

photographers moved their subjects around a bit to get different angles. When they were satisfied that they had enough shots, Rainey said, "Okay, Mr. Bradshaw, we've got it."

"I'll write up a release," Marianne added. " *'Devin Yorke Bradshaw, widow of L.A. GARB founder Paul Bradshaw, has been named the new president of the company's Pulled Together division in South-Central Los Angeles,'* et cetera. I'll send it over for your approval, Sam. And congratulations, Mrs. Bradshaw."

"Thank you, Marianne," Devin replied. "Give me your fax number and I'll fax you the stats on my background in the industry for your press release."

"Great," the young woman beamed.

"All right," Devin said, picking up her purse, "I'll hear from you later, Sam." She waved cheerily and again left the executive suite, followed by the couple from the PR department, who split off down the hall with their camera gear.

Alone in the office now, a grim-faced Sam pressed the button on his intercom and asked Alexandra Anson to come in.

"Yes, Sam?" Alex said, appearing in the doorway.

"Sit down," he directed, indicating the chair in front of his desk that Devin had just vacated. "I want to tell you about your new assignment."

29

Rosemary was enjoying Saturday afternoon quiet time in the living room of her stately old Tudor house in Mandeville Canyon. Startled suddenly by an odd noise, she looked up from a magazine she'd been leafing through. Someone was turning a key in the lock of the front door. She jumped to her feet as the door swung open, and a tall, gaunt man with a straggly beard and long, dirty hair shuffled into her entryway. He was dressed in torn, shabby clothes, no socks, and a pair of scruffy run-down moccasins that were badly ripped at the seams. It took her a minute to realize that it was her son.

"Pauly!" she cried, rushing to him.

"Hi, Mom," he said, not moving from the doorway. He looked worse than Rosemary had ever seen him. He looked like his next step was *dead*.

"I heard about Dad," he said.

"Come in, Pauly," she beckoned.

Seeing her son in this condition was devastating. She led him into the kitchen and sat him down at the big round oak table. Turning away from him, she busied herself with making a pot of coffee until she could pull herself together. She didn't want him to see the tears welling in her eyes, even though she doubted that he'd even notice.

Paul Nathan Bradshaw Junior was twenty-seven years old. He'd been abusing drugs for a decade, maybe longer. Since Paul had left her four years ago, Rosemary had worked very hard at putting her own shattered life on track, and she'd only lately emerged from denial about Pauly's drug addiction. Her top priority in life now was to deal with it, to get her son straight.

Once again he'd shown up unexpectedly at his mother's house, his old home. Usually it was just to cadge a meal and get a handout, but today Rosemary could sense that he had a larger agenda. Well, so did she.

"I have money coming, don't I, Mom?" he asked her now. Rosemary could see that his teeth were yellowed and decaying. "I need money," he said.

"I'm sorry about your father," Rosemary returned, setting a steaming mug of coffee in front of him, with a little bit of cream, the way he liked it.

"I don't give a damn about my father," he threw back. "He cheated on you, and he was too busy for me, so why should I care about him?"

"Don't talk that way," Rosemary scolded gently. "Whatever you think your father did to you, it's not a license for you to waste your life this way. Your brother and sisters are doing fine."

"They're not like me," Paul Junior said.

"And what does that mean?"

"They're like him. I'm like you, Ma."

It was true. Pauly had been the sensitive one, the child who looked into people's hearts and found insight into their souls. Pauly had always needed more love than the others. And although she'd never admitted it to anyone, not even to him, Pauly had always been her favorite. Now he was breaking her heart.

So the news had finally filtered through his drugged-out haze that his famous father was dead, and he'd come here to find out how to get his hands on his inheritance. He wanted his money to support his habit. But having serious money would only escalate his downfall, she knew.

Rosemary had had no way to contact him when his father was killed. He'd never given her his address on Third Street, if indeed he had one. He had no phone, or at least he'd provided her with no phone number, and she knew no one who knew anything about his current life. Paul Senior's personal attorney, Irv Chapman, had advised her that as soon as young Paul surfaced, it was incumbent on her to contact him. At his first opportunity, Irv had to advise Pauly of his inheritance and explain his options, he'd told her. Rosemary had leveled with Irv; she had no idea when that would be. The only times she had seen her boy in recent years were on the rare occasions when he dropped in unannounced.

But today she was ready for him. Tough love! She had researched, studied, and mastered the approach. She was convinced it was the only avenue left that could save her youngest son, her baby. She had already contacted the Los Angeles County Sheriff's Department and gone downtown to meet with two narcotics detectives. She'd told them the next time her son showed up at home, she wanted to turn him in.

They took her through the steps. The sheriff's detectives would come out to the house, and if Pauly was carrying illegal drugs, they would arrest him for possession. They would take him in to the station, book him, incarcerate him, and he'd be brought up before a judge.

She'd known that Pauly's father would never countenance such a plan. When she'd once broached it to Paul Senior, he'd roared about negative publicity for the family. Years ago he'd washed his hands of Pauly and his problems. But during this past summer, she'd made up her mind to do it anyway.

Now Paul was dead. He could no longer stand in her way. Nor could she ever again count on him for help with their son. Only she could save Pauly now, she was convinced, and his precipitous slide was obviously getting steeper. It had to be done, and she was ready.

Last week, on the afternoon of the funeral, she had talked it over with Irving Chapman, told him what she was planning to do. She hadn't been able to bring it up to Irv when Paul was alive; she knew that her ex-husband would throw up a roadblock. Now Irv had assured her that he would represent her son. And since it would be Paul Junior's first offense, they hoped, Irv would probably be able to plea-bargain his sentence and have her son sent to a medical facility for drug diversion. Pauly would probably do his time in extended drug rehab at a county clinic, Irv counseled, and he suggested that Rosemary, since she was able and wanted to take responsibility for her son, should offer to reimburse the county for the cost of his treatment. The deputy district attorney would look favorably on that.

This would be hard time. No fancy private rehab house that Pauly could walk away from. His release would be subject to the standard evaluation by the county. And the detectives had made certain she understood that the bust would depend on whether they actually found drugs in her son's possession. Rosemary intended to take no chances.

It was warm in the kitchen, and the hot coffee was making Pauly sweat. Or maybe it was the drugs. Rosemary could see that he was stoned, his perennial state on these visits home. Or maybe all the time, she feared. She got up from her chair, picked up a white linen napkin from the table and patted his forehead with it. Then she helped him off with his beat-up leather jacket and threw it over a chair.

"You drink your coffee, Paul, and I'm going to find Claudie and have her fix you a good lunch," she told him. "Then we'll talk about your money."

Rosemary disappeared into the butler's pantry and buzzed her longtime housekeeper on the intercom. She told her that Pauly was home.

"He looks even worse this time," she prepared the woman, who'd known and loved Rosemary's four children during most of their growing-up years. Rosemary asked her to come into the kitchen and make some sandwiches for Pauly.

She ducked into the library then and took the card with the detectives' names and number out of her desk drawer.

Studying it, she made the call. Her fingers were unsteady, but her features were set with determination.

"Squad room, Jacoby speaking," a voice answered her ring.

"I'm calling Sergeants William Smits or Jay Rinaldi," she said, reading from the card.

"Hold on." After a minute Jacoby came back on the line. "Hello, ma'am ... Smits and Rinaldi are in the field," he said.

"Can you get a message to them?"

"Depends. I'll try."

"Please," she said. "Tell them Rosemary Bradshaw called, and now's the time. My son is home. Tell them to come over as soon as possible. I'll try to keep him here." She gave Jacoby her address and phone number.

"They'll know what this is about?" he asked.

"Yes. And it's extremely urgent."

She went back into the kitchen and sat at the breakfast table across from her son. Claudie had put a plate of turkey and roast beef sandwiches in front of him, and a bowl of her fresh German potato salad. He hadn't touched any of it. He was smoking.

"How do I get my money, Ma?" he asked her. She saw that his eyes were glazed and bloodshot, his pupils dilated. His hand trembled when he picked up his coffee cup.

"There's a clause that says you can't have any of it while you're on drugs," she lied. In fact she was breaking the law by telling him that, but she'd gone this far, she reasoned, and she wouldn't be deterred.

"I'm not on drugs," he responded adamantly.

"Then you'll have to take drug tests," Rosemary replied. She saw a tear escape from the corner of one of his eyes, and it tore her heart out. Pauly, her sensitive one. He was in such pain.

She couldn't stop herself. Tears streamed down her own cheeks. "Sweetheart, I love you so much, do you know that?" she asked.

He didn't answer. He looked away. Finally he turned back to her. "I have to leave, Mom," he said in choked tones.

"Please don't go, Pauly. Please stay, eat your sandwiches, talk to me. I love you. Stay the night in your room, where it's warm ..."

"I ... I gotta go," he stammered, and he stood uncertainly. Rosemary got up and put a hand on his arm to detain him.

"Wait, come sit with me, let's talk for a bit, and I'll give you some money."

He looked up at her, hesitated. "A lot of money," she promised.

She steered him into the warm, comfortable living room. She asked him to light a fire. As a boy, he'd always loved that task. He busied himself unsteadily at the fireplace, setting kindling. Rosemary said a silent prayer.

The doorbell rang. The detectives, Rosemary prayed. For a half-hour or more she and Pauly had been sitting side by side on one of the living-room couches in front of the fire. Talking about his father's will and how he and his brother and sisters would be receiving a regular income from the Bradshaw Family Trust. She'd need an address—Irv Chapman would have to know where to send it, she was telling him.

Pauly's attention was wandering. He wanted money now, and he wanted to leave. Rosemary had the feeling that if she handed him a hundred-dollar bill from her purse he'd be out the door, without giving a thought to the millions in company stock that could one day be his.

She had asked Claudie to go upstairs to Pauly's room and pack up some of his clothes. Clothes Rosemary hadn't touched for six years, since the day her son had moved out of the house. Times before, when he'd shown up, to get money from her or to steal it, she'd been too angry with him to offer his clothes, and he'd never asked. Probably he didn't even remember that his things were here. He'd never set foot in his old room since the day he'd left with just the clothes on his back, without telling anyone where he was going. Without so much as a good-bye. Now two large shopping bags stood on the floor in front of them, packed with sweaters, pants, shirts, a plaid, woolen duffel jacket, shoes, socks, underwear. Some of the clothes were still new, and all of them were expensive.

Claudie came into the living room then and told Rosemary there were two men at the door to see her. Rosemary stood. Her knees were weak. As the women walked across the room and out of earshot of Pauly, Claudie whispered that the men said they were detectives. And there, in the paneled entryway, stood the officers Rosemary had met with months before at sheriff's headquarters downtown.

"Thank you for coming," she spoke softly. "He's in the living room. And," she said pointedly, "his jacket is in the kitchen."

Rosemary gestured to the far end of the living room where Pauly was still sitting on the brightly flowered, chintz-covered couch, his back to them. She stood aside to let the officers pass, then went upstairs to her room. She didn't want to hear it.

The detectives had found a packet of crack cocaine in Pauly's jacket pocket. A baggie that Rosemary had kept at the ready to plant on him. After she'd made her decision back in late summer, she'd told Francisco Diaz, a young man who did handiwork for her, what she needed. She didn't tell him it was for her son. An intervention for a friend's daughter, she'd said. Cisco had nodded sagely, and mumbled something about knowing someone who knew someone ... And one day he brought her the small plastic bag of rocks. Crack cocaine, he'd told her. She gave him fifty dollars.

Rosemary could hear Pauly yelling downstairs now. Protesting that the drugs weren't his, she figured. Then she heard the front door slam. And Claudie rushing upstairs and into Rosemary's room, clearly distressed.

"They took Pauly," her housekeeper cried. "They took Pauly away!"

"It's all right, dear," Rosemary soothed the woman, though her own stomach was racked with nervous contractions. "He's going to get some help now."

"His clothes .. . he didn't take his lovely clothes ..."

"We'll get them to him. Take the bags back into his room, but leave them packed. He'll be needing them," she said. She hoped.

After Claudie left the room, Rosemary picked up the phone. It was Saturday; she called Irv Chapman at home. Told the teenager who answered to tell his dad it was urgent. Irv was summoned from his tennis court.

"Hello, Rosemary," he said, a little out of breath. Rosemary breathed a sigh of relief that she had found him home.

"Irv, it's happened," she forced out the words. "Pauly came home today. An hour ago. I called the detectives. They found drugs . . ." The attorney had no idea that Rosemary had planted them. No one did.

"Okay. I'll jump in the shower and get down there. Don't worry, Rosemary. I'll take care of everything," he said.

It was the first time in her life that Rosemary Cullen Bradshaw had knowingly defied the law. But this was the day of deliverance. If Pauly continued on his present course, he would surely wind up dead. With money in his pockets he would buy larger quantities of drugs. Or he would be murdered for his cash.

So she broke the law. For her baby.

30

Maneuvering her black Jag through the sizable parking lot outside the plant, Devin came upon the spot next to the side entry that was marked *PAUL BRADSHAW*. She pulled into the space, turned off the ignition, got out, and locked her car.

It was ten minutes to eight on Monday morning, and Devin was excited. She'd carefully chosen an understated Donna Karan burnt coral jacket and matching pants, with a white cotton man-tailored shirt. Her only jewelry, besides small diamond-stud earrings and her watch, was a pair of solid gold monogrammed cuff links that she'd had for seven years. Her lucky cuff links. The owners of Pieces had gifted her with them after that company's first outstandingly successful year.

She found her way up the stairs to PT's executive suite, such as it was, and found a surprise there. Big surprise! Seated at the scruffy desk in the anteroom to Paul's old office was her late husband's longtime assistant, Alexandra Anson. Devin stopped short in the doorway.

"Good morning, Mrs. Bradshaw," Alex said, barely raising her eyes, her words tinged with ice.

Devin took the few steps over to the desk where Alex was sitting, the desk at which Devin intended to station an assistant of her own choosing. Well, maybe not at *this* desk, Devin made a mental note. This desk looked like it had come from a closeout sale on bad second-hand furniture.

"Why are you here?" Devin demanded.

"Mr. Bradshaw assigned me here," Alex replied. "Sam Bradshaw," she offered then, in case there was any doubt. "To be your assistant."

"Really!" Devin managed. "When was that decision made?"

"Geneen Landers has taken over my old job as assistant to the CEO in Santa Monica. Now Sam is the CEO, and I've been relegated here. I'm yours," Alex flipped to Devin with a definite grimace, making it no secret that she planned to hate every minute of it.

"I didn't ask you *why* this decision was made," Devin said. "I asked you *when.*"

"On Friday," Alex answered. Of course, Devin thought. She nodded and walked into the inner office, closing the door behind her.

Devin set her tote bag on the floor and sat in the scarred, vinyl-padded chair behind her new desk to digest this. Her first day on the job, before eight in the morning, and already it starts, she thought with chagrin.

Her first inclination was to dismiss Alex immediately, then call Sam and read his beads. To assign Alex as her personal assistant without so much as consulting with her or even informing her was a nasty power play, a move designed to show Sam's contempt for her and to establish right off the rules of engagement in the cold war between the two of them. Even more significant, Devin felt, was Sam Bradshaw's obvious ploy to have Alex Anson spy on her.

She opened one of the creaky desk drawers to put her purse inside, then changed her mind. The paper lining was ripped and dirty, and there was a dead spider in one corner. She set her purse on top of the desk, folded her hands, and proceeded to think the situation through. There was an intercom to her left, she noticed after a bit. She buzzed it. Alex picked up.

"Is there any coffee in this place, do you know?" she ventured.

"I'll find some," Alex responded. "How do you take it?"

"Black, thank you." Devin clicked off. So far, so good.

After Alex had brought her coffee without saying a word, and after Devin had analyzed the pros and cons of Sam's Monday morning gift, she came to a conclusion. Or at least a temporary conclusion. She decided that in fact there was probably no better personal assistant for her than Alexandra Anson, who knew every facet of the workings of L.A. Garb. And knowing the nuts and bolts of the business, it wouldn't take Alex long to get up to speed on the Pulled Together division.

Above all else, Devin wanted to succeed, and Alex could turn out to be a real asset, she knew. And Devin certainly didn't have anything to hide from Sam Bradshaw. She decided she would keep Alex, give it time, see how it worked with them. She would not go to the mat with Sam on this one. Who knows, she thought, maybe she should call and thank him. That would fake him out!

That decided, she looked around her. The place was a slum, and that was an understatement. Her first official move at PT was to take her Rolodex out of her tote, place it on her desk, find the number for her decorator, Bailey Senn, and call him. She told him she needed her offices remodeled—yesterday—and she made an appointment to see him at PT that afternoon.

"Where?" Bailey fairly screamed into the phone.

"It's on Florence Avenue near San Pedro Street in South-Central Los Angeles." She gave him the address.

"*Mon Dieu,* what on earth are you doing down there?" he demanded to know. Devin chuckled.

"Come on down, darling, and I'll tell you all about it," she said. "Two o'clock. And don't drive your Rolls." She hung up, smiling.

First and foremost, Devin was a designer. She'd pulled the mansion together, and no interior job could have been more complex. To make this place comfortably habitable would be a piece of cake. She took a quick, exploratory look around. The furnishings were junk. The building was unimaginative but new. In a cursory scan, she was able to envision what she'd need in her office. She buzzed Alex and asked her to come in, with a notepad.

Alex pushed open the door, walked in, and stood in the middle of the room, pad and pen in hand. Ignoring the

look of insolence her new assistant trained on her, Devin
gestured to one of the beat-up chairs in front of her desk.

"Okay, first order of business," she dictated. "Set up an
orientation meeting with the entire management staff as
soon as production shuts down for the day. Of course,
you'll have to figure out who they are," she said with a grin.

"What time?" Alex asked.

"Three-thirty. The end of the production day is the same
here as in Santa Monica. Let me know if there's anyone
who can't make the meeting. If more than a couple can't
be here, reschedule for the first available time tomorrow."

"Fine," Alex said.

"Personal agendas now, yours and mine," Devin went
on. "Production starts at seven A.M. I'll be in every morning
by eight, and I'd like you to be here when I arrive. As you
were this morning," Devin smiled again.

"And I'll need you to stay until six, Alex, and sometimes
later when it's warranted. I'll try to give you advance notice, but you know this business; that's not always possible.
And just as you did with Paul, I'll expect you to take a
reasonable lunch period and breaks at reasonable times.
Okay?"

"Okay."

"Good. Now, we're going to remodel this office suite so
we can stand it," she said, making it a point to be affable
and pleasant. Alex's expression didn't change. It was arrogant bordering on rude. Devin appeared not to notice.

"So," she went on, "I want you to be thinking about
what you need and what you'd like in your own office. One
thing I do want out there is a large worktable with a few
stools apart from your desk, a place where you and I can
go over samples, fabrics, orders, what have you, and meet
with designers. An excellent decorator will be here this afternoon at two, and we'll get him going on sketches. Bailey Senn."

"*The* Bailey Senn?" Alex raised her eyebrows.

"He'll like that," Devin smiled.

"Expensive, isn't he?" Alex threw out.

"Uh-huh. And fast, and good. And we deserve him, because we are going to make a lot of money for this company," Devin said.

"Two o'clock," Alex confirmed, an intimation of disapproval shading her already sour expression.

"Two o'clock," Devin echoed cheerfully. "Also," she continued, "I want you to order a state-of-the-art computer setup for the two of us. Much like what you had in Santa Monica, only better. Updated. And get it installed and hooked in to the company's mainline system. Okay?"

"Okay," Alex said again, writing down Devin's instructions. "And who should I bill for it? Sam?"

"No. Bill it to me," Devin said firmly. "Our accounts are going to be reestablished totally separate from the Santa Monica operation."

"That'll take some doing," Alex said.

Devin knew that Alex was thoroughly familiar with the way PT accounts were now conveyed through the CEO's office. "No, it won't," she told her. "We'll just do it. It'll be much more efficient for us."

"Are you going to clear this with Sam?" Alex asked.

"That's not for you to worry about, Alex," Devin said, still smiling.

"Anything else?" Alex asked, not missing the gentle rebuff.

"That's it for now," Devin said. "Get back to me as soon as you have anything on the management meeting or the computer setup. And if you have any ideas at all about how we can turn this place into efficient and pleasant working quarters before we meet with Bailey, let me know. Okay?"

"Sure," Alex said, and she got up and left the room.

Watching the woman retreat to her own office, Devin shook her head. Still, she knew from her years with Paul that whatever Alex was—and certainly she'd been difficult with him, too, after Devin had come into his life—there was no disputing that she was brilliantly capable. Alex would have a meeting with key personnel arranged in the conference room at the earliest possible time. And she would know exactly what computer equipment to order and where to order it, both for their private files and for access to the rest of the company's programs. Alexandra Anson knew the overall workings of the company probably better than anyone else in the entire L.A. Garb system. If Devin had brought in a new assistant from the outside, as she had initially planned to do, they would both be in the dark today, feeling their way.

Her intercom buzzed. She clicked on. "Yes, Alex."

"Ruby Johnson to see you."

"Great. Send her in."

Ruby appeared in the doorway, looking crisp and efficient in a trim tan Byblos suit with matching heels. Seeing Devin, her face lit up with a huge smile. Devin got up and went to her, gave her a hug, and steered her over to the tattered vinyl-covered couch where they both sat down.

"God, am I glad to see you!" Devin said. "Want coffee?"

"Uh-uh ... I've had a cup this morning. If you've sampled our coffee, you know that one cup a day is all a body can stand. How's it going?"

"Well, aside from the fact that I've got Lucretia Borgia in my outer office, it's going fine for the first hour," Devin grinned.

"Alex Anson? Yes, that was a surprise to me," Ruby observed.

"Surprised me, too. It's a long story. Don't ask. But I'm going to try to make it work. Meantime, my advice to you is don't get too close—I think she bites!"

"Hmmm ... Well, I'm sure you know what you're doing," Ruby said dubiously.

"Not necessarily," Devin countered, and they both laughed.

The two women chatted for a bit. Ruby went over what was in the pipeline in production and provided her with a list of the names and extension numbers of everyone at the plant.

"Anyone you want the lowdown on, just call me," she told Devin "What I don't know, I'll find out."

"You are a breath of fresh air, Ruby," Devin said gratefully.

"Well, I'm so glad you're here," Ruby smiled. "I know it's going to be good—for all of us. I'd better get back to my department now," she said, standing up to leave.

"Thanks, Ruby. I needed this. And I don't mean the list, though I needed that too."

"Oh," Ruby said, "I have a copy of the list for Lucretia, too. I'll drop it off with her on my way out. And anything either of you need, just whistle!" She paused at the door and gave Devin a wink over her shoulder. One ally, Devin noted. One ally, two rabid enemies, and about twelve hundred unknowns.

*   *   *

Alex could not foresee a time when she'd be happy again. For seven years she'd been the executive assistant to the top company officer, ensconced in plush offices at corporate headquarters in beautiful Santa Monica. Now she was exiled to this dump in riot-torn South-Central Los Angeles, working for a woman she loathed. She couldn't imagine ever getting over Paul, who'd been the love of her life. She was beyond exhausted—she couldn't sleep. Her migraines were virtually constant now. And this had been a day from hell.

She did have to admit to herself that Devin had accomplished a great deal on their first day. They'd met most of the management people at Pulled Together at the afternoon meeting. And, grudgingly, she'd been impressed with the way Devin had handled it. Their computer equipment would be installed on Friday. She also ordered a new computerized typewriter for herself and other basic equipment she would need.

The decorator was something out of a drawing-room comedy. Martin Short from *Father of the Bride,* on uppers! But he had some great ideas. Her whole office was not only going to be redone, but Bailey Senn and Devin had decided to nearly double its size by knocking down one of the walls. And they were going to install a washroom for her, and even a small kitchen so that she could make palatable coffee, instead of ingesting the rotgut they'd had this morning out of the machine down the hall.

Still, she hated it here. She wondered if she could drive home in the dark without getting shot at. Or carjacked. And needless to say, she couldn't stand her boss.

It was six o'clock. She buzzed Devin and said she was leaving. Devin told her she wanted to see her. Alex already had her coat on.

In the inner office, Devin asked her to sit down. She was perusing a file on her desk. Alex could see that it was her company personnel file—Devin must have had it messengered over from Santa Monica, Alex determined. After a beat, Devin removed her glasses and looked up.

"I'm cutting back your pay by one third, effective today, your first day at Pulled Together," she told her. "Even with the cut, your job will still pay much more than comparable jobs in the industry," she observed. Alex looked stunned, but said nothing.

"Also," Devin went on evenly, "I'm going to recall your company car. You'll be given the opportunity to buy the

Mazda Miata you're driving at the Blue Book price for the make, model, and year. You can have payments deducted from your paychecks through the company credit union, if you'd like. Or arrange for some other method of monthly payments. If you don't want to purchase the car, I'll expect you to turn it in by the end of the week.

"And one more thing," Devin went on, referring to notes she'd made. "You will no longer be accorded vacations totally paid for by the company."

Alex felt the blood rush to her face. A vein in her left temple was throbbing. "Will you tell me why you're doing this?" she demanded, with barely controlled rage. Devin squared off and looked at her evenly.

"Yes, I will," she said. "The reason I'm doing it is that I don't feel the need to grossly overpay you."

"I'm worth it."

"How would I know?" Devin asked. "I've never slept with you."

Alex stared at her, outraged. Ignoring her fury, Devin calmly told her that there was something else they had to address. If Alex wanted to keep this job, she said, she was going to have to have a major attitude adjustment.

"I have no intention of putting up with the kind of crap you've been handing me all day," she leveled.

"What are you talking about?" Alex demanded.

"You know perfectly well what I'm talking about, Alex," Devin snapped. "And if you don't, then we really can't work together. But I'm willing to make an honest effort, if you are."

Devin told her to take the next day off and think it over. And to look for another job if she wished. She was to let her know by Wednesday if she wanted to continue at PT, or ask Sam for other placement within L.A. Garb, or leave the company altogether. It was up to her.

"Also," Devin added, removing a crumpled piece of paper from the top of the file and scanning it, "if you do decide to leave the company, you won't be getting the excessive settlement that Paul offered when he fired you the night before he was killed. You never signed this. You'll get the standard company policy severance pay."

Alex was staggered. The damned resignation letter! How the hell did Devin get it? She didn't ask. But if this bitch wanted to play hardball, she would teach her a few plays.

31

"Yes, yes, yes, I'll make it all up in your paycheck, you won't lose a dime," Sam Bradshaw told an irate Alex Anson, who had whiffed past Geneen this morning, demanding to see the boss. It was just after nine o'clock on Tuesday, the day off that Devin had insisted Alex take to "think things over." She had planted herself in Sam's office before he got there, and waited for him to arrive. Before he could get himself seated, she'd launched into a blow-by-blow account of her first day on the job as Devin's assistant, capping her rant with the way the bitch had chopped her pay and benefits. Now she was loudly demanding that Sam give back everything that Devin had taken away, and he was wearily shaking his head.

"So I'll keep exactly the same salary? And the car, too?" she badgered.

"Yes, the car, too. You'll make payments through the credit union, and I'll see that the money gets filtered back to you," Sam said, with just a hint of annoyance. He didn't like his day starting with a banshee screaming at him, and he sincerely hoped that his hefty investment in the feisty woman his brother had meant to fire would pay off.

Sam had seen her "letter of resignation," dated the day before Paul was killed. The next day, while the family waited for his brother to arrive for lunch at their mother's house, Sam had called Geneen and told her to search Paul's office complex for a clue to his whereabouts. Scouring the suite, Geneen had found the letter. Alex hadn't come in yet, but she was on her way. Out for the morning with a headache, but more likely it had been about the letter, Sam figured in retrospect, and the showdown that she and Paul must have had the day before. As he realized now with chagrin, that Thursday had been a day of showdowns for his brother.

Geneen had brought the letter in to the full staff meeting

on Saturday morning and discreetly slipped it to Sam before Alex had arrived. She'd found it crumpled up in the trash basket under Alex's desk, she said. And she pointed out that the letter had to have been written by Paul, not by Alex, because it looked sloppy—it wasn't centered on the page, and there were a couple of typos. Alex would never put out a letter like that. So this wasn't Alex wanting to resign, Geneen had whispered, it was Paul wanting her out. Alex was her friend, of course, but she'd assured Sam that her first loyalty was to her boss, and she felt he should know about that letter. Paul was dead, after all, and the police were saying that he'd been murdered.

The letter included a complete addendum of severance benefits that Alex was to receive. That signaled to Sam that his brother had been serious about letting Alex go. Sam had had a front-row seat for the Paul and Alex show for years. He'd been very much aware of their volatile relationship, which had become even more volcanic since Paul had excised Alex from his personal life. Maybe Paul wanted to sleep with her again and Alex wasn't having any. Maybe the two of them had had a fight, then kissed and made up, and Alex had tossed the resignation letter in the trash.

On the other hand, seeing that letter had triggered in Sam's memory something that Paul had told him on that same fateful Thursday when he'd had his own confrontation with his brother over "the report." Sam had hardly been able to focus on anything but his own situation that day, but later he remembered Paul telling him that he was going to fire Alex, and the reasons why. However, it certainly wasn't in Sam's interest by then to act on Paul's intention. Besides, somewhere on the back burner of his libido, Sam lusted after her himself, and he didn't want to let that sexy little vixen get too far away. Not yet, anyway. He'd told Geneen to put the crumpled letter into Alex's personnel file, for future reference if needed.

"And what about my all-expenses-paid vacations?" Alex was grilling him now.

The woman had balls, no question. A week ago she was on the glide path to the unemployment lines, and now she was making demands. Next, she'd be asking him for a raise.

"The vacations, Sam!" she insisted.

"Jesus, Alex," Sam ventured, "Paul gave you those vacations, just like he gave you the fur coat, and the car, and the jewelry, because—"

Alex cut him short. "Sam, that's not the point. If you want me to *work for you,*" she said pointedly, "I don't want to lose any of my ... benefits."

"Alright. For now. And we'll see how you do," Sam told her, also pointedly.

"What does that mean?"

"It means that if you deliver, you'll keep your 'paid for' vacations, even though you're the only person in the company who gets to put a trip to Barbados, all expenses included, on the company credit card. Even I can't do that."

"Oh, I think you can do that *now*!" Alex threw out. Sam let that one go past. He didn't want to encourage another one of her hissy fits.

"But since, as you say, I'm on probation, depending on the *results* I turn in, I think it's only fair," she persisted, "to expect an increase in pay if I do bring you some, aah ... interesting data."

There it was, Sam thought. Sure as hell, she was asking for a raise! Well, who knows, maybe she *would* get a raise, he half smiled to himself. If she took on some new duties down the road, that is—duties that involved Sam Bradshaw.

"We'll see," he maintained, "we'll have to see," but he smiled at her when he said it.

Alex's business with him concluded, she stood and offered her hand. They shook on their agreement, and she gave Sam one of her adorable quicksilver Irish grins.

"Let's go to work, boss!" she bantered with a wink, and with that she turned, allowing him the pleasure of watching her perfectly put together little backside sashay through his office door. Hard to resist, Sam acknowledged to himself.

Their collaboration could work. Immediately after Devin had hit him over the head with her outrageous demands on Friday, Sam had proposed to Alexandra that she take on the position of personal assistant to Devin at Pulled Together. It was a logical move for the company, he'd told Alex, because she knew the business inside and out. She'd be invaluable getting Devin's operation up and running, and keeping things on a smooth track at PT.

Sam would quite frankly like to see Devin fail dismally, of course, but the woman had him dead to rights on the fraud issue. If she were to follow through with her threats, she could ruin him. He couldn't take that chance. He had no choice but to let Devin have her head at Pulled Together.

He also needed to get some strong numbers out of the PT line. As head of the company, that would reflect well on him, but much more important, he needed to resist taking the company public. Bruce Henning, Irving Chapman, Charlie Fine, the Solomons, everyone was recommending selling shares as the only expedient way to raise the capital they needed to pay the tax man. But that would almost certainly lose Sam Bradshaw control of the company, and he had no intention of letting that happen, so he'd devised a two-pronged plan. One: he would severely tap L.A. Garb's lines of credit at several banks to come up with needed cash flow. And two: he would siphon money out of the Pulled Together operation just as fast as the division could bring it in.

The Solomon Brothers' appraisers were pulling every trick they knew to lower the valuation of the company and its assets and to push back the due date while the tax amount was being settled. Still, the day would come when payment was due, be it six months or a year from now, and Sam needed PT to be his cash cow. So it was important that they didn't throw out the bathwater down there in South-Central. Just the baby. The baby executive, Devin Bradshaw.

There was another reason why Sam had planted Alex at Pulled Together. He wanted her there to *keep an eye* on Devin, to operate as a corporate spy. Common enough practice in today's business climate, but Sam's reasons were personal first and business second. He needed Devin's 10 percent vote to revert to the Bradshaw Family Trust. He needed Devin on a slow boat around the world. He needed Devin in an ashram in Tibet. He needed Devin dead.

Instead, she'd set herself up right under his nose as head of the new division, in a position she created herself. And Sam wasn't able to stop her. But with Alex on the case— bright, crafty Alexandra Anson with all of her Paul Bradshaw-trained business savvy—he was working on it!

The question was, would Devin put up with Alex? Probably so, for a while anyway. Devin was anything but dumb, and she would see in Alex a wealth of company knowledge and know-how that she could access to help her succeed at

PT. Especially if she intended, as she'd flatly stated on Friday, to right the wrongs at the factory by pouring money into payroll and benefits for the South-Central workers.

If she could do that and still pull down profits, that would work in Sam's favor. If she couldn't, she'd be gone, which would also work in Sam's favor. Even Charlie Fine would back him if it turned out that Devin made a loser out of Pulled Together. Still, the best-case scenario, for Sam's purposes, was for PT to make money but for Devin Bradshaw to take a fall.

Alex had initially balked at the assignment. With every bit of her fiery Irish passion, Alex Anson hated Devin Bradshaw. She made it no secret; everybody knew that. Devin knew that, for God's sake. But Sam had dangled in front of her big brown eyes a solid gold carrot on a stick. "Let me know when, where, and how Devin screws up," he'd told her in their locked-door session on Friday morning, "and if there are enough significant instances to justify her removal, I promise you, Alex, you're next in line for her job."

Alex left the L.A. Garb building and thought about how she would spend this day. Her lovely free day, for which she'd be paid. And paid her full salary. This was the first minute she'd felt some of the old Anson esprit since her horrible fight with Paul a week ago Thursday, then the harrowing day he was killed, followed by the complete upheaval of her life. Today was the first day she didn't feel confused, depressed, and frightened for herself and Rosemary. Today, finally, she was able to look ahead to a brighter future.

Thanks to Sam Bradshaw. A quintessential jerk! Not only would she take over Devin's position as head of Pulled Together, but it wasn't at all outside the realm of possibility that from there she would someday replace Sam at the top. Even now, she was better equipped to run the company than he was, and they both knew it.

Sam had made a big mistake replacing her with Geneen as his assistant in that office. Geneen was a nice woman, and efficient enough at her former duties, but she was way over her head when it came to the business of the CEO of L.A. Garb. As was Sam, of course. That had become glaringly apparent to Alex when they'd all worked together during the long days and nights of transition. And the workings of Sam's former financial department had been anything but efficient. Frequently over the years, Paul and Alex had had to put out fires originating from Sam's operation. Big fires! Sometimes they had barely been able to head off major fiscal disasters. But Sam was Paul's big brother, and Paul had always cleaned up after him. Now, however, there was no Paul to do the catching in the rye. And there was no Alex there to back him up.

While working to bring Geneen up to speed, Alex had found herself holding back just a bit. Maybe more than just a bit. She'd briefed Geneen on only about 60, 70 percent of the CEO's systems. Alex had justified it by telling herself that she didn't want to load Geneen up with more information than the woman could absorb in such a short time. She would always be on the other end of a phone line to bail Geneen out if needed. Call on me any time, she'd told her, and she was sure she would. Because she'd have to. One of the top corporate rules for succeeding in business, Alex knew well, was to make oneself indispensable. She'd done that with Paul, certainly, and it had paid off handsomely in every way. And because Paul Bradshaw had run such a tight ship, had let no one but herself totally into the loop, Alex Anson was now indispensable to the smooth operation of the giant company.

As for Devin, she wasn't going to be a pussycat, Alex had found out yesterday. But she should have realized that. After all, Devin Yorke had headed up a very successful business in the high-stakes Los Angeles garment industry. And, realist that she was, Alex also had to admit that the woman had managed to wrest Paul Bradshaw out of her own clutches. That still nettled, even after all these years.

So yes, her new supervisor was going to be a major challenge, but Alex intended to prove that she was a better man than Devin She was off to a fast start, and she had her ducks lined up for the fight. She had the big guy on her side, paying her to spy on Devin's every misstep.

But Alex intended to go further than that. She harbored delicious thoughts of actually engineering some of those screw-ups herself, and making sure that they had Devin Bradshaw's name on them. It would be easy for Alex, because only she really knew where all the company bodies were buried. In fact, Alex smiled to herself, this could be fun.

So how should she spend this lovely day, she mused, as she maneuvered her white convertible out of the L.A. Garb parking lot in Santa Monica and headed east. Her cream puff of a buggy that was no longer an endangered species. In fact, she decided, she would start turning in her gas and oil and repair receipts on her company expense account. To Sam, of course, not to Devin. She had no doubt that Sam would sign off on them.

She really did have Sam Bradshaw over a hefty barrel. It probably hadn't occurred to him, but at any time she might just suggest to him that if she ever decided to blow the whistle on their little clandestine arrangement, Sam would be in big trouble with the board, most especially with its newest member by virtue of her present status as a major stockholder, Devin Bradshaw.

On Friday, Sam had taken Alex quite by surprise with his proposal for her to spy on Devin for him, but today Alex had come to the office prepared for espionage. Up on the desk between Alex and Sam, inside her porous Adella Rogers ribbon purse, her Sanyo Mini Talk-book had been rolling. The meeting they had just taken was all on tape, loud and clear and in its entirety.

Yes, this was going to be fun. So today she would celebrate. She picked up the car phone, called Vera Brown at her famous Retreat in the Glen, and scheduled a facial and a massage. Next, she booked Cristophe, Hillary and Bill Clinton's Beverly Hills hair stylist, for a trim. And maybe she'd have him lay in a few sun streaks, to match her ebullient mood. Then she'd swing by Theodore on Rodeo Drive and pick up some new clothes. Freshen up her look. Theodore had Calvin, Gaultier, Thierry Mugler, Richard Tyler, all the hot designers. Maybe she'd walk over to José Eber's then and have her nails and toes done. A head-to-toe pamper day. She'd earned it.

And along the way, she would casually tailor the speech she would give to Devin when she went back in to work tomorrow. She'd say that she'd given it a great deal of thought, and she very much wanted to stay on at PT. Her demeanor would be appropriately sincere. She would apologize for her behavior, saying that with Paul's sudden death and her subsequent job change, she'd been under tremendous strain. However, she would concede, that did not excuse her deplorable behavior on Monday.

She would assure Devin that the woman was entirely right, her attitude had been immature and unacceptable. She would suck up big-time, tell Devin she was a superb manager, that she'd handled the situation expertly. She would say she realized now that the best thing she could have done, as Devin had suggested, was to take a day off and thoroughly think things through. And she'd done that.

She would tell Devin that she had all intentions now of going forward in her new position in a spirit of hard work, good cheer, and loyalty, and she'd like the chance to prove it. She and Devin could make Pulled Together soar.

Devin would be expecting her to bring up the issue of renegotiating the cut in pay and benefits that she'd hit her with yesterday. She would be mystified when Alex didn't mention it at all. Devin wouldn't know that Alex's money situation had already been very nicely settled, thank you. And it was all on tape, she smiled to herself, giving her purse an affectionate pat.

Alex pulled into a spot behind Vera's elegant salon in Beverly Glen. Today would be a day of luxurious indulgence. And tomorrow, let the games begin!

32

"So where's your uptown assistant?" Billy Hilgarde asked Devin with a grin. He hadn't failed to notice that Alexandra Anson's office was empty today and that Devin had done her own calling around to set up this meeting. It was close to ten-thirty on Tuesday morning. Billy and Ruby Johnson were in the conference room with Devin, waiting for the other managers to arrive.

"I gave her a day off to go have her attitude tuned up and lubed," Devin grinned back.

"Good move," Billy said. "But it might be beyond repair."

"Oh, have you two. . . ?" Devin started.

"Oh yes," Billy jumped in, "we two have tangled. Twice just yesterday, in fact. Alex Anson and I have a long history of tangles. Excuse me if she's your best friend, Mrs. Bradshaw, but the lady is a world-class bitch."

"Call me Devin, and she's not my friend," Devin chuckled. "You and Alex go back, huh?"

"Oh, yeah. The chick put me down inside, upside, and every way from the middle when I was trying to get an appointment with your husband . . . aah, late husband."

"She was probably just doing her job," Ruby observed. "If the man didn't want to see you, what was she supposed to do?"

"Ruby is being generous," Billy told Devin. "And yes, I know Alex had to be told to shine me on, but it was the way she did it. Woman has a way of making you feel like a nigger," Billy laughed humorlessly.

"So what's the deal?" Ruby asked. "Is she coming back?"

"I told her to take today off and decide if she intends to continue acting like a world-class bitch—though I didn't put it in your words exactly," Devin smiled at Billy.

"Or what?" Ruby asked.

"Or go work somewhere else. We'll know tomorrow. She's talented, and knowledgeable and smart. I'd like it to work out. But I assure you, if she does come back, I won't have her here insulting us all. So we'll see."

"And if she doesn't come back?" Ruby asked.

"Then I'll get somebody else. Someone with experience as a garment executive assistant and who knows sportswear, hopefully. I have some contacts from my years in the business, and I'm sure you two know some good people. You'll help me find somebody terrific, right? Unless you'd want the job, Ruby?"

"Oh no, no, no . . . you can't do that!" Billy Hilgarde jumped in. "Production is this far away from total chaos," he said, holding up his index finger and his thumb with a hairbreadth of space between. "If Ruby leaves the department, we'd fall two seasons behind on her first day away."

"Well, thank you very much, Mr. Hilgarde, my good friend," Ruby said indignantly. "Please don't let *me* decide if I'd like to accept a better position with this company!"

Devin laughed. "Guys, it's my second day on the job.

Ease up," she said. "I haven't had a chance to look at production yet, but if Billy's right, if it would fall apart without you right now, Ruby, then I withdraw the offer, at least until I can get a handle on the problems in your area. Meantime, as far as I'm concerned, a better job means better money, and you're definitely getting a raise, Ruby."

"See, babe?" Billy Hilgarde grinned at Ruby. "I got you a raise!"

"No, you didn't get her a raise, Billy," Devin laughed. "I did get to look over the payroll numbers yesterday. You get a raise, Ruby, starting Monday. I plan to bring some equity to this place."

"All right!" Billy exclaimed. "And how about me, Mrs. B.? I get a raise too, huh?"

Devin laughed again. She liked these two. "Sorry, Billy," she said, "but it didn't escape my notice that you happen to be making very good bucks. They had to ante up big to get you over here from GUESS?, huh?"

"Can't blame a guy for trying," Billy said, flashing his magic grin again. "And I'm glad to see you standing up for equality for blacks."

"Dum-dum," Ruby scowled at Billy, "in case you've failed to notice, most of this entire factory is black. Mrs. Bradshaw is addressing equality for *women!*" Billy did one of his elaborate, sheepish shrugs and had the two women chuckling again.

Henry Lewis from shipping arrived then, and the conference room started filling up with department heads and the rest of the PT management team. Devin sat at the head of the table. Most had met her at the brief orientation meeting the day before. They exchanged greetings, and when all were seated and quieted down, Devin called the meeting to order.

"First of all," she said, "I want you to understand the chain of command, just in case Sam Bradshaw and the corporate higher-ups in Santa Monica failed to make it clear. No one here answers to anyone there any longer. You answer to me."

"What about payroll?" asked John Quethe, the factory paymaster.

"Payroll, too," Devin said. "John, I'll be working out the transition with corporate over the next week or two, then you and I will sit down and restructure the system. The same goes for all accounts, payable and receivable. We'll get to that."

"Sounds good," Quethe said. That settled, Devin stunned the assemblage with her next order of business.

"Now," she said, "we're going to go around the table, and I want to hear from each of you. And today, I don't want to hear what's right with your departments. We need to get to what's wrong here. All of it. From inferior equipment to lack of supplies, to laziness, to corruption, to fraud, to whatever it is, I want to hear it. Who's going to start?"

The room was stone silent.

"Well, if you're not comfortable talking about it in front of everybody else, tell me that, and we'll make an appointment for a one-on-one. But I'm here to get things done, and if we have to do it that way, it's going to take a lot longer to get results."

A couple of department managers darted glances at others around the table. Billy Hilgarde could hear the wheels turning in their heads and see the fear behind their eyes. He raised a hand.

"Since you all have been listening to me bitching for months," Billy announced, "why don't I start?" His words were an icebreaker. Tense shoulders relaxed.

"Go for it, Billy," Devin encouraged, and smiled. In the absence of an assistant, she'd asked Ruby Johnson to keep a record.

"Okay," Billy started, "you know that I've been trying to organize PT as a union shop, and you know why. But Mrs. Bradshaw isn't up to speed on all the reasons why, so I'm going to go through my laundry list, and if you've heard it all before . . ."

There were laughs and groans around the room. They *had* heard it all before, many times, but it was apparent to Devin that they very much liked Billy Hilgarde and looked to him as their leader.

Billy began to outline the omissions, outright wrongs, and fraudulent practices that he and Ruby had sketched to Devin the night they'd had supper with her at the Benedict manse, but now his litany was corroborated by cheers and elaboration from other department managers around the room.

Ruby sat at Devin's left, writing furiously, taking names, keeping notes on the different speakers' titles, positions, backgrounds, even dress, in some instances. At one point she found herself jotting beneath the head pattern maker's name: "wearing Brook's stonewashed blue denim work shirt, series 305A (collar is skimpy)." She couldn't help herself. Ruby was in the rag business, and she knew just about everybody's goods in the trade, especially goods that competed with PT.

As Billy got warmed up and rolling, the rest of his colleagues took the cue. Layers of intimidation fell away, and one by one, men and women in the room loosened up, forgot fears for their jobs, and told Devin what was on their minds and in their hearts. And what was going on within their respective departments.

Devin asked questions. Billy Hilgarde jogged some memories. Ruby Johnson occasionally asked for something to be repeated. At one point, Devin told Billy to pick up the phone and send out for sandwiches—lots of them. Egg salad, tuna, roast beef, ham on rye. And salads. And coffee, soft drinks and bottled water, and fruit and desserts.

This meeting was going to be a long one, she could see. And very productive.

33

Devin was trying to remember the last time she'd had sex. Where was it? In a suite at the Four Seasons Hotel in Washington, D.C. How was it? Rushed. When was it? Weeks ago. How about the last time she'd had *good* sex? Much longer.

And then there was *great* sex. She and Paul had definitely had some great sex. But thinking back, there seemed to have been none that fell into that exquisite category for years.

Last Thursday she'd buried her husband, she reminded herself. Six days ago. How rotten a woman did that make her? she wondered, thinking about sex this morning, good, great, rushed, or otherwise. Thinking about sex so intensely that she could smell it, taste it.

The giant black-rimmed clock on the mirrored wall of the gym indicated that it was 6:52 A.M. She tried to concentrate on her leg extensions for strengthening quadriceps. *Inhale, lift, exhale, six; inhale, lift, exhale, seven . . .* She looked over at Tanner, doing identical leg curls on the machine opposite hers.

Wonder how many women he has? Devin mused. *Inhale, lift . . .* Probably hordes of them. He wasn't married, but he never talked about dates. He had to have them. He was gorgeous. He was in great shape. He was a lawyer. Blondes, redheads, brunettes, short, tall—he probably had them all. Probably got laid every night. Or maybe he had a special woman. Of course he did, he must! He was probably engaged . . .

God, what the hell was wrong with her? she wondered, trying to wrest her mind away from her raging hormones. *Exhale, ten . . .* From under lowered lids she watched the outline of Tanner's chest heaving as he breathed, his nipples outlined under his tight gray T-shirt stained with sweat, sleeves rolled up to his shoulders.

She wanted to touch them. Not his shoulders, his nipples. Oh God, she thought, she needed a shrink! But who had time? *Inhale, lift . . .*

They'd spent most of their first hour this morning talking about Devin's second day at PT. The incredible meeting she'd had yesterday with her department chiefs. She'd told him how funny and adorable Billy Hilgarde was. And how dedicated. And about wonderful Ruby Johnson. And bitchy Alex Anson, her late husband's assistant. Her late husband's mistress for more years than Devin had been married to him. Now *her* assistant. Maybe. She'd know at eight o'clock. Strange bedfellows. Or would that be bed gals?

Devin realized she was telling Tanner everything now. That used to be against their rules. But if it hadn't been for Tanner and his ingenious plan, she probably—no, certainly—would not be head of Pulled Together now. Besides, she was sure he would tell her all about his life if she asked him. But she didn't want to know. And besides, again, he gave great feedback. She wondered if he gave great head.

Stop it! she reprimanded herself. They'd reached the

point in their workout when they were too short of breath
to do much talking. So she was thinking. Wonder if he ever
thinks about me? In bed? Of course not, she scolded herself. He had a life. And she only wanted him because he
was here. And she was horny.

She needed a sex therapist. No, she needed sex. God
help her, she thought, she was twelve days a widow. They
should pin a scarlet letter on her: *S,* for *Sick.* Or *Sex-
starved.*

She'd always been faithful to Paul. She'd had men before
she married. After all, she was single until she was thirty-
one. But marriage was sacred, no matter how disappointing
it had turned out. She'd taken vows. She was a good Pasadena girl. She wouldn't cheat. She was going to divorce
him, but she would never cheat.

Oh, she'd thought about it, especially in the last year.
And almost always with this man: Tanner. Smart. Funny.
Great-looking guy. Incredible body. But that wasn't why,
she was sure. She'd fantasized about sex with Tanner because he was *here.* Lot to be said for that.

Besides, what was wrong with fantasizing? Everybody did
it. Ask Shere Hite, the guru of sexual fantasies. Devin had
her own secret garden. And all the damned healthy, full-
blown, moist, dripping flowers in it looked like ... Tanner!

"You're slumping," he was saying. Slumping? she
thought. Ha, I'm thinking about screwing, and he's thinking
about slumping. I need help. I need a vibrator, maybe.

He was standing behind her now, his two hands on her
waist, pulling her back against the backrest, forcing her to
sit up. He smelled of sweat mixed with Floris. Ten of his
fingers burning ten holes around her waistline. She wanted
to take his two hands in hers and slide them slowly up her
tight, white leotard and over her breasts.

Maybe she *should* see a shrink. A sex specialist? For
what sex? There was no sex. No sex for her. She was twelve
days a widow!

Mercifully, the morning workout was over.

34

Bailey Senn was a man who wasted no time. When Devin strode into her office suite at a little before eight o'clock on Wednesday morning, he was there, along with his army. And all of Devin's furniture was stacked up out in the hall.

She stopped in the doorway and peered at the disarray. They had already torn up the cheap faded gray industrial carpeting in both offices and laid strips of plastic on the floors to try to keep the dust down. Which was only minimally effective.

All that remained of what had been in both rooms yesterday were the two desks, Devin's and Alexandra's. Even the chairs were gone, replaced with a few temporary folding chairs that Bailey had brought from his showroom so the women could work. Devin had instructed the guards to give Bailey access at any time after hours, and she'd stressed to the decorator that the whole operation must not put her out of commission for a minute.

One man was masking the windows; another was measuring the walls. A woman seated on a workbench was taking notes on specific pieces of furniture that Bailey wanted purchased. Another woman was arranging swatches of fabric across Devin's desk for his perusal. Three men were up on ladders, applying paint with brushes and sponges to the newly sanded walls. Another couple were breaking down the appliances in Devin's washroom. Two more with axes and hammers were knocking down the east wall in the outer office. Others were scurrying about, doing only Bailey knew what. All of them wore white porous antipollution masks.

In the middle of the chaos, on one of Bailey's small metal folding chairs, her ankles crossed, her arms folded around herself, clutching her purse, sat a confused-looking Alexandra Anson.

"Good morning, dahling!" Bailey gushed with elaborate good cheer when he looked up and spotted Devin in the doorway.

"My God, Bailey, when did you start?" Devin asked, remaining rooted between the door jambs.

"Eight, nine o'clock last night," he said. "My people have been staggering in at different hours. Espresso?" he offered gallantly, indicating a portable worktable he'd set up in a far corner, on which stood a steaming, stainless-steel European coffee maker, along with trays of fresh fruit and croissants. Devin ventured across the threshold.

"Good morning, Alex," she said, curtly acknowledging the woman who may or may not be her assistant, who was looking actually meek now, a demeanor rarely observed in Alexandra Anson.

"Good morning," Alex responded with a hesitant smile. "I think." Devin sailed through the room on the arm of Bailey Senn, who ushered her into the inner office.

"Some decisions by you, sweetness," he instructed, "and then we're gone. You'll work. We'll buy furniture. Keep the windows open all day for the paint fumes. And please, have *le crappe* in the hallway removed. Salvation Army or something. Makes my stomach queasy looking at it," he complained, wrinkling up his nose.

"And clean out your desks today please, ladies," he said, raising his voice to reach Alex in the outer office. "Because tomorrow they are gone."

"What's taking you so long, Bailey?" Devin laughed now.

"Believe me, *ma belle Deveen,* you know how dearly I adore you, but I do not wish to be one millisecond more than I must be in this . . . this *place!* Are you sure you know what you are doing here, *chérie?*"

"I hope so," Devin offered with a diffident smile.

"All right then, have a look at these swatches, now, and we choose. First, your couches . . ."

She and Bailey went about the business of selecting from the attractive and serviceable fabric samples assembled on Devin's desktop. That done, Bailey cleared out with his troops, leaving the two women alone to face the day—and each other.

Reluctant to initiate the inevitable confrontation, Devin

consulted her Rolodex and called Ruby Johnson in the production office.

"Ruby, hi, it's Devin. Can you come up here for a sec?" She punched off the speakerphone and looked up to see Alex standing in her doorway.

"Come in, Alex," she beckoned, without smiling. "Pull up a chair if you can find one." Alex picked up one of the metal chairs that was leaning against a wall. She carried it over to the front of Devin's desk, unfolded it, and sat down.

"So how was your day?" Devin asked her pointedly.

With that, Alex launched into what sounded to Devin like a very carefully worded speech, delivered with effusive sincerity, no doubt feigned. Devin smiled inwardly. What she was hearing was really not much different from what she herself might have said to her boss had she been in the same position, and had she wanted to hold on to a very good job. Not at all dumb—full of shit, though, Devin noted, as she focused on Alex's explication, her insistence that she was ready to go forward in a spirit of good cheer, loyalty, and yata-yata-yata.

Devin wasn't fooled. The woman would really like to scratch her eyes out, she knew. But she smiled and accepted Alex's offer of a new leaf, a peaceful working relationship. It suited her—for now.

There was a tap on the door.

"Come on in," Devin called, and Ruby burst through the door, a look of horror on her face.

"Good Lord," she said, aghast, "this place looks like the riots all over again!"

"Hi, Ruby," Devin said. "Not to worry. Bring over one of those funky chairs and join us. I've got another oddball assignment for you."

"Lay it on me," Ruby winced.

"I want you to find homes for the stuff you probably stumbled over on your way in here," Devin told her, indicating the scarred and scruffy but still usable furniture piled up outside the doors to the executive suite. Ruby knew a great many of the people who worked at Pulled Together, and some of their families.

"Pick out some workers who could use the things," she said, "and get a couple of guys from shipping to truck it over to their homes. Can you do that?"

"Of course," Ruby told her. "I've got a few good candidates in mind. When do you want it out of here?"

"Yesterday!" Devin told her with a grin.

"You've got it, boss," Ruby smiled. "Now listen, I think I should go down to the carpentry shop and bring you ladies a couple of face masks if you intend to work in here without getting lung disease. What say?"

"Thanks, Ruby," Devin smiled, "but Alex and I are on our way down to the design center to educate ourselves, find out exactly what we're selling and what we're not. Then we're going to lunch. By the time we get back, we should be able to breathe in here."

Alex's phone was ringing. She went out into her office to take the call, and Ruby rushed off to play Santa Claus with two roomfuls of furniture. Devin walked around the suite, making sure the windows were open as wide as they'd go.

Alex came back into the inner office, a somber look on her face. "The police are here," she told Devin. "Evidently they've been talking to several of the workers. Right now they're downstairs in the marking department interrogating Billy Hilgarde."

35

"We're going to make this a long working lunch," Devin smiled. She was sitting across from Alex Anson in one of the apricot silk-chambray padded booths at the Ondine, a tasteful little French restaurant near the Music Center in downtown Los Angeles. Devin had chosen it because it was away from the hustle and din of the usually packed South-Central eateries. While their offices were airing out after the all-night attack-and-destroy mission by Bailey Senn's flying wedge of subcontractors, this would be their executive suite.

"This is a wonderful place," Alex said, looking around at the softly lit hand-textured peach plaster walls, the secluded booths, and the tables set with crisp white linen, gleaming silver, and crystal bowls of joseph-coat roses. Later tonight the Ondine would be crowded and boisterous, when it would host both the before- and after-theater crowds, but on days when there were no matinees, lunchtime was usually quiet.

"I love it," Devin said. "I used to take clients here when I was at Pieces. It's ten minutes from the garment district, the ambience is pleasant, and the food is superb."

"A good place to know about," Alex returned, scanning the menu. "What's terrific?"

"All of it, actually . . . but I recommend the sole almandine. Or the chopped salad is excellent, if you're in the mood." The waiter brought a basket of cheese toast and a bottle of Evian.

"Drinks, ladies?" he asked.

"Iced tea," Alex smiled.

"Good idea. I'll have the same, " Devin echoed, "with lots of ice and lemon, please." The waiter poured Evian water into stemmed goblets.

Devin was acutely aware that she and Alex were operating according to the unwritten protocol of a declared truce. Two bright, efficient, high-powered women, both very good at what they did—the atmosphere between them fairly bristling with strained politeness.

And each with a definite agenda. Devin's, of course, was to succeed at Pulled Together. To take an already high-profile line of casual clothes, multiply its output tenfold, and put it on the global map. And she was sure that Alexandra Anson had the talent and the drive to help her do it. If she wanted to, that is.

At the moment, Devin was also sure that Alex's agenda was entirely different. Her guess was that the attractive, poised, smartly dressed young woman sitting across from her smiling, chatting, behaving with civility and charm, would like nothing better than to see Devin Bradshaw fall mightily on her ass.

Interesting challenge, Devin mused, studying Alex while Alex studied the leather-bound menu: to channel the hostility that raged just beneath her assistant's tightly controlled cool into the intense high energy that Devin knew she was capable of and the productive creativity needed to accomplish her vision for PT.

Maybe the dynamic would work. And maybe it wouldn't.

But if it didn't, Devin knew that she would need to be keenly alert to the signs, so she could jettison Alex before the woman could do any significant damage.

"I'm going with your suggestion," Alex said then. "I'll have the sole. With a small green salad to start."

"Me too," Devin replied. "It's been a long time since I've had it here, but if Jacques Montil is still the chef, we're in for a treat." The waiter came over and took their orders.

After he'd brought their iced tea, refreshed their water goblets, served them butter chips, then bustled off, Devin leaned back against the plush cushions of the booth and looked into Alex's eyes: dark brown velvet eyes with glints of amber light dancing in their pupils, evincing the intelligence behind them. Devin tented her hands.

"Let's talk a little about my business philosophy," she began then, "specifically as it relates to what I want to do at Pulled Together." Alex returned her gaze with rapt attention.

"I have a million ideas about our product," Devin went on, "but before we even begin tackling design, production, distribution, and the rest of the nuts and bolts of everyday business, we have a complex situation at the plant that is top priority. It's also extremely delicate and deadly dangerous."

Alex's already gigantic eyes grew wider. "My God, what?" she asked, for the moment completely dropping the guard gates on her practiced reserve.

"Take notes," Devin instructed. "This is big, and it's rotten to the core, and you and I have to jump in with both feet and clean it up before we can so much as open a sketch pad."

"You mean remodel the whole building?" Alex asked. She too had noted, though she'd spent barely a day and a half at the factory thus far, that the entire place was a disaster.

"I only wish that was our biggest problem," Devin said. "Yes, we'll refurbish as we go along, but that'll be easy."

Devin glanced around to see if any of the other Ondine lunch patrons happened to be tuned in to them. Satisfied that their conversation was private, without mentioning names she began describing the long list of ills spelled out by Ruby Johnson, Billy Hilgarde, and the entire management team she'd met with the day before. She knew it would all go right back to Sam, which was fine with her. Sam would know she wasn't bluffing when she'd told him she was hip to all the skulduggery going on at PT. For her part, Alex seemed genuinely astonished.

"I can tell you honestly that none of those conditions exist at the Santa Monica factory," she told Devin

"Would you know it if they did?"

"Oh, sure," Alex said. "I know every inch of that operation. I can't imagine what was in his mind—" She stopped herself, abruptly realizing that the man she was about to discuss was Devin's late husband.

"It's okay," Devin reassured her. "I don't know what Paul was thinking about either. Money, probably. But I do know we have to fix it, and right away, because the whole sorry situation is about to bite us in the ass."

"How do you mean?"

"I mean there's a reporter out there who's on to it," Devin said, lowering her voice even more. "Actually, I'd like to cooperate with her, assure her that if I can find out everything that's going on, I can fix it—"

"Is this going to ruin Paul's name?" Alex interrupted, her dark eyes suddenly taking on an intensely proprietary mien. My God, Devin thought, this woman is still in love with him.

"No," she responded, "because hopefully we'll diffuse it before it can."

"In other words, if the reporter tells you she learned such-and-such, and if you tell her now that you know about it, you'll get on it and correct the situation, she doesn't have much of a story. Kind of back-page stuff," Alex said thoughtfully.

"Right, and she gets credit for some high-level reporter involvement, so it balances out for her. You know, 'Maxi Poole'—that's who it is, the anchorwoman at Channel Six— 'helps management solve labor problems at inner-city factory,' that kind of thing."

"But how can you say that the fallout on Paul's memory won't be devastating?"

"Alex, listen"—Devin looked squarely at her—"you have to know that Paul wasn't lily white in all this. No way. But whatever the woman reports, if we *don't* cooperate, he's going to look a whole lot worse. Do you understand that?"

"Yes," Alex sighed. "I guess I do. And maybe it'll turn out to be a non-story, because you'll be taking all the sizzle out of the exposé. Maybe she'll back off it altogether."

"I don't think so," Devin responded. "First of all, she's working on the murder investigation, and from her reports I get the feeling that she thinks it could be tied in to corruption at the plant. And second, there's another potential scandal brewing, and she's on to it . . ."

"Tell me," Alex said with resignation.

"Okay. You're aware, of course, that the hangtag on every Pulled Together garment states that five percent of the purchase price of the item goes directly into programs that benefit the people of South-Central who were burned out in the riots?"

"Of course," Alex said. "Paul was very proud of that."

"Well, what you may not know, and what I have only recently learned, is that this five-percent plan is a myth. Doesn't exist."

This time Alex didn't look surprised.

"We're going to have to make it exist," Devin went on. "*Now.* Before Maxi Poole trumpets *that* to the public and no one ever buys another piece of PT goods."

She told Alex to make a note to ask the L.A. Garb comptroller for a strict accounting of all sales of PT garments since the line first went on the market several months ago. And since the retail price of goods was usually about double the wholesale price, Devin said, her plan was to actually donate *10 percent* of the factory price to PT's charity program, one that she and Alex would put in place as soon as possible.

That was the way Paul had spelled it out to the press when the division went into business, she told Alex. That was why PT got so much start-up publicity. That was why Paul Bradshaw got the U.S. Commerce Department medal from the President of the United States. That was why the line took off. And in Devin's opinion, she told Alex, that was what accounted for a lot of PT's business. The money they'd be contributing to this worthy cause was 10 percent of the gross that they wouldn't even have if people didn't believe they were doing something charitable when they bought garments with the Pulled Together label on them.

"I want you to set up meetings for me as soon as possible," she told Alex now. "With Mayor Bradley, with Dick

Riordan—because he's planning to run for mayor and he knows the ins and outs of the business world—with Peter Ueberroth, the head of Rebuild L.A., Reverend Cecil Murray from the First AME Church in South-Central . . ." Alex was taking notes.

"And find out who the most influential black leaders in the community are," she dictated. "Set up a meeting in the conference room with as many of them as you can find."

"And the purpose of the meeting?"

"Tell them we want to explore what services can best utilize the five percent of the purchase price of all PT garments that we have earmarked for the people of South-Central Los Angeles. Tell them we're ready to roll on it now."

It had been a brilliant idea, Devin went on. Paul's idea. To herself, she questioned whether Paul had really meant never to follow through. Wondered if he could possibly have thought that no one would ever call him on it. She asked Alex if Paul had ever said anything to her about that heralded 5 percent, and what exact plans he'd had to collect and disperse those funds.

Alex looked up at her but said nothing. Devin could see that the woman was wrestling with her emotions, which were bubbling very close to the surface. She watched Alex's eyes flicker and moisten. She looked alternately sad, hurt, protective of her ex-lover, and a little bit lost.

The realization suddenly hit Devin that Alex was grieving. *She's grieving over the death of my husband,* Devin thought, *and a great deal more than I am.*

36

There were three taps on Devin's office door. She looked up as it opened and her assistant poked her head inside. "Yes, Alex?"

"Two things," Alex replied. "Your three o'clock appointment, Nathalie Oliver, is here. Also, Billy Hilgarde is in my office. He'd left several messages saying he was waiting for you to get back from lunch. He needs to see you. He's quite insistent."

"Ask Billy if this can wait an hour," she told Alex. "If he says no, send him in, and tell Nathalie I'll be just a few minutes, okay?" Alex nodded. She went out and closed the door.

Devin didn't want to keep Nathalie Oliver waiting. She was a longtime friend and a busy woman, an executive at her family-owned company, Charles Oliver Shoes. Today's meeting was to explore the potential of licensing Charles Oliver to upgrade PT's line of footwear. It was also the reason Devin and Alex had rushed back from the refuge of the Ondine to the wreck and rubble of their office complex.

Devin's door opened again. This time, Billy Hilgarde hurried inside. He planted himself on one of the metal folding chairs in front of Devin's desk. Absent was his usual good cheer, the magic smile. He didn't even comment on the havoc of the office suite.

"This couldn't wait," he said to Devin.

"What's going on, Billy?" Devin asked. He shot a glance behind him, checking to be sure the office door was tightly closed.

"The cops were here," he said.

"I heard."

"They've been talking to everybody."

"That's no surprise, is it?"

"No," Billy said, "but I'm in deep shit. When they got around to me, they not only laid me out on the carpet, they impounded my car."

"Do you know why?"

"Sure I know why," he rejoined. "They say that Paul Bradshaw's Ferrari probably didn't skid out of control in the rain after he was shot. They have evidence that it might have been *pushed* over the cliff. By the killer, probably to buy time."

"What evidence? Did they say?"

"Yeah, they found a scrape on the back of it, with a transfer of black paint. They said it probably wasn't from an earlier rear-ender, because a man like Bradshaw wouldn't have driven his fancy car in that condition. He'd have had it fixed."

"Maybe not," Devin said. "The car could have been

rear-ended when it was parked somewhere. It might be an old scuff that Paul hadn't even noticed."

"Well, they let me know that they have this high-tech testing process that can pinpoint when it happened within hours," Billy countered. Devin raised her eyebrows.

"Anyway," Billy went on, "the cops talked to a lot of people on the production floor, and they knew I'd had a fight with Mr. Bradshaw the morning he was killed. I never talked to you about that . . ."

"I knew about it," Devin said. "Everybody in the plant knew about it. I heard about it on television, for heaven's sake—some fellow from shipping was interviewed on the news."

"Yeah, Reggie. I saw that too. Guy actually apologized to me. I think when that blond reporter chick asked him to go on her show, he got all starstruck."

"He's the one who saw you in the parking lot?" Devin asked.

"Him and Andy Kingston. They both happened to be in the lot when I was letting this crazo pal of mine try out my new car. Bradshaw . . . s'cuse me, your husband, came out of the building just then."

"They say you followed him," Devin prompted.

"Well, I'd been bitching about him because we'd just had that argument, see, and when I told my friend that the guy getting in his car right in front of us was Paul Bradshaw, he went tear-ass out of the parking lot after him. I kept yelling at him to back off, but he wouldn't."

"Why not?"

"Because he was ripped. I didn't know it when I let him get behind the wheel, but I should have. It was my fault."

Devin wanted to know how far the two had followed Paul, and what they'd seen, but she wouldn't let herself ask. With the police investigation circling closer to home, she needed to stay as detached as possible.

"But I want you to know what went on between me and your husband," Billy was saying now.

Devin listened. He gave a quick account of his confrontation with Paul on the morning he was killed. It was over the same old union business they'd been batting around, he told her, but this time Billy gave him an ultimatum, and Bradshaw threw him out of his office with threats of his own. Word had gotten around the plant about this, Billy

said, because everybody was aware of his union organizing
on their behalf. And after the fight, that's when Andy and
Reg saw him tail Bradshaw out of the parking lot, then
down Florence Avenue and onto the freeway.

"But I think that's all the police know," Billy told her,
"and South-Central L.A. is a long way from the top of
Mulholland Drive. Still," he said, "there's always some witness who comes out of the woods that you hadn't counted
on, and I can't lie to the cops."

"Billy," Devin interrupted now, "where are you going
with this?"

"Here's where I'm going, Mrs. B.," he said, leaning forward, his bulk barely supported by the small metal chair.
"I'm a black guy from South-Central. I had a fight with the
dead man on the day he was killed. They say it was a
murder done by someone in a black car, and they made
my black Trans Am in hot pursuit of Mr. Bradshaw just
before the man was whacked. If I lie to the cops, about
anything, and they nail me in the lie, my black ass will be
in San Quentin for a long time before they sort out the
truth. If they ever get around to figuring out the truth.
That's the way the system works for black dudes."

"What does this have to do with me?" she asked him
steadily. His brown eyes bored into hers.

"I don't think the cops know this," he said, "but I *was*
up on Mulholland Drive around the time of the murder.
And I saw you up there, too!"

Devin felt her stomach do flip-flops. "What do you mean,
you saw me? You didn't even know me then," she said
quietly.

"Mrs. B., you're like Ivana, everyone knows you," he
told her. Then, to back it up, he launched into a description
of her as she waited by the side of the road that day. In a
raincoat. A tan Burberry or London Fog. He was in the
rag biz, he reminded her—he noticed clothes. She was
wearing light-colored high heels in the mud. Standing next
to the car she drives to work every day. The black Jag.

Devin felt her blood run cold. "Why are you telling me
this?" she asked.

"Because the cops are going to come nosing around me
again, asking more questions . . ."

"And?"

"And if they find out I was at the scene, they'll ask me what I saw, and I'm going to have to tell them I saw you."

"So ... do what you have to do," she said, trying to sound unconcerned.

"I will," he said, "but I thought you should know. And I need you to understand that I'm between a rock and a hard place on this ... and I'm scared."

Billy didn't ask Devin what *she* was doing up there. And Devin didn't admit to being there. Nor did she ask what *he* was doing up on Mulholland or what he saw. The two regarded each other in silence for a time, but they made an unspoken pact that Devin was sure they both understood. To keep each other's confidence.

Abruptly, Billy got up. He said good-bye and left. There was nothing more to talk about. Almost immediately, Alex appeared in the doorway with a smiling Nathalie Oliver. Devin welcomed her friend, returning the smile, asking her to excuse the shambles in her office, suggesting they move into the conference room, where they could talk. But Devin was shaken, preoccupied. The last thing on her mind at the moment was shoes.

37

Billy Hilgarde, cruising west on Slauson, hung a left on Hoover, all the while scanning the streets, scanning the sidewalks, eyeballing empty lots and storefront doorways. He was looking for Scud Joe Jones. He'd been skimming Crips territory for thirty, forty minutes having no luck, and hoping the cragared-down heap he was driving wouldn't crack in half rumbling over one of the jagged South-Central L.A. potholes.

The buggy felt like a G-ride that had been snagged, stripped, and left to die. In fact it was a beat-up, rusted-out '74 Ford Pinto wagon with 172,000 miles on it, owned by a hardworking friend of Billy's who was a cutter at Pulled Together. The man had been good enough to lend him his wheels, since the cops had towed Billy's Trans Am into impound this afternoon.

The detectives had made it clear to Billy that they had a whole lot of questions to ask him about a week ago Friday, when Hilgarde and friend tailed the man on a death trip. First they were going to check out his ride, they said. Might make their job easier. In any case, they'd be back, and then maybe they'd be reading him his Miranda rights.

Billy needed to find Scud Joe again, fast. He hoped he'd find Joe in some shade of lucid. So far he hadn't found him at all. Just like a cop, Billy shrugged. Guy was almost always on the street, except when you needed him.

It wasn't as if Joe had an address. Or a phone. In fact, the guy didn't really have a crib, since he never slept at his mother's anymore. He usually slept where he happened to be. And that could be anywhere.

Billy gave up trying to spot him and decided to ask around. Most of the homeys in South-Central knew Scud Joe, but he'd have to pick his spots. Because to know Joe wasn't necessarily to love him.

He pulled up in front of a liquor store where half a dozen guys were hanging, two of them wearing flue rags tied around their foreheads, the blue-bandanna symbol of the Crips

"Yo," Billy called to the pack, to no one of them in particular. They turned in unison and gave him the red eye.

"What set you from?" one of the homeboys demanded, hostility blazing from his narrowed eyes.

"None," Billy said. "I'm looking for a cuz, Scud Joe Jones, you know him?"

One of the guys, a short wiry black in his twenties, with hair moussed straight up in a six-inch-high fade, broke into a wide grin, flashing a mouthful of huge gleaming white teeth. Except for one in front, which was missing.

"It's Billy Hilgarde!" he trumpeted to the others. "Hey, bro," he called out, ambling over to the idling Pinto.

"You know me," he said to Billy, still grinning. "I'm Tonio! I seen you with Scud Joe lotta times."

"Oh, right," Billy smiled back. "You know where Joe is? I gotta find him."

"Ain't seen him for a couple hours," Tonio said, leaning his elbows on the open window frame on the passenger side of the wagon.

"Any idea where he is?" Billy pressed.

"I heard he got hold of some twenty-cent bags he's dealin' over on Century. Be back out in a while, you know Joe."

"Tell you what, do me a favor?"

"Sure, Billy. Say, what happen to your cool ride, anyway?" Tonio quizzed him.

"Long story," Billy said. "Can you give Joe a message for me? Real important message?"

"Sure. Whazzat?"

"Get the word to Joe that Billy Hilgarde wants to buy him dinner tonight. Maurice's Snack 'n Chat on Pico, seven o'clock. Tell him Billy Hilgarde will meet him there. Deal?"

"No problem," Tonio said. Then he grinned even wider, and Billy found himself staring into that chasm in the front of his smile. Another small reality check for Billy. There but for the grace of God . . .

"So," Tonio was saying now, "big baller like you, gonna show me some snaps?" Still the big grin. Base-head looking for money to ask a guy to dinner for him. Billy knew he'd ask for money even if he was doing nothing for him.

He pulled out a twenty. The man's grin faded. He pulled out another twenty. Then another. Held the three of them in his hand in front of Tonio's leering eyes.

"That's all, man. That's all I got. You gonna tell Joe, or is somebody else gonna tell Joe?"

"Sure, Billy, I'll tell 'im," Tonio said, reaching for the bills.

"What're you gonna tell him?" Billy asked, pulling the money away.

"Chow tonight, seven straight up, Maurice's, be there or be square!" Tonio flashed his idiotic grin again, proud of himself.

"Good," Billy said, handing him the green. "And if you don't tell him, Scud Joe's gonna be pissed tomorrow! Don't want that," he said pointedly.

"Don't want that," Tonio echoed.

Guess he got it, Billy thought. He could only hope so. Tonio had to be as reliable as any other homey on the street, and this was the only game in town. Grace of God, he told himself again, as he coaxed the ailing Pinto back into traffic.

In the rearview mirror he could see Tonio waving at him,

the three dead presidents in his hand, dumb grin still on his face.

Alex drove her white Miata onto the A lot at L.A. Garb. She glanced over at her old parking space near the guarded rear entry behind the corporate complex. It still had her name on it, but Geneen's dull gray Chevy Nova was parked there. She felt a brief pang but told herself that maybe her new job was going to work out after all.

She pulled into one of the spaces marked VISITOR and hopped out of her car. Her cream puff was gleaming in the late-day Santa Monica sunlight, fresh from the car wash. She'd had some time to kill before she had to be here, so she gave her baby a little TLC.

Devin had decided that they might as well quit early today—because their offices were barely habitable, she said. But Alex sensed that the real reason was Billy Hilgarde. Whatever Hilgarde's business with her had been, he'd thrown the usually imperturbable Mrs. Bradshaw for a loop. Devin went home, she guessed, and Alex set up a late appointment at headquarters with Sam. It was twenty to six.

She'd made one other stop on the way, at the Rodeo Collection in Beverly Hills. She held her brand-new Prada purse, a creamy, caramel-colored leather shoulder bag, close to her hip now. And tonight she would move her essentials into the matching Prada leather wallet she'd purchased on her American Express account. All in the spirit of being extra good to herself. She still wasn't sleeping and she was hurting, but she was going to make it through.

She'd stuffed her notes inside the lustrous new handbag. Information for her first report to Sam Bradshaw. And pretty good stuff, she thought.

Passing the elevators, she skipped up the stairs to the executive complex. She was early. She popped into Geneen's office, her old office, gave Geneen a smile and a hello, and sank into the pillows on the cranberry silk-corduroy-covered couch, her old couch.

Geneen buzzed Sam to let him know she was here, then came over and sat on a chair opposite her. She studied Alex for a minute.

"You look good," Geneen said at last.

"I'm okay," Alex responded. "Don't love it down there, but I must say, it's never boring."

"How are you doing with the famous Devin Bradshaw?"

"Okay," Alex said. That was the party line.

Sam appeared at the doorway to his office and beamed at the two women. "Together again," he said, "the dynamic duo who run this place. Come on in, Alex."

Alex hustled into the inner office and sat in one of the big studded hunter green leather chairs. It still gave her a jolt every time she saw Sam behind the signature mahogany desk instead of Paul.

"How's it going?" he asked her.

"Well, the lady is making some big moves," Alex said, reaching into the Prada bag for her handwritten notes.

Their computer setup wasn't installed yet, and besides, Alex wouldn't chance putting information like this on a hard disc, even though it could be deleted as soon as it was printed. You never knew what computer nerds were capable of retrieving that could someday come back to haunt you.

"She's having meetings," Alex said. "She's picking people's brains, and she's changing things."

"Like what?" Sam asked.

"Like this," Alex said, reading from her notes:

> *No more leaning on employees to work long past the time they've clocked out.*
> *No more kickbacks from suppliers of fabrics, threads, belts, buttons, trim, even machinery.*
> *No more favors in the way of gifts, trips, or money to certain buyers from high-volume department stores and boutiques around the country for their orders.*

Alex glanced up at Sam to assess his reaction.

"Go on," he said, his face unreadable.

"She told me to start looking into setting up a medical and dental plan, a day-care center, credit union privileges with low-cost loans, and other benefits for the PT employees."

"Jesus Christ, she's been on the job for fifteen minutes," Sam groused.

"Well, I'll tell you, Sam, the workers already love her. They think she's some kind of savior. She gets calls from employees, people phoning to say thank you for the new coffee maker in the lounge, thank you for the furniture ... Oh, the furniture!" Alex exclaimed.

"What furniture?" Sam breathed, a vein on the right side of his temple protruding now.

"She got rid of all the furniture in our offices; gave it away to anyone who wanted it. She's having a big, high-priced decorator redo the executive suite from scratch. Same guy who did the Benedict Canyon mansion. She says she's going to get around to renovating the whole factory."

Sam rolled his eyes. "Is that all?"

"One more thing," Alex said. "One more big thing ..."

"What, what, what?" he demanded.

"The ten percent that the PT hangtags promise to the South-Central community—"

"*Five percent*," Sam cut in.

"Well, Devin says five percent of retail translates to ten percent of the wholesale price. She's called for an accounting of all sales receipts, and she says she's going to kick in ten percent of the gross, retroactive from day one. She intends to set up a Pulled Together giveaway program right away. Says it's what Paul promised the people, and she's going to make good on that promise."

Sam groaned. "And what exactly does she plan to do with the funds, has the lady said?"

"She's having me set up meetings ASAP with the mayor, Peter Ueberroth, and every civic and religious leader I can find in South-Central. She's going to have them consult on where to funnel the money to do the most good ..."

"Jesus! Is that all?" Sam asked again.

"Isn't that enough?" Alex chuckled, then realized immediately that Sam was not amused.

"Anyway," she told him, "that brings you up to date." She waited expectantly for him to comment on the job she'd done. He was staring out the window, as if she wasn't there.

"Sam?" she said, after several moments.

"Yeah?" he responded, looking over, looking almost surprised to see her.

"I'm going to run, unless there's anything else. You can have these," she said, pushing the several sheets of notes across the big desk toward him. She had copies.

"Oh, thanks, Alex. You did good," he said then. Alex gave him a tentative smile and left.

Sam was suddenly very tired. He put his head back and closed his eyes. Ten percent of PT's sales was a whopping amount. What he and Paul had intended to do was fund programs that would cost nowhere near the amount stated on the hangtags. Five percent of the purchase price was just a public relations number.

The brothers had talked about doing something highly public, a mobile book-lending service combined with a Meals-on-Wheels type of thing, a high-profile, low-cost operation that would guarantee a lot of good human interest press.

And all her fucking reforms and benefits, he thought dismally. Renovate the building? The plant in South-Central was practically new. Cheap, yes, but new, and certainly serviceable.

Behind closed eyelids, he saw thousand-dollar bills with wings flying in droves out the windows. Just when he was desperate to drain every available nickel out of the PT operation to pay down the damned estate taxes. And Ms. Uptown Bitch was doing designer couches!

But he knew he had no choice on any of it. He had to leave Devin alone for now to run Pulled Together the way she saw fit, or she could make good her threats and blow the whistle. He had no idea how far she'd go, but he couldn't afford to find out. So far, it was worse than he ever could have imagined, and this was just her first week on the job!

He had to figure out how to get her out of his way. Out of the company. Off the planet would be nice.

An hour later, at five to seven, Scud Joe Jones was shuffling along Pico Boulevard headed for Maurice's Snack 'n Chat. He'd had a lucrative day, he was a little high, and he was in a good mood. He was looking forward to having dinner with his pal Billy Hilgarde.

Suddenly, from a spot to the left and just behind him, the sound of semiautomatic gunfire ripped through the night. Joseph Bernard Jones Junior was gunned down in a drive-by shooting. Sprayed all over the sidewalk in his L.A. Lakers jacket. Dead.

Police, an ambulance, a car from the coroner's office, a TV camera crew, a couple of print reporters, and a gathering of neighborhood lookie-loos filtered onto the scene in succession, crowding around the body.

Eyewitnesses talked to police. Some of the homeboys talked to reporters. The text of the dead man's life was being pieced together. With Scud Joe, said those in the know, it could have been any number of people who wanted to waste him. Gang related, drug related, gun sale related, female related, any kind of grudge, and on and on.

Billy Hilgarde never showed up.

BOOK TWO

FEBRUARY 1993

38

Devin stood in front of the mirror in her massive bathroom, quickly dabbing a touch of blush to her cheeks. She was almost dressed—in a pair of teal blue Armani slacks, not belted yet, and a matching silk Armani shirt, not buttoned yet. It was after seven, and she was hurrying to get on the road. Morning rush-hour traffic through downtown Los Angeles was always a bear.

She picked up a brush to run through her hair, then let out a terrified shriek and sent it crashing onto the marble countertop, overturning several expensive bottles of perfume. Behind her, reflected in the mirror, she saw a man standing in her bathroom.

Devin clutched at the front of her shirt, holding it closed. The man didn't move, just stood rooted to the floor, staring at her. She wheeled around and faced him squarely. He was fifty-something, thin, of medium height. Gray hair, gray eyes, gray complexion, gray suit: a gray person. He gave her a wan smile.

"What the hell are you doing here?" Devin demanded, her hands trembling.

"Looking at the house," the man said, still smiling. A rotund woman suddenly appeared at his side. She was as garish as he was dull, her face slathered with heavy makeup tending to orange, accented with blazing red lips and thick black brows, and topped with a stiffly lacquered upsweep of midnight blue hair. She wore a tight red suit with huge gold buttons straining at her ample bosom. A quilted black bag swung from her shoulder by a strap of gold chain entwined with leather. The interloper was overdone, overblown, overweight, and overdressed for an early morning foray into a stranger's bathroom. Devin took all of her in as she struggled with the adrenaline rush that was still making her hands shake and her heart pound.

"What a lovely house you have, dear," the woman said

in a loud raspy voice. Her gray ghost of a husband, if indeed he was her husband, stood ramrod straight beside her, still smiling stupidly.

"Excuse me," Devin blurted, "did you say you're here to view the house?"

"Yes," the woman said, breaking into a broad smile, revealing a swath of Revlon's Fire & Ice smeared across her front teeth.

"Where is the realtor?" Devin demanded.

"Downstairs somewhere," the woman croaked, obviously the spokesperson for the pair. "He knows we like to wander around by ourselves. We do our looking nice and early before Rodney has to be at the office," she elaborated. Devin was speechless.

"You're Devin Bradshaw," the woman rattled on. "I recognize you from your pictures. We just saw your divine closet. My, what lovely things you have!" she gushed, idly picking up an antique silver-framed hand mirror from the marble countertop and turning it over to examine it.

Devin bolted around the pair and fled from the bathroom, buttoning her blouse as she ran. She bounded down the stairs and went looking for Todd Julia. The listing broker. Sam's choice, of course. Unhappily, she was getting to know him a lot better than she cared to. Thirty-something. A tanning-salon glow. His light brown hair was highlighted with dyed sun streaks. He smelled of gardenias. Beneath the modish veneer, a mean-spirited, dishy queen who was desperate to make this mega-commission sale. Letting clients wander unescorted among homeowners' personal belongings was unethical, unprofessional, and unheard of, but Devin had learned the hard way over the past several weeks that Todd Julia would do anything to kiss up to potential buyers. What did he care if they lifted a few baubles into fake Chanel purses?

She found him perched on one of the couches in the game room. She was astounded to see that at seven in the morning he had helped himself to a snifter of brandy from the bar. He sat idly leafing through the latest issue of *Vanity Fair* that he'd picked up from a coffee table.

"How dare you let people rove unattended through my home!" she blurted at him. "And you're supposed to let me know in advance when you plan to bring clients."

The broker raised his eyebrows without raising his eyes

from the pages of the magazine. "Sam authorized me to do whatever it takes," he said dryly, turning a page.

"I don't give a damn what Sam said," she snapped. "This is my home—"

"That's not what Sam told me," he interrupted, still not looking up at her.

Devin snatched the magazine out of his hand and slapped it down on the table in front of him. He looked up at her and widened his eyes in mock surprise.

"Aren't we touchy!" he exclaimed. "This isn't an easy property to unload, you know. We really can't afford to offend the customers willy-nilly. Besides, Sam assured me that the house and all of its contents belongs to the Bradshaw Trust. To quote him exactly, he said, 'Sell the place and everything in it, up to and including the mistress's underwear.' "

The only thing that kept Devin from smacking him was the certain knowledge that he'd be thrilled, and go running off to a lawyer to file a giant lawsuit against her. Her eyes narrowed, and she looked at him with controlled rage.

"Listen, *Julia*," she said, "get upstairs now and escort those people through the house, then escort them the hell out of here. And don't ever again bring anybody here, or use the key Sam gave you, without calling first and checking with me. I'll let you know if it's convenient."

"Sam said—"

"I don't give a good goddamn what Sam said," she jumped on him. "If you don't do as *I* say, I'll yank the listing from you. And don't for a minute doubt that I can do that."

She wasn't at all sure that she could do that, but she was gratified to see the disagreeable Todd Julia pull himself up with a huffy sigh, stride out of the room and up the curving marble staircase to find the Odd Couple. Devin heaved a sigh of her own and hurried upstairs behind him to grab a belt, her jacket, and her purse. She was late for work.

As she maneuvered the Jaguar in bumper-to-bumper traffic on the Santa Monica Freeway toward South-Central Los Angeles, Devin took stock of her life over the past two months since her husband had been killed. The murder investigation was heating up, blowing like autumn winds in skittish swirls and eddies, up and over and around the realities of her world. Not yet touching her, but she had the sense that it was moving ever closer. Meantime, she forced herself to keep going forward, business as usual.

Her salary for heading up the Pulled Together division was minimal for the job, $85,000 annually with standard benefits. It was a fraction of what she'd made at Pieces in her last years there. When Sam had quoted that figure it didn't surprise her, nor did it deter her. She'd known that he wouldn't offer her a fair wage; in fact she was sure at the time that he was counting on her to turn it down. She did manage to get him to agree to a yearly bonus, to be based on operating profits. Pieces had given her incentive bonuses that had increased substantially as she'd built the company's sales. That perquisite, she knew, could turn out to be a bonanza if she was successful with PT. And she intended to be.

Irv Chapman had met with her, as he was obligated to do, and had definitively spelled out her financial situation. On her ownership of 10 percent of the company's stock, she would earn dividends amounting to about $3 million a year. Close to $750,000 quarterly. The figures had staggered her. It was taxable income, he'd said—she would realize a little more than half that amount in spendable income.

Devin had had no idea that she stood to be so wealthy. She said nothing to the lawyer, but the magnitude of the numbers he'd dished up with such equanimity had struck her with the force of lightning. She didn't hear his subsequent elaboration on how she was to receive payment. Her soul had not yet returned to her body. This news was going to take a lot of coming to grips with.

At their meeting that afternoon in his Century City offices, Chapman had spoken dispassionately. He was clear, thorough, courteous, and forthright in his explanations. He'd provided her with a portfolio of pertinent papers, which he suggested she keep in a safe-deposit box. He'd told her not to hesitate to call him at any time if she had questions. He handed her cards bearing both his office and home phone numbers.

Then, maintaining his impersonal tone, he gave her one final piece of information. He was obligated, he'd said, to advise her of something she probably already knew. That the law prohibits a person from inheriting goods or money from another whose death he or she is proven to have

knowingly and maliciously caused or in any way contributed to, directly or indirectly.

His words had hung on the air, bearing not a hint of
emotion or innuendo. When Devin's face registered nothing in return, he added that if a beneficiary was found culpable by law *after* any payouts had been made, those
monies would be immediately due and payable to the estate
of the deceased. Having said that, attorney Irving Chapman
had removed his glasses, stood up, and offered his hand.
Their meeting was concluded.

It was almost eight o'clock. Traffic was being held up by
an accident on the freeway just before the Harbor interchange. Three dented cars off to the right, three irate drivers arguing. She would be late for her first appointment.
Devin's fevered pace at Pulled Together had escalated. She
was putting in twelve-hour days at the factory, then taking
work home that consumed most of her evenings.

Her wonder drug was exercise. She continued working
out religiously with Tanner every morning. Or maybe reli-
gion had nothing to do with it, she mused. Maybe much of
her motivation was carnal. Her sex life was strictly on a
fantasy level. She had definitely joined the growing ranks
of the celibate in the nineties, she thought ruefully. And
she was still nursing a somewhat achy right wrist as her
bothersome hairline fracture slowly healed.

Her office suite at PT had been made attractive and efficient in record time by the indomitable Bailey Senn, who
had since forged ahead on the showroom, the conference
room, the fitting rooms, even the rest rooms. All the areas
apart from actual factory production space were either already refurbished or in the process of being done over. The
plant's ongoing face-lift provided a definite morale boost
among the workers. Devin could feel employees' spirits lifting higher with every change she effected, and that was as
gratifying as the fresh, new style numbers she'd put into
work.

And perhaps most gratifying of all, Devin had PT's
South-Central community program in place. After a series
of meetings with civic and black leaders, she'd formulated
her plan and put the wheels in motion. Pulled Together
would create, fund, and staff a comprehensive community-
training center in South-Central Los Angeles, to be housed

in a three-story building near Jefferson Boulevard and Main Street that had been gutted during the riots.

She'd concluded the deal for a very good price and a short escrow, and long-suffering Bailey Senn had taken on the task of reconstituting and renovating the spectral hulk. Shaking his head balefully when he first stood with Devin on the site, Bailey had insisted that the owners should have paid *her* for taking the abomination off their hands. He'd whined for days that he would rather take a stiff beating than tackle that dirty stinking job, and in truth the premises did still smell of wet and rancid burned-out wood and plaster. But Devin had no intention of letting Bailey off the hook, and when she insisted, of course he couldn't turn her down. Nobody, Devin knew, could get the building up and running and even looking good in less time than Bailey.

The center would provide cost-free job training in many disciplines. The city's RLA office was helping out, recruiting specialized teachers and guest lecturers from businesses all over Southern California, men and women who would volunteer their time to come down to South-Central on a regular or semiregular basis and teach the skills they knew. Computer software, automotive repair, data processing, commercial photography, and paramedic training classes were already scheduled.

They would also provide such services as reading classes for the functionally illiterate, first-aid techniques in the home, beginner typing, even basketball coaching. And, Devin's favorite, they would offer courses in garment industry skills, taught by Billy Hilgarde, Ruby Johnson, Henry Lewis, and other PT personnel. Besides providing job training for South-Central residents, those classes would produce qualified workers from the community for the Pulled Together plant.

Devin was very excited about the center, and in true Paul Bradshaw fashion, she had garnered a fair amount of positive advance press, with the promise of much more to come. Good for business, she knew, and sales of PT garments over the past month already reflected that.

And there was another big plus on the ledger. Because the division was kicking back 10 percent of its wholesale price on each garment to fund social programs for South-Central Los Angeles, the city was giving Pulled Together some excellent tax breaks.

Most important, the proposed community-training center, with all of its potential, all the opportunities it would create for people in this economically depressed community, made Devin feel good. Very good. Finally she was doing work that counted.

Now her focus was on advertising the PT look. She wanted the retail customer to buy the line not just because he or she was doing a good thing for ravaged South-Central Los Angeles, but because the clothes were hot. And they were going to sizzle. She had spruced up design from top to bottom, from sequined crop tops to thigh-high hose, for a less funky and more trendy look, very colorful and still very affordable. Now she was planning a comprehensive ad campaign that would hit when the new lines came out, the first under her banner. The ads would be black-and-white and wildly sexy in the established L.A. Garb style, but with a definite Pulled Together look. A look that Devin had designed with the company's advertising agency creative director and his crew.

They had determined that the distinctive look for the ads should reflect South-Central Los Angeles: hot, sexy, tantalizing, and outrageous. They would create three-person ads, to be shot everywhere—on sandy beaches, in steamy desert terrain, atop snowy mountains, on horseback over the Vasquez Rocks, in trendy downtown dance clubs, at L.A. Laker games, and more. Ads that would show that PT clothes were comfortable, great looking, and appropriate for the whole Southern California experience. Later they might go on to San Francisco, New Orleans, Chicago, New York, London, Paris, and beyond.

They needed three fabulous signature faces. They had decided on a hunky black man, an exotic black woman, and a gorgeous Southern California blonde. Consumers worldwide would see these three in every imaginable situation, in all kinds of poses. In magazines, before movie trailers, on billboards, on the backs of buses, in television commercials, on MTV. Everywhere.

The public would get to know the three people in the ads. But they wouldn't know who was doing what with whom. Was it the black man and the black woman? Was it the black man and the white woman? Or the black woman and the white woman? What about all three of them together? The different poses would suggest every possible alternative. It would be a salacious, seductive mystery story, and ongoing. And always the three would be wearing PT, but often the garments would be grubby, dirty and torn, or unbuttoned to the waist, or used just to cradle their heads on a rocky cliff. Unexpected, unusual, steamy, sexy, hot!

Devin herself had come up with the ménage à trois notion. When she'd finished outlining her sexy, bordering-on-illicit scenario for the ads, she became aware that the artists and ad men and women sitting around the table in the PT conference room were all staring at her, open-mouthed. She'd felt her face go crimson. Then the account exec started clapping, and the tension broke. Everybody began talking at once, congratulating her and chattering about the concept. They loved it.

Intense! exclaimed the ad people. Provocative! Titillating! Hugely commercial! It'll work! They were bubbling over with ideas and couldn't wait to get to work sketching out the story boards. At this morning's meeting she would see their first drafts, and review head shots they'd rounded up from the top agencies in town to begin the selection process in the hunt for the perfect threesome.

So she hadn't shocked any of them after all. She later realized that the only person she'd truly stunned was herself. What was a nice, conservative, Pasadena girl doing with these lascivious thoughts running loose in her head? And promulgating their display, with her good name attached, in a vast public arena?

It has to have something to do with my sex life, she thought now, as she dodged the morning midtown traffic. Sublimation, Freud called it. The more she got zero sex in real life, the wilder her sexual fantasies became, along with the natural desire to act them out. And she'd found a way to do exactly that, vicariously—through her ads.

She would like to put Tanner in the ads. Tanner was certainly featured in all the wild sex scenarios she played out in her head. Exclusively. Doing it all. And only with her. If he only knew, she thought. He'd probably run for high ground!

39

Julius Jackson had a heavy heart. Julius was a black man, 61 years old. He and his wife Essie had three married children, seven grandchildren, and an old droopy-eared cocker spaniel named Jim. They'd lived for years in Baldwin Hills, a middle-class, nicely groomed, largely black section of Southwest Los Angeles. Julius had a reputation in his community as hardworking, reliable, proud, a principled person, a family man, a good neighbor. He had worked for L.A. Garb as Paul Bradshaw's chauffeur for more than three decades.

The boss had been dead for two months now. That in itself caused Julius to wake up every morning feeling sad. A lot of people said a lot of terrible things about Paul Bradshaw. Julius had overheard plenty over the years while sitting at his station in the L.A. Garb lobby in Santa Monica. But Paul Bradshaw had always treated Julius like family. Paul Bradshaw would always be *the boss* to him. And Sam Bradshaw would always be the boss's brother.

Julius had known Sam for years, of course, had driven him when he rode with his brother, but he could never bring himself to like the man. And he knew that Sam had always sensed his disapproval. As professional, as detached, as dignified as Julius was, still, given enough time, people can always read other people. Words aren't necessary. His father used to say that folks shouldn't bother telling lies about themselves. That the truth of a man is written in volumes and hanging around his neck for the world to read. Julius could read what kind of a man Sam was, and Sam could read that Julius didn't like him. And now Sam was in charge.

Julius would never forget the black Friday when Paul Bradshaw was killed. He'd somehow made it through the weekend, feeling numb, praying there had been some mistake. But on the following Monday, the company's official

day of mourning, reality set in. A quietly grieving Julius
reported for work as usual. And Sam had made it clear to
him that he was now the man to reckon with. Sam now
owned the limousine, so to speak, and that meant he owned
Julius along with it.

Unlike Mr. Paul, who'd loved tooling around on his own
in his little red Ferrari or in his sleek black Viper J/T, Sam
used the limo exclusively. He seemed to love his brother's
customized silver-gray stretch Mercedes limousine. Sam
would use the limo just to go a couple of blocks to chat
with his son, Myles, at the auto shop. He would sit back
against the plush cushions, sipping a crystal glass of chilled
Stolichnaya over ice, talking on the phone, and giving Julius
orders: go faster, go slower, stop here, go pick up some
cigars.

What was weighing heavily on Julius's mind today was
the secret file. Paul Bradshaw had kept a file consisting of
highly sensitive material right in the limo—in a large hidden compartment in the passenger section. He'd called it
his "Julius" file. The boss used to stash documents in it
that he didn't want the staff, his assistant, or anyone else
to see. Also personal items, like women's phone numbers,
addresses, letters, lists of underwear sizes, even underwear.

And a gun. His old service revolver. Oiled and loaded,
he'd told Julius. He'd acknowledged that he was not eligible for a permit to carry a concealed weapon in the city of
Los Angeles, but in case they ever encountered any kind
of trouble in the car, he had it at his fingertips, he'd use it,
and he'd explain later. It was for their protection in this
crazy city, he'd said. Julius fervently wished that he'd been
driving the boss when somebody used a gun on him up on
Mulholland Drive. Everything would be different today.

The only person besides the boss who knew about the
"Julius" file was Julius. Paul Bradshaw had made that very
clear when he'd stressed the importance of never, ever,
letting anyone know about it. He'd explained that the file
was the reason why he didn't want his brother, or his kids,
or staffers, clients, or anyone else running around in the
limousine when he wasn't using it himself. Even when he
was out of town, and even though Julius was on the clock.
Because of the "Julius" file. If anyone asked Julius to "run
them somewhere"—and they often did—Julius was to say
that he wasn't authorized to do that. Period. The fact was,

Paul Bradshaw wanted to know exactly where the limousine and that file were at all times.

Often Mr. Paul would come bounding down the stairs at L.A. Garb, ignoring the elevators, and he and Julius would go for a ride, just so the man could take care of some business with the "Julius" file. If someone observed him from the street, from another car, from the sidewalk outside a restaurant, Mr. Paul could be reaching for liquor behind that built-in paneling. No one would suspect it was secret papers that he was pulling in and out of the back cabinet. It simply looked, even to family, as if Paul Bradshaw very often worked in his limousine, as busy, powerful people do.

Julius had very little idea what the documents in the file were and no particular interest in them, but he did know that the file was very important to his boss, and top secret. Sometimes when Julius was sitting at his station in the downstairs lobby or in the car, Mr. Paul would come by, give him a wink, and hand him an envelope. Julius would know that the envelope was to be locked up immediately in the "Julius" file.

With Sam Bradshaw in the car every day now, several times a day, the knowledge that he was harboring the eyes-only file had been bothering Julius tremendously. He'd loved Paul Bradshaw, and he felt a strong loyalty to the man and to his memory. He wanted to do the right thing. For weeks Julius had been giving the matter of the late Paul Bradshaw's top-secret file a great deal of thought. What was he to do?

This morning he had come to the conclusion that he had to tell Sam Bradshaw about the file. After all, Sam was now the head of the company. For all Julius knew, some things in the file could be crucial to the running of the company. Julius decided that Mr. Paul would want him to turn them over to his brother. And if he waited too long to tell Sam about the file, or if Sam happened to discover the hidden panel and ask him what it was, he would be very angry at Julius for keeping it secret. He might even fire him.

After first ascertaining that Sam would not be needing the limousine until lunchtime, Julius said that he was going to take the car for a wash and polish, but instead he drove it to his small house in Baldwin Hills. And backed it into his own garage. Of course it didn't fit—the front half of the sleek machine jutted out from under the overhead doors—but at least there was a modicum of privacy there.

Essie was visiting her sister in Compton. No one was home except Jim, who wagged his tail with joy to see his master in the middle of the day. Julius found two large empty cartons in his garage, and he filled them up with everything that was in the hidden cabinet. He carried the two heavy boxes into his house and locked the door.

His intention was to remove the incriminating things, out of loyalty to the boss. Like the little black book with models' phone numbers, their sizes, and Paul Bradshaw's personal notes by each name. And the black lace G-string, the Frederick's of Hollywood bra with the holes for nipples, and some pictures of the boss with different women, dating back from his marriage to Rosemary right up to just awhile ago.

Julius scanned through everything. Including the B.S.&S. folder, which he knew was very important and highly confidential. His plan was to leave everything that was obviously company business in the file and to remove and destroy all the things that fell into the category of personal, especially hanky-panky, business.

He was not sure what this B.S.&S. business was about, didn't care really, but he did know that this set of documents happened to be very high priority with the boss. Paul Bradshaw had put these papers in the file shortly before he died. He'd handed Julius successive documents to add to the same thick folder, which he was very secretive about.

Julius had already made copies of the pages in this folder marked "B.S.&S.," as well as many of the other documents in the "Julius" file that seemed to be important company business. Years ago, Julius had started duplicating the documents at a nearby copy shop. After carefully placing the originals back inside the "Julius" file cabinet in the limousine, he would take the copies home and put them into a large accordion file container. He kept it locked up in his old oak rolltop desk in the corner of the living room of the immaculate little house that he and Essie had lived in for years, and he'd never mentioned it to anyone, not even his wife.

What started him making the copies was a scare he got when one of Mr. Paul's limos—an earlier incarnation but one that was also customized with the secret "Julius" file compartment—was being detailed. This was long before Paul Bradshaw had set up Bradshaw Automotive for Sam's son, Myles, before they'd started taking all the company trucks and vans, the corporate cars and vehicles, the family cars, and of course the limousine there to be serviced. Back then, Julius was using a detailer named Big Benny Cano, a jovial black man working out of a grungy garage on Venice Boulevard, a filthy shop from which the guy turned out spotless, immaculate, white-glove-proof cars.

Big Ben was a tall rangy guy with a gold tooth in front who laughed a lot, sang a lot, did great work, and had more business than he needed, and the boss being a meticulous sort, Julius took the limo to Big Ben for detailing about once a month. Julius would stand around the shop and jive with Benny while he worked on the car, which usually took the better part of a morning or afternoon. Ben used to ask why the hell didn't Julius take in a flick, shoot some pool, go get a sandwich, get some poon, for God's sake? Why hang around this dump for hours, man? Julius would tell him that his job was to be with the car, so wherever the car was, that's where he was, that's why.

Once, when Julius was coming back from the sooty vending machine out front with a couple of cold Dr. Peppers for himself and Big Ben, he heard Benny loudly exclaiming, "Wow-ee! Well I *will* be damned." And there was Benny holding up a bright violet, sequined mesh garter belt! In his fastidious technique of automobile detailing, Benny would unscrew and remove cabinet doors to spit and polish them. He had never before noticed that the well-disguised panel fronting the secret cabinet that housed the top-level file was removable, but this time he'd inadvertently stumbled upon that fact and uncovered the "Julius" file.

He'd only got as far as the delicate lady's undergarment, which he was dangling in wide-eyed awe between a giant, greasy black thumb and forefinger, when Julius let the soda cans crash to the concrete floor and pounced on him. Julius grabbed the silken goods, shoved the thing back into the cabinet, and screwed the panel back on himself, then watched Benny like a hawk, in silence, until the man was finished detailing the car. Then he drove it out of the shop—and never went back.

And never again did Julius for a minute take his eyes off the limousine in his charge, whatever was being done.

He wouldn't even let the stretch town car go through the local car wash—he'd have it washed by hand right under his nose. But careful as he was, he knew that anything could still happen. The car could get stolen! So he'd started copying all the papers that went into the "Julius" file, for Paul Bradshaw. Without telling him. Maybe Mr. Paul wouldn't like it. But he was protecting himself. And he was protecting stuff that was obviously very important to the boss.

The boss also made a point of discussing sensitive issues in the limousine, purposely so Julius would overhear. So he would have a trusted witness if he ever needed one, he'd often told him. And sometimes Mr. Paul would even have a paper written up in advance attesting to what was said in the car, which he would sign, and have Julius sign, for the record. Then Mr. Paul would tuck the document into the "Julius" file. In other words, Paul Bradshaw was casually loose-lipped in front of Julius for a reason. He'd once told Julius that he trusted him, his driver of thirty years, more than he trusted anyone else in the world, even his own brother.

This morning, after Julius had finished carefully sanitizing the "Julius" file for the boss's sake, he placed the gun and a small bag of ammo back inside, locked up the hidden panel door, then drove the big car back to the Santa Monica plant. On the way, he stopped at a key maker's kiosk that he'd used before in a crowded minimall, and had his own key to the file duplicated. He had no idea where Paul Bradshaw's key would be. And he was sure whoever found it would have no idea what the key was for.

Then he sat at his usual station in the lobby and waited for Sam Bradshaw to come down to go to lunch. Sam came off the elevator alone. Julius walked out to the car with him and opened the rear door. When Sam was settled in the back seat, Julius said quietly that there was something he had to show him. He pointed out the secret compartment in the limousine and briefly explained its purpose.

Then he opened it up, showed Mr. Sam its contents, and handed him the key.

40

Devin had spent the last hour poring over agency head shots of prospective black models to test for her first ad campaign. Hundreds of photos were strewn about the table. Handsome men and women, all, but none that hit a visceral chord, no real candidates for their featured *big three*. With her in the newly enlarged and refurbished PT conference room were Bill Janus, head of L.A. Garb's in-house advertising and publicity department, and Parker Sorensen, account executive with the company's outside ad agency. Also grouped around the polished walnut conference table were several artists and copywriters, all of them sifting through the photos.

The three principals in the ads had to be right the first time around. The effectiveness of the campaign would depend on the consumer getting to know these three from the get-go. Devin wanted to avoid having to put in substitutes in midstream. And the three models had to be actors. Good ones, hopefully. Besides having the right look, they must be able to walk and talk, because they'd be performing in a long slate of diverse commercials and videos. And most important, they had to look great in the clothes.

Each would be tested individually to see how he or she came across on both film and video. And when the three were tentatively chosen, they would have to be tested again in scenes together, to determine whether they had what their account exec called "group chemistry." What's more, they had to be available to sign exclusive contracts so that no other products could claim their faces. And the group gathered around the conference table had decided that the three should be new, or relatively new, so they were not already overexposed or deeply associated in people's minds with some other company.

In the first ten minutes of the meeting, Devin had made one immediate, sure selection from among the photos. She had decided on the model who would play the blonde: Marva Modine. Sunny, hot, sensuous, and devastatingly beautiful, with the long, lean California-golden-girl look they were after. True, the public already knew her, but only in connection with this company—Marva Modine was what they called a "brand name" in advertising. She was ideal; there was nobody sexier. And Marva could certainly move, Devin knew. She'd watched her making expert moves on her own husband. It had been a dazzling performance, Devin remembered, wincing as the cozy dinner party scene between the two replayed across the insides of her eyelids.

Okay, so the woman had come on to her husband. Didn't matter now, Devin told herself—her top priority was to succeed at Pulled Together, and the ad campaign she was about to mount was crucial. She couldn't let personal rancor interfere with her business judgment. Devin didn't like Marva, and she hoped she wouldn't have to spend much time with the woman, but Marva it would be. And everyone around the table applauded the choice.

Devin had given up trying to find any real potentials among the photos of black women being passed around. She asked if they could find any others. Susan Proctor, the company's director of publicity, who'd done the canvassing, told her that she would keep looking, but she had already conducted a very extensive search, not only among the many top model and theatrical agencies in L.A. but at all the big New York houses as well.

That was when Devin had a flash of inspiration. She'd gotten to know one of the PT in-house models, beautiful Vanna Brylock. Vanna had a quality of pride and even hauteur mixed with a vulnerability that was very alluring, very sexy. She asked Parker Sorensen to set up a few tests with Vanna if she was willing, a combination film, video, and photo session.

Now what about the man? she asked the group. The stud? Critical to the success of the campaign. But beautiful men in this line of work were not nearly as plentiful as beautiful women. Fabulous male actor-models who weren't already tied up were hard to find.

The Pulled Together man had to be a big guy, drop-dead gorgeous yet outdoorsy, rugged, maybe a little dangerous looking, but not turnoff dangerous, not scary. Older than the women but still young. And black, of course, with a touch of cream. Devin knew the look she wanted, but she didn't see him among the hundreds of submissions.

They talked about the kind of man they envisioned. Each person in the group had ideas about him. Great ideas. He should be a surfer, a skier; he must be able to climb mountains, sail, play basketball. He had to look good on a horse. He should be strong enough to pick up the women with ease, maybe both of them at once. And he couldn't have any of that typical male-model swagger. Also, of course, he had to look sensational in Pulled Together clothes. That meant broad shoulders, small waist, and muscular chest, arms, and legs. And he had to be naturally friendly. Able to charm the world, not just the women.

The more they talked up this mythical fellow, the more elusive he became, Devin thought with a sinking heart. The others were starting to feel that way too. Did this perfect black Adonis exist?

That's when the door to the conference room opened and one of PT's more popular employees strode in carrying a magazine ad that he'd promised to get for Devin. As the young man walked across the floor—tall, trim, straight, muscular in his faded denim shirt with the sleeves rolled up, handsome, radiating confidence, flashing a broad, magic grin—the room went silent. Mouths gaped—including Devin's.

It was Billy Hilgarde.

Across town in Santa Monica, Sam Bradshaw sat in his brother's office with the doors closed and locked, his desk strewn with the contents of the "Julius" file.

He was astounded at his luck. He had ascertained from B.S.&S. that there had been only one copy of the L.A. Garb report issued. That the company's policy was to print just one hard copy and to process one disk, both to be given only to the person who had ordered and authorized payment for the report. And that after having delivered its report, the company's policy was to delete all work relating to said report from its database. For security reasons.

Even then, Sam's contact at the consulting firm told him, information had been known to seep out in the past. Details potentially damaging to clients had been excerpted from reports by unscrupulous employees and sold to the media. Or had landed on the desks of the competition. The company couldn't totally safeguard against such leaks—no company could, not even the government—but B.S.&S. did everything possible to prevent that from happening.

After searching thoroughly through the CEO's files, both computer and hard copy, Sam had found no trace of the incriminating B.S.&S. report that Paul had talked to him about at lunch on the day before he was killed. Now, inside this nutty file in a secret compartment in the back of his brother's limousine, he had laid hands on both the hard copy and the disk, the only existing imprints of the damning "report" that Paul had been about to act on but never got the chance.

After Geneen went home tonight he would shred the hard copy and split the diskette in half and cut up the Mylar disk inside. Then he would take the scraps home and burn them.

41

Two men sat in the reception area in the executive suite's outer office at Pulled Together, waiting for Devin to return from her meeting with the advertising staff. Both had again displayed to Alex Anson their gold-and-blue LAPD shields in worn leather holders, along with laminated ID cards. The tall dark man with curly black hair in the charcoal pinstripe suit had made it a point to identify himself again as Detective John Furrino. The shorter, red-haired, red-faced man in khaki pants and a rumpled tweed jacket was Detective Richard Ryan. When Devin walked in, they stood.

"Mrs. Bradshaw, can we talk to you again?" asked the taller man.

"Of course," Devin smiled.

The two had questioned her several times before. In the beginning they'd asked about Paul's recent activities, any conflicts she might know about, and other details of her late husband's life. Through the succeeding weeks, however, their questions had focused more and more upon herself. They'd asked where she was in the hours leading up to the lunch at Regina Bradshaw's. She'd told them that she was at home. And mentally crossed her fingers. It wasn't technically a lie. Now she tried not to let them see how much they frightened her.

Leading the way into her office, she forced a cheery hello to Alex as she passed her desk. Inside, she invited the detectives to sit down on one of the couches, then settled into a chair opposite them.

"Coffee?" she asked.

"No, thank you," Furrino said. They both looked at Ryan.

"No, thanks," he echoed. Irish, Devin thought. Irish and Italian, these men. Both forty-something. The pair was becoming an odd, grating, threatening fixture in her life. She looked at them expectantly, a half-smile still lighting her features.

Furrino started. "Mrs. Bradshaw," he said, consulting his notebook, "our records show two firearms registered to you and your husband. Two Smith & Wesson thirty-eight-caliber handguns. Registered on the same day, March eighteenth, nineteen ninety. In the names of Paul Nathan Bradshaw and Devin Yorke Bradshaw. We'd like to see those guns."

"One of them is in the drawer of a table beside my bed at home," she told them. "Paul kept the other one in his desk at the house, but it's not there now. I remember him saying some time back that he was going to take it down here, to the South-Central factory."

"Whose gun was that?" Furrino asked.

"Whose?" Devin asked, perplexed.

"Yes, whose?" Furrino repeated. "Was it the one registered to your husband, or to you?"

"Oh," she said. "I wouldn't know."

"Is it still here on the premises?"

"I have no idea," Devin answered. "If it is, I don't know where he kept it. This was before I worked here."

"Aren't you the boss here? Samuel Bradshaw said that you're the president of Pulled Together," Furrino went on. "If a handgun is kept on the premises, maybe even your own, shouldn't you know where it is?"

"Yes, but I hadn't even thought about it. I'll make it a point to find out."

"Do you know how to shoot it?" Furrino asked.

"Yes," Devin said. "Paul and I took classes at the Beverly Hills Gun Club. It was his idea. He said we should be able to protect ourselves."

"What guns did you use in the classes?" This from Ryan.

"Those two pistols," Devin said. "We always took the one from beside the bed, and Paul would have Julius bring the other one to the house on class days."

"Julius?" Furrino asked.

"Julius Jackson, Paul's driver," Devin said. "Then Julius would bring one of the guns back the next day. Presumably here. You can ask him. Now that I think about it, he probably knows where the other gun is kept. I can give you his numbers, in Santa Monica, at home and in the limousine." Ryan was taking notes.

"We'll come by your house tonight to pick up the gun you have there, okay?" Ryan asked then. "To have it checked."

"Sure," Devin said. "Checked for what?"

"Checked to see if it's the gun that shot your husband," he responded evenly.

"Something else," Furrino said. "You've said that you did *not* go to lunch at your mother-in-law's house on the day that your husband was killed. Is that right?"

"Yes," she said, "that's right."

"But your husband's brother said you were on the guest list. You were supposed to be there."

"That's right," she said again.

"So why weren't you there?" John Furrino asked, displaying just a shade of annoyance that he'd had to ask.

"My husband told me he didn't need me to be there."

"When did he tell you that, Mrs. Bradshaw?" Furrino asked.

"On the day of the luncheon."

"What time?"

"After noon," she replied, furrowing her usually unlined brow. "About twelve-thirty, I think."

"That's just a half hour before the lunch was scheduled," Ryan put in.

"That's right," she said.

"Weren't you all ready to go?" he asked.

"As a matter of fact, I was."

"Did Mr. Bradshaw tell you in person not to go to the lunch?" Furrino asked.

"No, he told me on the telephone. From his car. That I didn't have to go."

"And did he tell you *why* you shouldn't go to the lunch?" Ryan put in.

"No. He just told me it wouldn't be necessary."

"Didn't you ask why?" Ryan asked again. "Didn't you think it was odd? You being all ready to go, and him telling you not to go at the last minute? There must have been a reason."

"If there was a reason, he didn't say," Devin persisted. "He just told me that I didn't need to go. That there was nothing on the agenda that affected me. I guess he thought I had better things to do."

"Like what?" Ryan asked. "What did you have to do?"

"Well, nothing, really ...," Devin managed. "But Paul was known to change his mind on the spur of the moment. He had just scheduled that luncheon on the day before. The fact that he told me at the last minute that I didn't have to go didn't surprise me."

The two detectives remained silent, looking at her.

"I'm sure if I'd wanted to go to the luncheon, I'd have been welcome," she lied.

"But you didn't want to go?" from Furrino.

"No, I didn't particularly want to go. If it wasn't necessary."

"Even though you were all dressed up and ready?" from Ryan again.

"Even though I was dressed and ready," she smiled.

"Why wouldn't you want to drive over to lunch with your family, fifteen minutes from where you live, if you were all ready to go and it was lunchtime?" Ryan queried.

Devin paused. She looked pained. After a beat, she said softly, "I didn't want to go to the lunch because my husband's family doesn't like me."

The two police officers digested this information. Furrino broke the silence. "And your husband knew they didn't like you?"

"Yes," she said.

"And you think he was trying to spare you, is that it?"

"If he didn't need me there, yes," she lied again.

Furrino and Ryan looked at each other, then stood. They

made an appointment to pick up the Smith & Wesson .38 that was in her bedroom early that evening, after she got home from work. They took Julius Jackson's address and phone numbers, which Devin copied on notepaper from the Rolodex on her desk. Then they thanked her and left.

Devin watched the pair retreat. Her heart was pounding wildly. If they'd asked her again where exactly she was in the hours leading up to her husband's murder, she was prepared to tell them. At this point, she was afraid not to. But they didn't ask. So she still hadn't told them that even though she didn't go to lunch at Regina's house, she *was* in fact up on Mulholland Drive on the day that Paul was killed.

42

Rosemary Bradshaw had a date. A blind date. She felt like a kid again. No, she felt like a silly old woman. Actually, she felt good. She looked at herself in the full-length mirror in her newly remodeled master bathroom. This was the house where she'd lived with Paul Bradshaw for more than thirty years. The house where they had brought up their family. A comfortable old Tudor on the affluent Westside, in rustic, established Mandeville Canyon.

It was hard to believe that Paul was dead. She had spent many, many days and nights over the years wishing he were dead. There were times she was sure she actually could have killed him. No, he wasn't at all the man she'd thought she married, but that was so long ago. They were both so young. How could a woman possibly know at that age? And then you were in it. People didn't run off getting divorced back then. You did your best.

Now she had no more rancor left in her heart for her husband of thirty-three years. Funny, Rosemary thought, when he'd left her for Devin Yorke, she had literally wanted to die. But in retrospect, that's what it took for her to get a grip on her life. For her to become healthy, whole, the woman she was looking at in the mirror, a person she liked again. She learned in time that Devin Yorke had done her a favor.

She felt blessed. Pauly was doing better than she'd ever dared hope and was being released from drug rehab this weekend. She'd had the house completely redone earlier this year. Now this bathroom was three times its former size, and it had a bidet. Her decorator, the wonderful Bette Leon, had insisted on the bidet. If not for you, she'd told Rosemary, you have to think about resale. Rosemary had never used the bidet, but she loved it—it was wonderfully decadent. Her new bath was done in rosy-colored granite and wall-to-wall mirrors. Rosemary checked herself again. She looked good.

She'd had a facial at Vera's this afternoon, and she'd had her sunstreaked chestnut-colored hair done in a loose, casual style. Her body was looking its absolute best since before she had the kids. Thanks to exercise, with the accent on regular. No more fits and starts for her. Sessions with a trainer three times a week, four-mile walks on the other days. To look like this, you had to do that, it was that simple. She smiled, approving her trim, five-foot-six, 118-pound figure. Whoever said that bringing up kids was enough exercise for women was dead wrong. It was exercise, that's for sure, but the wrong kind. And chasing after four kids and a giant sheepdog all day made a woman want to reward herself with a box of chocolate fudge, Rosemary remembered. She finally had it right. And she'd had her face done. Another good move. God bless the brilliant Dr. Frank Kamer and his magic sculptor hands. Yes, she liked herself now, inside and out. She was sixty years old, going on forty.

She was wearing a trim, lightweight wool, black Chanel suit with black suede heels, not too casual, not too dressy. With classic gold knot earrings and an understated Schlumberger diamond bracelet. This was Rosemary's first actual date since her husband had left her four years ago. She was a whole different woman now. A little nervous, but what the hell, she was going to have fun tonight. No, she corrected herself—as Dr. Jenny had taught her, she wasn't nervous, she was excited.

Who was she kidding? she smirked, spritzing Lalique on her throat and wrists. She was terrified. She told herself again that this was no big deal, for heaven's sake. Just dinner with Alex Anson's father. They'd talked on the phone. He was taking her to Georgia, a new, high-profile restaurant on Melrose. Rosemary had noticed it mentioned often in the columns. Alexander Anson was a talent agent. He dated starlets.

She felt old again. But just for a second. She refused to allow herself that self-defeating nonsense. Al Anson was lucky to be having dinner with such a terrific woman, she told herself, smiling at her reflection in the glass. She picked up a brush and ran it through her medium-length hair, softening the hairdo José Eber had styled that afternoon. She had a good cut, a good line, her hair fell into place but it wasn't stiff. She'd long ago abandoned the hair-sprayed look. That was for insecure women, she'd decided, who couldn't live with a hair out of place. The kind of woman she used to be. No more. She shook her head, watching her hair move gracefully, pale gold streaks catching the light.

Satisfied, she twirled on her heels and headed downstairs, dimming lights along the way. Classical music played softly through the house. Ravel. And a fire crackled on the huge stone hearth in the comfortable living room. She'd always loved her home, and since the remodeling, it was a showplace. There was only one thing wrong with it, Rosemary mused. It was empty. Not that she didn't enjoy being alone; she had finally become comfortable with that. Her days and nights were filled with activities and family. It was just that the house was so lovely she sometimes felt a little sad not to be sharing it with someone.

Al Anson was picking her up here. They would have a drink in the family room. She looked around. The whole place looked wonderful. Fresh flowers everywhere. Claudie had left a platter of pâté, cheeses, water crackers, and cornichons on the bar. And per Rosemary's instructions she'd left a good bottle of Taittinger's Blanc de Blancs chilling in a silver bucket.

The doorbell rang. Rosemary straightened, smoothed her skirt, and smiled, ready to brave the front door.

43

"They're asking me a lot of questions," Devin told Tanner.

"What kind of questions?" he asked, in spite of the red flags he saw waving at him from all directions, warning him to leave it alone. Don't ask! they signaled.

"Questions about the guns Paul and I owned. They took one of them last night to check it, to see if it's the gun that shot Paul."

"Is it?" Tanner asked, against his better judgment.

"Of course not," she said. "I mean, I don't think so."

It was just after six-thirty in the morning. They were in the gym. It had been nearly ten weeks since her hairline fracture, and Devin's wrist was almost totally healed now. She was pumping big weights, big for her, almost back up to full tilt.

And spilling her guts to Tanner again. And the more Tanner wanted no part of it, the more he found himself being seduced. The Paul Bradshaw murder case was one of the most highly publicized news stories in the country. He was seduced by her situation, by her story. Face it, pal, he told himself, he was seduced by her!

"The point is," he began, going for it now, and annoyed at himself for doing so, "do you have anything to hide?"

His question hung on the air, which was silent except for the creaking of the twin weight machines each was working vigorously. Her silence told him that she didn't want to say, and in fact he really didn't want to know if she had anything to hide.

"Yes," she said finally, startling him with the answer he didn't want to hear. Don't ask her what! he ordered himself.

"What?" he asked her.

"Plenty," she said, and he could see that she was committed to telling him the tale. Slam the door shut now, he warned himself. Tell her it's not appropriate for me to know. Remind her you're a lawyer, Counselor. Tell her to go confide in a friend, a sister, a mother. Not me. But he said none of this to her.

"I was up there," she blurted out then. "Up on Mulholland Drive on the day Paul was killed. Standing in the rain. Waiting for him to drive by on the way to his mother's."

"Why?" Tanner asked, dreading the answer.

"Because I wanted a divorce," she said simply.

"A divorce?"

"A divorce."

"But why Mulholland Drive in the middle of a rainstorm?"

"Because I'd made the decision, and I had to tell him and be done with it before I changed my mind."

"So what happened?"

"He came by, I flagged him down, and we had a fight."

"A fight?" echoing her again, stalling for time.

"An actual, physical fight," she said. "He slapped me, hard, and I socked him back, and gouged his eye with my ring hand, my good hand."

"And the police don't know this?"

"No."

"Who knows this?"

"Just you." Oh God, he thought, why me?

"Why me?" he asked her.

"I don't know," she wailed. "Maybe because I have to tell someone."

"Don't you have anyone to talk to, Devin? Someone to tell?"

"I'm telling you," she said. That simple. A responsibility he didn't need, didn't want, absolutely couldn't take on.

"So tell me, then," he said, appalled at the words he'd heard himself utter.

She told him again that she was up there, on Mulholland Drive, waiting for her husband to drive by on the day that he was killed. And again, she told him why. Because she'd decided to divorce him, and she needed to tell him of her decision immediately. She explained why it couldn't wait until later that evening when he got home. Because he would talk her out of it. *Sweet*-talk her out of it. He was that persuasive. Leaving Paul would actually be easier than telling him she was leaving. That would be the hard part, she insisted, the telling. She had to tell him right away, then move out. By the time he came home after work she'd be gone.

Tanner listened with a sense of dread. Did she kill him? Should he ask her the bottom-line question? No, absolutely not. He didn't want to know. Must not know if she was responsible for pulling the trigger on a gun that shot her husband dead while she was physically slugging it out with him with one hand in a cast on Mulholland Drive in the rain. All kinds of scenarios played fleetingly across John Tanner's consciousness. Self-defense? Temporary insanity? How would a jury read it?

He clearly didn't want to hear any more. It could technically make him an accessory after the fact. Worst case, he could even be disbarred. He shushed her when she started to speak again. With a petulant frown, she fell to working out in silence, and both of them could feel the tension building between them, sucking the oxygen out of the room. She wanted to talk, and he didn't want to hear it.

As they plowed through their exercise routines, the silence in the room weighed heavily. Tanner was uncomfortable, felt that he'd created the tension by putting her off, hushing her up. He wanted to clear the air, but without treading back on dangerous ground. Like murder.

When they'd finished their cool-down regimen, Devin quietly suggested that they go into the sauna for a few minutes to relax their muscles. They'd taken occasional steaming saunas together before, when the workout had caused them more than the usual amount of aches and pains.

She was on his wavelength, he considered, feeling the same way he did. Not wanting to part with this slight pall of restiveness hanging over them. Tanner saw her suggestion as an unspoken pact to spend a few minutes in the sauna together and let the steam heat melt the moderate chill between them. Good idea, he thought. Then he'd jump into a cold shower before he rolled down the canyon to his place to change and skid into the office.

Tanner already knew the drill. He went into one of the twin changing rooms off the gym, took off his workout clothes, and put on one of the fresh white terrycloth robes that hung on wooden hangers in a niche opposite the shower. When he came out she was waiting for him, but she wasn't wearing a robe. She was wrapped in an oversized white velour towel tied in a giant knot just over her breasts.

Together they walked down the hall and entered the teak-lined sauna, and he closed the door behind them. The immediate crush of intense, concentrated heat was overwhelming at first. Tanner checked the thermometer on the wall: 114 degrees Fahrenheit. He lifted a metal tumbler from a hook, held it over a small wet bar, and filled it from the tap. As he poured water over the hot rocks, a sudden *whoosh* of scalding steam permeated the cubicle. Replacing the tumbler on the hook, he sat down next to Devin on the upper bench. Leaning back, he closed his eyes, letting the heat envelop him, feeling rivulets of sweat gushing from his pores.

"Hot, isn't it?" he heard her say after a few moments. "This is probably what hell feels like in the first few minutes. Before you catch on fire." He opened his eyes and looked over at her.

"Guess you have doom on your mind," he said.

"Guess so," she returned evenly.

"It can't be that bad," he said, leaning his head back against the boards and closing his eyes again. "Get a lawyer, Devin. Don't you have a lawyer?" It was getting hotter.

"I have lots of lawyers," she said.

"So?"

"So I'm not sure what I should do. If anything. And I'm not sure why I'm telling you these things. But please, nobody else knows, any of it. I'll figure it out. Please promise you won't tell anyone—"

"Of course I won't," he stopped her. "I never heard anything, okay? It's better that way."

"Okay," she said.

"Okay," he said. "So, do you think we're cooked yet?" he asked then, wiping away the sweat pouring into his eyes.

"Speaking of cooked," she mused, "if you were going to the gas chamber, what would you order for your last meal?"

"Doom again," he observed. "Two cheeseburgers, medium rare, with lettuce, tomatoes, catsup, mayo, and sliced dill pickles."

"You wouldn't have something gourmet? Like baby veal medallions with shallots, roast poussin. . . ?"

"Uh-uh. Oh, and a side of fries. Large. Make them crispy."

"You don't eat that stuff, do you?"

"No, but it's my last meal."

"That's true. Any dessert?"

"No dessert."

"I'd have dessert," she said, mopping her forehead with the back of her hand.

"Oh yeah? What's your dessert fantasy?" he returned idly, not looking at her.

"You," she said, and she reached over and ran a finger down through the sweat on Tanner's chest, forcing the terrycloth robe open down to his waist. Tanner jumped, and clutched at his robe.

"Don't do that, Devin ... no touching!" he yelped, grasping her hand and pushing it away. "Not fair! I'm human, you know ..."

"Be careful of my wrist," she murmured. "It's still a little sore ..." More unfair advantage, he knew, as he softened his grip on her hand. She slipped it out of his and reached up again to his chest, entwining her fingers in the damp, sandy, curly hair. Then she slid her hand to the left and began slowly, gently, rubbing his nipple between her forefinger and thumb. Tanner slumped, leaned back on the wooden bench and closed his eyes, for the moment defeated.

Taking the cue, Devin got up and turned to face him, then she climbed up on him, straddling his lap. She loosened the belt on his robe, and with both hands she worked both his nipples, lightly, tenderly. Sitting on him, her towel askew, his robe slipping open, he could feel her naked bottom on his flesh. He could feel himself getting hard. He opened his eyes. The knot in her towel had loosened, and it had slipped down over one of her breasts, baring a firm, pink nipple. His eyes focused on it, his cock was erect, and his brain had turned to mush. "Oh God," he moaned.

He reached around her and nudged the towel the rest of the way off, then slid both hands slowly down her back from her shoulders to her waist. She was oily wet. He lifted her gently and pulled her toward him, until one of her breasts, the one first bared, the one he'd lusted after, was about two inches away from his mouth.

He closed his eyes and made one last, futile attempt to muster the will to resist, then opened them just a slit and gave up. He urged her to him, taking the small hard nipple into his mouth. It was salty. And delicious. And probably addictive, he knew.

Still not too late to save himself. Rewrap the towel around her, scoot her off his lap, apologize for losing control, and escape. He was actually thinking about that while gently sucking on both her nipples, first one, then the other, and now she was moaning softly.

Pulling away from them reluctantly, he slid her sweaty bottom a couple of inches back on his lap, trying to summon the resolve to stop this before it was too late. That's when they both dropped their eyes and saw his penis, erect and rigid and begging for mercy. Like it had a life of its own. For a second Tanner had a flash that it wasn't his. He would disown it. What the hell was that thing doing here? But Devin reached her two hands down and began to stroke the trespasser, and it was all over.

He pulled her to him and kissed her, long and passionately, oblivious to the oppressive heat now. Running his hands down her dripping back and cupping them under her buttocks, he raised her up until she was poised over his throbbing cock, then lowered her slowly onto it. Mentally chiding himself for not being the good lover, for not fondling her and stimulating her. He was flunking foreplay. Couldn't help it. Couldn't stand it. Couldn't wait!

So John Tanner and Devin Bradshaw, on the second Tuesday in February at seven-forty in the morning, in the scorching sauna room on the ground floor of the Benedict Canyon mansion, made hot, lustful, steamy, sweaty love.

44

Devin sat on one of the canvas-covered couches at the far end of her now-cheerful office, looking incredulously at Billy Hilgarde perched at the opposite end. She had just offered him the deal of his life, at least five times his current salary and the chance to be a star, and he was protesting vehemently.

"It's not for me," he said again. But he was grinning, obviously flattered. And it was the first time Devin had seen that dazzling smile of his in a long, long time. Since the police investigation had heated up in earnest.

In fact, Devin was having trouble toning down a dazzling smile of her own this morning, just two hours after sex with Tanner. She could still feel his touch, his kisses, his wetness inside her. And she was soaring.

"Look," she cajoled, forcing herself to concentrate on the matter at hand, "all I'm asking is that you do some test shots for me, for the ad agency."

"I'm a production guy, I'm no model," Billy insisted. Then, mischievously, he added, "Don't you have to be gay or something?"

"You know, for a guy who is so politically correct, you're sure being a jerk."

"Just kidding," he chuckled. "But look at me—do I look like one of those male models?" he demanded, spreading his arms wide, showing his loose-fitting, rumpled PT chinos, his faded lemon cotton shirt with the sleeves rolled up, his scarred leather belt, the PT running shoes.

"No, you don't, and that's what's so right about it."

Looking at him now, hearing him protest, Devin was even more convinced that Billy was the man for the sexy PT ads. He was perfect. And that broad magic grin of his was devastating. Devin had often observed the effect he had on women at the plant. She saw them melt when he turned that smile on them. And no, as he had been quick to point out, he was not a pro; he wouldn't even know how to do any of that professional male-model posing. There was nothing slick about him. He was real, down to earth. Billy Hilgarde was a big, buff, lovable, sexy black guy who was loaded with charm and who happened to look great in PT clothes. The ad agency would flip over him, Devin was sure of it.

"What exactly have you got against doing it Billy? Tell me," she pressed.

"Everything," he said, serious now. "For starters, what's going to happen to my department? It's taken me half a year to get the whole marking process on computer, to perfect the technique, and it's very new for us. If marking takes ten steps backward, production will take twenty steps backward. Who's going to make sure it's done right?"

"Somebody you and I will pick and you will teach. Whom you'll look in on regularly, and whose work you'll review. It isn't as if you'd be going anywhere, Billy. You'd still be working for PT, you know."

"And when this big-deal ad campaign is finished, then what? Some other guy would be doing my job. What am I supposed to do then?"

"I guarantee you can have your old job back," Devin promised. "That is, if you still want it. If you're not off doing television commercials and print ads. You could even get some acting parts out of this, Billy. You could have a whole new, big career."

"Oh God no, please, no acting!" Billy put both hands up as if to banish the thought.

"Fine, you don't have to be a movie star," Devin laughed. "All I'm asking you to do is one lousy little session for the ad agency. Just twenty minutes of posing for stills. Then we'll look at them. Do it just to prove I'm wrong." Billy could see that his boss wasn't about to be put off. She was a lady who got what she wanted.

"Okay, okay, ease up," he said. "Who knows, maybe it could be fun."

"Not to mention lucrative, Billy. You have to think about that."

"I suppose," he said thoughtfully. "If it actually worked out, maybe I could put a down payment on a condo somewhere. Get myself the hell out of South-Central." He and Devin shook on it.

Billy sat hunched over one of several computer terminals in his crowded marking department workroom at PT, trying to trace out a particularly intricate pattern. Usually he relished tackling this kind of challenge, but he was having a great deal of trouble concentrating on the layout graphics.

He had told Devin that he'd give the advertising assignment a try because it might be fun and because he could use the money. What he didn't tell her was that he'd also welcome the opportunity to break out of his regular routine. Try as he might, he couldn't focus on anything for very long other than the Paul Bradshaw murder investigation. In the middle of every waking thought, his mind kept circling back to the fatal Mulholland Drive scenario—what he knew about it, what he heard on the news, his own part in it, what the cops said, and what seemed to be his options.

Scud Joe was dead. Billy didn't show at his funeral. The police had been buzzing around Pulled Together for weeks. And they'd shown up at his apartment with a search warrant and tossed the place. Looking for the gun that killed Joe. They'd questioned him several times—the same questions, asked in different ways. He didn't have an alibi for the night Joe was killed. His car was in police impound, and he was driving a rented car that night. A late-model two-door metallic blue Ford Taurus. The cops found the car and cruised it around the neighborhood near Maurice's Snack 'n Chat. They told him witnesses said they'd seen it at the scene that night, right around the time Scud Joe was gunned down. With Billy Hilgarde behind the wheel.

He told them that's right, he was supposed to have dinner with Joe. At Maurice's. Sure, they said. He told them Joe was dead when he got there, so he kept on going. You mean you didn't even stop when you saw your good friend splattered all over the sidewalk? they asked him, several times, in several different ways. No, he said every time, he didn't stop. Why? Because he was afraid. Sure, they said.

He knew they didn't believe him. They suggested that he whacked Joe Jones to keep him quiet about what went down that day on Mulholland Drive. But they couldn't prove it. They would ask how far he and Joe had followed Paul Bradshaw that day. He'd tell them they followed the man till they lost him. What do you mean, lost him? they'd ask. Lost him, Billy would repeat. You know, now you see him, now you don't. At one point, when they came around a curve, he'd told them, Bradshaw just wasn't there anymore. Must be convenient, one of the cops had said, that Joe Jones wasn't around to contradict his story. No, Billy said, it wasn't convenient at all, because Joe was there with him, Joe would confirm his story. Sure, they said.

He still hadn't copped to seeing Devin up there. Nobody had asked. They did ask if he and Joe saw anything that day that looked suspicious. That's probably when he should have told them about Devin, but he hesitated. He'd told himself that might be construed as suggesting that Devin murdered her husband. It was a judgment call. Not that he would go to the mat for Devin on this one. He'd made that clear to her. She understood that. Whatever the lady was

doing up on Mulholland that day was her business, her
problem. And he had his own problems. If they specifically
asked if he'd seen anyone up there who looked out of
place, he'd have to tell them about Devin. But the way
Billy read it, the cops were so convinced that Billy was the
killer that they hadn't bothered to ask him that. Yet.

Billy had no idea what Devin had to do with her husband's ride to oblivion that day. Something, he was pretty
sure; he'd seen her at the scene. When he'd confronted her
with that, she'd told him nothing. She didn't ask him any
questions about what he was doing up there either. Nor did
he offer her any information. They just didn't talk about it.
Still, the subject hung in the air around them like a gathering storm cloud, threatening to burst. And Billy could not
help wondering if Devin was holding out the high-paying
modeling gig now to make him indebted, to secure his silence. He was no model. That was the biggest reason why
he'd turned it down at first, though he didn't tell her that.
Then he'd relented, agreed to do the trial shots. Because
she had to know there was no deal, didn't she? He'd told
her point-blank that there would probably come a time
when he would have to tell the cops that he'd seen her up
on top of Mulholland that day. Within the same time frame
and at the exact spot where her late husband was murdered. Or maybe they already knew. Maybe Devin told
them. If she had nothing to hide, why wouldn't she?

Every time the detectives showed up looking for him,
Billy was terrified that they were going to arrest him. A
few days after they'd impounded his car, they came by the
factory, sat in his workroom, asked him more questions.
Then they gave him the address of the crime-lab garage
and told him to go pick up his car. Beyond that, they
wouldn't tell him anything. At the lab he'd asked about the
tests they'd done on his Trans Am, but the impound officers gave him no answers. In fact, they treated him like
scum. The LAPD was known to have no love lost for black
guys from South-Central who were implicated in a crime.

45

"What's B.S.&S., SAM?" Devin repeated. The first time she'd asked, he ignored the question, acted as if he hadn't heard her.

"Let me think," Sam responded vaguely now, scratching his head.

While going over the division's books to better understand what she was dealing with at PT, Devin had come across a notation for a check in the amount of $350,000, payable to something called simply B.S.&S.

They were in Sam's office at the Santa Monica plant now, at an afternoon meeting Devin had asked for. The stated purpose of the meeting was to go over Pulled Together's books. As the company's former chief financial officer, Sam Bradshaw, Devin figured, should have a handle on PT's accounts. Her real agenda was to find out what B.S.&S. was and why PT had paid a whopping third of a million dollars to those three initials in the form of a check that was dated the week before Paul Bradshaw was killed.

"Look, Sam," Devin said after he'd hesitated again, "PT's books are a mess. But most of the discrepancies are traceable, and most don't involve hefty sums. Except for this huge invoice from a company that I've never heard of. B.S.&S.," she repeated. "Who are they, and what do they do?"

"Oh, of course," Sam said. "It's a fabric company." Geneen was taking notes.

"But they're not on our list of suppliers . . ."

"That's because they've gone out of business," Sam said.

"What fabric, Sam?" Devin persisted. "The only fabric PT ordered in huge quantities in the last quarter was the parachute cloth, and that was from a company called Dexter J. And it certainly didn't amount to anything near three hundred and fifty thousand dollars' worth."

"It's a fabric company we were behind on payments with,

because they were slow shipping," he said. Devin looked at him carefully.

"Then they overshipped," Sam went on. "We paid the bill before we realized it. By the time we caught up with the error, the company had gone out of business. We couldn't get a refund, so we just kept the goods and laid some of it off to L.A. Garb. The rest we sold at outlet, or gave away. It was . . . cotton duck," he said.

"But B.S.&S. isn't listed anywhere . . ."

"Like I said, they've gone out of business," Sam smiled. Devin said nothing. Geneen didn't look up from her notebook.

"Okay then, I think that does it for me," Devin said after a beat. "Do you have anything else, Sam?"

"Why would I?" Sam threw out. "This was your meeting." He stood up, snatched his jacket off the back of his chair, and left the office.

Devin was puzzled. On the midafternoon drive back downtown to the PT plant, she thought about Sam's reaction. True, Sam was almost always snappish or unpleasant with her just on general principle, but there was something else going on. Sam was lying about B.S.&S., she was sure of it.

Sam grunted at Julius as he passed him in the L.A. Garb lobby, which the chauffeur took to mean, rightly, that the boss wanted to go somewhere. Sam had decided to visit his health club, take a steam, and try to work out the stress kinks at the base of his neck that his nettling sister-in-law had caused. This royal pain-in-his-ass woman was on to the report. Sam was pretty sure she hadn't swallowed a word he'd tried to feed her about *cotton fucking duck*. It was just a matter of time before she got to the bottom of the mystery fabric company.

She had taken him completely by surprise with her inquiry about B.S.&S., but enlightened him at the same time. Provided him with the last piece of the puzzle. So that was how Paul had managed to keep the report totally secret, he thought. In order to hide the B.S.&S. study on cost cutting from him—as well as from Alex, the rest of his staff, and everybody else at the main plant—Paul had paid for it and written it off on the Pulled Together accounts in

South-Central. Then, of course, he'd hidden the report itself in that screwy file in his goddamn limousine.

Now Devin was hot on the trail, and if Sam was any judge, that meddlesome bitch would not stop digging until she dredged up the whole sorry business. He knew that if Devin were to find out about the B.S.&S. study, and if somehow she were to get a load of the information in the report as Paul had spelled it out to him, Devin could definitely do him in. She could take the information to Charlie Fine—and she probably would. She could swing her 10 percent vote to the Bradshaw Foundation block, and together she and Fine could force him out. Though Charlie was a gentleman, Sam could hardly miss the fact that he had never had much respect for him. And more to the point, Fine, in the best interests of the company, would certainly take his orders from his longtime friend and business associate Paul Bradshaw, from the grave.

Sinking back into the limo's plush glove-leather cushions, Sam heaved a mighty sigh and closed his eyes. And allowed himself to trip into his favorite, recurring fantasy of late. He visualized the headlines: DEVIN YORKE BRADSHAW FOUND DEAD! or, WIDOW KILLED IN TRAIN CRASH. How about, DISTRAUGHT WIFE OF MURDERED GARMENT KING TAKES OWN LIFE!

He could dream, couldn't he? With Devin out of the way, Sam Bradshaw would control the company's majority vote and have clear sailing for the rest of his life.

46

Devin wheeled her Jag into the parking spot that was still marked PAUL BRADSHAW, by the side doors at the Pulled Together plant. She dashed up the steps and down the hall into the executive suite, saying hello to Alex on the way into her office. Alex barely nodded. Preoccupied with Sam Bradshaw and the B.S.&S. business, Devin didn't notice the two men until she'd moved past them and settled in behind her desk. And looked up.

There they were again, the Italian and the Irish, sitting on her trendy canvas-covered couches, looking uncomfortable. What were their names? They'd talked to her just yesterday, she had their cards in her desk drawer, but she always had trouble remembering their names. Blocking them out, she was sure.

And Alex had got her again. Score another point for Alexandra Anson, her trusted right hand. Alex had deliberately failed to mention that the two detectives were sitting in Devin's office, waiting for her. Knowing full well that they would make her uneasy. But she wouldn't chastise Alex for it, wouldn't give her the satisfaction of knowing she'd scored a hit. She carefully chose the bouts she got into with Alex. Most of the time she pretended not to notice her assistant's little parries and thrusts. It was Devin's way of neutralizing them. Alex was still on probation with her, and at this point it was looking like she wouldn't make the cut. Not that she wasn't excellent at her job. But she was getting failing grades as the person Devin wanted closest to her at work, and all of her knowledge and efficiency were becoming increasingly less worth the aggravation.

Devin smiled at the detectives. "Hello, gentlemen," she said, "Forgive me, I have so much on my mind I didn't even notice you sitting there."

"What do you have on your mind?" asked the Irish.

"Does that question have to do with your investigation, or is it just a 'penny for your thoughts' kind of pleasantry?" she flipped back. She didn't dare ask their names again. They'd probably arrest her for stupidity.

"Just wondering if you were thinking about your husband," he threw out, not returning her smile. "Your dead husband," he added. As if she didn't know which husband.

"Is there a reason why I should be?" she queried, raising her eyebrows.

Since this encounter was opening on a rather nasty note, she made no attempt to make the two less uncomfortable, to walk over and join them on the couches, or invite them to come sit by her desk, or ask if they'd like something to drink.

"Oh, just because it's been two months and five days

since your husband was killed," said the Irish. "But who's counting? Not you, huh?"

Ryan, Devin remembered. The one with the faded red hair was Ryan. And the other one was Furillo, Furrino, something like that. John Furrino. And Richard Ryan. Maybe his friends called him Dick.

"What can I do for you, officers?" she asked. She still wore the smile, frozen in place.

"We got something for ya," Ryan returned, and he stood up and sauntered over to her. He put his hand in the pocket of his rumpled, ill-fitting glen plaid jacket, pulled out a gun, and tossed it on her desk. It was the .38 Smith & Wesson the two had picked up from the Benedict house last night.

"And?" she asked, looking from the pistol up into his squinty, sky blue Irish eyes.

"And it's not the gun that killed your husband," Ryan said, with a definite note of disappointment. " 'Course this one isn't *your* gun. This one's registered to the late Mr. Bradshaw."

Devin had no response. She continued to look at the man expectantly. Then Furrino, still sitting on one of the couches across the room, was heard from.

"We want to know where the other one is," he said.

"I told you," Devin returned, "I don't know. Did you contact Julius?"

"We did. Mr. Jackson says Mr. Bradshaw kept it in the top left drawer of his desk in this office, which drawer he kept locked. Mr. Jackson says Mr. Bradshaw kept the key to the drawer taped to the underside of the middle of the desk, where the kneehole was." This from Furrino.

Devin glanced down at her desk, which wasn't a desk at all. It was a marvelous old Italian Franco Raggi stripped and polished pine table that Bailey Senn had brought in. With just a horizontal bank of shallow drawers slung beneath its smooth surface. No kneehole.

"That would be Paul's old desk," Devin told them. "It's gone."

"Gone where?" they asked in unison.

"Gone ... gone!" she offered. "Gone I don't know where. We gave the old furniture away. To employees. Ruby Johnson would know. But there was no gun in the desk," Devin added.

"How do you know?" Furrino quizzed.

"I know because I looked through the desk thoroughly before we got rid of it, of course. There was nothing in the drawers except the usual pens, pencils, envelopes, paper clips and assorted junk, which we cleaned out. And one large dead spider. Definitely no gun. And none of the drawers was locked."

"We'd like to take a look at that desk," Furrino said.

"Fine. See Ruby Johnson, ask her whom she gave it to," Devin said, jotting Ruby's name, number, and extension on a piece of notepaper.

Ryan took the sheet of paper from her and turned on his heel. He walked out the door, with Furrino following behind. No good-bye, no go to hell, nothing. *Nice guys,* Devin thought. *They're sure I did it.*

47

It was ten to six, not yet light. Devin was in the gym doing her morning stretches against the balance bar. Waiting for Tanner to come. This was the first morning in her life that she showered *before* her workout. What was it about the sexual urge that was stronger even than fear, she wondered. Maybe it was just her. A regular nympho! Or maybe it was a mechanism to mask the fear, diminish it. Whatever, since yesterday morning she'd been hard pressed to keep her mind on business, whether police business or PT business.

Today was a big day, an important day. Today they were going to start the massive Pulled Together advertising campaign shoots. It was crucial that she keep herself totally focused. Yet images of the smell and touch and feel of Tanner kept intruding on the periphery of her thoughts. And she found herself going with them, welcoming them.

How would he act this morning? Would he behave as if nothing out of the ordinary, nothing special, had happened between them? Does he have a woman? Or a lot of women? Devin was anxious, even fearful. And she was fresh and scrubbed and sweet-smelling and eager, and hungry for him to touch her again.

But maybe he wouldn't. Maybe he wouldn't even come. Maybe he'd thought about the potential hazards and decided he wanted no part of her. Or maybe he didn't really love it yesterday, like she did. Maybe he didn't think she was sexy; maybe he wasn't even turned on. After all, she'd practically raped him.

Half of her had thought he might call last night. Just to say hello, to say that he was thinking about her. Validate that it had really happened. But he didn't. Maybe he was busy trying to *in*validate what had happened, come up with a way to pretend it never happened and just go on. Maybe . . .

Suddenly he was in the doorway, tall, tanned, fit, and drop-dead gorgeous, one shoulder leaning against the doorjamb. Her heart skipped a beat. Four or five beats. She looked up at him, and she had to remember to breathe.

"Good morning," he said.

"Good morning," she echoed, and she gave him a tenuous smile, then directed her eyes back to the wooden bar she was pressing.

Tanner made his way over to the far side of the room, where he dropped his jacket and gym bag by the wall. Then he straightened and slowly turned toward her. Devin went on with her stretches, doing her best to ignore the man.

Oh God, I'm such a fool, she thought. When did I turn into this simpering adolescent, all ga-ga over the drugstore soda jerk or the lifeguard? She dropped lower and harder into the stretch, until the pain was too much.

Stretched over to the opposite side, head down, she felt his hand on her shoulder. A light touch, but she jumped. She looked up at him, and he drew her to her feet. And into his arms. Where she leaned into him, her face buried in the curve of his neck and shoulders, small tears escaping from her eyes. Oh God, he felt so good.

"You're all I've thought about for twenty-four hours," he whispered into her hair.

"I thought you'd call . . ." She stopped herself. She felt so dumb. She felt so wonderful.

"Call? I wouldn't dare call you! I was afraid you'd hang up on me."

"Why would I—" He stopped her with his mouth on

hers. A deep lingering soul kiss that melted her, left her weak. Then he held her at arms' length.

"Let's work," he said.

"I feel like a teenager," she started. "A silly—"

"Shhh," he put a finger up to stop her. "Let's not talk about how we feel. Because we don't know how we feel. Neither of us. Please," he said again, "let's work."

They did. They got into their respective rhythms and went through their programs, easing up emotionally as they drove themselves physically. It was nearly an hour before Devin felt she could trust herself to behave with some level of normalcy. That was when she threw out a normal question, not really expecting any information.

"Have you ever heard of a company called B.S.&S.?" she asked Tanner. She hadn't found it in any directory, which was no surprise. She hadn't expected to find it listed by its initials, but those initials were all she had to go on.

"Oh, sure," he said, to her amazement. "Bragg, Schlemmer & Schultz. Everybody knows the Bragg boys in this era of company streamlining."

"The Bragg boys?" she repeated, hoisting ten-pound weights over her head. "Do they make fabric?"

Tanner laughed, hefting his own twenty-five-pound weights. "No," he said, hefting between breaths, "they make enemies. They get people fired. They're efficiency experts. New York-based. Considered by most to be the best in the business."

48

It was sunny on the beach, but not warm. The ad people had chosen early February to begin the PT shoots because the morning cloud cover wasn't usually heavy at this time of year, the light was often nearly perfect, and it was still cold; it wasn't beach season, so the crew would not have to cope with sun-worshiping Southland crowds. Devin had set up her workstation on a canvas drop cloth stretched on the sand against a cluster of rocks. She'd dressed for comfort, in jeans, a black crew neck sweater, and deck shoes with no socks. She had a thick sheaf of notes clipped into a loose-leaf binder, and she was ready to work.

Crouching down, she shielded her eyes with one hand and surveyed the scene like a camera—clean-swept sand, sparkling whitecaps pounding onshore, gulls swooping low over the water searching for food. They were on beautiful Malibu, just above Latigo Canyon, where a wide stretch of combed, sandy beach built back to rugged rocks and pampas grass. An occasional stroller or jogger went past, and only a handful of hardy souls braved the winter surf.

The location was a scramble of activity. This was to be a combined still photography and videotape shoot, and both crews were busy preparing their setups. Close to the water's edge, a pair of trainers were walking a beautiful white Andalusian stallion that would be used in the shots. Devin had insisted on an Andalusian, the huge, all-white, muscular breed of horse whose lineage goes back to an era of knights and kings. Farther up the beach near the rocks, under wide striped umbrellas where makeup and hairstyling stations had been set up, Marva Modine and Vanna Brylock sat in facing high-backed director's chairs. While expertly applying creamy base to Vanna's luscious molasses-colored skin, Joni Lawrence, a veteran makeup artist, was telling war stories that were making all within earshot howl with laughter. And Sandy Bailey, one of the busiest hair stylists in this La-La Land of movie stars, was manipulating Marva's massive mop of sun-streaked hair, lifting, ruffling, spraying, tussling, working it into that fell-out-of-bed, lolled-on-the-beach, did-nothing, it-just-happened-this-way look that would take half an hour to achieve.

Ad agency reps bustled about giving orders, and wardrobe people wrestled with cases, boxes, and racks of Pulled Together garments. Billy Hilgarde was walking around barefoot in cutoff jeans, poking into every department's business, grinning, asking questions, scanning story boards, examining equipment. He was enormously curious. He had no clue what was going on, and he was having a great time.

When the two women were ready, it was Billy's turn, but there wasn't much work to be done on him. He closed his eyes while Joni sponged his face, neck, and ears with tawny base, and he laughed and squirmed when she insisted on making up his arms and hands as well.

"Sit still," she scolded him good-naturedly. "I want you all the same color."

"Are you gonna do my legs, too?" he quizzed, scrutinizing his golden brown muscled calves beneath frayed jeans.

"No, honey," she shushed him, "but I *am* going to do your entire chest, so don't even think about jumping out of my chair. I'll let you know when you're dismissed." Joni talked stern, but her face lit up in smiles dealing with this unlikely, reluctant star. The Billy Hilgarde charm was infectious.

Devin kept half an eye on all of it. Time was precious, and they had a lot to accomplish. They'd taken out a permit to shoot for one day at this location, they'd hired the best people in the business, and they'd scheduled photography to take advantage of all the different phases of light on the Southern California beach—cool morning light, going into harshest light at highest noon, and mellowing to the prettiest light, magic time, when the afternoon sun waned over the sea.

They would piggyback the video with the stills. Some of the still photography would be color, but most would be in dramatic black-and-white. The designer in Devin knew exactly the look she wanted the shots to achieve and the image she needed them to project. She knew style, she knew the PT line of clothes, she knew exactly what she was after, and she was a stickler for perfection.

When the models and the handsome white horse were in place for the first setup, and before actual shooting began, Devin had the still crew take Polaroid exposures, each of which she studied carefully until she was totally satisfied with the aspect, the attitude, the garments, the accessories, the background, the framing, and the look that would be caught on film and tape.

By late morning, the work was progressing well. Billy Hilgarde was a natural. He took to the assignment as if he'd been doing it all his life, and incredibly, he was almost always perfect on every take because he didn't try. Vanna Brylock was stunning and sexy. And Marva was Marva, the ultimate pro, with the blinding smile, the exquisite face, the great bones, the superb body, and tons of attitude that lost not a decibel when it was translated onto film.

Watching the photographers working with the models while the advertising design teams supervised, and the crew of more than fifty people involved in the effort doing their respective jobs, Devin let her mind drift down the beach to where the young Paul Bradshaw had staged his very first advertising campaign shoot for L.A. Garb. He had told her all about it, laughed at the memory. It was more than thirty years ago. Paul was in his twenties then, and the fledgling company had no money to create ads. He, too, had decided to shoot on the beach, just a few miles south of where they were today, on Santa Monica beach a couple of blocks away from the company's first, small brick building.

Paul had told her how he'd packed a canvas garment bag full of clothes, taken an old Brownie box camera, and coaxed one of the showroom secretaries who happened to be a very lovely redhead onto the stretch of beach closest to the shop. There, the secretary wriggled in and out of one outfit after another, from bell-bottom, hip-hugger jeans to sixties' tie-dye creations, while Paul shot the clothes from several different angles. Until the police showed up and demanded to see his permit.

First Paul told them the girl was his sister, and he was taking family snapshots. With a professional garment bag full of goods on the sand, the cops knew a fashion shoot when they saw one, so that didn't wash. But they didn't cite him, because Paul said he was sorry, he'd just started his business, he didn't know he was supposed to have a permit, and he promised to leave and get one. And he gathered up the clothes and his "model" and walked off the sand—only to drive a mile up the beach and try it again. Until the two got chased away by yet another pair of officers assigned to cruise the beach.

Never one to give up, Paul finally did succeed in setting up at still another location and getting the bulk of his shots. But by that time the clothes were wet and dirty, and the girl was salty and disheveled, not to mention weary, annoyed, and completely out of patience with her young boss. But having gone to so much trouble, Paul said, he took the damn pictures anyway.

And what Paul liked to call his two-dollar snaps turned into a campaign that rocked Madison Avenue! The grainy black-and-white blowups of a gorgeous woman looking pouty and cold, with very little makeup, no lipstick, her long, dark hair all askew and her clothes wrinkled and muddy, were considered the sexiest fashion poses ever done. These off-the-wall L.A. Garb images showed up everywhere, the young line took off, and a brand-new, daringly innovative, award-winning style of ultra-hot fashion photography was born—quite by accident.

Devin sighed. There had been so much wonderful creativity in Paul Bradshaw. So much wit, so much drive, so much genius. That's what she'd fallen for, and who wouldn't? Only to learn over time that he had very little soul. And in the end, after the dinners and the parties and glitz and the glitter times, at home alone behind closed doors, she'd found out what really counts in a relationship. If she ever had another one, she promised herself, she would look long and hard beyond fun and successful and handsome, into the heart and soul beneath. Yet another of her mom's old clichés ringing true, she smiled to herself— *handsome is as handsome does.*

Devin was nudged out of her reverie by a tap on the shoulder. Turning, she was more than a little surprised to see Marva Modine, in black leggings and a loose-fitting men's gray sweatshirt, squatting beside her in the sand, digging into her oversized model's tote.

"Hi, Devin," she said, still rummaging through her bag. "We're breaking for lunch, and I brought you a sandwich. Tuna on La Brea Bakery's seven-grain bread, with lettuce and fat-free mayo."

"You're kidding," Devin said, astonished. "You made a sandwich for me?"

"I sure did," the beautiful Marva told her. "I knew with a body like yours, you would definitely not want to eat the fat-loaded sandwiches or the congealed pasta salads off the catering truck."

"Well . . . I . . . You're right, I hadn't even thought about lunch," Devin stammered, genuinely dumbfounded by Marva's gesture.

Devin had met Marva only twice before, the first time at her and Paul's last, ill-fated dinner party, and again a few days ago when Devin gave her final approval of the clothes the woman would model for this shoot. Both times were brief. At the dinner party she'd wanted to smack this ravishing creature who was flirting shamelessly with her husband. And at the fitting there was nothing not to approve of; the most innocuous rag looked nothing short of extraordinary on Marva.

"I grabbed some plates and napkins from the truck," Marva was saying now, "and I brought some fresh-squeezed carrot juice from home." She poured rich orange liquid from a thermos into two large plastic cups. "Try it," she said with her dazzling smile, handing one of the cups to Devin.

Devin sipped the juice, and it was truly delicious. Then Marva offered her a sandwich she'd partially unwrapped, healthy-looking tuna chunks on thick homemade bread. Devin glanced around at what the rest of the crew was lunching on. They jockeyed plates heaped with what looked like some kind of gray meat with brown sauce, stewed vegetables, heavy pastas and pot pies, and burgers and hot dogs with small bags of potato chips.

"This is terrific," she told Marva, munching on the tuna sandwich. She hadn't realized how hungry she was, and they still had long hours of work ahead of them.

"Good," Marva said, taking a huge bite out of her own sandwich. "This fat-free mayo isn't half bad once you get used to it, and it saves you about a million grams of fat in a sandwich like this."

"Weather turned out great, didn't it?" Devin offered, making small talk. What the hell, she thought, maybe Marva always sidled up to the boss.

"Perfect," Marva returned, settling herself more comfortably against the rocks behind her back.

The two women were sitting on one of the canvas drop cloths that the video company had spread out on the sand for the crew. Marva poured some celery sticks and fresh cherry tomatoes out of a plastic bag onto a paper plate and offered it to Devin

"Thanks, Marva," Devin said gratefully. "This is totally unexpected, and much appreciated."

Then Marva threw her another curve. "How about lunch tomorrow?" she asked. "I know a great little place on Broadway near the California Clothing Mart. Just a few minutes from the PT plant. I'd like to talk to you."

49

Devin left the West Coast Office of Bragg, Schlemmer & Schultz on Wilshire Boulevard's Miracle Mile with nothing much in hand. After Tanner told her what B.S.& S. was, the company was easy enough to find, and she'd made an appointment for nine o'clock this morning. She wanted to find out exactly what Pulled Together had paid $350,000 for.

A comprehensive efficiency study of the entire L.A. Garb operation from top to bottom, ordered by Paul Bradshaw several months ago—that's what they'd paid for, she was told. And yes, the study had been completed, and the report had been issued. But as everyone knew, B.S.&S. reports were strictly confidential, as was all related data.

Sol Schlemmer's son ran their L.A. office, and it was he who met with and explained it to Devin. For obvious reasons, this lanky, balding, thirtyish, colorless, and quite humorless gentleman told her, Bragg issued a finished report only to the person who commissioned it. Also for obvious reasons, after that person had received and signed off on one hard copy and an accompanying disk, Bragg did not even keep copies itself. Once any given report was completed and gone, company policy was to delete everything to do with it from its computer files. For obvious reasons.

Devin asked Sol Schlemmer's son what the obvious reasons were. In a tone that sounded like he was explaining something to a three-year-old, he told Devin it was so nothing could ever rear its head in the press. So there was no possible danger of insider trading on the information. So employees wouldn't get advance word of firings, layoffs, department cutbacks, plant closures, and the like. And for any number of other obvious reasons.

The bottom line, according to Sol Schlemmer Junior: his company was not about to divulge any of the contents of the commissioned, delivered, and paid-for L.A. Garb report to Devin Bradshaw. Or even to the new head of the company, Paul Bradshaw's brother, Mr. Samuel Bradshaw. That gentleman could always order a new study, Mr. Schlemmer said. But the report already issued had been erased from their hard drive, and it was erased from their memories. End of story. End of meeting.

"Oh, and sorry about your husband," Schlemmer Junior had added while showing Devin the door.

In the underground parking garage of the high-rise that housed the Bragg boys, as Tanner had called them, Devin found her Jaguar and made her way out into the sunshine of Wilshire Boulevard. So, the report was something that Paul had ordered, and knowledge of its contents had gone to the grave with him. Maybe. But unless they had been destroyed, somewhere there existed a hard copy and a disk. What information did the report contain that was worth a third of a million dollars to Paul? And who else, if anyone, knew about it? Devin was more than curious. Wherever the material was, and whatever it contained, one thing was sure: Sam Bradshaw had lied to her about it, and she wanted to know why.

Devin drove east on Wilshire toward the Harbor Freeway and South-Central Los Angeles. As it happened, she had a meeting with Sam at the PT plant at ten-thirty. He'd left a message with Alex this morning, and she'd reached Devin in her car. Sam Bradshaw in the morning! That was enough to put a woman in a bad mood. She had no idea what was on his agenda. To discuss business, Geneen had told Alex. Probably he wanted to dish up more of his high-handed, supercilious bullshit, which was his signature way of trying to show her who's boss.

Still, why would he be coming all the way in to South-Central? His usual MO was to summon her to Santa Monica, leave the driving to her, and try to belittle her on his turf. And it was just yesterday that he'd lied to her about B.S.&S. He had to know that she knew he was lying. The man hadn't even bothered to try to lie convincingly. Even Geneen had had the grace to be embarrassed for him. You would think he'd want to keep his distance for a while, see if that bit of business would blow over. Oh well, Devin sighed, it was just another illustration of his contempt for her.

Dodging in and out of the heavy midmorning traffic, she

decided to focus on more pleasant thoughts to even out
her mood. Gee, what would she think about? As if there
were anything else she *could* think about. Tanner! She
would allow herself the luxury of ten minutes of drive-time
fantasies about Tanner. About sex with Tanner.

She had actually taken him into bed this morning. Tuesday morning it was in the sauna, Wednesday it was in one
of the showers off the gym, and this morning she'd led him
upstairs into the master suite, locked the door, and leaped
into her silk-covered, down-feathered, king-sized bed with
him!

She wondered if Maria could tell when she made up the
room. Maria would probably be horrified. The marital bed!
Just two months and ... what had that detective said the
other day? Two months and five days, two months and
seven days now, after her husband had been killed, but
who's counting? Good Lord, what was wrong with her?

It wasn't what was wrong with her, she reassured herself,
it was what had been wrong with her marriage. And her late
husband. She had long since lost any sexual sparks for Paul.
The short-circuiting began almost three years ago when she
was lunching at Jimmy's with a well-meaning friend, who'd
lowered her voice and raised her eyebrows and suggested
that Devin might want to keep her husband on a shorter
leash. Something about a whispered dalliance with the very
attractive daughter of a business associate of Paul's. The
daughter was only twenty-three, the woman said, and had
been talking a lot. Simply too many people knew about it,
my dear, said the woman.

Devin had decided to ignore it, until Paul suggested a
few weeks later that they have the Stewarts over to dinner
and invite their daughter Daina to come too. Devin flushed
even now, remembering the humiliation. That one, and the
dozens of others, until finally she simply didn't care about
sex with Paul anymore.

But sex with Tanner was something else. This morning
it was heaven. Fast, but unbelievably divine. They were
both all sweaty and ripe after their workout, and there'd
been no time to jump in the shower before they jumped
into bed. They were both pushing the clock, so the sex
was urgent.

Or maybe it was just urgent anyway. At the photo shoot
on the beach yesterday, when Billy, Marva, and Vanna

were grouped in every conceivable hot, sexy pose, with the horse and without the horse, Devin kept seeing herself and Tanner in the picture. Without the other three. But sometimes with the horse, she had to admit.

She loved to think about his hands on her. Ten minutes of Tanner touching her could keep her on a high all day. Powerful stuff, the feeling that went with thoroughly intoxicating sex. Be nice if she could package it and market it, she smiled. No drug on earth could compete. She'd be a billionaire, there'd be no more wars, the world would be Utopia, and everybody would feel like she did when she thought about sex with Tanner.

She pulled into the big PT gates. Time for a reality check—now she had to face Sam Bradshaw. He would condescend; she would be sweet and nod her head. Or he would rant, and she would be quiet and listen. She'd learned that being passive was the easiest and fastest way to get him off her case.

In fact, whatever he said was of little consequence to her. Sam couldn't afford to really cross her—she had the upper hand, and they both knew it. Maybe at some point this morning she could catch him off guard with a question about the B.S.&S. report. She was convinced that Sam knew something and he was anxious to keep it secret.

Alex was her usual Mona Lisa self, with the smile for Devin that said, *You're my boss, and I'm pretending to like you, but I'd kill you if I could get away with it.* Devin shuddered. She went into her office, and closed the door. And braced herself for Sam. But no amount of preparation could have fortified her for what Sam Bradshaw had come to assail her with today.

He strode in unannounced, thank you very much, Alex. He fairly slammed the door behind him, looked around—rather disdainfully, Devin thought—at her now tastefully decorated office, parked himself on one of the couches, and without even a hello, he beckoned her to join him. A power play. He wouldn't sit in front of Devin's desk. Devin rose and walked over to him and settled opposite him on a chair.

"Good morning, Sam," she said pleasantly.

Without preamble, he threw a bombshell at her. "I know that you were up on Mulholland Drive on the day Paul was killed," he said.

Devin met his gaze, her mind racing. Perhaps Billy Hil-

garde had to tell that to the police and hadn't had a chance
to let her know yet. And probably the officers then told
Sam, to see how it would play, see what it would get them.
That seemed to be routine with them. Then came the real
shocker.

"I also know that you were up there telling Paul that
you were about to divorce him," he said.

Now she was stunned. Nobody knew that! Wait a minute—*Tanner* knew that. *John Tanner was the only person
she'd told that to, and in strict confidence. On the same day
she'd had sex with him for the first time! In the sauna!* My
God, would Tanner have gone to Sam with that information? And if so, what else would he have told him? Tanner
knew so much. But why? For money? People you least
expect will do unheard of things for money.

What did she know about Tanner, really? Nothing! Foolish girl, for trusting him. The age-old trap. Women were
known to invest a man they had the hots for with all manner
of marvelous attributes. Raging hormones short-circuiting the
brain cells. There was no other way Sam Bradshaw could
know that divorce was the real purpose of her frenzied run
up to Mulholland in a downpour. Staring Sam down now,
Devin wrestled with pain and rage. She felt royally *had* by
a wild-card gigolo stud called John Tanner.

"I want to know exactly what went on between you and
my brother up on Mulholland Drive that day," Sam demanded now.

"You're out of line, Sam," Devin returned evenly. "I
don't intend to discuss this with you."

"Well, you were up there, weren't you?" he pressed.

"That's not your business, Sam."

"You're damn right it's my business," he barked. "You
killed my brother."

"I don't have to take this," Devin threw back, raising
her voice a little now. It occurred to her fleetingly that on
the other side of the closed door, Alex must be enjoying
this.

"Tell me this, then," Sam went on. "I happen to know
that you were up there with Paul on that day, at that time,
in that spot. If you didn't do it, what did you see happen?"

Something in the way he'd asked the question made
Devin doubt his righteous anger. Maybe Sam wasn't really

asking her what she did, maybe he was asking her what she *saw*!

"I didn't say that I was up there, Sam. You did."

"Oh yeah, you were up there all right," Sam shot back. "You were up there to let my brother know you were checking out, and when opportunity presented itself, you opted to check out as a rich widow instead of a divorcee!"

"Sam," Devin said then, getting up from her chair. "why don't you take a flying leap into hell!" Sam got up and stormed out of her office, slamming the door behind him.

Devin sat down again and remained perfectly still for a few moments, trying to think this through. Tanner. Yes, it had to be. She'd confided in him, and he violated her trust. There was no other possible explanation. It had to be Tanner, because she hadn't told another soul.

Could the police have known that she'd confided in Tanner? Tracked him down and questioned him about her? Not likely, she thought. And even if they did, certainly he should have told her. She'd been spilling her guts to him, and doing it before, during, and after sex. And he'd betrayed her.

She picked up the phone and punched in the number she had for Tanner, where she often left him messages, always brief. *Don't come next week, I'm out of town. Can you come an hour earlier tomorrow—I have a breakfast meeting.* Well, this message would be brief too.

His machine clicked on.

"Hi there. What's up?" the familiar voice said. Her heart skipped a beat. So he still had that effect on her, so what? The beep snapped her out of it.

"This is Devin," she said into the phone. "Don't come anymore. You're fired."

50

Sitting at a corner table at the Café Maxx opposite Marva Modine, Devin couldn't believe what she was hearing. This was the second time that she had been stunned by what someone was telling her, and it was still before lunch. First Sam and his murder accusations, and now Marva.

"Did you hear me, Devin? I said I slept with your husband," Marva repeated.

"I heard you," Devin said quietly. "Why are you telling me this?"

The Maxx was maxed out, as it always was at lunchtime, filled to the rafters with garment trade patrons. People both women knew were nodding to them, waving, stopping by the table to say hello.

"I'm telling you this because I like you," Marva answered. "Because I want us to get to know each other."

Devin looked at her askance. "I must say you've picked a hell of a way to break the ice," was the only response she could come up with.

"Well, I know you knew, or at least you must have suspected, and I didn't want that hanging fire between us. I mean, now that we're working together," Marva added, flashing that dazzling smile of hers. Devin thought she must be in the twilight zone.

"Look, let's order," she managed.

"Can't we talk about this?" Marva persisted.

Devin sighed. This was definitely a day from hell. "Sure," she breathed. "What do you want to talk about, and why?"

"I want to talk about the night I slept with Paul Bradshaw. And it was only once," she added with a solicitous look, as if that made everything okay.

Devin just looked blankly at her. There was no way on earth she was going to be able to stop this woman, she realized. She was about to get an earful, whether she needed it or not. Of course she could just get up and walk out of the place.

"It was the night of your big dinner party. The night before he was killed," Marva said.

Devin stole a surreptitious glance around her, checking to see if anyone else in the packed restaurant was tuned in to this preposterous conversation. Incredibly, Marva kept on talking.

"He showed up on my doorstep that night. In the rain. I guess he knew my address. It's in the personnel files. I mean, he'd been flirting with me from the day I went to work there, but that was the only time I slept with him."

Devin suddenly noticed one of PT's belt suppliers hovering at their table, a man Devin had bought goods from back when she ran Pieces. How long had he been standing there? she wondered. This has to be a scene from a Woody Allen movie, she told herself, flashing the man a somewhat lackluster smile.

"How nice to see you, Alan," she said, and introduced him to Marva. For a few seconds she found herself weighing the propriety of introducing the man to the woman, or should she have introduced the woman to the man? She pondered this as he made small talk, shook hands, told Devin he'd be calling on her soon with new items, and left. Devin thought about just telling Marva that she didn't feel well all of a sudden, she had to run.

"You know my sister," Marva said then.

"Your sister?" Devin echoed blankly.

"Yes, my sister Gabby. Gabrielle Modine. She told me that a couple of years ago she met you at the L.A. County Museum, at an art exhibit. But she didn't realize who you were until she read about your husband being killed. That's when she told me about meeting you, because she knows I work for L.A. Garb. Gabby's a nut for art. She works at Sotheby's." None of this was registering with Devin.

"You know, I really don't feel good," she started. Then suddenly she remembered. "Oh, does your sister have red hair?"

"Yes," Marva smiled. "She's my half sister, actually. She told me she put you together with a fitness trainer."

"I remember. I liked her. What does this have to do with your sleeping with my husband . . . ?"

"Nothing," Marva jumped in, and her exquisite California-sunny features broke into a cheerful laugh.

Either she's crazy, or I am for listening to her, Devin thought. But she couldn't seem to extricate herself from this outlandish dialogue. Something perverse in her wanted to find out where the hell it was going.

"I brought you a present," Marva said then, throwing her another screeching curve. Devin said nothing. Marva was fishing in her large, woven-leather Bottega Veneta carry-all bag.

"It's a new herbal face spray for after you shower," Marva said, handing Devin a lovely cobalt blue bottle she'd taken out of tissue wrapping.

"It's divine," Marva went on. Devin was truly speechless. She accepted the bottle like an automaton. Looked at it. "REVEIL de la ROSE—Face and Body Mist," the label read.

"When you get out of the shower and you towel off, but you're still a little damp, you spray this all over yourself," Marva beamed. Devin continued to stare at the bottle, not having the slightest idea how to respond.

"You'll think you died and went to heaven," Marva was bubbling. "I use it all the time. I stock up. I have tons of it. So I brought you some. You'll love it."

"You said you were going to tell me why you slept with Paul," Devin finally uttered, almost sheepishly, holding onto the bottle, looking up at Marva, feeling absolutely ridiculous.

"Oh, yeah," Marva said, her glorious face turning serious on cue. Devin became aware that another man was standing at their table now. She looked up at him.

"Hi, I'm Randy," said a tall, thin young man with round tortoise-shell glasses and an orange-colored buzz cut. "I'll be your waiter. Ready to order?"

"In a minute," Devin waved him off.

"Sure," he grinned, and he made a jack-rabbit sprint over to another table.

"Uhh . . . you were saying?" Devin pressed.

"I slept with him because he showed up at my house at one in the morning," Marva offered. "I didn't particularly want to. But he was the boss, after all. And I didn't know you at all. There was no reason not to." That simple, Devin marveled.

"Marva, you don't have to tell me this because *I'm* the boss now," Devin said, trying to bring some sense to this exchange.

"Oh, I know ..." Marva started, but Devin shushed her.

"You already have the job," she said. "And this new campaign could go on for years if we're successful. I chose you for the Pulled Together ads because you're perfect for the spots. You don't have to explain anything to me, Marva. In fact," Devin added evenly, "I really wish you wouldn't."

"Okay, fine," the irrepressible Marva grinned. "It's just that we're working together, I knew you knew, and I wanted to get it out there. And put it behind us."

"And so you did," Devin served up, thinking that Lewis Carroll must have had conversations like this. "Let's have lunch now, okay?" she almost pleaded.

"As a matter of fact, he wasn't very good in bed, was he?" Marva remarked off-handedly, to Devin's astonishment. She debated fleeing from the restaurant on that one.

"Look," Marva said, leveling her gaze into Devin's green eyes now. "Say something to me. Tell me I'm a slut. Slap my face. Or tell me it's okay, you couldn't stand the bastard anyway. Because that's the feeling I get."

"Why would you say that?" Devin couldn't help asking.

"Because he was all over anything in skirts, and you're too smart not to have known that. And much too classy to have put up with it for long. So say something, Devin. Don't just act like this conversation isn't happening."

That got Devin's attention. She looked at Marva with new respect. She still had no idea why the woman had forced this issue, but force it she did. This was definitely Devin's exit cue; Neil Simon couldn't have written a better one.

Still, something kept Devin rooted to her seat. Nobody had ever been that brutally honest with her about Paul. There was something compelling about this impossibly beautiful woman whom she hardly knew, daring to be candid to the core. With her new boss.

"All right," she heard herself saying, "I forgive you. And you're right, I suspected. But I no longer much care."

This off-the-wall supermodel's outrageous candor was actually refreshing, Devin considered. And probably conta-

gious. Because she astounded herself then by blurting out
to Marva, "And yes, he could be lousy in bed."

Marva broke into reverberant peals of laughter. Which
was infectious. In spite of herself, Devin started laughing
too. The two women sat across from each other at the small
table and laughed out loud for three minutes solid, causing
diners around them to look over and smile. Until Devin
caught their waiter's eye as he darted past their table again.

"Randy," she called out. The young man jumped to attention. Still chuckling, Devin said, "We're ready to order."

Alex and Rosemary were shown to their table at the Ondine. Rosemary looked around with approval at the softly
lit peach-and-apricot decor, the French stained-glass chan-
deliers, the small tables with crisp white linen, sparkling
crystal and silver, and bowls of fresh, peach joseph-coat
roses.

"I love it," she told Alex. "When you said downtown, I
didn't expect a place like this."

"Well, I owe you so many lunches," Alex told her, settling into her comfortable, damask-covered chair, "that I
wanted to take you someplace special, but I don't have
time to stray too far from the factory. This restaurant caters
to the theater crowd, and the food happens to be wonderful."

"How did you find it?"

"The bitch took me here," Alex threw out, wrinkling up
her small Irish nose.

"How's it going with you two?" Rosemary smiled.

"It's going okay," Alex returned. "We just give each
other a wide berth and do our jobs."

"You two work together in close quarters," Rosemary
observed. "What kind of relationship do you have?"

"Please, too boring," Alex stopped her. "And you are
not getting out of it, Rosemary Bradshaw. Now, I demand
to hear about your date with my dad."

Alex had tried grilling her father about it, but he'd put
her off, said he was with a client, couldn't talk. Then he'd
managed to avoid her calls for two days. And Rosemary
had done the same, simply said it was a pleasant evening
and changed the subject every time she asked. So Alex
invited Rosemary to lunch, figuring if she held the woman
captive in a restaurant for an hour, she'd get full disclosure.

"It was lovely," Rosemary responded vaguely, picking up her menu and scanning the entrées. "What do you recommend?"

"Do you *like* him?" Alex demanded, exasperated.

Rosemary looked up at her with a twinkle. "What did *he* say?"

"What is it with you two?" Alex threw up her hands. "He says nothing. You say nothing. I figure either you can't stand each other, or it was love at first sight. Which is it?" she begged.

"Neither," Rosemary answered. "What about the red snapper? Have you had it here?"

"Okay, just answer one question," Alex persisted. "Are you going to see him again?"

"Yes."

"Really! When?"

"Tonight," Rosemary smiled. "Now, I'm going to try the grilled snapper, and an endive salad to start."

Clearly, that was all she intended to say about her new relationship with Alexander Anson, but it was enough to satisfy Alex. She smiled back and summoned their waiter.

The two women enjoyed lunch and caught up. Alex talked about the workings of Pulled Together and how the division seemed to be flourishing. She carefully avoided any talk of Devin. Rosemary spoke glowingly about Pauly. How great he was doing, how proud she was of him. Neither woman mentioned Paul Bradshaw, Rosemary's ex-husband, Alex's former lover. They finished with coffee and fresh berries, and Alex called for the check.

"Rosemary, this has been wonderful," she said, then she sighed heavily. "Unfortunately, I have to get back to the witch now."

"Alex," Rosemary said, turning serious, "are you so sure that Devin is a witch?"

"How can you even ask?" Alex demanded. "She stole your husband, didn't she?"

"Look, Alex," Rosemary countered, "I don't mean this as a low blow, but isn't that exactly what *you* tried to do?" Alex visibly reddened.

"What I mean is," Rosemary went on, "maybe that doesn't make her a witch. Maybe nobody could have stolen my husband if my marriage was sound. Maybe it lasted longer than it should have. All I know is I haven't been this happy in years. Maybe I should thank her."

"Rosemary," Alex challenged, "I really admire your personal growth, your hard-won emotional evolvement, but I'm not there. Your homilies can't dissolve my hate. I'm stuck with it."

Rosemary was taken aback, but she tried not to show it. She really did feel good about herself, she really was the happiest she'd been in years, she looked forward to seeing more of Al Anson, and she really did consider Alex a friend. Yes, there was a time when she wanted to kill this woman, and Devin too, but she was light-years beyond that now.

"Okay, look at it this way, then," she said to Alex. "Your hate is doing you no good. It's just eating you up, making you miserable. Meanwhile, your hate isn't hurting Devin at all."

"Don't be too sure about that," Alex said tersely.

51

"Jesus, Jer, what the hell *is* this?" Devin asked, squinting at the color sheets spread out in front of her.

She and Jerred Quigg, one of the company's most creative designers, were sitting at the worktable on the far side of Alex's office. They were looking over his latest sketches for PT's back-to-school line.

"It's hip-hop," the young black man said with a wide grin, pushing his round, black framed glasses up on his nose. "All the kids are wearing it—"

"All the kids in South-Central Los Angeles, maybe," Devin broke in, "but we have to sell Indiana too, Jerred. They're not going to buy big baggy ripped jeans in Indiana."

"No kidding, Devin, this slouch thing is raging—"

"No!" Devin said, sharper than she'd meant to. The designer fairly winced.

"Look," she went on, "I think a very small percentage of kids across the country wear this stuff, and the ones who do are not going to buy it from us. They want to decimate their own jeans. They don't want their holes in the same places as some other kid's pants. They create their own stuff. Or destroy their own stuff, I should say."

"Well, we can rip 'em in different places—" Quigg started.

"Nope. Won't work," Devin snapped. "What are the odds that a hip-hopper will go into a store and find the exact pair of jeans he wants, in the exact color he likes and the size he needs, and the damn *schmatta* will also be ripped exactly where he wants it ripped? Zero! Our pants will have a gash above one knee, and he'll want them torn in the crotch. Forget it."

"Okay," Quigg said. "Do you still want the sags and rags?"

"I have no objection to baggy pants and bandannas," she answered. "But what's with these giant sweats? And T-shirts down past the knees?"

"It's happenin'," he insisted.

"I'm telling you, I don't buy it," Devin said, with a hint of annoyance in her voice. She knew she was being overly hard on the young man, but she couldn't seem to curb it.

"Rethink this," she said to the designer, who now had a hurt look on his face as he scanned his meticulously drawn sketches. "Keep the sags, mix them up with straight jeans and pants, lose the el huge-o T-shirts, give me a lot more wearable numbers, and don't take your inspiration from MTV rappers. Got it?"

"Got it," Quigg said quietly, gathering up his sketches. He'd come into this meeting exuberant, and now he looked defeated. Sketches under his arm, head lowered, he slipped out the door.

Devin slid off the stool she was perched on and glanced over at Alex. She could see disapproval etched on her assistant's face.

"Did you see Jerred's sketches?" she asked her.

"No, but obviously you hated them," Alex said with raised eyebrows, without looking up from her paperwork.

Devin went back into her office and closed the door behind her. She had to get a grip. Quigg's designs weren't the problem, Tanner was. She was terrified by what he might have said, and to whom. And she was enraged. Not to mention humiliated, hurt, and furious with herself. She'd compromised her principles for what amounted to a cheap E-ticket ride at Disneyland, a few rolls in the hay. A stupid, gigantic, dangerous mistake.

He'd called and left messages for her yesterday, one at work, two at the house. Asking what on earth was wrong. Saying he'd try her again later. Never leaving a number where she could call and talk to him. Not that she would. But the only number she had for Tanner reached a voice mail. Him and his damn secrets. She had no idea what kind of life the man really led or why he would betray her. Money was the only reason she could think of.

It occurred to her that Sam would probably have seen records of the monthly payments made over the last couple of years to John Tanner at his post office box address. Sam's department, his financial people, had always handled the family's business and bills as well as the company's. It would have been easy enough for Sam to trace John Tanner, and since Tanner was someone Devin saw every day, she wouldn't put it past Sam to get to him, feel him out. Sam would probably quiz anyone he thought could possibly be in a position to compromise her.

Or maybe it was just loose lips. Tanner talking about her to someone, chatting up his proximity to one of the principals in a murder case that was making national headlines. Idle gossip. And someone told someone who told someone who brought it back to Sam Bradshaw. Something like that.

Sitting here raging and panicking was doing her no good, she knew. And it was doing the business no good, certainly. She would have to apologize to Jerred, tell him he was on the right track. Admit to him that she bit his head off because she was in a foul mood about something that had nothing at all to do with him. She knew better than to stifle a designer's creativity by acting the way she did. She picked up the phone and punched up his extension.

Quigg sounded relieved, enthusiastic again. That fire out, Devin slumped back in her chair. She knew only too well that if the police were aware that she was leaving Paul that day, she would be a prime suspect. Don't divorce him, silly, kill him if you can manage it, and be rich. That's what Sam had insinuated. Even Debra DeAngeles had picked up on her new status. Devin would never forget her words at the funeral reception: *"You're free now, darling—and you're rich!"* Outrageous Debra, who always said exactly what was on her mind. How many people who would never dream of saying a thing like that were thinking that exactly?

How difficult could it be to find out where John Tanner works? she asked herself now. It shouldn't be hard; she'd just never tried before. Devin picked up the phone and called Los Angeles information. He was listed. She called the number. "Good morning—Brigant, Hale, Tanner & Lowe," a cheerful voice answered. Devin asked for the address of the law firm. She jotted it down. And thought of little else for the remainder of the morning.

At lunchtime she headed up the Harbor Freeway to the Santa Monica Freeway and over to Century City. She found the high-rise building on Century Park East, and saw the name BRIGANT, HALE, TANNER & LOWE on the glass-enclosed directory in the lobby. In the firm's suite of offices, she told the attractive Asian woman at the reception counter that she needed to see John Tanner. The woman nodded and made a call.

"Mr. Tanner is out to lunch," she relayed to Devin after a moment. "May I have your name?"

"I'll wait," Devin said, ignoring the request for her name.

"Do you have an appointment?"

"No," Devin responded, "but it's an emergency."

"And what is it in regard to?" the woman asked, eyeing Devin obliquely. It occurred to Devin that she probably looked a little strange. A bit agitated, and rather furtive.

"He'll know what it's in regard to when he sees me," Devin asserted, and she started to turn away.

"Fine—his secretary will call me when he gets in," the receptionist said, handing Devin a business card and giving her another odd look before turning her attention to other matters.

Devin accepted the card and took a seat. The woman probably thinks I'm here to slap a paternity suit on the bastard, she thought. She intended to confront Tanner on his turf. Demand to know exactly what the hell he'd said about her and to whom. Face to face, he couldn't wriggle out of it, and if she knew, maybe she could do some damage control. Camped on a stiff chrome and black leather chair in the reception area, she kept a stony watch on the double doors at the front entry.

Many people, singly and in groups, came pouring through those doors. But no Tanner. After about thirty minutes, the woman at the reception desk startled Devin by addressing her by name, which she was sure she hadn't mentioned.

"Mrs. Bradshaw, Mr. Tanner will see you now," she said.

Good God, Devin thought, *how did he get past me? And how did this woman know who I was?* Then it occurred to her that all of Los Angeles probably knew who she was: the socialite—trophy wife—rich widow of the very wealthy, very powerful, and very murdered Paul Bradshaw.

"Right through here," the woman said, indicating a doorway to the right.

Devin walked stiffly through the door and down the hall, which led to a group of office suites. That's when she glanced down at the card she was still clutching. Below the name of the law firm it read: *John P. Tanner.* And under the name, in small script: *Criminal Law.*

She opened the door marked JOHN P. TANNER. A tall, leggy, very pretty redhead—his secretary, Devin presumed—looked up at her expectantly.

"Go right in, Mrs. Bradshaw," the young woman smiled.

Devin could actually hear her heart beating. Her knees felt like Jell-O, but she pulled up straight and walked through the door to the inner office. And stopped short. A very attractive older man with a thick crop of white hair, perhaps in his sixties, stood behind a wide glass-topped desk and extended his hand.

"Hello, Mrs. Bradshaw," he said. "I'm John Tanner."

Oh God, Devin thought, the wrong John Tanner. It was probably a common enough name. But this man was a criminal attorney, and he knew who she was. He probably thought she'd come to see him about representation, and now she was having a case of cold feet. He was probably thinking maybe she did it and she needed a top criminal lawyer. Or maybe she didn't do it but felt she needed protection. Devin stood rooted to the spot, halfway between the door and the man's desk, arguing with herself on the antique Oriental rug.

"Why don't you sit down," he said then, kindly, she thought, "and I'll get you a cup of coffee."

"I . . . I've made a mistake," Devin managed to stammer. She backed her way out the door then and turned and fled from the office suite. Mortified. She rushed blindly to the bank of elevators, her cheeks flaming. She became aware that people were staring, or at least she thought they were staring. Suddenly it seemed to her that the world knew who she was, and everybody in it thought she'd murdered her husband.

She rushed across the crowded lobby and out of the building, and down the wide granite steps toward the parking structure. In her haste, she glanced up for just a moment, then stopped in her tracks. There, on the steps, heading into the building, was Tanner. Her Tanner!

He saw Devin at the same time. Her heart skipped a beat. She had never seen him in anything but exercise gear and sweats. He looked very California-handsome in a dark gray-and-white striped shirt, the top button unbuttoned and his tie loosened, his trim hips in charcoal pants, a suit jacket thrown over his shoulder, a briefcase in his other hand, sandy hair blowing.

"Devin!" he uttered. "What are you doing here?"

"Looking for you!" she blurted out.

"Well, you've found me," he said, and walked the short distance between them. "What on earth is going on?"

"It's come back to me that you've said I was up on Mulholland that day to tell Paul I was leaving him," she sputtered. "Whom did you tell? Sam Bradshaw? I need to know."

"Who . . . ? I never told anyone," he protested. "Not *that* . . . not *anything* about you. I've never even told anybody that I work with you."

"You're a liar," Devin spit out.

Tanner glanced around. People were noticing them. "Look," he said, lowering his voice, "let's go across the street to the coffee shop and talk . . ."

"I don't want to go anywhere with you," she hissed. "I just want to know exactly what you've said about me, and to whom. And I want to know why you would betray me like that!" Her heart was in her throat. She felt totally out of control, foolish.

"Devin, I don't know what you're talking about. I never betrayed your trust—"

Devin turned on her heel and sprinted the rest of the way down the steps. She didn't want to hear it. No one else on earth knew that she went up to Mulholland that

day to tell her husband she was divorcing him, no one. Now
Sam was dishing that incriminating piece of information up
to her. And Tanner was about to hand her some lies. Well,
she wasn't going to listen to them.

Reaching in her purse for her car keys in the underground parking structure, she realized she still had the business card in her hand. She looked at it again. BRIGANT,
HALE, TANNER & LOWE. *John P. Tanner.* The older man in
the office must have been John Tanner Senior, the partner.
And John Tanner Junior was the rat!

52

Billy Hilgarde sat on the low concrete wall bordering the
stairs to PT's side entrance, the same set of steps he
and Scud Joe had watched Paul Bradshaw sprint down on
the day they'd tailed the man on a joyride into the hills. It
was lunchtime. Next to him on top of the wall was a sack
containing two burgers and a Coke from a nearby fast-food
joint. Billy didn't have much of an appetite. He was watching the entrance to the parking lot, waiting to head Devin
off when she came back from lunch. When her black Jaguar
appeared at the big PT gates, Billy hopped off the wall and
stepped over to her parking spot, and when she'd nosed
her car into it, he opened the passenger door and jumped
inside.

"We have to talk," he said in hushed tones, "and I don't
want to talk in your office."

"What's up, Billy?" she asked. She looked agitated too,
Billy noticed.

"The cops grilled me again," he said, "and this time they
didn't wait till I got to work. They hauled me out of bed
at six in the morning," he said tersely.

"And . . . ?"

"And among other things, they pumped me about you."

"I'm not surprised," Devin said. "And you told them I

was up on Mulholland where Paul went over the cliff, right?"

"Nope," Billy said. "They told me."

"They told you?"

"They told me," he repeated.

Devin hugged herself, as if warding off a chill. "Tell me this," she said, leveling her gaze into his brown eyes. "Did you say I went up there to tell Paul I was going to divorce him?"

"No, I didn't," he said. "But they told me that, too."

"They told you *that*?" she asked incredulously. "This morning?"

"Yes. The cops asked me if I was aware that you were about to leave your husband. Asked if you'd ever mentioned that to me."

"And what did you tell them?"

"I said no, of course. You've never said anything to me about a divorce."

Devin didn't respond. She turned her head away from Billy and stared out the window. The two sat in the front seat of Devin's Jaguar and said nothing for an uncomfortable minute, until Billy broke the silence with another bombshell.

"Devin, listen to me. These guys are convinced that one of us did him. Me or you."

Devin sat alone in her office with the door closed, trying to think things through. It was just a matter of time before the detectives would come back to her, interrogate her again, she knew. Billy Hilgarde had shaken her badly. Before he'd let himself out of her car, he said something that chilled her to the core. He told her that he was looking over his shoulder, day and night. That he was afraid. He said that was the biggest reason why he'd agreed to take the new job, to change his daily routine. And why he was relieved that he'd be going out of town a lot.

Then he told her about Scud Joe Jones. How Joe was the guy who was with him that day, and how Joe was scraped up off the sidewalk in South-Central. It was the week after Paul's funeral, Billy said. He was driving down Pico Boulevard to meet his friend for dinner at Maurice's. Joe was just getting there, and Billy saw it happen. A drive-by shooting. A drive-by killing. And his instinct was not to

get involved, Billy said. Something told him to just keep
on going.

Billy told Devin that with Joe it could be anyone in the
'hood out to do him, even a brother Crip dog who was
stoned. But it also could be someone connected to Paul
Bradshaw's death who somehow knew that Joe was up
there, figured Joe saw something, knew Joe was a loose
cannon, and wanted to shut him up. And if the shooter
knew that Joe was at the scene, then he knew that Billy
was up there too. And maybe intended to shut him up,
too. So he was wary and watchful, he said. Looking over
his shoulder.

"And that same pair of eyes might have seen you up
there, too," Billy told her. "So you better be careful too,
Devin—because those eyes just might be watching *you*."

53

"I have to go with the divorce angle," Maxi Poole was
insisting to Ruby Johnson.

"You really shouldn't without talking to Mrs. Bradshaw
first."

"Well, as you know, I'd love to talk to her," the reporter
rejoined with not a little exasperation in her tone. "But the
woman won't talk!"

Maxi was on deadline and running late. Story of her life,
she sighed to herself. She'd had a tip from one of her
LAPD sources that Devin Bradshaw had been with the
victim just minutes before his murder, at the murder scene,
telling him she wanted a divorce. This looked incriminating,
and Maxi wasn't surprised that the widow Bradshaw
wouldn't comment.

In fact, the crime scene was looking like Grand Central
Station, so the newsroom jokes went, with not only Billy
Hilgarde and his pal in hot pursuit, but any number of
family members possibly having traversed the deadly spot
to get to lunch at the senior Mrs. Bradshaw's house.

If Maxi's source was correct, she wanted something, even a "no comment," on camera. Just a shot of Devin Bradshaw's face would tell volumes about the woman's state of mind. Even if she didn't say a word, Maxi knew that it would make good television, and making good television was her job.

Maxi had prevailed upon Ruby to ask her boss to give her a statement. She'd made it clear that she intended to lead tonight's newscast with the newly surfaced information. The public would hear it and make judgments, Maxi told Ruby, and if the woman was innocent, she should tell her side.

But the door to the suite discreetly marked DEVIN BRADSHAW remained closed, and Ruby had just relayed the message to Maxi that Mrs. Bradshaw wouldn't see her. She was like Jackie O., Maxi thought ruefully, who in a lifetime of accusations leveled at herself and her famous family never once deigned to dignify those accusations with comment. Very classy, to be sure, but a dead end for journalists. Give me the Donald Trumps, the Ivanas of the world, Maxi thought, people who loved publicity and courted the press. Viewers might get tired of hearing what they had to say, but at least they said it. And said it, and said it. But this woman, Devin Yorke Bradshaw, said nothing.

Well, that wasn't exactly true. She had talked to Maxi a few times, when Maxi specifically asked about questionable practices she'd uncovered at PT. And inevitably Maxi would learn later that the labor irregularities they'd discussed had been stopped. Maxi decided that Devin Bradshaw might really be on the level, might really intend reform at the Pulled Together plant, and she was using the reporter to get that message across in the press. That was the only explanation Maxi could fathom as to why Devin allowed her and her crew, and no other media, into the PT building. But that was fine; it was a two-way street. The Paul Bradshaw murder case was a glitzy news story, played up on all the talk shows as well as legitimate news outlets. Reporters from everywhere were dogging the principals, showing up at doorsteps with relay trucks and camera crews, trying to land interviews, get information or confirmation, or shots of the key figures coming and going. But because of the access Devin gave her, it was Maxi Poole from Channel Six in Los Angeles who had the inside track, who was the reporter with a leg up, as they say, on the Bradshaw murder story.

The detectives were talking to everyone who'd surrounded Paul Bradshaw, even his sainted mother. They were leaking selective bits of information to different people to see what would bounce back, and many of those leaks and responses found their way to Maxi. And her reporter's instinct told her that the widow Bradshaw had something to hide.

Devin had locked the doors of her office. She knew that Maxi Poole and her news crew were in the building again, probably right outside her door. When she had learned that the high-profile reporter intended to investigate worker abuse at the PT factory, Devin had opened the doors to her, promising to correct any ills the woman could find. Now, with the focus shifting from the aborted workplace fraud to the murder investigation, and with Devin being pulled into its vortex, for her to bar Maxi Poole from the building would look suspicious. So Devin had made an exception for the aggressive Channel Six reporter. She had decided not to stop her from coming and going at will, but she made it a point to stay clear of her. Now she was actually holed up and hiding.

Devin dropped her head into her hands. She was scared. When the rioting had broken out in South-Central Los Angeles and had spread west across Hollywood to the edge of Beverly Hills, Southland citizens bought guns in great numbers. That's when her husband had acquired the pair of .38's, along with permits to keep them. Although Devin had gone along with Paul, had taken the classes with him, she'd never been totally committed to the concept of protecting herself with a gun. Until now. Checking the Rolodex on her desk, she picked up the phone and punched in the number for attorney Irving Chapman. He was in his office.

"How are you, Devin?"

"Fine, Irv. I need your help with something."

"Sure," he said. "Can you tell me over the phone, or do you want to come in? Or I'll come to you."

"No, we can talk about it now," she said. "Remember those two handguns that Paul bought last summer?"

"Yes, two Smith & Wessons," Irv affirmed.

"Right," she said. "Can you have the permit for Paul's weapon put in my name?"

"Yes, of course," he said. "And what about the other one?"

"The other one seems to have vanished," she told him.

"Vanished?"

"Yes. I know that Paul brought it down here to the South-Central plant after the riots, but I've never found it."

"We'll have to report that," Irv told her.

"The police already know. They came looking for it."

"That's not good enough, Devin," he advised. "We have to file a formal report that the handgun registered in your name was lost or stolen. I'll look for the paperwork on those guns and have a statement drawn up, and you can sign it."

"And you'll have the other one put in my name?"

"I'll have Paul's gun reregistered in your name, yes," he assured her.

Devin closed her eyes and breathed deeply. She couldn't shake the fear—of the authorities bearing down on her, and also of the *unknown eyes* that Billy Hilgarde felt were lurking out there.

"Irv," she said in a small voice, "I think I need to carry the gun around with me."

"For God's sake, why?" he demanded.

"Because I work in South-Central L.A., the most volatile part of the city, maybe the country—"

"Absolutely not, Devin," he broke in.

"Irv," she reminded him, "you know that Paul and I took regular target practice. I know how to handle a gun."

"Devin, it's against the law," the lawyer said. "Unless you're in law enforcement, there's no way that you, me, or anybody else can get a permit to carry a concealed weapon in the city of Los Angeles."

Devin dropped the subject. She made arrangements with Irv to sign the missing gun report and said good-bye. She knew that Marva Modine carried a small gun in her model's tote. She'd first caught a glimpse of it the day they'd lunched at Café Maxx, when Marva was rummaging in her bag for her wallet. At the time, Devin had put it down to the stunning model's penchant to shock. But now she thought about that gun. It was an antique-looking thing, but Marva had assured her sotto voce that it was in perfect

working order, it was loaded, and she knew how to use it.
Marva told her she carried the gun to protect herself from
the crazies she seemed to attract. That without it she felt
naked, vulnerable. And now that Devin was driving to
South-Central every day, Marva contended, she ought to
carry a gun for protection too.

Devin knew that more and more people were arming
themselves in this increasingly dangerous city. Especially
women. She had asked Marva if she was carrying that gun
legally. Marva had laughed her throaty laugh. "Who the
hell cares?" she'd shrugged. "Better to shoot first and
worry about not having a permit later. At least I'd still be
alive to pay the damn fine!"

54

It was the Ides of February—the thirteenth day of the
second month in the ancient Roman calendar. And a
rare, crystal-clear Saturday afternoon in twentieth-century
Los Angeles. A day he'd been looking forward to with both
anticipation and dread. For Paul Nathan Bradshaw Junior
it was graduation day—the first day of the rest of his life.

The lone graduate, clean-shaven and almost painfully
thin in white T-shirt and jeans, sat behind a screen at the
far end of the center's recreation room, watching as guests
came through the doors and settled on the metal folding
chairs grouped around the perimeter. He could see them,
but he couldn't yet be seen. It was a surreal experience for
Pauly, scanning the faces of family and friends, seeing each
person from a distance and yet, perhaps for the first time
in years, very clearly.

His eyes settled lovingly on his mother, his intervener.
Rosemary looked happy, relaxed—beautiful, in fact. He
knew that on this day she was finally proud of her youngest
son. Certainly she'd saved his life by nailing him the way
she did, and he admired her courage. They'd never talked
about it, but he knew that she was the one who'd planted

that bag of rocks in his jacket pocket. Initially, in his drugged-out haze, he'd wanted to murder her for having him slammed into this place. But he had come to realize, after hundreds of hours of therapy, that *he* was the hurtful one, *he* was the jerk, *he* was the screwup who was damaging himself and others with his substance-abuse reaction to whatever ills, real or imagined, he felt had been done to him by the rest of the world.

His brother and two sisters were out there. Over the last several weeks he'd talked to each of them more often than he had over the past decade. And he could see Myles Bradshaw, the cousin he hardly knew, the quiet one, sitting by himself toward the back of the room. On the opposite side was his cousin Allena, who'd rerouted herself from Lisbon a day early to be here. And Uncle Sam and Aunt Lizbeth, with his grandmother between them. Pauly was deeply touched that the doughty Regina Bradshaw had come all the way downtown for him. His stepmother was out there, too, beautiful Devin, whom he'd only lately come to know. What a bunch, he thought, a group of people wildly discordant among themselves, but all united on this day in their support for him. The Bradshaws might not much like each other, he mused, but they sure did stick together, and he was grateful for that. Never before had he needed his family as much as he did today.

There had been times over the last two months when he thought he'd never reach this day. Somehow he'd made it through the agonizing first week of rehab, the gut-wrenching detox period, the pure physical hell of endless days and nights of drug withdrawal when he feared he was going to die, wished he would die. After he'd started intense therapy, his counselors encouraged him. They told him they were sure he was going to make it. They suggested that he had taken to the grueling drug rehabilitation program with the same fight and dedication with which his father had been known to tackle business. So he *was* success-oriented after all, they told him.

Seeing the bulk of the formidable Bradshaw clan out there now, Pauly remembered the day a month ago when he'd first reached out, called each in turn from the pay phone at the center. It was at that point in classic rehab where the addict's assignment is to call the people he'd hurt the most and tell them flat out what an asshole he'd

been. Of course he called Rosemary first. He'd told his
mother, then and many times since, that without her he'd
be dead, that simple.

Next came thoughts of his father. He was able to see
some of the good as well as the bad in his father now,
which was another first for him. Now, too late, Pauly knew
that in spite of everything, in his own way he had loved his
dad, and he regretted that he'd never get the chance to tell
him that. So he'd picked up the phone and called his father's house, he wasn't even sure why. When Devin answered and surprised him by being warm, friendly, and
responsive, he found himself spilling out his feelings about
his father to her. Oddly, they were simpatico. Devin began
dropping by to visit with Pauly at County-USC Medical
Center, which was east of downtown Los Angeles and close
to the PT plant. They talked candidly about Paul Senior.
And she'd told Pauly that just as she was part of his therapy, so, too, he had become part of hers.

The recreation room was nearly filled now, and Pauly
was watching for his cue from Doctor Taggert to come out
and take the seat reserved for him. During the fifteen minutes he'd sat behind the screen, studying, one by one, the
main players in his life, he'd gone through the gamut of
human emotions. He had made it through a tunnel from
the farthest reaches of a bottomless pit to arrive here today,
and the tunnel was like a mile-long, rusted-out, ragged
length of six-inch pipe through which he'd been stuffed and
shoved and dragged, body and soul, whipped, bruised and
bleeding, until light-years later he'd come limping out the
other end. Now these people here today, most of whom
he'd so badly let down in the past, were offering their hands
to help him up and onward.

His eyes kept circling back to Devin. She sat alone, apart
from the rest of the family, tall and regal and coolly stunning in a soft cream-colored cashmere sheath that clung to
her perfect body. Each time he looked out at Devin, Pauly
again felt the sexual stirrings he couldn't seem to control.
Instead, to his consternation, they had grown in intensity
by great leaps over the past several weeks, and he knew it
was something he was going to have to deal with.

It was not going to be easy. One of the lessons he'd
learned in rehab was to be brutally honest with himself.
And at this point on the long uphill trek to sobriety that

stretched before him, he was painfully aware that there was nothing he desired more than to put his hands squarely on Devin's hips, to draw her to him, to put his tongue in her mouth, to take her to bed, kiss her passionately, and drive his cock deep, deep inside her.

His therapist had told him not to worry about it too much right now. It was a sign that he was coming back to health, back to life, she said. He hadn't cared about sex in years—only his next fix and where it was coming from. His therapist said that once he got back out into the world, clean and sober, he would meet appropriate young women, and his libidinous feelings for Devin Bradshaw, his own stepmother, would vanish.

Dr. Taggert cued him to come into the room now. Rising from his seat, his legs were weak and his heart was pounding wildly. When he emerged from behind the screen, a tenuous smile on his face, the whole room erupted in tremendous applause. Biting his lip to keep from weeping, he made the long walk up the middle of the huge semicircle of friends and family and took his seat.

The graduation rites were bittersweet, both joyous and painful for Pauly. Three of his counselors spoke. Doctor Taggert observed that of the seventeen drug addicts who had started the nine-week rehab program together, only three had made it to the finish line. And one of their group, a teenager from Studio City who'd busted out after less than a week on the grueling program, was dead now, they'd heard. Of a heroin overdose.

Another of the therapists outlined ways in which people who loved Pauly could help him get back on his feet in the real world. Told them that he needed their help. Told them not to lie to him, not to enable him or indulge him in any way. This was not the end of the road to recovery; far from it. Today was just the beginning for Paul Bradshaw Junior, who had a tough, tough road ahead.

When the formal remarks were finished, a symbolic coin was passed around to all in the room who were part of Pauly's life. Each person was asked to hold the coin and speak from the heart about the candidate for sobriety, be it about his past or his future. When Devin held the coin, she told how Pauly was going to come to work at Pulled Together. He would train in the business, starting at the bottom, she said, and she was convinced that he would display the business acumen she was sure he had inherited from his father.

When the coin had gone around to everyone and had come back to Pauly for his turn to speak, he paused, rubbing it between his two hands. There were tears in his eyes. The coin, touched by all who had expressed caring and support for him, was now fraught with symbolism and meaning. He began by promising the group that he would carry that coin with him always.

Closing his hands over it, he outlined his future plans. First, he and his mother would find an apartment for him. He was going to have his teeth fixed, he said, and embark on programs to build up his health, including exercise and proper diet. And he pledged that he would adhere to the requisite "90 in 90"—ninety meetings in the next ninety days, in therapy sessions, AA meetings, Twelve Step groups, and the like. After the ninety days, he explained, he would be allowed to taper off to a schedule that met his needs, according to evaluation by his therapists.

And starting next week, he would begin work at Pulled Together as an apprentice in the accounting department. He and Devin had planned a program for him at PT, he explained, in which he would learn all departments and all facets of his father's business. Rosemary looked over at Devin with new eyes at that, her smile filled with genuine gratitude. Pauly thanked everyone for coming and for caring, and he promised that he would earn the love and support they were showing him.

Paul Nathan Bradshaw Junior was twenty-seven years old. Standing before the people who loved him, holding the symbolic coin on this, his commencement day, he felt as if he had just emerged from the depths of hell and his life was just beginning. His mother would be taking him home tonight to sleep in the room where he'd spent his childhood, and from there he would have to learn all over again how to crawl and walk, then finally fly.

55

It was Sunday, Valentine's Day. Devin closed her eyes for a moment, trying not to let the owner and the two realtors see that she had fallen in love with this house. She'd just stepped through the lovely front courtyard, with its bubbling three-tiered fountain enclosed within sienna-colored walls, all ablaze with luxuriant bougainvillaea. Now she stood in the open living room with its graceful Spanish arches, and although she hadn't seen a square foot of the rest of the house, she already knew. She had known immediately that this was home.

Tucked away in the hills of Bel Air, it was a newly built California Mediterranean, sophisticated, in glorious taste, small, secluded, and, most important, secure. It was hidden behind a pair of sturdy ornate wrought-iron gates, through which only a profusion of exotic plants and trees and colorful flowers could be seen from the street. Being here felt safe.

She toured the rest of the house, moving slowly from room to room, and as she walked through each doorway her heart leaped higher. She loved it, from the modern, fully equipped kitchen to the rich wood-paneled library, the inviting family room with its built-in entertainment center and oversized hearth, and upstairs to the cozy master suite with gleaming hardwood floors, smoky teal green hand-painted cabinets, and wonderful limestone fireplaces, even in the bathroom.

Within the master suite was an enormous room-sized closet and a mirrored gym. And off the mezzanine below, there were three generous guest suites with wide outdoor terraces. She would make one of them her office, and the other two she would reserve for guests—at the moment she couldn't imagine whom, but she'd get there. Outside, the grounds were Shangri-la! A lush paradise surrounding a sparkling black-bottom pool, with decking done in multi shades of terra-cotta slate.

Devin thanked the realtors and said she'd be in touch, she'd be back, even though she knew she didn't have to see the house again. It was as if it had been built with her in mind. She would have Irv Chapman handle the sale. She'd tell him to put the house in a short escrow; she'd move in as soon as the routine tests and inspections were finished. She couldn't wait to get out of the mansion, with all its disturbing memories. This house would symbolize the start of her new life.

She climbed into the Jaguar and turned up her favorite music on the CD player. Driving back home along Sunset Boulevard, she felt a wonderful surge of well-being and hope, rare these days. The Benedict house was still on the market, no solid nibbles yet. It was a tough sell, but that was the estate's problem, not hers. It was listed for sale completely furnished, with all the elegant antiques she had brought in from around the world, the exquisite uphol-stered pieces she'd worked so hard with Bailey to design, the luxurious drapery, tapestries, the paintings worth mil-lions, the avant-garde sculptures, the books, china, crystal, silver—everything. She wanted none of the "things" she'd so zealously devoted most of her time and energy to gather-ing and assembling. Each artifact and piece of furniture represented a period in her life that she wanted to put behind her.

She had already scaled her lifestyle way down. She'd let most of the staff go, including Gussie, the downstairs maid who had so expertly run the kitchens; Andres, her brilliant chef; and Laguya, her sweet second housekeeper—she'd been able to get Laguya a job with a friend of hers. Bruno, her houseman and butler, and even Peggy, her in-home secretary, were gone. She didn't need them anymore. She was left with just Maria, her housekeeper, and José, the gardener who came in daily to tend the grounds.

There were times when Devin wondered how she man-aged to get through these days. The detectives showed up repeatedly—at her home, at the office, once when she was coming out of the beauty salon. She had no idea how they'd known she was there. And they kept asking her the same question over and over. *What exactly happened between you and your husband on Mulholland Drive on the day he was killed?*

And again and again she dished up the same answer, skidding widely around the truth. She repeated how she'd gone up Benedict Canyon to Mulholland Drive to intercept Paul because they had been talking on his car phone and the line went dead. They'd lost the signal in the hills. Paul had been talking about the luncheon at Regina's house, she'd tell the officers, and in the static just before they'd lost contact, Devin thought he was saying that she didn't have to go, but she had to be sure.

And no, she told the police repeatedly, she did not go up there to tell Paul she wanted a divorce. Whoever told them that was lying. She hoped they didn't notice her cheeks coloring when she said that, but, she reasoned, no one actually heard what she did or didn't say to her husband on that nightmarish day.

The detectives let her know that her whole rap rang phony with them. "You would do that in one of the worst rainstorms in L.A. history?" one or the other would ask incredulously. They'd give her long, sideways looks, but she never flinched. That was her story, and she was sticking to it.

The job of running the galloping Pulled Together division was nearly overwhelming, with all her reorganizing, massive policy changes, the overhaul of product design, manufacture and shipping, and the complete renovation of the plant. And she still wasn't sure what to do about Alex. The woman was maddeningly inconsistent, unpredictable. One minute Devin wanted to toss her bodily out of the building, and the next, she'd do something bordering on brilliant to expedite their work.

On top of it all, the expensive PT advertising shoots were going full tilt. They were in their second week, and everything that could go wrong had already gone wrong, as was almost always the case with photo shoots, in Devin's experience. And these daily extravaganzas were no mere photo shoots, they were *Gone With the Wind*! Devin managed to get out to the location for at least a few hours every day. And surprisingly, Marva Modine continued to make an effort to get close to her. When Devin was on the set, Marva would join her for lunch, or gravitate to her when the crew was on a break. And Devin didn't discourage her. She found she really enjoyed the woman's company. Marva was charming, friendly, helpful, always entertaining, and outrageously funny. She was fresh air. Marva cheered her up, and God knows she needed that.

Back at the plant, Marva had taken to dropping by to see Devin, often bringing her thoughtful little gifts. The new *teint peche* bronzing blush that Chanel had just come out with, a great pair of earrings she'd picked up on Montana Avenue, or a bottle of new Beaujolais she wanted her to try. After they'd exchanged home phone numbers, Marva would often call in the evenings just to chat. She would ask how she could help with the shoots or with anything at all, since Devin was doing about six full-time jobs getting the division launched under her tenure.

It was during these chats that Marva had started confiding in Devin. Telling her about her recent devastating breakup with her longtime lover. And that she was laughing on the outside—that was her nature and even her job—but really she was hurting. Devin would listen, and she felt for the woman, but she couldn't bring herself to reciprocate; she could not confide in Marva. God, she felt really alone.

Still, she enjoyed Marva enormously. She found herself looking forward to seeing her, hearing from her. Marva had become a sunny diversion from Devin's very real problems. And for all the luscious model's drop-dead gorgeous looks—the long lean body, the tawny complexion, the marvelous mess of tousled streaked-blond hair, the tiger green eyes, the package that made men of all ages want to kill for her—Devin could see that beneath the surface glitz, Marva was a very vulnerable young woman.

Also, contrary to the young model's fiercely independent persona, she seemed overly eager to please. At least eager to please *Devin*. Marva actually got flustered at times, even blushed in her presence. Devin was beginning to think that—*Marva Modine seemed to have some kind of a crush on her!*

56

Maxi Poole looked up through the glass wall of her office to see the lanky frame of Martin Berman, the Channel Six news director, approaching her door. He poked his dark, unruly head inside.

"What time are you shooting today's piece at Pulled Together?" he asked.

"I'm meeting my crew at two," Maxi returned. "Why?"

"Because I'd like to be there."

Maxi flashed him a mischievous smile. "What on earth for?"

"Because it's one of the biggest stories in the country. Don't you think it's a good idea for me to be there?"

Protesting too much, Maxi thought. Of course it wasn't a good idea for him to be there. He was beyond busy running a major news operation with a staff of hundreds, putting six hours of news on the air live, seven days a week. His presence was certainly not needed on any news shoot. But he wasn't fooling Maxi at all.

"Martin, wouldn't it be a lot easier if you just picked up the phone and invited her to lunch?" she grinned.

At that, Berman opened the door the rest of the way and came inside. Scooting a pile of books and papers to one side, he dropped onto her faded blue couch.

"I did," he said then, crossing his long legs, tenting his hands in front of him, signaling that he wanted to talk about it.

"And?"

"And she turned me down."

"What was her excuse?"

"Busy," Martin said.

"So ask her again."

"I did," he replied, grim-faced. Maxi suppressed a smile. The man was taking this very seriously.

"No luck?"

"No luck. But I doubt that luck had anything to do with it," he said, a scowl darkening his features.

Maxi shrugged. She didn't have a lot of time to devote to the issue of her bachelor boss's latest attraction. In the short time he'd been in the Los Angeles market, the good-looking Berman had been seen around town with several hot L.A. ladies. And unlike cold, windy Chicago, La-La Land certainly had a lot of hot women.

Still, Martin looked altogether serious about this. Maxi watched as he ran his fingers through his overgrown mass of thick, curly hair. No news director in the business ever seemed to have time to get a haircut, Maxi knew. He must really be smitten with Alexandra Anson if he was willing to drive all the way down to South-Central on the off chance that he'd run into the lady at the PT plant.

Martin had first seen Alex Anson on tape in Maxi's coverage of the complex story that had begun with a rumor of workplace abuse and had escalated to murder. Oddly, Martin had seemed fixated by the woman. He'd made a habit of dropping by the edit room, asking Maxi how the story was going, lingering a bit too long. And after one too many questions about Paul Bradshaw's widow's personal assistant, it hadn't come as a big surprise the day he'd mentioned, with studied nonchalance, that he would be riding with the crew on a shoot that morning at the PT factory. And while they shot an interview with Ruby Johnson, Martin had waited in the executive reception area, also no surprise. And he'd achieved his objective; he'd met Alex Anson, had a cup of coffee with her, chatted with her a bit. And apparently, since he was fretting about her now, he still hadn't been able to get the lady off his mind.

"Doesn't it bother you that she's a suspect?" Maxi threw out now.

"Oh, come on, Maxi," Martin protested.

"Come on, nothing! You know that our sources say the victim fired her the night before he was murdered, and a guard heard her threaten him—"

"She has an alibi," Martin broke in.

"That she was having lunch at the Bistro Gardens? With Bradshaw's ex-wife? People at the restaurant say the two of them all of a sudden bolted out of there—*before* they got around to lunch. They had plenty of time, and you know it!"

Maxi was baiting him, she knew. The women had told police that Alex had a migraine headache that was worsening, so the first Mrs. Bradshaw drove her home and stayed with her awhile. The two were each other's alibi. But even if Alexandra Anson wasn't a murderess, from everything Maxi had heard about the woman from her coworkers, the feisty Irish beauty had a reputation for being an unequivocal bitch. Maxi hated to see her new boss, whom she'd come to have great affection for, waste any of his precious little time, or worse, his emotional energy, on a woman people described as some sort of rancorous piranha.

"You *do* know she was Paul Bradshaw's mistress, don't you?" she lobbed another ball at Berman.

"Oh yes, you remind our viewers of that every single time you mention her," he half sneered.

"For years!"

"Uh-huh-I'm surprised you don't chyron her with VIC-TIM'S MISTRESS in six-inch letters, instead of BRADSHAW'S ASSISTANT."

"Oh, great idea," Maxi grinned. "It has a cachet—"

"You're impossible!" Martin stopped her, getting up to leave. On his way out the door, he threw back over his shoulder, "I'll see you at the shoot."

"Perfect," Maxi sighed to his retreating back. "You can hold my clipboard."

57

Marva Modine and Devin Bradshaw—fashionable Westsiders raised eyebrows upon seeing the two women together so frequently lately, not on the habitual circuit of in-crowd parties, art openings, or charity bashes, but usually in a secluded corner at an offbeat restaurant, talking quietly, definitely in a world of their own. Seemingly two polarized sides of the same person. The good twin and the evil twin. Both of them tall, both blond, both impossibly thin, both tanned, toned, and tawny, both strikingly beautiful, both oozing sexuality and sensuality. They were a pair of wealthy, self-assured, powerful women, very good at what they did, extremely successful, hot personalities sought after in any social mix. But opposites.

Devin, the older, the elegant, the sophisticate. A paradigm of the conservative Pasadena socialite, in designer clothes worn with carelessly devastating chic, in perfectly understated makeup and short, sleek, shiny hair that fell naturally back into place after every saucy toss of the head. The ice queen with the imperious, autocratic demeanor. Without having to say a word, she gave a man the impression that if he was really good, really special, and if he was really lucky, he just might be the one for whom she'd tear off her expensive, well-cut couture clothes and take on the sexual romp of his life.

Marva, the younger, the trendsetter, off the wall, outrageous in hip-length skirts, thigh-high boots, sheer silks and rough leathers, diamonds and torn jeans. And always the dazzling cleavage, dramatic eye makeup, and the lion's mane of wild, unruly multi-colored, spun-gold hair. One major hot babe who gave a man the impression that she was hopping in and out of bed with everyone on the planet except him, poor sucker.

Marva and Devin. Ms. Sizzling Hot and Ms. Icy Cool. Together they turned every head when they walked into a room, and made men want to leave their wives and children for them.

Devin sank back into the pillows on her king-sized bed and thought about the two of them. They had got to giggling tonight at Spago, after they'd both had one martini too many. Which, of course, was one martini. Neither could much tolerate hard liquor, because except for an occasional glass of wine, they rarely drank at all. Devin had to preserve her faculties, and Marva had to preserve her face. But tonight they'd been caught up in the usual gaiety at Wolfgang Puck's celebrated Sunset Boulevard eatery, a premier gathering place for L.A.'s rich and famous, and they'd talked each other into having a martini.

Wolf, who'd made Spago world-famous by the sheer magnetism of his whimsical personality and love of fun, had personally brought a very special bottle of Petrovskaya to their table. This was without question the smoothest, the subtlest, the most superb vodka made, he told them. We can't buy it in the United States, he said, only in Europe, but we can bring it in. And Wolfgang did, he laughed, every chance he got. After allowing the two women to examine the ornate label, he ceremoniously poured for each of them a double shot, or maybe it was a triple, over crushed ice, into which he stirred no vermouth, just a swizzle stick that speared two giant pimento-stuffed olives. Then he stepped back, raised his own glass, and toasted them in his marvelous Austrian-accented English: "To the two most beautiful women in my place!"

And that was saying a lot. Cher was at the next table with her bagel-boy boyfriend, Rob Camiletti. In a far corner sat blond, leggy supermodel Linda Evangelista, who was dining with actor Kyle MacLachlan. Adorable Winona Ryder was with a group of raucous young people, celebrating somebody's birthday. And in the middle of the main room, as conspicuous as possible, was Heidi Fleiss, known to the rich and hip of La-La Land as the youngest, trendiest, hottest Beverly Hills madam, with a half-dozen young women who looked like scrubbed, wholesome, captivating coeds, obviously "Heidi's Girls."

Spago was always a circus, more European than American, more left bank than right, a nightspot where anything goes as long as it's chic, where if you weren't somebody you probably couldn't get a table. Nor would you want one, because you'd feel dreadfully out of place.

Marva and Devin fit right in at Spago, and they'd really had a good time tonight, loosened up by Wolf's special vodka. They'd got a little silly, but at Spago nobody took special notice. At Spago you could walk in naked and hand-painted from head to toe. People would probably think you were just Demi Moore doing another *Vanity Fair* cover, and let you enjoy your dinner.

Devin reached over to the night table, switched off the bedside lamp, and snuggled contentedly into the luxurious satin sheets. She wondered for a second if Sam was also going to sell her Porthault sheets along with the house. Oh, who cares, she chuckled, she'd buy more. It had been great fun to let her hair down a little tonight, to get her mind off the police, the murder investigation, Tanner's betrayal, her dreary brother-in-law and his irksome family, business pressures, her lonely life, her uncertain future. Marva was a tonic, and Devin was hooked.

There had been something different going on with Marva and Devin tonight. Or maybe it was just something that Devin hadn't noticed before. Or hadn't allowed herself to notice. A wisp of sexual tension between the two women, fragile but palpable. Marva had even teased about it, treating it like a joke, but Devin knew she was kidding on the square. Knew that if she'd encouraged her one little bit, Marva might have put her hands on her in the libertine atmosphere of midnight at Spago Devin smiled as she thought about Marva unconsciously flirting with everyone in the place, including the corpulent Marvin Davis, including the ebullient Wolfgang Puck, including her.

And no, Devin admitted to herself in the still of her bedroom suite, dark now except for the scented Rigaud candle flickering on the side table, tonight was not the first time. Her mind drifted back to the week before, one late afternoon at the end of the workday, after Alex had left. Devin was sitting at her desk looking over some late orders when Marva bopped into her office, in jeans and a sheer cream-colored Armani silk shirt, unbuttoned almost to the waist. She was braless, and as she perched on a chair in front of Devin and animatedly related an amusing incident that had happened at the location that day, a pert, rosebud nipple would occasionally escape for just seconds, until Marva would reach up and make a reflexive little tug at her shirt, covering herself again, all the while continuing her narrative. And all the while knowing exactly what she was doing, Devin was sure.

Stretching languorously in the cushy down featherbed now, still feeling a little tipsy from the vodka, Devin allowed herself to think about that afternoon. And tonight. Marva the flirtatious vixen, outrageously flirting with *her!* She supposed that all women have fantasized at some time or another about caressing and being caressed by another woman. A beautiful woman with a beautiful body. Especially when there happened to be no man in her life. She'd asked herself a time or two if that was normal and had no answer, but she didn't spend a lot of time dwelling on it. There were too many other pressing concerns on her mind of late, and Marva Modine, a nationally known, much more beautiful version of the flagrant Madonna, was one of the few fun, pleasant, and exciting things in her life right now.

Devin closed her eyes. Gently, slowly pulling her white silk nightshirt up over her hips, she thought about Marva. Fantasizing about that naked rosebud breast peeking out behind sheer, creamy silk, she slipped her hand between her legs. She was dripping wet with desire.

58

Alex stood behind Devin, looking over her shoulder at the thick sheaf of order sheets fanned out on the worktable in the outer office. Devin was about to review a large order for the new PT summer line, written by the central office of the Federal Group. Since its recent series of mergers, Federal had become the largest chain of retail stores in the country.

"Looks like a terrific order!" Devin said, riffling through the dozens of sheets.

"It's the biggest they've ever written with L.A. Garb," Alex confirmed.

"Thank you, Federal," Devin breathed. "This is definitely going to help."

Idly, she reached for a packet of fabric swatches on the table, squares of imported sand-washed silk in each of the colors PT's most popular summer group would be cut in. She fingered the silky snippets of fabric in black, white, and several pretty, bright citrus colors. Pretty except for the bottom one. Puce!

Devin shook her head as her eyes lingered on the muddy-colored swatch. Puce was a particularly ugly shade of dirty brownish purple, with threads of a green-tinged mustard color running through it. The reason she was shaking her head was because she saw that it was the very first color designated on the Federal order.

"Awful, isn't it?" she murmured absentmindedly, looking back again at the top order sheet.

"Ugh!" Alex confirmed. "I can't believe Federal is buying any pieces at all in that color. What woman in her right mind would wear it?"

"Hard to say," Devin responded. "We put out samples in it because for some strange reason it actually tested well with a couple of focus groups."

"I still never thought anybody would order it, did you?" Alex asked her.

"Somebody's bound to write it; there's no accounting for taste, God knows. But I agree, it's ghastly," Devin said, holding the offending swatch against her wrist. "It makes your skin look sallow."

"Well, they'll be marking it down at the Federal stores, but who are we to argue with the customer?" Alex shrugged.

"You said it, the customer is definitely right," Devin laughed. "Especially a colossal customer like this one. So let's get the goods made."

"Absolutely," Alex said. She left Devin to check the order sheets and made her way back to her desk, where a mountain of work awaited her.

Alex sat at her computer terminal, flexed her fingers, and sighed. Her job at PT had become a juggling act. She found herself constantly putting on an amenable face for Devin, all the while looking for ways to stab her in the back. That put her out there on very thin ice, skating full speed ahead with her eyes on her backside. She had to be efficient and helpful enough so that she wouldn't get fired, yet always on the lookout for ways to sabotage the operation that would reflect badly on Devin

Like the day the power went out in the factory during the Claremont quake. Rufus Greene, the plant manager, immediately called upstairs to ask for an okay to fire up the generators. Alex told him to hold off, she'd check it out. Then she said nothing at all to Devin. And just as she'd suspected, Devin wasn't aware that the plant had backup generators. Before she found out, Devin had shut down work and sent everybody home, and they'd lost almost a full production day. Because of that, PT didn't make its delivery date on a big order from the May Company. And the problem compounded itself. The next time the May Company buyers ordered, they wrote with short pencils. They couldn't afford to be low on inventory, and they no longer completely trusted the young Pulled Together line to come through with the goods.

And the time when Robert Winters, the head of transportation at PT, rushed into Alex's office with a big grin on his face and blurted out that he had to get home right away, his wife had gone into labor. Alex looked up at him and told him flat out that he couldn't leave the plant if he wanted to keep his job, that was Mrs. Bradshaw's policy. Young Winters was stunned at first, then his eyes hardened.

"My wife is having a baby," he'd said. "Our first."

"It's up to you," Alex had returned, just as hard.

"I'm gone," Winters threw at her then, turning on his heel. He never came back. And Devin never found out the real reason why a very valuable employee had quit in a huff and gone to work for Caribou Sportswear three days later.

Sometimes the subversion backfired, and Alex knew she'd come close to getting nailed more than once. She was traversing a precarious tightrope at the PT factory, and she hoped she wouldn't be left out there twisting for too much longer.

Then there were her weekly reports to Sam at headquarters, where he expected her to come up with even more ways to topple her boss without tipping their hand. It was all very tricky, and dangerous as well. But Alex was clear on her agenda. She would continue to discredit Devin in ways large and small, in hopes that the cumulative effect would result in the widow Bradshaw's eventual dismissal. The whole process was no mean feat, because in single-handedly taking on the challenge of turning Pulled Together around, Alex had to admit, if only to herself, that the woman had been doing a masterful job.

Sam wouldn't, or couldn't, simply let Devin go. Although he'd stopped short of explaining why, he'd made that very clear to Alex. Devin was in the job on a trial basis, he'd said, and the board would have to vote her out if she was seen to have made too many costly or embarrassing mistakes. There were three things the board would not countenance, Sam had told her: incompetence, bad press, or ongoing losses on the ledgers, and not necessarily in that order. With all her fancy innovations, Devin had been spending money by the carloads, and so far PT wasn't making up the outflow with compensating new business. In fact, Pulled Together was deeper in the red than it was before

Devin had taken over. With the innovations she'd effected, that was to be expected, but if the cash-flow picture didn't turn around soon, Sam said, the board would be taking a good, hard look at the mistress at the helm. And he continued to assure Alexandra that she was next in line for the presidency of the division.

On top of everything else, Sam made it patently obvious that he wanted her in bed. His clumsy grabs and passes were escalating, and Alex had all she could do to keep from openly cringing. So far she'd managed to keep him at arm's length, at the end of which she held out a fistful of promises. Tacit promises that when she got hers, he'd get his. She shuddered to think about how she'd have to handle it when he came through for her. But she would not let it stop her from going for the gold. Do in Devin, then do Sam, maybe a few times if she had to.

Devin came by and dropped the Federal order on her desk. "It looks good," she said. "In fact, it looks great!"

"Shall I process it?" Alex asked.

"Yes, put it in work," Devin fairly sang, and she disappeared through her office door.

Alex glanced at the order. It represented hundreds of thousands of dollars, and much more in repeat business if the stores did well with the summer line. She glanced through several pages, scanning the numbers, and suddenly her face lit up. She saw a massive mistake that Devin had apparently overlooked. She smiled broadly. Time to make hay. Or more precisely, time to make hell for the boss lady again. And this one would be costly. It would be embarrassing. It just could be the straw that did milady in!

On the multipage computer printout order sheet there were small squares for the customer to fill in item, quantity, style, size, color, and price. Each differential was represented by a number. The color puce was number 09. The first item Federal buyers ordered was a blouse, 650 in quantity, varying in sizes, one style, 09, or puce, in color, listed at $39.75. The next item was pants, 300 in quantity, varying in sizes, and the color space was blank, which meant it was to be repeated, the same as above, because it would be sold as a group. So, more puce.

The glaring error was that none of the other tiny color squares were filled in with numbers. It was an obvious oversight by the Federal order desk. Devin had understandably concentrated on the quantity and the dollars, and evidently hadn't noticed. That meant, if left as is, every single garment in the huge Federal order would be cut in ... the color *puce!*

Alex could save the day. She could bring it to Devin's attention, whereupon the pages would be faxed back to Federal's central buying office and the color squares filled in. Or she could let it go through and say that she never bothered to look at the order, she just sent it down to production, because Devin had okayed it.

The ramifications were delicious. PT would cut thousands and thousands of garments in puce. Federal would not accept the huge shipment, of course. They would say it was such an obvious error that PT should certainly have caught it. PT would have to eat the goods, because the company would need to try to keep such an important client happy. And it wouldn't even be able to dump the stuff at outlet houses in San Pedro for a dollar apiece. Even they couldn't sell tons of puce shit, Alex chuckled.

Worse, hundreds of Federal stores across the country would not get the PT inventory they'd ordered, advertised, and counted on for a huge chunk of their summer selling. They'd have empty racks. Pulled Together was still new. Still trying to prove itself. Once burned, the giant Federal chain could not be counted on to come back to the well.

Alex thought about it for just a few seconds, a wicked smile lurking behind her dark Irish eyes. Then she sprang out of her chair, snapped up the Federal sheets, and headed down to production to send the order through.

59

"Mrs. Jackson, we've checked with the police, we've checked with the hospitals, all we can do now is wait," Sam Bradshaw repeated, trying to soothe the quietly distraught woman seated in his office.

Nobody knew where Julius was. Late that afternoon, the

chauffeur had driven Sam over to the Sports Connection in Santa Monica to take a steam. Fitting himself into his dead brother's life, Sam was now using Paul's membership at the health club. Julius was to go back to the factory and wait for a call to pick him up, Sam said, but he'd never returned to L.A. Garb. He and the limousine had been missing for several hours. It was dark now, nearly eight o'clock, and Essie Jackson was alarmed. It was not at all like Julius to go off somewhere without calling.

"Mrs. Jackson," Sam said to her now, "it makes no sense for you to wait here. Julius will come in to drop the limo off, then he'll take his own car and go home. I'm sure he'll be back soon, with an explanation. Probably the damn car broke down—"

"He hasn't answered the car phone all night," Essie broke in.

"Well, if the car's not functioning, the phone won't ring," Sam reasoned.

"Julius would have called," the woman returned.

"Not if he got stuck out in an area where there aren't any phones . . ."

"What area, Mr. Bradshaw?" Essie Jackson demanded. "You said yourself you didn't send him anyplace."

"No, but someone else might have called and sent him on an errand—I'm not as rigid as my brother was about the car. If it's needed elsewhere and I'm not using it—"

"But don't they tell you?" she asked incredulously.

"Well, I was in the steam room at the gym . . ."

"Miss Landers says she wasn't told Julius was sent anywhere," Essie said with finality.

Sam sighed. He wanted to go home. Lizbeth had two couples they were friendly with from the Bel Air Country Club coming to dinner tonight, and he was already a half hour late.

"Mrs. Jackson, I want you to go home, and I'm going to ask Geneen to follow you and stay with you for a while. She'll help you make calls to anywhere you think Julius could possibly have gone. And I'm sure he'll walk in on you in the process. Will you do that?"

Essie Jackson hesitated. Sam called out to Geneen, who was still at her desk in the outer office, waiting with her boss until the problem was resolved. She appeared in the doorway and looked kindly at Mrs. Jackson.

"How can I help?" she asked. The presence of another woman seemed to topple the petite black woman's wall of control. Tears welled up in her eyes.

"Somethin' terrible's happened to my Julius, I feel it!"

Geneen sat on the couch and put her arm around the woman. Essie dropped her head in her hands, and her shoulders started to shake. She was weeping. For a moment Sam was in awe. He had no idea what it was like to love your partner as much as this very proud woman obviously loved her husband of more than forty years.

Sam was finishing dinner with Lizbeth and their guests when the call came in. Julius had been found in a deserted back alley in a run-down section of South-Central Los Angeles, slumped over the wheel of the L.A. Garb limousine, dead. Shot in the head. His wallet and gold watch had been stolen, and the several bottles of liquor in the ice chest of the car's passenger section had been lifted as well.

Sam went back into his dining room, looking solemn. He told Lizbeth and their guests that Julius Jackson, the company's longtime chauffeur, had just been found robbed and murdered near the Pulled Together plant in South-Central. Devin must have called him down there, he observed. Detectives were on their way here, he said, to take his statement. Then he excused himself and went into his den and closed the door. And sat down to think about the situation.

The only thing Sam had left inside the secret compartment, the space that Julius had said with pride that Paul called his "Julius" file, was an illegal gun and a small box of bullets. The gun had belonged to Paul, some ancient service revolver that his brother had brought home from the Korean conflict as a kid. Sam remembered the gun; Paul had been very proud of it when he'd returned home a war hero. As far as California state gun control was concerned, that unregistered pistol didn't exist. But Paul, who was a crack shot, had evidently kept it in perfect working order, loaded, and inside the "Julius" file cabinet. "Just in case," Julius said he'd told him.

Sam had forgotten about that gun years ago, until Julius opened the hidden cabinet for him, and along with the rest of the assorted stuff in the secret file, there it was. He removed all of the documents from the file, but he'd left the gun and the ammo in there. Why not? Still "just in case," he'd reasoned. As far as he knew at the time, only two people besides himself knew about that gun, his brother Paul and Julius, and Paul was dead.

Now they were both dead.

60

It was a little before noon on the last Wednesday in February. Warm, sunny, clear blue skies with big puffy clouds presaged an early Los Angeles spring. Alex sat at her desk at the PT plant, absorbed in some advertising copy that Devin had asked her to look over, when she was interrupted by a short knock at the door. She looked up to see it slowly open and a man poke his head inside.

Removing her glasses, Alex had to think for a moment, then she remembered. It was that news executive from Channel Six who'd been here a couple of times with Maxi Poole. He'd called and asked her to lunch, twice. And she'd turned him down, twice. He was smiling at her now as he came inside.

"Hello, Alex," he said. "You have to have lunch with me today. I'm here, and I won't take no for an answer." Martin Berman, that was his name. He stood squarely in front of her desk, a huge grin lighting up his face.

Alex studied him for a minute without responding. Pretty confident, she thought. Or was it cocky? Very attractive, though. About six foot four and in great shape. Good-looking. Intelligent face. Needs a haircut. Backwater tweedy in a black fleck Polo jacket with patches at the elbows, white windowpane-check chambray shirt unbuttoned at the neck, loosely knotted black knit tie from Calvin Klein's summer silk collection. Basic charcoal corduroy pants. Classic black, soft leather penny loafers. Alex wondered if women who were not in the garment business scrutinized men's clothes. Probably not. In any case, she wasn't interested in him. Or in any man.

"I can't go to lunch," she offered finally, not returning his smile. "Too busy."

Undeterred, Berman said, "Well, you have to eat, don't you?"

"I'm having lunch at my desk today," she returned, giving him a curt smile of dismissal before dropping her eyes back down to the copy in her hand.

"What time?" he asked.

"Wh ... what?" she responded, looking up at him again, her expressive Celtic face registering some surprise that he still stood there.

"What time will you be having lunch at your desk?"

"I don't know," she said, a hint of annoyance flickering in her eyes now.

"What time do you think?" Berman persisted.

"Twelve-thirty, one o'clock," she blurted, with just a bit more irritation.

"Great, don't order anything in," he told her. "I'll be back with lunch. We'll eat at your desk."

He was out the door before she could protest. Harmless, she decided, shaking her head. Persistent, certainly. Intriguing, even. Any woman would enjoy that kind of flattery, she supposed. Maxi Poole had introduced him as head of the news department at Channel Six. He seemed to vibrate with energy. Jewish. Thick mop of curly hair. Good clothes. Great body. She wondered if he really would come back. But no, she was definitely not interested. Besides, he probably just wanted to pick her brains for information about the murder case.

He strode back into her office at twelve forty-five, loaded down with bags and boxes. This time she did smile. He looked like an indulgent uncle at Christmas.

"That's lunch?" she asked.

"This is lunch."

"How many are you feeding?"

"Just us. Unless you'd like to invite somebody else," he submitted.

"No ..."

"Good," he said.

"Well, we can eat over here," Alex acquiesced, indicating the worktable at the far end of the office. It was littered with papers, swatches, pens and pencils, sketch pads, pots of India ink and brushes, piles of fashion magazines, boxes

of buttons, bolts of fabric, and more. Alex walked over to
the table and began to clear a space.

"Nope," he said, "we're eating at your desk. Like you
said. Like you would if I weren't here."

He carefully picked up a few items on her desk and
placed them to one side. Then he took a small, red-and-
white checkered tablecloth out of one of his bags and
smoothed it out across the desktop. And proceeded to lay
upon it a veritable feast. Two kinds of pâté, a plain goose
liver and a fancy one with truffles and brandy, and a ba-
guette of crunchy French bread. Sophisticated. A delicate,
fresh-tossed spinach, endive, and walnut salad, which he
spooned onto two white ceramic salad plates. Luscious.
Reaching into another of the bags, he came up with a bottle
of chilled California Chardonnay, a corkscrew, and two
gleaming wineglasses. And stainless-steel cutlery. No plastic! Where the hell did he get this stuff in less than an
hour in funky South-Central Los Angeles? He had to be
enormously resourceful. For dessert, he put out a plump
bunch of green grapes, strawberries, small nectarines, and
some fresh-baked chocolate-chip cookies.

Berman pulled out two white cloth napkins then and
placed one on her side of the desk. Next came a beeswax
candle, which he worked into the end of an empty wooden
thread bobbin that he'd picked up off the worktable. Inven-
tive, she noted. He set the bobbin upright on the desk and
lit the candle with a flourish, then pulled up a chair and
sat down opposite her. The whole business took him about
three minutes. Alex was totally charmed. Who wouldn't
be? she asked herself. She spread the napkin on her lap
and broke off a piece of the French bread, while he poured
the wine.

It was the most delicious lunch she'd had in years—since
the cursed day that Paul Bradshaw had met Devin Yorke.

61

Devin sat next to Essie on the worn flower-print couch in the Jackson living room, sipping tea. The tiny room was crowded with family and friends. Essie's three married children were there, along with their spouses and all seven grandchildren. And Essie's best friend, Ella Snow, a rotund, chocolate-skinned woman with short-cropped salt-and-pepper hair, sitting on a wooden folding chair that was much too small for her ample girth, venting loud intermittent sobs. Jim, the family's old cocker spaniel, lay at Essie's feet looking sad, as he always did when Julius wasn't there. Devin smiled and kept a conversation going, but her heart was breaking for the frail proud black woman who had buried her husband this morning.

The funeral service was held at the First Baptist Church in Culver City. Rosemary Bradshaw, who'd ridden with, known, and loved Julius for more than two decades, delivered a warm and moving eulogy, telling how Julius had been like a second father to her children, ferrying them to swimming lessons, to Little League practice, birthday parties, the orthodontist, and all the while soothing, comforting, admonishing them, giving them advice, even bandaging skinned knees when Rosemary wasn't there.

Essie's cousin Marta Rae sang "Amazing Grace." And hundreds of people from the company filled the church. Some of the blacks who worked at the PT plant were friends and neighbors of the Jacksons, and most of the employees at headquarters knew Julius, had chatted with him daily when going through the lobby. Julius had been a long-time fixture at L.A. Garb.

After the service, the minister announced that there would be a reception at the home of the deceased, and he carefully read the address and gave directions. Devin had known that the employees would have to get back to work. And that Sam wouldn't be bothered going to Julius Jackson's little house in lower-middle-class, mostly black Baldwin Hills. Rosemary was there, of course, but Essie had to be hurt that after all her husband's years of loyal service, the sole representatives from the company who came to her house to lend comfort and support on the day he was buried were herself and Billy Hilgarde.

When the two were about to leave, Essie asked Devin to wait just a minute, she had something for her. Standing with Billy in the small entryway, Devin watched as Julius's widow removed a key from the pocket of her black rayon suit jacket and opened up the front of an old oak rolltop desk in the corner of the modest living room. Essie came back into the entry carrying a large accordion-file container that appeared to be stuffed to overflowing with papers.

"Take this, Mrs. Bradshaw," she said, handing the bundle to Devin. "It belongs to you."

"What is it?" Devin asked the woman, baffled.

"I don't know," Essie said. "It's something Julius kept that has to do with the company, he told me, but he wouldn't say what."

Devin looked at the bulging container. "Shouldn't you look through it?" she asked. "Make sure it isn't something Julius wanted you to have?"

"I'm sure it isn't," Essie Jackson returned. "Julius was mum about it; said it didn't concern me none, it was important stuff belonged to Mr. Paul."

"Then maybe Sam Bradshaw should have it—"

"Julius didn't like that man," Essie broke in emphatically, shaking her head.

"But Sam is the head of the company and the executor of Paul's estate," Devin demurred.

"No, I don't think my Julius wants me to give him anything," Essie insisted. "If you think this business concerns Mr. Sam Bradshaw, then fine, you go ahead and give it to him."

"But why are you giving it to me, Essie?" Devin asked, not wanting to be in possession of Julius's papers if it were in any way inappropriate.

"Because Julius loved Mr. Paul," she said simply, "and you're his missus."

Rumbling east across town on Slauson Avenue toward the Pulled Together factory in South-Central Los Angeles,

Devin sat quietly in the passenger seat of Billy Hilgarde's
Trans Am, holding on her lap the tightly tied package of
documents that Essie Jackson had given her. She and Billy
had driven together to the early morning church service for
Julius and on to the funeral at Holy Cross Cemetery in
Culver City, then back to the Jackson house for the sad
reception.

"Maybe we should stop for lunch, Billy," Devin said,
breaking her contemplative silence.

"Are you hungry?"

"Not really, but I don't feel like going back to work right
away. Aren't you depressed?"

"More than depressed," Billy murmured. "This whole
thing stinks."

"What do you mean?"

"I'm not sure what I mean ... I keep going over and
over it in my mind. Where do you want to eat?"

"Is there anything decent between here and the plant?"
Devin asked dubiously, looking out the windows at the
bleak topography of battered storefronts, laundromats, gas
stations, and fast-food joints along this seedy stretch of
South Los Angeles.

Billy looked over at her and smiled. "Oh yeah," he said.
"Oh yeah! I'll take you for the greatest soul food you ever
ate in your life!"

"I'm not sure I ever ate *any* soul food in my life," Devin
laughed, enjoying his enthusiasm.

"Then it's way past about time," Billy said, hanging a
left on Fairfax Avenue. "We're going to Maurice's Snack
'n Chat."

"For soul food," Devin confirmed.

"For Maurice's famous soul food and *chat!"* Billy said.
Sobering then, he added, " 'Cuz I'd really like to chat about
how come Julius Jackson all of a sudden gets himself killed
in a part of town he's not even supposed to be in, and it
happens to be down here in our backyard."

Billy was right. The food was delicious. He'd ordered for
both of them, pan-fried chicken with honey, and creamy
mashed potatoes. To hell with the calories, forget the fat
grams, Devin decided. This was comfort food, and she
needed some comfort.

"Terrific lunch," she said to Billy, actually licking her fingers.

"It is. But I brought you here for another reason besides the food," he told her.

"Probably not the atmosphere," she smiled, glancing around at the sparse, down-home furnishings.

"No, not the atmosphere. Did you know that this is where my friend Joe Jones was killed?"

"He was killed *here*?"

"Right out front, on the sidewalk," Billy confirmed, cocking his head toward the entrance. "They wrote it off as a drive-by, but like I told you, I had my doubts. Now, with Julius hit, I got bigger doubts."

"Hit? What do you think happened to Julius?"

"I think it was not the routine South-Central robbery they're saying it was, that's what I think."

"Who's *they*?"

"The cops. That's what they're saying on the news."

"But you don't buy it?"

"I don't buy it. You knew Julius, I knew Julius. Would he go anywhere in that car except on legitimate business?"

"Of course not. Unless he was having something fixed . . ."

"Doesn't Bradshaw Automotive service the limo, along with all the company vehicles?"

"Yes, and the shop is in Santa Monica."

"And if he had personal business, there's no way Julius Jackson was dumb enough to take that glitzy silver bullet down to South-Central. He'd have driven his own wheels."

"That's one of the reasons I never call for the limousine down here—too dangerous," Devin offered.

"So, nobody at PT called, and nobody at the Santa Monica plant sent him over to PT for anything. And we agree that Julius would not go down to gangland in that high-profile car unless he had an assignment. So why was Julius in South-Central?"

"You're saying someone must have called for him? Someone had to assign him there?"

"Absolutely. Looks to me like he was set up."

"But why?"

"I think because Julius knew something," Billy responded. "Something that could incriminate whoever killed your husband."

"What could Julius possibly have known? Then again,"

she amended thoughtfully, "Julius was closer to Paul than anybody. Closer even than me, in some ways."

"So here's what I'm getting at," Billy went on, looking hard at Devin. "Where the hit on Scud Joe could have been unrelated to Bradshaw's murder, the hit on Julius makes that look less likely."

"Because they both knew something?"

"Because the killer *thought* that. Maybe thought Joe saw something. Maybe had reason to believe Julius knew something."

"And the killer might think you or I saw something up there too," Devin said quietly, following his logic.

"That's assuming *you're* not the killer," Billy remarked then, only half smiling.

"And assuming *you're* not," Devin shot right back.

"We're testy," Billy said, signaling for the check. "But you're right, Julius was my pal. If I really needed him to come down to the factory for some reason, I could have called for him."

"And you're right too—certainly I could have summoned the limo," Devin said.

"And it ended up on *our* turf! Not in Santa Monica, not in Beverly Hills, not downtown. In South-Central. About six blocks from PT."

"Not a coincidence?"

"Hell, no," Billy said. "If at some point it stops looking like a robbery to the cops, and it starts looking like a hit to shut Julius up, then it's gonna look like someone at PT did him, don't you see?"

The two were quiet for a few moments, each thinking the situation through. Billy broke the silence. "Who else could order the car?" he asked.

"Well, Sam, of course," Devin responded. "Or Geneen, or Alex."

"Or any executive or department head, right?" Billy added. "Or anyone who made it sound like some kind of emergency ..."

"Okay, if you're right, who's doing it, Billy?" Devin asked, her eyes locking on to his. "If somebody has killed three people, who is it?"

"I don't know," he said, "but believe me, like I told you before, I'm looking over my shoulder every minute. And so should you. For that pair of eyes we talked about, Devin, remember?"

"I remember."

"I think the person behind that pair of eyes silenced Julius and silenced Joe Jones," Billy said evenly, "and isn't done yet."

62

Marva had the cabbie drive her right inside the gates at the Pulled Together parking lot, where the guards were expecting her at the side entrance to the building. It was a little after seven in the evening, the factory was closed, and Marva did not want to be alone on the dark street for even a couple of minutes in that dangerous neighborhood. She'd come to the plant to meet Devin, who was working late. They had reservations for dinner at eight at Rex, a tony restaurant ten minutes to the north in downtown Los Angeles. Marva had taken a cab to PT so they could drive there together in Devin's car. It was not a good idea for a woman to drive alone in South-Central after dark.

Marva didn't dress for Rex, she'd dressed for Marva, totally original as usual. Torn stonewashed hip-hugger jeans sashed with a gold solid-link Gucci belt. A sexy see-through loose-patchwork-knit sweater that stopped three inches above the waist, exposing her long smooth golden midriff. Black leather lace-up high-heeled boots that added another four inches to her already impressive height. Her mane of tussled blond hair was loosely pushed up under an L.A. Dodgers baseball cap thrown on backwards. She looked exquisitely tossed together and absolutely stunning. Marva Modine was an L.A. celebrity who could go anywhere at all dressed anyway her whim dictated, and without trying, she managed to make other women in the room feel that *they* were the ones who were dressed all wrong.

She burst into Devin's office with a noisy whoop that

made the other woman smile. The overhead lights were off; Devin was sitting in shadows behind her desk with just a high-powered halogen spot illuminating the work she was studying.

"Sexy lighting!" Marva said, coming into the room.

"I'm giving my eyes a rest," Devin told her. "It's been a day from hell."

Marva had insisted on taking Devin to dinner tonight because her friend was down, saddened by the funeral of the company's longtime chauffeur this morning. Marva was determined to cheer her up. She scooted behind the desk and gave her an affectionate hug, then shrieked when she saw what Devin was working on.

"Whoa!" she gasped. "When did these come in?"

"Today," Devin returned, smiling now. "And they are really fabulous!"

Spread out haphazardly across the top of Devin's desk were dozens of eight-by-ten prints from the first two PT fashion shoots. Marva dove into the pile of pictures, pushing them around on the desktop. Each of the black-and-white photos showed the three models in strikingly erotic poses.

"My God, these are wild!" Marva howled.

"Fantastic, aren't they?" Devin beamed.

There were several different shots of Billy Hilgarde, Vanna Brylock, and Marva all crowded together on the back of the muscular white stallion on Malibu beach. Vanna sat in front and Billy brought up the rear, both of them dressed stylishly in Pulled Together casual chic. And Marva was jammed in the middle, between the two—stark naked! At least she looked naked. She'd been wearing a nude body stocking during the shoot, but in the finished pictures all traces of it had been airbrushed out.

Another sequence of shots showed the beautiful three-some sitting on the jagged rocks above the beach, entwined in different highly suggestive poses, Marva again looking as if she were totally nude, while the massive white horse stood down on the sand nearby, untethered, watching them.

"I hope we don't all get arrested when these ads hit the streets," Devin laughed.

"I'm the one who's gonna get arrested!" Marva wailed. "I'm the one who has no clothes on!"

"It seems to me that pseudo-au-naturel pose was your idea," Devin pitched at her mischievously.

"I was hoping you'd forgotten that," Marva chuckled. "Oh well, will you testify at my trial that I was actually wearing something?"

"Oh, they won't believe me," Devin smiled, studying the brilliantly retouched photos. "But I'll bring you a cake in prison. What do you want baked inside of it?"

"Umm ... a huge bottle of Sebastian creme rinse. They probably don't issue that in county jail."

The two women laughed and shuffled through the pictures for a few minutes, then Devin got up and put her hands on Marva's shoulders and eased her down into the chair behind the desk.

"You look these over," she told her, "while I do one last thing. I have to run down to the showroom and check out the new sample groups that go out in the morning. Then we'll go to dinner."

"Okay. God, these are fun," Marva laughed, enthusiastically digging through the shots.

"Enjoy," Devin said, turning toward the door. "Pick out some of the ones you like best. I'll be back in ten, twenty minutes, depending on what state the samples are in."

"Wait, wait, wait!" Marva shrieked, pulling out an outrageous shot of her and Vanna astride the magnificent white Andalusian stallion. Billy Hilgarde, in a loose collarless white shirt, white cotton pants, and barefoot, was walking ahead along the edge of the surf, leading the horse by a pair of silver-studded reins. Both the women were dressed in PT's sheer-silk summer citrus group. Vanna was in front, and Marva sat close behind, and it looked as if Marva had both her hands up under Vanna's silk shirt and squarely on the beautiful black woman's breasts. She didn't, but the way the picture was shot, it *looked* as if she did.

"Bitchin'!" Marva screamed, throwing her head back in howls of laughter.

"God, that's sexy," Devin rejoined, bending over Marva to study the shot more closely. "Do we *dare* use that one?"

Suddenly, Marva put her two hands on Devin's waist and pulled her down onto her lap. Devin shouted with laughter at the horseplay, and Marva held her down, saying, "Yes, you're going to use it ... yes, you're going to use it ... chicken time if you don't use it!"

Marva raised her hands a bit up over Devin's waist. "See, here's the way we took the picture," she told Devin, remaining perfectly still for a few seconds, her hands just lightly touching the undersides of Devin's breasts. She was amazed that Devin didn't move, didn't leap out of her lap.

"But here's how the picture *looks*," Marva said then, a catch in her throat. Gently and sensuously she moved her hands up over Devin's small, firm breasts. She felt Devin's nipples harden through her delicate cashmere sweater. Marva let out a soft moan, then tenderly stroked Devin's nipples between her thumbs and forefingers.

"Oh God," Devin whispered, moving Marva's hands away. "I can't, Marva," she said. "It just isn't me."

Devin quickly moved off Marva's lap and hurried out the door.

63

"I've rented an Eddie Murphy movie," Billy Hilgarde said to Vanna, waving a tape of *Harlem Nights*. "Want to watch it with me tonight?"

"I don't know, Billy," Vanna said doubtfully. "I'm really tired. I thought I'd get to bed early with my new Sue Grafton novel."

Billy Hilgarde was spending all his evenings with one woman lately, but it was not a "date" thing, it was a "friend" thing. He had long been close with Vanna Brylock, who'd been one of PT's in-house models, and who was working with him now on the Pulled Together ad campaign.

Vanna was hip to the whole police buzz and gang buzz that had been swirling around Billy's head since the day he'd had that portentous fight with Paul Bradshaw, and like most people at the company, she knew that Billy was a prime suspect in the man's murder. After Scud Joe was killed, Billy had confided to her that he was scared. He didn't go anywhere that he didn't have to—he mostly just stayed home at night, he told her. That's why Vanna would insist from time to time that he come over to her house after work, so she could feed him and cheer him up.

Then, after Julius Jackson was murdered last week, Billy told her he was convinced it was no accident. He had the feeling there was a killer out there, and he was on his list. Or hers. He'd had a second dead bolt installed on the door of his South-Central apartment, he'd told her. That's when Vanna suggested that he stay overnight at her house for a while, until the case was solved.

Vanna owned a small tastefully decorated home in Encino in the San Fernando Valley, twenty miles away from his flat in South-Central. The arrangement was working out well for both of them. Over the past several days, Billy had become a kind of temporary member of the family, like a visiting brother from out of town. He slept on the comfortable corduroy-covered couch in the family room, and he used the little guest bathroom off the entry hall.

Vanna had a child, an adorable three-year-old named Tiffany, who loved her mom, loved her puppy, and loved life. And she was now crazy about Billy, who had a dozen ways to make her giggle. It was the closest thing to paternal he'd ever felt, and he actually found himself enjoying it. His kid fix, he called it. He was in no hurry to have any of his own.

"Okay, it's me and Eddie Murphy," Billy said to Vanna now, sitting at the table in her cheery kitchen.

"You'll make a lovely couple," Vanna laughed.

"I'm gonna turn in soon, too," he smiled back. "We've got an early call at Raging Waters tomorrow and it's an hour drive. Are you ready to go down the jaws-of-death water slide in nothing but your PT cotton-knit sling bikini, model number 602?" he grinned.

"No way I'm going down that thing," Vanna protested. "You'll go down the monster slide, and Marva and I will watch for you adoringly at the bottom!"

Billy laughed. "Well, don't be surprised if they make me take both you women down the slide on my lap." The PT shoots were explicitly outrageous, on the edge. They seemed to be going well, Billy felt, and he had to admit that they were fun.

"Ugh!" Vanna shrugged. "Maybe I'd better fall into bed as soon as I put Tiffany down. I'm going to need my rest."

"What about dinner? Want me to run out and get some barbecue?"

"No barbecue, Billy!" Vanna scolded. "I stopped at the market on the way home, and I'm doing fresh grilled vegetables. Lovely zucchini, green and yellow peppers, mushrooms and tomatoes, with brown rice. You're welcome to join us."

"You're going to keep me healthy," Billy groaned.

"I'm going to keep Tiffany and me healthy," Vanna told him, "and if I can teach you some good habits in the process, I'll get points in heaven."

Billy knew Vanna wasn't kidding. She was so unlike most of the women he'd known. Vanna was wholesome, hardworking, and had a strong set of values and a definite bent toward the spiritual. And she was interesting. He saw Proust and Kierkegaard on her bookshelves, as well as the latest mystery novels, which she would pull out of her model's tote when they had a break on the set.

Vanna was also a devoted mother. Tiffany's father, a musician, had been killed in a freeway accident before Tiffany was born. Vanna talked lovingly about him to Tiffany when the little girl asked questions about her daddy.

There was something else about Vanna. Now that he was seeing her in the evenings, without makeup, her long dark hair falling loosely around her shoulders while she went about feeding the dog, scrubbing vegetables, cooking, fussing over Tiffany, or relaxing in sweatshirt and jeans, Vanna Brylock was the most naturally beautiful woman Billy had ever seen in his life. Of course that shouldn't be any big surprise. Vanna made her living at being beautiful. But Vanna had a quality of beauty that went much deeper than her fabulous face and model's body.

"I'm gonna go buddy up with Tif," Billy said. "Maybe she'll watch the movie with me."

"She's not a big Eddie Murphy fan," Vanna laughed. "Maybe if you watch *A Hundred and One Dalmatians . . .*"

"She's seen it five times since I've been here!" Billy protested.

"Probably twenty-five times in all," Vanna chuckled. "It's her favorite right now."

"I gotta have a talk with her about those damn dogs," Billy smiled, and he got up and went into the family room. He pushed a Miles Davis CD into the system and got down on the Oriental rug, where Tiffany was busy coloring. Without stopping, she moved her little body and her coloring book closer to him.

"Excellent horse," Billy observed after a bit, as Tiffany continued coloring the animal a bright purple, using bold strokes that veered way out of the lines.

"My pony," Tiffany corrected, with a broad, dimpled grin for Billy.

"Of course, your pony," Billy confirmed. "What's his name?"

"Umm ... I don't know," Tiffany pronounced thoughtfully. "Do you know his name?"

"I think so," Billy said. "I think his name is Meatloaf."

"Yes," Tiffany giggled. "His name is Meatloaf!"

After the three had dinner, Vanna went upstairs to bathe Tiffany and put her to bed, while Billy popped in the Eddie Murphy movie and sat back to relax. He stayed with it for about a half hour. The film was disappointing, and he was about to hang it up and turn in himself when Vanna came into the family room to say good night.

"Do you have enough blankets?" she asked him. "It's chilly tonight. It's supposed to rain."

"Plenty of blankets," Billy smiled. "You're spoiling me, Vanna, I'm never gonna go home."

"Yes, you are," she said. She knew that Billy was living for the day when the Paul Bradshaw case was solved and the madness was over. Vanna sat down on the couch beside him and looked up at the oversized television monitor.

"You didn't tell me Richard Pryor was in this," she said. "I love Richard Pryor!" The two sat quietly and watched the movie for a few minutes.

"Pretty bad, isn't it?" Billy commented finally.

"It's just as well," Vanna said. "I really want to get to bed early."

"Don't you ever go out on dates?" Billy asked her then.

"Not a lot," she said. "I'm too busy, and dating is very time-consuming."

"You never talk about the men in your life."

"Funny you mention that," Vanna said, a dreamy look coming into her eyes. "I just met a man who is *very* interesting."

"Oh yeah? Who?"

"He's a new pediatrician at Tiffany's well-baby clinic," she told him. "Really nice, and incredibly good-looking ..."

"Who says he's really nice?" Billy asked. "What do you know about the guy?"

"Nothing, really, but I'd *like* to get to know him," she said with a twinkle.

"How do you know he isn't married?"

"Well, he doesn't wear a wedding ring, and he acted very interested. I get the feeling that if I encourage him he'll ask me out. Tiffany has her regular checkup on Friday, and I've been thinking about moving on him a little."

"You mean you're just gonna flirt with him ... ?"

"Yes, Billy. You're a big boy. You know how that girl-boy thing works," she laughed.

Billy knew how it worked. He knew all the moves, and they had always been easy for him. He'd had probably hundreds of women in his lifetime. Of course, he'd been so busy trying to survive and strive all his life that he'd never sought out a woman for a real relationship, just basically for sex. There had always been plenty of those, and there had always been plenty of that. But he couldn't see Vanna in that role. He knew her well enough to know that she wasn't interested in casual sex with guys. Vanna Brylock was a *serious-relationship* kind of woman. Something Billy had consciously avoided all of his adult life.

With Vanna, Billy treasured their friendship. She was black, she understood a lot, and she was a pal. Working with him on a regular basis, they were thrown into sexy situations daily, up close and personal, but to both of them it was business.

He'd discovered that hanging out in the evenings with Vanna and bubbly little Tiffany was comfortable. That had come as something of a surprise to Billy Hilgarde, who'd been basically a loner since he'd left home. At first, staying at Vanna's house was simply expedient, but now he found himself looking forward to their homey evenings. Vanna was there, but unlike most of the women he'd brought home to his bachelor apartment from time to time, she didn't hang on him. She didn't need him. She cooked, and when he wanted to join the little family for dinner, he was invited, and when he didn't, that was fine with her. It was different, refreshing, spending time with a woman friend who wasn't a lover.

Tiffany's nanny was a robust, no-nonsense, sixty-something Irishwoman named Bridie who had dyed red hair pulled back into a bun, an outgoing, cheerful demeanor, and ceaseless energy. Bridie came in six days a week and did all the housekeeping for Tiffany's busy working mom, and she stayed late on the occasional nights when Vanna went out. Billy had been staying in the well-run Brylock household as a temporary guest for a week now, and he'd found to his frustration that there was nothing much he could do to help. Bridie even did the gardening, in which she took great pride, and she would not allow him to touch a sprig. And Vanna refused to accept money from him to contribute to the household. "But I owe you," he'd told her. "You don't owe me," Vanna had insisted. "I know you'd help me if I needed it. That's what friends are for."

He watched her now, sitting next to him on the sofa, her bare burnished-brown feet with red-painted toenails resting on the coffee table in front of them, her huge brown eyes idly following the action on the flickering screen.

"Yes, Vanna, I know how the girl-boy thing works," he responded now. "But you have to be careful. There are a lot of men out there who just want to take advantage of you," he said, a frown creasing his wide forehead.

"And what do they want from me?" she chided. "My daddy's oil wells?"

"Does your daddy have oil wells?" Billy asked, raising his eyebrows.

"No," she laughed. "My daddy has a dry-cleaning business in Tarzana. And he and Mom spend all their extra money loading Tiffany up with toys. By the way, they're coming by for brunch on Sunday after church. You'll meet them if you're around."

"Do they know I'm staying here?" he queried, a little nervously.

"Of course they do," she said. "Tiffany told them all about you, and Dad demanded to know what the story was. He's going to be looking you over pretty thoroughly, but don't worry, that's just Daddy. I swore to him that we're just friends, but he's suspicious. I'm his only baby, you know."

"Oh God, what time's brunch?" Billy asked. "I'll go shoot some hoops. Or stop by my place and water the plants."

Vanna laughed and stretched. "You know, I think I'm going to leave you alone with Eddie Murphy and Richard Pryor. I'll bet they both wish they'd never made this stinker," she smiled. "And don't forget, it's your turn to drive tomorrow. What time do we have to leave?"

"I think we should hit the road by seven, just to be safe," he said. "Traffic will be heavy."

"Okay. Sleep well. Sorry you're about a foot longer than my couch," she giggled, then she reached over and planted a quick kiss on Billy's cheek. She smelled like fresh flowers.

Something came over Billy that he later tried to explain to himself and to her. Suddenly he pulled Vanna to him and kissed her. And kissed her. And to his amazement, she didn't pull back. Vanna's response astounded him. If she'd just swatted him off and laughed at him, that would have been the end of it, but she didn't. She parted her lips and hungrily welcomed his probing tongue.

He stood her up and pressed her long, lean, delicious body to his own, running his huge hands up her back and down over her buttocks. Then up under her T-shirt and onto her breasts. She shuddered.

"My God, what's going on?" he murmured against her hair.

"I don't know," she whispered. "We're lonely . . . ?"

"Maybe we're horny," he whispered back, leading her toward her bedroom. She didn't resist. Suddenly he picked her up and carried her, almost running with her.

"Billy Hilgarde, you are mad!" she giggled, clinging to him.

"Shhhh," he cautioned, "don't wake Tiffany. Or the pooch, or we've really got trouble."

He carried Vanna up the stairs and into her cozy bedroom, backed up to the door to close it, and set her down on the ivory-quilted antique brass bed. Standing, he closed his eyes for a moment and tried to collect his thoughts, think this through, control himself. But he couldn't, and she was no help. He felt her hand on his and opened his eyes, as she gently pulled him down onto the queen-sized bed with her.

Billy put his two immense hands around Vanna's tiny waist, and he marveled at the feel of her. He reached up under her short-cropped T-shirt, and this time he unfastened her bra. And lightly touched her naked breasts. And felt his erection almost hurting. He lowered his hands and slipped her elastic-waisted silk trousers down over her hips. He kissed her smooth stomach, then pushed her pink lace bikini panties down and finished undressing her. And stared down at her for a few moments. He'd seen her nearly naked so many times during the sexy PT shoots, but now he was overwhelmed. She was breathtaking. Something had changed, and it wasn't Vanna, It was him, Billy Hilgarde, wanting this woman right now more than life, but afraid at the same time,

She opened her eyes, sat up, and smiled at him. Moonlight filtered into the room through rose-colored gauzy curtains tied back with Victorian satin ribbons, and Vanna was glowing.

"What's wrong?" she asked quietly.

"It's too right," he said with a catch in his throat, and he felt tears welling up behind his eyes. Vanna reached up and touched his cheeks with both her hands.

"I know," she said. "Let's not analyze it. Because no matter what, Billy, we'll never not be friends."

Billy stood up and fairly jumped out of his shirt, jeans, and underwear. Then he drew Vanna off the bed and pulled back the bedclothes. He lifted her onto the cool creamy sheets and ran his hands ravenously over her body. Then down between her legs.

Vanna arched her body up to meet his probing fingers. She was wet. He put two fingers up inside her and gently stirred until she moaned softly. When he removed his dripping fingers, she opened her eyes. She watched as he put his fingers in his mouth and slowly licked them.

"Delicious," he whispered.

"Come inside me," Vanna begged.

"What about the pediatrician?"

"Who?" she mumbled, as she put both her hands on Billy's throbbing penis.

64

The click of Devin's heels echoed in the stillness as she hurried down the empty halls from her office suite to the PT showroom. It wasn't unusual for her to work into the night; she often did. Still, she'd never quite got used to the chill that seemed to permeate the huge factory after the hundreds of workers had all gone home.

She shivered. Maybe it was because the massive plant was deep in the heart of South-Central Los Angeles, where just outside these walls was arguably the most volatile and dangerous inner-city district in the country. But with more than a dozen armed guards patrolling the building throughout the night, she knew there was no reason why she shouldn't feel safe.

Or maybe it was because Marva had actually made a pass at her. More than a pass. Devin's cheeks were still burning, her heart still racing after Marva had sensuously stroked her breasts. It bothered Devin. It bothered her because she'd liked it. But Devin had never in her life had lesbian leanings. Of course, when you're brought up in Pasadena, you wouldn't, she reasoned.

Still, she had to admit that she had been wildly turned on. Could she be a latent lesbian? Certainly all her relationships with men thus far had been less than successful.

No, she dismissed her own self-doubts, picking up her pace down the dimly lit hallway toward the showroom. She truly loved great sex with wonderful, sexy men, No question that having a *man's* hands on her, in her, was the ultimate turn-on. It was just that she hadn't been to bed with a man in weeks, and she didn't see any great sex, any sex at all, in her immediate future.

She thought about Tanner for a moment, and it hurt. And made her angry all over again. Since the day she'd confronted him at his Century City office he'd called several times, left messages on her answering machine. Saying

she was wrong, asking her to call. And now he *was* leaving
alternate numbers, work and home numbers. She never returned his calls. He'd even shown up, once at the house
and once at the factory, but he couldn't get past either
Maria or Alex. Wouldn't you know, it was the one time
Alex was doing her job, screening visitors. If Tanner had
burst into her office, she might have melted on the carpet.
As it was, she'd wavered a few times, wanted to call him,
wanted so much to see him, but her good sense prevailed.
He could charm her, he'd already proven that. If she gave
in, she'd be back in bed with him; she knew it, she ached
for it. But she also knew that the leaks to police about her
final confrontation with her husband had to originate with
John Tanner. Connecting with him again would not only
be foolish, it could be dangerous.

She forced him out of her mind. You never really knew
someone until you knew them, she told herself, and she'd
never really known John Tanner. So she got burned. Real-
istically, she knew that her husband's murder case was not
going to turn on stories that Tanner might have told out
of school, but she wasn't about to get near him again.

No, Devin thought, she was not a lesbian. But she did
love Marva Modine. She winced when she thought about
how abruptly she had fled from the office. Marva was probably hurt. She would talk to her at dinner. Explain that she
meant what she'd said; it just wasn't for her, but that didn't
mean she'd been repelled by Marva's advances. In fact, she
had to admit that she had been aroused, that she did have
some kind of primal desire for Marva. She knew it was
only natural, she'd tell her—that we're all bisexual to some
degree. Greek and Roman art was filled with women touching, stroking, lying with, loving other women. And because
her life was in such turmoil, because she'd been going
through hell on every level, it was a great temptation to be
soothed, to be loved, even to be sexually fulfilled by Marva
right now, even if just for a little while, if just for a night.
But Devin couldn't dare give in to it, she would tell Marva.
She was afraid it would confuse her even more. She would
make Marva understand.

She smiled at the thought of Marva sitting back at her
desk, whooping her infectious laugh as she rummaged
through scores of what had to be the sexiest fashion photos
ever shot. The erotic scenarios had photographed even

more intriguing, wilder, more dazzling than anyone had hoped. And the edited videotape would be ready to view by the end of the week. This provocative new PT campaign was going to sell a whole lot of clothes, Devin felt sure, and it was going to make instant stars of Marva, beautiful Vanna, and the irrepressible Billy Hilgarde

Devin let herself into the newly remodeled showroom with her master key. She groped for the bank of switches just inside the entry and flicked on all the lights. Thanks to Bailey Senn, the showroom was truly a showplace now, done in gleaming hardwoods mixed with wide expanses of polished limestone in shades of taupe and ivory, providing an elegant but not overpowering backdrop to show off the garments, and posh, comfortable seating for buyers to write the line.

Walking quickly across the floor of the main salon to the far wall where the more than sixty new samples were hanging, Devin breathed a silent prayer that there wouldn't be many mistakes. Or any big ones, at least. PT was expected to put out five major collections a year, plus additional smaller groups each month. There was no time to do any significant alterations; the samples had to get out to the sales force tomorrow, or PT would fall behind the curve in the upcoming selling season.

It was a very long line, a washed-silk midsummer group in muted earth tones—celadon, sapphire, raspberry-and-cream, topaz, cornmeal, wheat, heather, biscuit, pearl. After several groups done in bright primary hues, Devin was going to attempt to educate the PT customer to subtleties of coloration.

She pulled out the samples one by one and gave each number close and careful scrutiny. Ultra perfectionist that she was, her designer's eye occasionally spotted deviations in her specs—a dart put in at a slightly wrong angle, a cuff that should be half an inch wider, a collar that would lay better if it were cut on the bias. These small glitches produced a few sighs, but time was crucial and costs had to be kept in line, so she didn't tag the pieces for changes. She would correct them in production.

There were only two mistakes that she couldn't live with. A long flared jacket that had flat bone buttons instead of the filigreed silvertone buttons she'd called for, and a daytime dress that had a fabric-covered belt instead of the

distressed-chamois leather belt she'd switched to in the final
design check. The metal buttons and the leather belts for
all three dozen groups of samples were in the house, she
knew, so neither change would cost significant time or
money.

Devin tied the two offending garments together with a
heavy elastic band around their hanger tops and carried
them over to the "change" rod. Hastily she scribbled out
a note, "See me about these two pieces ASAP before you
bag samples—DB," and pinned it onto the jacket in front.
When the changes were made on both garments in each of
the collections of samples tomorrow morning, all the sample lines would be bagged and shipped to sales representatives throughout the country.

She rubbed her hands together and took a last look
around before turning off the lights and locking up the
showroom. Not too bad at all, she thought. The samples
looked quite good. Her staff was learning, getting faster
and better with every line.

As Devin made her way back up the long hall, dimly lit
by the plant's reduced night lighting, a sharp, reverberating
crack stopped her in her tracks. My God, she thought, it
sounded like a gunshot. But it couldn't be. A backfire? No,
it had definitely sounded *inside* the building. Coming from
where? she puzzled, cocking her head. Somewhere up
ahead of her in the darkened halls. Perhaps it was just a
clank from the extensive plant heating system, which was
cranked up by day against the early March chill, but was
turned off now during evening hours, the metal pipes
contracting.

She heard noises up ahead then, and froze. Besides the
security guards, there was no one in the mammoth factory
except herself and Marva. Eyes narrowed in the dim light,
her heart leaped as she saw three men materialize out of
the shadows, running from different directions, guns drawn.
Terrified, Devin hurried forward, when suddenly what felt
like a bear of a man bolted up from behind and grabbed
her, restraining her, squeezing the breath out of her, One
black gloved hand tightened around her; in the other, he
was holding a gun.

"Don't move," he breathed in terse tones against her ear.

"Let me go!" Devin shrieked, struggling as the huge man
held her in place, pinning her arms against her sides.

"You have to stay back till we find out what this is about, Mrs, Bradshaw," the man said then. She whipped her head around and saw that he was one of PT's uniformed guards.

Devin began to tremble, dreading the worst now. Down the hall she saw another man run out of an open door that threw light into the darkened corridor. As the man ran toward them, Devin could see that he, too, was one of the factory guards.

"Keep her out of there, Pete," he shouted to his colleague.

"What's happening?" Devin demanded.

"Somebody's been shot!" he said, stopping in front of them and pulling a portable cell phone from one of his pockets. Devin could see that he was dialing 911. Abruptly, she yanked free and ran the thirty yards down the hall to her office suite. Stumbling dizzily through Alexandra's area to the open door of her own office, she stopped short and screamed in horror. Marva was slumped over on the desktop, her mouth open, the baseball cap tipped off her head, her voluminous sun-streaked hair fallen loose over her shoulders in tangles. The jumbled piles of black-and-white fashion photos on the desktop were awash with blood.

Marva's right arm extended out over the surface of the desk, and in her hand was her own small, ebony-handled .22-caliber snub-nosed pistol, the one she had proudly shown off, like a sensuous treasure, so many times to Devin.

65

Phones were jangling. Strobes were flashing. Voices were trumpeting in a discordant clamor. Through the misty yellow haze that swirled around Devin's head, she could see the room teeming with people doing a ballet in slow motion. Men in gray suits, men in yellow rain slickers, rangy men in police blues, young men in sweats and windbreakers, technicians in white lab coats, security guards in

gray-green uniforms with black stripes down the sides of
their pant legs. And there were women in the murky mix,
each of them wearing what women wear. Womenswear—
that was her business. Devin was lightheaded, woozy, drift-
ing in and out of reality. She had heard someone say that
she was probably in shock.

"You say you heard a shot, Mrs. Bradshaw?" a disem-
bodied voice asked her. She recognized it. It was Irish, of
the Irish and the Italian.

"Try to drink some tea," said another voice, one that
threw her into a paroxysm of fear.

She opened her eyes narrowly and peered into the face
of a huge terrifying black man with a grizzled beard, holding a cup of tea in his hand. It was the bear who had
tackled her in the hall. A killer with a teacup. Devin was
in the rabbit hole.

No, she was in her office suite, sitting on a couch in the
anteroom, she realized, opening her eyes a little wider and
straining to focus. Too many people there, too much noise.
She closed her eyes and dropped off the planet again, her
chin falling onto her chest.

"Why did you leave your office, Mrs. Bradshaw?" She
heard the words from what seemed like a million miles
away.

"Leave the office," she murmured, feeling her head bob
from side to side.

"Mrs. Bradshaw, we can't drive you home," the teacup
killer seemed to be whining. "They won't let any of the
guards leave the building. Who do you want to call?"

"Who you gonna call?" Devin slurred, then she chuckled
a little. "Ghostbusters," she said.

"Get one of the paramedics over here."

"They're gone. The deputy coroner has just come in."

"Mrs. Bradshaw, we have to call your family, or a friend.
Who should we call?"

"Call a friend," Devin mumbled, opening her eyes again.

"Who's your friend?"

"Marva's my friend," Devin said to the teacup killer,
though he didn't look so menacing now as her eyes adjusted to the light.

"Where's Marva?" she asked him.

It was as if her question triggered all the sound in the
room to stop, and that's when she remembered. Marva was

dead. Devin looked from face to face at the strangers in the room. Clarity was returning with a wave, and with it came a terrible, terrible pain. Marva! Killed herself? Why? Marva was on top of the world. Then she remembered what had gone on between them. Marva putting her hands on her, Devin wrenching free and fleeing. But suicide? Could Marva really have been that fragile? Devin broke down in tears then, dissolving into great, wracking sobs.

"She's not gonna tell us anything tonight, Dick," she heard the Italian saying to the Irish.

"Yeah, somebody should get her home."

"She can't drive. Who's gonna take her?"

Funny, the two detectives, the men in charge of her husband's murder case, seemed to be the only people in the room she knew. Her new best friends. She wanted to ask them about Marva. What in God's name had happened? But she couldn't. Tears continued to stream down her cheeks, and she couldn't bring herself to speak coherently.

"She has to get home, out of South-Central, and she sure as hell can't drive alone," one of them was saying now. The Italian.

"Yeah, a dish like her in that fancy Jag would be asking for it."

"The cops won't drive her. The guards ain't going nowhere. No cabbie's gonna come down to South-Central. And we can't send her home with just anybody. Maybe we oughta call an ambulance."

"No ambulance," Devin piped up, still weeping, but steadily regaining control.

"Okay," said the Italian. "Who should we call?"

Who could she call? she wondered. No one. There was no one. Not Paul. Not Tanner. No relatives. No close friends, really. Only Marva. But Marva was dead. Alex, her assistant, would love to see Devin dead, she was sure of it. She had never felt so alone in her life. Or so devastated.

"My Rolodex," she said to the detectives. "It's on ... my desk."

Pain stabbed her heart again. She knew Marva was still in the other room, still stretched out across her desk. Devin still held out faint hope that this was all a terrible dream, a nightmare. She watched the Irish lumber off toward her inner office.

"Call Billy Hilgarde," Devin said quietly, when he came

back and handed her the Rolodex. "Hilgarde," she repeated. "His number is in here." Devin was clumsily flip-
ping through the cards.

"Let me help you find it," the Italian said. Furrino.

They called Billy Hilgarde's number in South-Central
Los Angeles, and got his machine. "Hello, I'm not home
now—please leave a message. Beep.

"Try Pauly," Devin said. "Paul Bradshaw, my stepson."

Paul Junior was working at PT now. He was doing well.
He was clean and sober. He and Devin often grabbed lunch
together. They had grown even closer. She could trust
Pauly to get her home.

Furrino dialed, and Devin took the phone. It was after
nine o'clock. He was at home, in his apartment in Venice,
a beach community south of Santa Monica. He was about
a half hour away, he told Devin, but he'd be out the door
in thirty seconds. Don't cry, he told her. He was on his way.

Don't cry, she thought, mopping at the tears. What kind
of a woman was she? She'd come into Paul Bradshaw's life,
and he was dead. She'd never intended it, but nonetheless,
that's what happened. He'd be alive now if he'd never
known Devin, And now Marva was dead. Was Marva's
death her fault? Had she somehow implicitly led her on,
sent her mixed signals? She felt certain that Marva, so full
of lusty life, would be alive tonight if she hadn't been here
at the factory with Devin,

She had never felt such agony, such deep, hopeless de-
spair. Maybe everything was her fault.

66

Billy Hilgarde didn't get the detective's message left on
his answering machine the night before; he'd stayed at
Vanna's house last night and had come directly to work
from there. Vanna had an early call from PT's ad agency
advising that the photo shoot at Raging Waters had been
canceled. It had started to rain during the night, and she

and Billy had assumed the shoot had been postponed because of weather. Billy didn't hear about Marva's suicide until he'd arrived at the factory this morning.

Like everyone else at the plant, he was stunned. And Vanna was inconsolable. The three had become very close. Beyond that, Billy was troubled. It just didn't add up. No way would the Marva Modine he knew kill herself, he was sure of it. Not beautiful, lusty, outrageous, outgoing, fun-loving Marva, Couldn't happen!

Billy had been trying to reach Devin all morning. The buzz at the plant was that Marva had been alone in Devin's office when it happened. That Devin was down in the showroom checking the new samples. Accessing his calls from work, Billy only then found out that the cops had tried to get hold of him last night. They'd wanted him to come down to the factory and drive Devin home. Poor Devin, She'd been through so much, and now this. Billy knew that Devin and Marva had become close friends.

By ten o'clock, Devin still hadn't come in to work. Nor had she checked in, according to Alex. She wasn't picking up her calls at home, either. Who could blame her? Billy thought. But he had to talk to her. So he'd jumped in his car and headed out to Benedict Canyon through the still-congested, late morning rush-hour traffic. Light rain was slowing everyone down. It was almost eleven when he pulled up at the east gate to the Bradshaw mansion and leaned on the bell. After a few moments, a woman s voice crackled over the intercom.

"Who is there, please?"

Billy recognized the genteel voice of Maria Kozma, Devin's European housekeeper. "Maria, it's Billy Hilgarde," he answered. "Is Devin there?"

"I'm sorry, Mr. Hilgarde, but Mrs. Bradshaw is not available," the woman said.

"Maria, please tell her I'm here and I need to see her."

"One moment, please," Maria responded, and he could hear the system click off.

Minutes later, the big iron gates rolled back and Billy drove through. He went up the long curved drive and parked his Trans Am on the courtyard at the mansion's imposing entrance. Maria met him at the front door. Without saying anything, she beckoned him inside.

The big house was strangely still. Maria led him into Paul

Bradshaw's darkened study, and when his eyes adjusted to the gloom, he saw her. Devin, sitting in a corner, huddled in a white terrycloth robe, ashen, red-eyed, her hair disheveled, looking very small curled up in a huge overstuffed chair. When she saw Billy standing in the doorway she let go, started to sob. Quickly, he went into the room, knelt by her chair, and put his arms around her.

"Shhhh ... It's okay, Devin, it's okay," he whispered, holding her quivering body close. She felt frail in his big arms, weak, all semblance of the Devin Bradshaw power disintegrated.

Maria came back into the office with hot tea. Setting a silver tray on the coffee table in front of Devin's chair, she busied herself putting out cups and pouring. Straightening then, she looked sadly at Devin.

"I'm glad you came, Mr. Hilgarde," she said softly.

Billy saw that Maria looked unusually drawn and tired too. He realized that Devin had very probably been up all night, and loyal, caring Maria would have stayed up with her and was feeling helpless that Devin was not to be consoled. He nodded thank you, and Maria left the room.

"We have to talk," he said to Devin then, holding her by the shoulders, looking squarely into her red-rimmed eyes. Billy pulled another chair up very close to hers and sat down.

"Oh God, Billy, you don't know—" Devin began.

"I know one thing," Billy stopped her. "I know that Marva didn't commit suicide."

"But she had her gun in her hand ..."

"I think she was trying to get a shot off at someone else. Someone who had come into your office."

"But the guards said no one had come into the building," Devin protested.

"I think they're wrong," Billy said. "Or maybe it was one of them who shot her. I heard that none of the guards was allowed to leave the building until they were all questioned."

"But why would one of our security guards kill Marva?"

"I don't know. Maybe somebody paid one of them to do it. Money makes people do terrible things."

"But what on earth could Marva have done to make someone want to kill her?" Devin asked, sitting up in her chair.

"Devin, listen to me," Billy said then. "I've given it a lot of thought. Marva would never commit suicide. Someone killed her, I'm sure of it, because that someone thought she was you."

"What?" Devin demanded, incredulous.

"Think about it," Billy insisted. "You work late a lot. Marva was alone in your office after hours. She was sitting at your desk. The two of you look enough alike . . ."

"She had her hair pushed up under a baseball cap," Devin murmured, fingering her own short-cropped blond hair.

"That would make her look all the more like you," Billy interjected. "Were all the lights on in the office?"

"No," Devin said. "Just a floor lamp behind my chair. It's a high-density spot. It was trained on some pictures I had on the desk. Marva was looking at them . . ."

"So she would have been in shadows. Who knew that Marva was going to be in your office last night? In your chair?"

Devin thought for a moment. "No one," she said.

"Don't you see, Devin?" Billy argued. "The killer, that pair of eyes we talked about, mistook Marva for you!"

67

LAPD detectives John Furrino and Richard Ryan were en route to the Benedict Canyon estate of the late Paul Bradshaw, They were going across town to the high-rent district, as Ryan put it, to question the widow Bradshaw, who, as he also put it, was looking to be in deeper doo-doo daily. On the drive from downtown to Beverly Hills, the two compared notes on the case.

They had been called to the Pulled Together factory in South-Central Los Angeles the night before, after the model was reported dead. At first blush they both suspected a connection to the Paul Bradshaw homicide, and neither had entirely bought Devin Bradshaw's "swoon act," as Ryan characterized the boss lady's behavior. Nor had they ever been convinced that she was not the one who shot her old man, then shoved him into eternity.

Now they had some big questions about last night, and they wanted to talk to the lady. Production at the plant had shut down at three-thirty as usual, and the rest of the employees were gone by about six. All factory entrances were routinely locked by security after six, they'd been told, and there was no sign of forced entry through any door or window, According to the chief of security on site, at precisely 7:26 P.M. there wasn't anybody inside the cavernous Pulled Together factory except the guards, Devin Bradshaw, and the dead woman.

A statement from one of the security guards, Peter Tilten, said that he found Mrs. Bradshaw down the hall outside her office after the shot had been fired. But the guards had not come running, of course, until *after* they'd heard the gunshot. According to Art Frankel, owner of the Beverly Hills Gun Club, Devin Bradshaw was a very good shot. So who was to say, Ryan conjectured to his partner, that Mrs. Queen of Cool didn't fire off a round from near the office door, then split down the hall to where Tilten ran into her?

This Marva Modine broad seemed to be a close friend of Mrs. Bradshaw. Several people they'd talked to at the plant this morning confirmed that the two women had been seen together a lot lately, both on the job and socially. Stands to reason the model could know something that the widow Bradshaw didn't want to get out, Ryan mused.

"Could a woman kill her best friend?" Furrino asked idly.

"A woman with ice in her veins could," Ryan replied. "And if she'd killed before, and the friend was a threat, she not only could, she'd have to, wouldn't she?"

"How come she only had one friend anyway, a rich, beautiful woman like that?" Furrino queried.

In the course of their investigation over the past months, they had not been able to unearth one person who claimed to be a close friend of Devin Bradshaw. Except this glitzy model, who seemed to be a rather unlikely candidate for a socialite's best friend and confidante. And now the model was dead.

They had arrived at the Benedict Canyon estate. They

knew the place; they'd been there several times before. Furrino rolled down the window and pressed the bell.

"Hello, who is there, please?" a woman's European-accented voice greeted them over the squawk box.

"She wants to know *'Who is there, please?'* when she can plainly see it's the same two cops who have been dropping by this joint for weeks in the same butt-ugly, shit brown, twelve-year-old, black-wall Plymouth," Ryan groused sotto voce, directing a glance and a phony smile at the security camera mounted over the gateway.

"Police! Let us in, please, ma'am," Furrino answered back to the intercom.

"I'm sorry, Mrs. Bradshaw is resting," the woman's voice drifted back at the two detectives.

"No, *we're* sorry," Ryan barked, "tell Mrs. Bradshaw we have to see her now or we'll be back in an hour with a warrant for her arrest. You got that, lady?"

"One moment, please," the genteel voice responded, and the two officers heard a click.

Ryan looked over at Furrino behind the wheel. "Nice digs, huh?" he said. "Think you and me are in the wrong business?" Ryan said that every time they pulled up at the tony Bradshaw mansion gates.

"You keep forgetting that the fellow who lived in the lap of luxury here is now dead," Furrino reminded his partner. "What good is rich if you're dead?"

"True enough," Ryan agreed, and he spit out the window into the lush crimson oleanders fronting the sumptuous villa. The big gates swung open then, and the men in the battered unmarked car drove inside. They were met at the entrance by the pretty, middle-aged woman they'd encountered there before.

"The housekeeper," Furrino mumbled.

"No shit," Ryan snarled. These rich people did not put Ryan in a good mood.

"Mrs. Bradshaw will see you in the small sitting room," the woman said.

She led the officers to a room they were familiar with. When she'd left them there alone, seated uncomfortably on two of the French bergère chairs upholstered in a classic silk Louis XIV gold-and-black bee pattern by Clarence House, Ryan muttered the same remark he always did when they were in that room.

"Fucking *small sitting room's* bigger than my whole fucking apartment."

"Right," Furrino said, shooting him a condescending look that said you couldn't take this cretin anywhere. Even if this dame was a stone killer, John Furrino, whose Sicilian ancestors were probably Mafia dons, had a very healthy respect for wealth.

A few minutes later Devin Bradshaw came in, looking shaken, weepy, vulnerable. Ryan wasn't moved. He was thinking that this little lady could be one cool cucumber, and all her tears could be one big crocodile act. Still, even he had the good manners to stand when she entered the room.

"Mrs. Bradshaw, we want to ask you some questions. Please sit down," he said, cavalierly extending a hand toward a nearby couch, offering the lady of the manor a seat in her own parlor. Devin didn't see it, but Furrino rolled his eyes. She seated herself on the edge of the Tarra straw-silk cushions.

"Before we begin," Furrino said, "we want to inform you that you have a right to have an attorney present."

"I don't need an attorney,'" Devin mumbled.

Furrino and Ryan exchanged glances. From their years of experience, they knew that most amateurs, citizens who suddenly find themselves in trouble with the law, will decline to have an attorney present because they think if they say they want a lawyer, that'll make them look like they're guilty of something, whereas every pro, every two-bit car thief and crack dealer, starts hollering for an attorney the second you show up on his turf.

"Are you *certain* you don't want an attorney present?" Furrino repeated.

"Quite certain," Devin reiterated, with just a slight edge of irritation.

"Fine," Furrino said. "Now, if at any time you feel you would like an attorney present you can just say so, and we'll stop, even though you are waiving that right now. Do you understand that?"

"Yes," Devin said flatly.

Ryan and Furrino took turns throwing out questions. Devin told them the same story, albeit with more lucidity, that they had heard from her the night before. About going down to the showroom to do a final okay on the samples, and how she and Marva had dinner plans downtown. And where she was when she heard the shot, and how Tilten encountered her in the darkened corridor. After they'd gone over the same material several times , Furrino looked at her hard, and trod back on old ground.

"Mrs. Bradshaw," he said, "tell us again if you will, exactly why you drove up to Mulholland that day, in your black Jaguar XJS V12, to head off your husband in the pouring rain." When Devin hesitated, he added, "Please tell us again what was so important that you had to talk to him right away, it couldn't wait."

Devin stiffened a bit, then launched into the scenario she'd told them before, several times. About how the car phone went dead, and how she wasn't sure that Paul did not need her at the luncheon after all. In midsentence, Ryan held up his hand to stop her.

"Isn't it true, Mrs. Bradshaw," he asked, "that you went up there to tell your husband that you were going to divorce him?"

"Whoever said that was wrong, I've told you that," she insisted, not flinching, not surprised anymore by the repetitive questions.

"But isn't it true, Mrs. Bradshaw?" Ryan persisted.

"No, it's not true."

"Marva Modine didn't commit suicide," he said evenly then. "She was murdered."

Both detectives were scrutinizing Devin's reaction. Again, she didn't register surprise. Again she remained impassive, said nothing.

"Aren't you even curious to know what happened?" Furrino asked her. "This Marva Modine was your good friend, wasn't she?"

"I don't know what you want me to say," Devin said quietly.

Ignoring her response, Ryan reached into the inside pocket of his jacket and pulled out a small notebook. He flipped it open and took a moment to find the right page, then loudly cleared his throat. "The gunshot to the head that killed the Modine woman was fired from a Smith & Wesson .38," he read, "not from the gun the victim held in her right hand."

"Tell us," Furrino asked then, bending to remove an evidence bag from his briefcase and holding it up, "do you recognize *this*?"

"Recognize what . . . ?" Devin started. Furrino held out the clear plastic bag in front of him so she could see it plainly.

"It's a gun," she said.

"It's a thirty-eight-caliber Smith & Wesson handgun," Furrino clarified.

"A handgun that happens to be registered in your name," Ryan added.

"It was found at the Pulled Together factory this morning, stuffed into a cranny behind a heating pipe in the hall outside your office," Furrino said.

"It's been tested," Ryan went on. "It's the gun that killed your girlfriend." Devin looked from one to the other, wide-eyed.

"What about it, Mrs. Bradshaw?" Furrino asked.

"I . . . I don't know anything about it," Devin stammered.

"Well, we'd like to talk about this gun," Ryan said, "because it's your gun, and it was found about ten feet away from where a woman was shot to death with it, and you happened to be in the exact place at the exact time that it happened."

Devin assimilated that last piece of information with a look of growing distress. "Just a minute," she said then. "Can we stop? I think I'd like to have a lawyer present."

"Good. Call your attorney," Ryan said, sinking back into the plush, overstuffed chair. "We'll wait."

68

It was early afternoon at the Pulled Together factory, and the mood was somber. The executive suite was off-limits, secured with yellow crime scene tape. Alex Anson had set herself up in a temporary office on the third floor. The shocking death of Marva Modine in Devin's office the night before had cast an icy pall over the building. According to news reports, ballistics tests had ruled out suicide—the bullet that killed the famous model did not come from her own gun. Marva Modine was murdered.

Alex shivered. Devin had not come in to work. She and Marva had seemed to be very close, but the shocking buzz at the plant was that Devin was the prime suspect in Marva's murder. Maybe, Alex considered, she wouldn't need to think up sabotage ploys much longer. Maybe the California justice system would blow the woman out of here.

Martin Berman had called as soon as the news of Marva's death hit the wires. He asked Alex if he could get Maxi Poole and her crew inside Mrs. Bradshaw's office to tape news footage of the spot where the murder took place.

Reporters and crews had been clamoring at the PT gates all day. None of the others had called Alex to ask for permission to shoot inside the building, but then, none of the others knew her. Sam Bradshaw had dictated that all media inquiries be directed to L.A. Garb's PR department, and they had kept the press outside. But Martin Berman was another story. Martin Berman and Alex had enjoyed a quasiromantic lunch together last week at her desk right outside the room where the murder took place. Company policy dictated that she direct him, like everyone else, to public relations, but she told Berman that she would check directly with Mrs. Bradshaw. Who knows, she reasoned, if Devin was in some kind of tortured state, maybe she could slip this one past her. Then Channel Six would show her bloodstained office on the news, and every station in the country would pick it up. Not a good image for the lady president of Pulled Together.

When Devin had finally returned Alex's several calls to her private number at home, the woman had sounded totally destroyed. Alex told her she didn't want to bother her with business, but there were a few things that couldn't wait, like getting the samples shipped. Though obviously distressed, Devin explained about the two garments that needed changes. She told Alex what to look for, told her to go ahead and give the garments a final okay when the right buttons and belts were in place, and to get all the sample collections bagged and sent out to the PT sales reps around the country.

The two talked about a few other business matters, but Alex sensed that Devin was barely there for the conversation. Finally, she slipped in Martin Berman's request for

special treatment for the Channel Six news crew, since
they were the ones who did the last glowing piece on Paul
Bradshaw and his Pulled Together operation and since
Devin had been granting Maxi Poole entrée to the factory
right along. On that, Devin had broken down in tears,
something Alex had never witnessed since she'd known the
ice queen.

"No! No reporters!" Devin had sobbed. "Marva doesn't
deserve sleazy tabloid treatment . . ."

Alex quickly agreed and made attempts to soothe her.
She told Devin to try to get some rest and not to worry
about the office; she would take care of everything. Oddly,
Alex detected in herself a flicker of—what? Actual human
feelings for this woman? It couldn't be. She'd been forcing
civility with Devin for so long that for a millisecond she
almost believed she gave a damn about her.

There was a knock on her office door, then it opened a
few inches and someone peered in. Martin Berman's usual
entry style. She wondered for a second how he'd found her
on the third floor, then realized he was a newsman; of
course he'd find her. She could see a big smile on his face
as he put two fingers inside the door and wiggled them by
way of greeting.

"No ," she wailed at the partly open door. "I told you
no! Mrs. Bradshaw says no cameras."

He came inside, holding both hands in the air. "No cameras, I promise! The crew is outside shooting the gates, the
sign, the mural . . ."

"Then what are *you* doing up *here*?" she asked.

They both knew the answer. "I wanted to see you," he
grinned.

"Okay, sit down, but for just a minute," she conceded.
Alex suddenly realized that she was quite pleased.

"I don't know how long I'll be camped here," she offered, referring to her temporary quarters.

"Not long," Berman informed her. "I just came from
your office. They ran me out of there, but the crime lab
techs are hard at it, taking samples, doing their job. Usually
they don't take longer than a day."

"Did you find out anything?"

"Yeah, the cops are working on two theories," Berman
said. "We're going with this on the news tonight, so you

have to promise that between now and then you won't share this information with anyone."

"I promise."

"Okay. Theory number one—your boss did it. Mrs. Bradshaw was alone with the victim in the factory last night."

"That's been buzzed around here," Alex said, glancing up to be sure the door was closed. "But why would Devin kill Marva?"

"Maybe she knew something about Paul Bradshaw's murder," Berman said. "That's a possibility."

"Marva was close to Devin . . ."

"Exactly. Maybe your boss confided something to her, then as the investigation heated up she regretted it."

"My God, Devin would be facing life in prison . . ."

"In this state she'd be facing the gas chamber," Berman put in. "Multiple homicide is a special-circumstances crime."

Alex tried her best not to look gleeful. "So what's theory number two?" she quizzed.

"Aha, theory number two—much more plausible," he smiled. "Theory number two is that someone mistook the model for Mrs. Bradshaw and killed the wrong blonde."

Two police theories, and both scenarios featured Devin dead. If Devin were dead, Alex would be president. She felt her face redden. She hoped he hadn't noticed, but of course he did. Berman was looking at her curiously. She was learning that there wasn't much that escaped his notice.

"What kind of woman is Mrs. Bradshaw?" he asked then.

"That's not an appropriate question," she threw back at him.

"I know," he said, flashing his disarming grin again. "But that's how newsies are. Always putting our noses where they don't belong."

"Look," she said, "I've got a lot of work to do . . ."

"Okay, I'm leaving," he said. "But not until you promise to have dinner with me this weekend."

"Umm . . ."

"Friday night," he said, still grinning. "Or Saturday. Lady's choice."

"I'll let you know," Alex said.

"Not good enough. I'm not leaving until you say yes,"

he persisted. Then he put his two hands on her desk and leaned in conspiratorially.

"Do me a big favor, Alex. Say yes, because if I don't get out of here right now I won't get the news on tonight, and I'll be among the ranks of the unemployed. Then I'll be homeless . . ."

"All right, all right, yes," Alex gave in with an exasperated sigh. "Now will you leave?"

"I'm gone! Call you Friday," he said, and sprinted out the door. Alex was smiling.

69

Devin sat in her late husband's study with the door closed and locked. An attorney? She had no idea whom to call. Since the detectives had told her that she could stop at any time if she felt she wanted an attorney present, she had assumed that if she halted the proceedings they would just go away, give her some time to think this through, get some advice. But, no! They were waiting, poised like two looming hounds from hell, ready to pounce the minute she emerged from the room.

Now she had to come up with an attorney, but who? Bruce Henning was chief counsel for the company. Irv Chapman had been Paul's personal attorney and, as such, had helped her with matters relating to his will. She had heard women friends talking about their divorce lawyers. Devin did have a tax attorney. And a real estate attorney. What kind of lawyer should she call? She had to get somebody right now. Her mind flashed to Tanner, as it often did. He was some kind of attorney, and there was a time when she would ask him for advice, and he still called regularly and left messages, but of course she'd rather die than call Tanner.

Dear God, she thought, this was serious. The two detectives were waiting just down the hall. She stared at the telephone on Paul Bradshaw's desk. The number for John

Tanner's firm, scribbled on a sheet of paper she'd brought home the day she went looking for him, stared back at her.

Then it hit her. John Tanner's father! She remembered that he was a *criminal* attorney. He'd seemed so kindly on that dreadful day when she'd stumbled into his office. He probably didn't even know about his son's connection to her, Tanner and his damned secrets. She had no time to think this through. She couldn't even think whom to call for advice. Sam Bradshaw? Hardly. He hadn't even bothered to call with condolences about Marva. For lack of a better idea, she dialed the number on the pad.

"Good afternoon—Brigant, Hale, Tanner & Lowe," a woman sang cheerfully.

"Hello," she returned, somewhat hesitantly. "This is Mrs. Devin Bradshaw. I'd like to speak to John Tanner Senior."

"One moment, Mrs. Bradshaw, I'll ring."

Almost instantly the attorney was on the line. She recognized his congenial voice and pictured the tanned, handsome face and shock of white hair she remembered from a day she would otherwise like to forget.

"Hello, Mrs. Bradshaw," he said. "How can I help you?"

Devin heard herself babbling everything into the phone. Last night's horror scene, the gun, the detectives camped in her sitting room. Tanner Senior listened. At some point Devin broke down in tears again, and couldn't go on.

"Mrs. Bradshaw," the attorney said then, "give me your address."

Devin sobbed out the number of the house on Benedict Canyon Drive. Tanner repeated the address slowly, and she confirmed it.

"Good," he said. "As you know, I'm in Century City, very near your home. Listen to me carefully. Tell the officers that your attorney is on the way. Say nothing else. Then excuse yourself, and go wash your face and pull yourself together. I'll be there in fifteen minutes."

Devin heard the bell ring. She was feeling a little better. She had already taken her new attorney's first piece of advice. She'd gotten out of her robe, taken a quick shower, dabbed on some lipstick and blush, and brushed through her hair. She was back in Paul's study now, dressed in a pair of black Go-Silk pants and a matching shirt. Black for

Marva. And for her mood. There was a knock on the door of the study.

"Who is it?" she called out shakily.

"It's Maria, Mrs. Bradshaw. Mr. Tanner to see you."

"Yes, Maria, show him in, please," she said.

The door opened, and Devin looked up to see Maria and the elder Tanner. The two detectives were standing behind them, raring to get at her. She'd been tottering on the edge of control, intermittently weeping for the past twenty hours, and she lost it again. Tears flowed down her cheeks. The person who stood between her and two very menacing police officers was this man Tanner, and she didn't even know him. What the hell was happening to her life?

"Okay, ma'am, your lawyer's here. Let's talk," the Irish blustered then.

"Not so fast, guys," the elder Tanner said to the cops. "I've just come on the case. My client and I have to do some talking before I can allow her to say one word to you."

"Make it quick, will you, Tanner?" Ryan said to the attorney.

Devin's housekeeper was still standing in the doorway, looking helpless. Tanner gently touched her shoulder.

"Maria," he said to the woman, "why don't you take these boys into the kitchen and make them some sandwiches? I'll call you when we're ready."

Maria addressed the officers. "Will you come with me, please?" she offered graciously.

The cops reluctantly followed Maria. "Try not to take all day, Tanner," Ryan shot back.

"I'll do my best, fellas," Tanner rejoined, and he closed the study door behind them with a decisive click.

Already, Devin felt a little safer. Mr. Tanner was taking charge. He seemed to know what to do, and he was doing it. He walked into the study to where Devin was sitting, and the first thing he did was hand her a crisp white linen handkerchief. Devin accepted it gratefully and dabbed at her eyes. This man was at least comforting. His generation still carried handkerchiefs.

"All right," he said then, taking a seat a few feet away from her on the black leather couch. "Why don't you start at the beginning?"

"Well, my husband was killed three months ago—"

"Not *that* beginning," Tanner cut in, smiling. "I'm familiar with the Paul Bradshaw case—you'd have to live under a rock not to be. Tell me everything that's happened since last night, leading up to and since you walked in on the murder scene."

Devin managed to recount the horrible details in sequence, including Billy Hilgarde's visit this morning and his theory that the killer mistook Marva for herself. She wept when she talked about Marva, describing how she found her friend stretched across the desk in the inner office, her own small ornate gun in her hand. Tanner waited patiently each time Devin broke down, while she mopped her face with his handkerchief.

As devastated as she was, Devin couldn't help noticing that this man had many of "her" Tanner's mannerisms— the inflection of voice, the gestures, the mirth behind the same lapis blue eyes. *Her* Tanner? He was a rat! She put him out of her mind.

Tanner Senior punctuated her narrative with questions and made notes in a small black leather binder. When he seemed satisfied with the quick debriefing, he picked up the phone on the table next to the couch.

"Can I dial the kitchen on this?" he asked Devin

"Yes, press six," she told him. He punched the number and asked Maria to bring the officers back into the study.

"Now, don't you say anything at all to Ryan or Furrino," he told Devin, putting down the phone. "Even if they ask you a question."

"Did you know those two before?" Devin asked him. "They seem to know you."

"No, I hadn't had the pleasure, but I've spent a lot of years bouncing around the criminal courts building. I've probably brushed up against them in some capacity a time. or two."

At that, the men in question lumbered into the study and headed for a pair of chairs opposite the couch where Devin and Tanner were sitting. Tanner immediately got up.

"Uh-uh, don't sit, guys," he said. "I now realize I've got a lot of catching up, a lot of homework to do before Mrs. Bradshaw can speak to you."

The two made it clear that they were not happy, but they knew the attorney had the weight of the Fifth Amendment to the U.S. Constitution on his side.

"Tomorrow morning, Tanner," Furrino shot at him. "Nine o'clock sharp at Parker Center, Room 642."

"We'll be there," Tanner said.

"And tell your client to bring a toothbrush," Ryan added, as if Devin were not in the room. "After our little chat tomorrow, we may be arresting her on two counts of murder."

70

"She did it," Ryan spit, as the detectives made the turn out of the opulent gilt-tipped iron gates onto Benedict Canyon Drive. "That is one cool broad. I think she done 'em both. The old man, so now she's rich, and the model, 'cuz that one had something on her."

"It would help if we had some hard evidence," Furrino responded dryly.

"Hey, finding the lady's gun at the scene ain't too shabby," Ryan snapped.

"But it's got no prints," Furrino reminded his partner.

"So she wiped them off on her fancy clothes."

"Maybe, but that doesn't do us any good, pal."

"So if she ain't guilty, why did she hire a heavy hitter like Tanner?"

"Good point," Furrino conceded.

The two detectives were on their way to the Pulled Together factory in South-Central. So far they'd had no luck finding anyone, man or woman, really close to Devin Bradshaw, either family, friends, or business associates. They'd decided to go back to PT to see if they could stumble on anyone there who was reasonably tight with the lady. One individual they intended to seek out was her personal assistant, Alexandra Anson.

"The widow Bradshaw did not seem surprised when we hit her with the divorce bit," Ryan mused.

"Two possibilities," Furrino countered, wheeling the unmarked car onto busy Sunset Boulevard and heading east.

"Somebody already tipped her that we knew about that, or this woman is beyond cool."

"She's not that cool," Ryan observed. "She was pretty weepy."

"But that could be the height of cool," Furrino reasoned. "A smoke screen. Besides, if she bumped off the model, and the woman really was a friend, even *she* might feel a little bad."

"Right," Ryan shrugged. "Jeffrey Dahmer said he's sorry. Besides, you and I have seen buckets of tears shed outta just plain scared stiff."

"She has good reason to be scared," Furrino acknowledged. "Like I said, what good is rich if you're dead?"

"Or doing life," Ryan added.

Alex considered dinner with Martin Berman. The man was no Paul Bradshaw, but nobody was. And Paul Bradshaw was dead. She would have to get used to that and get on with her life.

She looked up to see the door to her temporary office open and two men shuffle in. It was the pair of detectives who had been coming around the factory for months asking questions. Her heart jumped. These guys made her nervous.

"Can I help you?" she asked, looking at them over her glasses.

"Yes, Miss Anson," the tall one said. As always, he pulled out his worn leather folder, and showed her his gold-and-blue LAPD badge. "We'd like to talk to you for a few minutes," he said.

"Have a seat," she offered, indicating a couch against the wall in the small cubicle. "Want coffee?"

"No, thanks," the two said in unison.

Without preamble, the officers informed Alex that her boss, Devin Bradshaw, had been up on Mulholland Drive talking to her husband just minutes before the man was killed. And, they told her, Mrs. Bradshaw did not happen to be on her way to lunch with the family at the time. Alex was wide-eyed. This was news to her.

"We suspect that Mrs. Bradshaw intercepted her husband to tell him she was leaving him," Furrino said. "She was divorcing him. Did you know that, Ms. Anson?"

Alex hesitated, and Ryan picked it up from there. "We

also know that Mrs. Bradshaw was planning to move out of her home that day."

"She had reservations at a downtown hotel for an indefinite stay," Furrino put in.

"That looks like divorce to us," Ryan added.

"Can you confirm that?" Furrino asked. "Had Mrs. Bradshaw told you she was planning to leave her husband?"

Alex looked from one to the other, computing the information. These two apparently didn't know that she and Devin did not confide in each other. It occurred to her that this might be an opportunity to nail Devin big time. Useless puce product was one thing, but prison would definitely finish the woman off. By now, Alex knew the PT operation backward and forward; she was ready for Devin's job.

And weren't these men just about telling her that they thought Devin Bradshaw killed her husband? If Devin was with Paul up on Mulholland just before he was killed, they were saying, then she was probably the one who killed him. Alex looked up at the officers, who sat quietly, waiting for her to respond. Yes, they thought Devin killed him, and they were looking for proof. Well, she was going to help them. Getting Devin had been Alex's main agenda since she'd made her deal with Sam, and she was about to drive another nail in the woman's coffin. And this one would be a big steel spike!

The officers were still looking at her expectantly. She assumed that in the course of their investigation they had probably picked up that Bradshaw and Alex Anson had been lovers. That was common knowledge. All the more reason they ought to believe what she was about to tell them, she reasoned.

"I was very, very close to Paul Bradshaw," she began, with a knowing look at the detectives. "I was his personal assistant and his good friend for eight years. And," she said pointedly, "you two have it backwards."

"What do you mean?" Furrino asked.

"The fact is," she said, "*Paul* was the one who was going to divorce *Devin*. He'd been confiding that to me for months before he was killed, agonizing over it really, and he had finally decided that he was going to do it."

"Divorce her?" That from Ryan, as the two hung on Alex's words.

"Of course," Alex lied. "If, as you say, Mrs. Bradshaw made a trip up to Mulholland Drive that day to talk to her husband about divorce, she would have been trying to talk him *out* of divorcing her before he went over to his mother's house and told the whole family about his plans."

Paul was very close to his family, Alex told the detectives then, warming to her subject. When he wanted to discuss important family issues with them, he would call these family meetings. He'd told Alexandra that this, though painful, was what he was going to address at lunch that day. That he and Devin were divorcing; that the marriage had been a mistake. And Devin must have known that; he surely must have told her that. That would be the reason why Devin wasn't invited to be present at the luncheon meeting at Regina Bradshaw's that day, she told the officers.

In fact, Alex had no idea what had been on Paul's agenda for the family meeting that day, but she didn't think anyone else knew either. She and Geneen had talked about it. Geneen didn't know, and that meant probably even Sam didn't know. Whatever Paul Bradshaw planned to tell his family that day had apparently gone to the grave with him.

The two officers looked very interested. "Well," Furrino started, "do you think Mrs. Bradshaw would have been able to change her husband's mind?"

"No," Alex said. "Paul had been thinking about divorce for a long time. He'd bounced it off me many times. He had finally made up his mind, and he told me that he was going to tell Devin as soon as their big dinner party was over."

"That was the bash the Clintons went to?" Ryan asked. "The night before Bradshaw was killed?"

"That's right," Alex confirmed. "Paul Bradshaw was a very decisive man, and when he made up his mind to do something, he did it. Most likely he told his wife that morning, the day after the party, that he wanted a divorce."

"So you think the reason Mrs. Bradshaw went up to Mulholland was to try to talk *him* out of divorcing *her*," Furrino reiterated.

"And he would have told her he'd made up his mind, it was a done deal," Ryan added. "So in your opinion, how would Devin Bradshaw have reacted to that?"

Alex paused, seemingly thinking about it. "I don't know," she finally answered, "I wasn't there. But I do know

that the woman always gets what she wants. She got Paul
Bradshaw away from his wife of thirty-three years."

"By the way, do you like her?" Furrino threw in.

"She's my boss," Alex said. "I was assigned to her after
her husband was killed."

After a pause, Ryan said, "Okay, let's talk about the
model."

71

Sam Bradshaw shifted position to face his guest on the
soft leather couch in front of the fireplace in his office.
He poured another glass of Veuve Clicquot Ponsardin for
Alex and lifted his own
crystal flute to hers.

"A beautiful champagne," he smiled. "Everything is
working out perfectly."

It was almost seven o'clock. When Alex told him she was
coming over to the Santa Monica headquarters after work
with news to report, he called Lizbeth to say he'd be working late. Now he drank in the luscious young Alex Anson
sitting two feet away from him. His brother's mistress intox-
icatingly close on his brother's designer couch while they
drank his brother's French champagne. Sam was warmed
by the wine, the fire, and the closeness of the woman he'd
coveted for much too long.

"Maybe it's a bit early to celebrate," Alex said cautiously.

"Oh, we'll have many celebrations," Sam said expan-
sively. "But tonight, we're celebrating the fact that Devin
Yorke is looking at the noose."

"The noose. . . ?" Alex started.

"Oh yes," Sam said with a smirk, filling his glass again.
"They found her gun, it was all over the news, and it's the
weapon that killed both Paul and Marva Modine. And the
little story you concocted for the cops that my brother was
going to divorce her provides the perfect motive. Let's drink
to that," he said, moving closer to Alex and raising his glass.

"Do you think she really killed them?"

"Well, she was in the right place at the right time, both times."

"But do you think Devin did it?" Alex persisted.

"Who cares?" he threw back. "But I'll tell you this—these were no crimes of passion. These were cold-blooded, premeditated killings for greed. I'm sure the state will be asking for the gas chamber for our interloping heiress. Drink up," he said. Alex obediently sipped her wine, but she looked troubled.

"Hey, why the long face?" Sam chided. "You've come through brilliantly on your end of the deal. You've earned your pay, baby, and much more."

"But what if Devin is convicted, and what if she does go to the gas chamber, and she didn't do it?" she asked him, suppressing a shudder.

"Alex, this is everything we both wanted," Sam said, smiling wickedly. "Devin will be gone. She'll be out of our hair, yours and mine. She can't inherit if she's convicted of murder. I'll have total control of the company, and you'll become president of Pulled Together. It couldn't have worked out better."

Alex was staring into the fire. She looked ravishing in the flickering light, like a young fiery Ava Gardner, her dark hair framing her face in a thick profusion of ringlets, her blazing eyes mirroring what Sam saw as the larceny in her soul. He slid over the few remaining inches that separated them and slipped an arm around her. He felt her stiffen. She was understandably nervous, he thought. That excited him.

"Sam, I'm worried," she murmured then.

"What's to worry about?" he whispered against her ear as he slid his other hand up under her sweater and found a small, firm breast.

"Don't, Sam," she protested, attempting to move his hand away.

"I've been waiting for this for a long time," he said, tightening his grip on her. "Don't be coy with me now, Alex. This is our night."

He put both his big hands firmly on her shoulders then and pushed her down across the length of the couch. Gliding his hands down to her waist, he pulled at her short wool skirt, ripping the button off and yanking the zipper down in one motion. Roughly, he tugged it off, revealing her black underthings beneath.

"No!" Alex shouted, struggling against his bulk.

"Yes," he said, tearing her silk panties away from her body. He rubbed his hands over her flat naked stomach, and up under the lace of her garter belt. He groaned. Alex was screaming now.

"Shhh! Nobody's here," he growled, clamping one big hand over her mouth, and forcing two thick fingers of his other hand up inside her vagina.

"*Please,* Sam . . . ," she managed to whimper.

"Be quiet, you little fool," he demanded. "Behave, and you'll get everything you want. Fight me, and I'll be forced to tell the cops you lied to them. And maybe for a reason. I'll have to tell them that you had a raging fight with my brother the night before he was murdered. And he fired you."

"No," Alex moaned.

"Oh yes," Sam breathed, opening his fly and reaching inside his trousers. "You weren't sure I knew that, were you? I'll also remind them that you have your own keys to the factory. And how you could easily have let yourself in last night and shot Marva, thinking she was Devin, whom you knew was staying late. I'll tell them how you hate Devin, how you plotted to do her in. I'll show them all the notes you've given me . . ."

"It was your idea," Alex cried. "I have it all on tape . . ."

"Oh, I'll admit that I wanted Devin out of the company," he said, "but I'll tell them that murder was something I couldn't countenance—I had to go to the police . . ."

Sam talked in cadence, all the while holding Alex down with one hand and rhythmically stroking his erect penis with the other. Alex was sobbing now, tears raining down her face and neck, her arms flailing in vain at the powerful man hunkered menacingly on top of her.

"And how, of course, you would have known exactly where Paul kept that gun—you knew everything my brother did," he went on, his breath coming in quick gasps.

Suddenly he scooped one huge paw under her hips, and with the other he forced his bulging member up into her. Then he locked both hands onto her narrow hips and fiercely jammed himself into her vagina, again, and again, and again, until finally he exploded inside her.

72

Wednesday, 9:03 A.M., at LAPD headquarters at Parker Center downtown. Outside it was chilly and overcast as the trailing edge of the storm that had moved in the day before rolled across the Los Angeles basin. Inside, the small interrogation room was just as gloomy, with its bare Formica table, six metal folding chairs, and single dirty window.

The group assembled in the cheerless room matched the mood. Detective John Furrino wore a navy suit, shiny where it shouldn't be. Detective Richard Ryan wore tan polyester pants an inch too short, with an ill-fitting plaid sports jacket, and he looked as if he had a hangover. John Tanner Senior was in a serious, dark Armani suit, with a white shirt and red silk tie. And a nervous Devin Bradshaw, sitting close to Tanner, had on a somber charcoal gabardine suit, with an ivory silk shell and black heels. She wore no makeup. Her eyes were red. For the second night in a row, she hadn't slept at all.

Ryan opened the meeting without bothering with hellos. He set a tape recorder on the table and pushed the *record* button, then pronounced in monotone the time, the date, where they were, and who was present. Next, he reached into his coat pocket and took out a card, from which he read to Devin her Miranda rights. Then he asked if she understood them. That done, he leaned back in his chair, folded his hands in front of him, and began.

"Okay, we're gonna start with murder number one, then we're gonna move on to murder number two. Mrs. Bradshaw, we wanna know why you went up to Mulholland Drive in the early afternoon on Friday, December fourth of last year, and this time we don't want to hear any crap."

"Just a minute, Mr. Ryan," Tanner said. "I'm going to insist that you don't use that kind of language with my client."

"Sorry," Ryan half snarled.

"Go ahead, Devin," Tanner said, smiling reassuringly at her. Devin nodded at Tanner, then faced the detectives across the table.

"You were right," she said. "I *had* made the decision to leave my husband. On that day, the day he was killed, I drove up to Mulholland Drive and waited at a spot where I knew he'd pass. I was going to tell him quickly, then leave. Let him digest it, and let him find me gone when he came home that night. My plan was that we would then communicate through attorneys, and that would be that. I wouldn't have to face him again after those few minutes."

Devin went on to explain what a powerful, persuasive, sociopathic personality Paul Bradshaw was, and why she wanted, needed, to do it that way. She got up top, she told them, and the wind and rain were even more ferocious up there. She knew if she stayed inside her car, out of the rain, he would likely roar right past her. He would be speeding in his Ferrari as usual, with his CD player blaring; the rain would be pounding on the roof; the windshield wipers would be slamming back and forth; the heater would be blasting against the chill; he'd be concentrating on the meeting at his mother's and he probably wouldn't even notice her parked by the side of the road.

During their lengthy briefing session the night before, she'd told Mr. Tanner all about their falling-out over the ruined dinner party in his honor and how her husband had blamed the debacle on her. And how she remembered thinking at the time that even if he *did* see her sitting there in her car, he was so irrationally furious with her that he probably would have ignored her anyway and whizzed right past. After all, he'd just hung up on her. And told her he did not want to see her at lunch at his mother's. But Tanner had said there was no need to get into all that with the cops; telling the detectives about the truculence between her and her husband was not pertinent to the story and would only exacerbate any suspicions they had of her guilt.

Addressing the two detectives slouched in the chairs opposite her and Tanner, she went on to describe the scene. She'd pulled her raincoat around her and stepped out of her car, she told them. She hadn't thought to bring an umbrella. She stood by the side of the road, in mud splashing over the tops of her high heels, bareheaded, water stream-

ing over her face and down into her collar, all the while
watching to the left, to the east, for her husband's Ferrari
to come tearing around the curve.

When it did, she stepped out into the street and flagged
him down. He screeched to a halt just in front of her. She
could see his face flush with anger as he mouthed the
words, "What the hell. . . ?" She waved him over to the
side of the road, indicating it was urgent. He pulled over
in front of her car with a jerk. Every nuance in his tanned
handsome face signaled to her that this had better be good.
He jammed at one of the electronic buttons, rolling down
the window on the passenger side a couple of inches to
hear her. He did not open the door, did not offer her refuge
from the rain. "What?" he'd barked. Without preliminaries,
she rattled off her speech, she said, before she lost her
nerve. Her husband was livid. "How dare you lay this neurotic crap on me now, here!" he'd bellowed.

"I'm not being neurotic," she'd told him quietly, stonily.
She was hardly the neurotic type, she'd said. It was sad
that he didn't respect her, value her, appreciate her, even
know her. There had been a major misunderstanding, she'd
told her husband, standing in the muck outside his sports
car in the pouring rain. It turned out they had wanted two
totally different things. She had genuinely loved him. She
wanted a husband, and she wanted children. But he only
wanted her to look good on his arm, to run his home, to
entertain brilliantly. He wanted to show her off. To Paul
Bradshaw, she said, she was just a shiny trophy on his shelf.

She remembered having a fit of sneezing as she shivered
in the downpour. He could have his extracurricular women,
she'd told him then, but he couldn't have *her, too*! She was
leaving. She would not be there when he got home. Her
lawyer would contact him.

That was it, she was done. She'd turned on her ruined
heels to leave, go back to her own car. But behind her,
Paul suddenly leaped out of his Ferrari in the driving rain,
grabbed her by one shoulder, and spun her around. He was
furious. "How dare you!" he'd ranted. "You're not going
anywhere, and you'd damn well better be home when I get
there. After last night's pigscrew was all over the press, I'm
not about to have you humiliating me even more!" And
on and on in that vein. She was looking him squarely in
the eye, she said, made defiant by the rain, the cold, and

her will to finish it. "It's over," she'd said again. "This was not an overnight decision." Blame it on the useless, social-climbing spin her life had become, she'd told him. His coldness, his womanizing, which was escalating, his abusive treatment, and more. His jaunt out in the storm to one of his whores last night, she threw at him, even before their last guests had left, obviously with no concern for her feelings, was simply the final straw. Her profound unhappiness was at the root of this, and that was not going to get better.

"So where *did* your husband go that night?" Ryan jumped in, interrupting her narrative.

"To Marva's house," she answered without thinking. Tanner looked at her sharply. Ryan immediately pounced on that bit of new information.

"No kidding!" he said. "Your husband was screwing the dead model?"

"Once—" Devin started, reddening.

"Don't answer that, Devin," Tanner interjected, putting a restraining hand on her arm. "She doesn't know, gentlemen. She wasn't there," he said.

"Fine," Furrino said. "Go on, Mrs. Bradshaw." Ryan was still smirking. Devin took a moment to collect herself.

Paul Bradshaw was shaking with fury, she told the detectives, but he made an effort to calm himself, to get control. He tried placating her. He told her to go on home, get out of her wet clothes. She was just exhausted after giving the disastrous party the night before. Get some rest, he'd said, and they would go out to a quiet dinner that night and talk this over calmly. He loved her very much, he told her. That's when she put both hands up to stop him, she said to the two officers.

" 'The fact is,' I told my husband, 'I don't love *you* anymore. To tell the truth, after the last few weeks, I don't even much like you.' "

At that, she said, he lost the fragile grip he'd managed to gain on his control. He hauled off and slapped her across the face with a force that made her head spin. It took her by such surprise that she didn't even duck. Devin had never been a victim, she told the detectives. No man had ever hit her before. She was almost thirty years younger than Paul, she worked out vigorously every day, and she was in top physical shape. She was very strong, and at that moment, after his physical attack, she was gripped by incredulity and fury. In a reflex action, she said, she reared back fiercely and landed a solid punch on Bradshaw's face. On his left eye. And while he was actually reeling, off guard, clutching his eye in pain, she ran back to her car, got in, and locked both doors, terrified of his reaction.

Jamming the Jaguar into gear, she backed away from his car, then roared off. She raced back down mud-slick Benedict Canyon and home, badly shaken. She had left Paul Bradshaw up on Mulholland Drive, staggering, clutching his eye, furious, soaking wet and bleeding, but *very much alive.*

Skidding through the rain, she'd glanced down at her trembling hands gripping the steering wheel. That's when she noticed her ring. Lately, she told the officers, she'd been wearing her diamond ring on her right hand. She'd been under a lot of stress and she'd lost some weight, and had come dangerously close to losing it a couple of times when it nearly slipped off her left hand. Like most right-handed people's, her right hand was bigger, she said, so she'd been wearing the ring there until she either put the weight back on or got the ring resized. It was a heavy, six-pronged, twenty-carat diamond solitaire. She saw that blood was running off the enormous stone onto her hand, and a jagged piece of torn flesh was caught on one of the sharp points of the platinum setting. Her ring must have raked across her husband's eyelid and ripped it open.

She stopped then. For a few moments, the only sound in the room was the faint buzz of the tape recorder.

"That's it?" Ryan asked impatiently. "You didn't shoot him?"

"I didn't shoot him," Devin said.

"Did Counselor Tanner here work this little story up with you last night?" Ryan persisted.

At that, Tanner looked threateningly at him and he backed down, which seemed to be a cue for Furrino to take up the cudgel.

"Mrs. Bradshaw," he asked, "why didn't you tell us all this on the several times we've questioned you before?"

"Because I didn't think it was germane—" she started.

"You didn't think it was *germane*?" Ryan yelped now. "Excuse me, did you say *germane*? Mrs. Bradshaw, please understand that our questions are not designed for you to arbitrarily eliminate information that you decide is not *germane!*"

"All right, all right, men," Tanner admonished.

"Well ... I was afraid," Devin said feebly. "I knew it would bring publicity, scandal, and suspicion crashing down on my head."

"And that's why you lied?" Furrino asked incredulously.

"I didn't lie," Devin protested. "When I got the call at home that my husband was dead, and I was being treated like a bereaved widow, I responded in kind. I really was sorry. I never wanted Paul dead, I just wanted out of the marriage."

"Huh!" Ryan threw out scornfully. "How about this for a much more plausible scenario, Mrs. Bradshaw. You knew that a divorce meant you would lose your big share of ownership in your husband's company. After Bradshaw got into his small car, which was parked right in front of your heavy Jaguar, while he was hardly able to see with his bleeding eye, and in the rain, you saw your chance. You followed him to his Ferrari, got in, and sat next to him on the passenger side on the pretext of making it up with him. Then you slipped your little .38 out of your raincoat pocket and plugged him! Then you coolly got back into your own car, right behind his little sports job, and tapped him over the edge. Easy. End of story."

"Okay, that's enough, boys," John Tanner blared. "You've got your statement."

"Not so fast, Tanner," Ryan said. "See, there's one more thing ... one more *big* thing here! We have a witness who tells us that you, Mrs. Bradshaw, were not going to divorce your husband at all, that it was the other way around. That he was about to dump *you*, cut you off with some kind of puny prenup settlement. So you went up there to try to talk him out of it," Ryan sneered, "before he made this big announcement to the rest of the Bradshaw clan at lunch. And my guess is you took your gun up there with you, had it in your pocket, to kind of back up your argument if you needed to."

Devin was stunned. "Who told you that?" she demanded. "Who said Paul was going to divorce me?" The detectives ignored her question. Tanner was watching her intently.

"Well, what about it?" Ryan demanded. "You're a pretty rich little lady now, aren't you! But you wouldn't be if

Bradshaw had lived to go through with the divorce, would you, now?"

"It's a lie!" Devin fairly screamed.

"Also, Mrs. Bradshaw," Furrino went on, "as you might have heard on the news last night, the gun we found in your factory, the Smith & Wesson registered in your name, was put through further testing. Turns out it's not only the gun that killed your model friend, it's also the gun that killed your husband."

Devin broke down in sobs. Tanner vaulted to his feet and pressed the *off* button on the tape recorder.

"Okay, that's all," he said to the two men, who'd remained seated opposite Devin and her lawyer, calmly watching them. "Unless you want to arrest my client, that's all for now." The detectives looked at each other and shrugged.

"Go ahead, Counselor," Ryan told Tanner. "But we'll be calling on you, you can count on it."

Tanner steered a sobbing Devin out of the dreary interrogation room, down the hall, into the elevator, and down to the parking structure. He helped her into his dark gray BMW, then headed the big sedan out of teeming downtown Los Angeles and back toward the quiet of the affluent Westside. He and his new client had to talk.

73

Tanner ushered Devin into Emilio's, a quiet Italian trattoria on Melrose Avenue. It was a few blocks off the trendy track, so it didn't get much of the high-profile, gossipy lunch crowd, and for that reason it was a favorite of Tanner's. Besides, they were early; it was not yet eleven-thirty, and there were just a few patrons scattered in the main dining room. They settled into one of the secluded, plush, red leather banquettes. The ebullient Emilio Baglioni appeared at their table almost instantly, carrying a bottle of chilled Pinot Grigio and two wineglasses.

"*Ciao, amico!*" Emilio greeted Tanner.

"Emilio, hello. This is Mrs. Devin Bradshaw," Tanner said. "Forgive me for not making a reservation, but this was spur-of-the-moment."

"You are always welcome, John," their host exclaimed, uncorking the Italian white and pouring a little for Tanner to sample. "Enjoy, with my compliments," Emilio said. "It's light, crisp. You like it, no?"

"Yes," Tanner smiled, after tasting the wine. "You are always more than gracious, Emilio. Would you have the chef make us just a little salad, and maybe a light pasta? Something simple."

"Of course," Emilio said. "Perhaps I cook for you myself, today."

Tanner knew that, besides beautiful women, cooking was Emilio's first love. He grew his own herbs behind the restaurant, and he spent many weeks a year in his native Italy, always bringing home new dishes to add to his already lengthy menu.

"Now that would be a rare treat," Tanner beamed. To Devin, he said, "Emilio is a brilliant cook. He used to be Jack Warner's personal chef at Warner Brothers, back in the golden days of the movie studios."

"Aah, that was when I was just off the boat," Emilio laughed, gathering the unopened menus from atop the table and moving off.

Devin seemed to be relaxing a little, Tanner observed. He wanted to get some food into her; then they needed to do some serious talking. In minutes, a waiter came to the table with a basket of hot fresh-baked Italian bread and two plates of crisp greens, and presented chilled salad forks. Devin ignored her salad, but she gratefully sipped the wine. After the waiter disappeared, both were silent for a moment.

Devin spoke first. "I'm in trouble, aren't I?"

"Let's talk about it," Tanner answered. "I was able to get some information out of Ryan and Furrino. They've been aware for weeks that you were up on Mulholland the day your husband was murdered."

"I know," Devin nodded. "They told Billy Hilgarde that. Somebody besides him must have seen me up there."

"A lot of people besides him might have seen you up

there," Tanner said. "Any of the Bradshaws could have passed you on their way to the family luncheon."

"Well, Lizbeth could have—she lives in Trousdale. The rest of them should have been coming from the west."

"But any of them *could* have come from the other side, couldn't they? From doing errands? Maybe shopping in Beverly Hills?"

"Sure, I suppose so."

"What I don't understand," Tanner said then, "is if any of them spotted you standing by the side of the road, why wouldn't they stop? Find out if you were okay, if you were having car trouble, whatever?"

"I have no idea," Devin responded. "Maybe because they hate me."

"That cold?" he asked incredulously.

"I was the outsider. The gold digger. The bitch who took Paul Bradshaw away from his wife and kids."

"And now?"

"Worse. They *had* to speak to me when Paul was alive. Now they don't bother."

"Well, anyway, a bunch of them were up on Mulholland that day, and most of them drive black automobiles. That's the reason the cops didn't pounce on yours right away."

"Did they check anybody else's car?" she asked.

"I don't know. Doesn't matter," Tanner told her. "Now that they know the murder weapon belonged to you, they want your Jaguar in the lab right away. They also want to take you up on Mulholland and have you show them the exact spot where your 'little scuffle,' as they called it, went down. I told them I'd be free tomorrow at noon—that all right with you?"

She nodded gloomily. His words reverberated in her ears: *Now that they know the murder weapon belonged to you . . .* Devin had explained to Tanner in detail the night before that she'd had no idea where that gun was, since long before it killed Paul Bradshaw. When he asked why she hadn't reported it missing, she said she didn't know it was missing—Paul took care of things like that."

"Something else," Tanner said then. "Somebody took a shot at Billy Hilgarde last night—in front of his girlfriend's house. Ryan and Furrino went out and took his statement."

"My God!" Devin exclaimed.

"This morning they asked me if I could verify where you were at approximately six forty-five last evening," he said.

"What did you tell them?"

"I told them you were with me, of course."

Devin sighed. "I can't remember the last time I drank before noon," she breathed, taking another gulp from her wineglass.

"There's another thing I want you to know," Tanner went on. "No one told the detectives there was a divorce in the wind. They figured that out."

"They told you that?"

"I asked them how they knew. I didn't really expect an answer, but they gave me one," he said.

"So how did they figure it out?"

"Easy," Tanner returned. "They'd subpoenaed your phone records from Pacific Bell. That's routine. You made a call from the Benedict house that morning to Checkers Hotel downtown. They found out from the hotel desk that you'd reserved a suite for an indefinite stay, beginning that night."

"So they assumed I was leaving my husband," Devin put it together.

"In Ryan's exact words," Tanner quoted, " 'Rich, married woman lives in a fucking mansion but is moving alone to a hotel in the same city indefinitely? That looks like divorce time to us!' "

"Charming," Devin responded dryly.

"So," Tanner asked her then, "why didn't you tell me about that hotel reservation?"

"Good Lord," Devin said, "with all that's been going on, it just slipped my mind."

She told him she'd made the reservation at Checkers that morning after she'd decided to leave Paul, but before she took off in her car. She didn't want to lose any time trying to book rooms after she confronted him, she said—she wanted to just pack up quickly and get out. Then, with the rush of events after Paul was killed, she simply forgot about it. She'd forgotten even to cancel, she told Tanner.

"And *you* were divorcing *him*?" Tanner asked her again. "*He* wasn't leaving *you*, right?"

"I swear it," she protested. "I was leaving my husband. It was not the other way around."

"So who could this witness be?" the attorney asked her

evenly. "Who would have told the detectives that Bradshaw was going to divorce you?"

"I have no idea," she said, "but it's not true."

"Not that it matters in the scheme of things, who was divorcing whom," Tanner said. "Either way, the result would have been the same. What does matter," he leveled at her, "is whether or not you are perceived to be telling the truth."

"Ask your son who wanted the divorce," Devin threw out after a beat. "Your son knew that's why I went up there, to tell Paul I was going to leave him."

"Well," Tanner Senior said quietly, "Johnny knows that's what you *told* him . . ."

"So, then it's my word against some damn lying *witness*?" Devin cried, visibly angered.

"In fact," Tanner said, in an attempt to calm her, "Ryan and Furrino might have lied about having such a witness, just to see how you'd react. Cops do that all the time."

Devin was silent for a moment. "I can't make any sense out of my world," she said then, looking utterly defeated.

Tanner studied her. "I can help you put it all right again," he said, "but you have to help me."

"How?"

"By not lying to me. Ever," he said. "And that means don't leave anything out, either. Only the truth, and all of it. Is it a deal?"

"Deal," she agreed.

"Okay. Now, I told you they're going to impound your car," Tanner said.

"Fine with me," Devin returned easily. "They won't find anything."

Tanner regarded the beautiful woman opposite him in the booth. She seemed to have regained her composure as quickly as she'd lost it. He tried to read her. Did she whack her late husband's Ferrari over the cliff, then have her Jaguar repainted in the past few months? If so, the techs at the crime lab would see that in a New York minute. In Tanner's experience, amateur criminals never realized that it was virtually impossible to get away with anything. Tanner was good; he'd won many more cases than he'd lost. But the sad fact was, most of the cases that made it through the criminal courts system did not turn on whether the accused was guilty or not. Most criminal cases were won because of a strategy that worked. That's what Tanner got paid for.

Even then, as every lawyer knew, litigation is always a crapshoot. Look at his friend, the brilliant criminal attorney Howard Weitzman. He got John DeLorean off after the whole world saw his client on tape with a suitcase full of cocaine. Yet he couldn't get Kim Basinger out of that simple *Boxing Helena* movie contract fiasco. The actress might have to spend years paying the production company millions of dollars just for not appearing in the movie. Maybe he'd win on appeal, but you never knew.

Tanner considered Devin Bradshaw. Experience had taught him that you could never count on really knowing anyone. Though she had just sworn to be truthful with him, he did not know this woman. Beneath the seeming vulnerability, the disorientation at times, the intermittent tears, he could see down to a deep core of icy cool. She was relentlessly beautiful. And now she was enormously wealthy. The cops were right: she would not be megarich if she'd become an ex-wife that day instead of a widow, no matter who was divorcing whom. Looking at her now, he *wanted* to believe her, but he couldn't be entirely sure what kind of woman he had on his hands.

"I'm going to call my office and send one of our runners over to your house," Tanner told her now, taking a cell phone out of his briefcase. "I want to get your car in to the crime lab."

"Won't the police pick it up?" Devin asked.

"I would rather send it down there before they impound it."

"Fine," Devin said. "It's at home. Maria knows where the extra keys are. I'll call and tell her someone's coming for it."

"Okay. Do you have something to drive in the interim?" he asked her. "Or would you like my office to arrange a rental?"

"No, I'll just use one of the company vans. Would you drop me at the factory so I can pick one up?"

"Sure. We'll go from here," he said.

"How long will they be keeping my car?"

"That depends," Tanner responded pointedly.

"On what?"

"On what they find," he said. "It could be a day, a week, or . . . indefinitely."

"Then I'm sure they won't need it long," she said.

"Good," he returned. Still, Tanner couldn't read her for

sure. Devin returned his level gaze. There was something on her mind now; he could see the wheels turning behind her intelligent green eyes.

"What are you thinking?" he asked. Tanner's purpose in taking her to lunch today was to get to know his client better. Any insights would help him do his job.

"I'd like to know what you know about your son and me," she asked now, and for just a second, the slightest flicker in her emerald eyes belied her cool exterior.

"Why do you ask?"

"You must know I blamed him for betraying me—otherwise I don't think you'd have bothered to find out that the police were *not* told about my divorce plans, that they'd figured it out on their own."

"Yes, Johnny told me about his relationship with you, after he learned that you'd asked me to take your case," Tanner replied, watching her carefully. Then he reached into his inside coat pocket and produced an envelope and handed it to her across the table.

"Read this later," he told her. "I was going to give it to you when I dropped you off." She glanced at it, saw that it was from his son, and tucked it into her purse.

"Alright, I want you to listen to me now," Tanner said, leaning in across the table. "I want you to reinstate that reservation at the hotel and move there, or somewhere that as few people as possible will know about."

"Well, I'm planning to move very soon anyway," Devin told him.

"How soon?"

"In a few weeks. I've bought a small house in Bel Air. Escrow closes the first week of April."

"Not soon enough," Tanner said.

"What do you mean?"

"Devin, you're not safe at home," he responded tersely. "Everyone knows where you live, in that highly visible Benedict Canyon landmark. Anybody can get to you there."

"Get to me. . . ?"

"And you're not safe at work, either," he said. "Don't ever stay after hours again. If *you* had been sitting in your chair instead of the model . . ."

74

Devin sat in silence, hunched against the plush silver-gray upholstery of Tanner's big BMW, vaguely aware of traffic teeming on the busy Harbor Freeway as they headed through the heart of downtown Los Angeles. Mentally she was attempting to wade through the miasma of complexities that swirled dizzily around her, trying to sort out pieces of the puzzle and put together a cohesive picture. It wasn't working. She was frightened, she was severely sleep-deprived, and she couldn't focus.

One crazy thought cheered her a bit. So *her* Tanner *didn't* tell anyone about her decision to divorce Paul, after all. The cops had checked her phone records, took a stab at the truth, and probably tried it out on Sam to see if he could confirm that divorce was in the cards for his brother and his wife. Tanner did not betray her trust. It was the least of her problems, but it actually sent a warm rush through her system.

"So, don't move to the Beverly Hills Hotel," she heard Tanner Senior saying now.

"Wh ... what?" Devin looked over at the lawyer, perplexed.

"Everybody in this town who expects to be doing some hotel living for more than a few days takes a bungalow at the Beverly Hills Hotel," he went on, keeping his eyes ahead on the crowded freeway lanes. "I don't want you there. Those bungalows are too accessible, too unprotected."

"Okay. I'll try again to get rooms at Checkers," she answered absently. "It's right over there." Devin raised a hand, vaguely indicating the downtown Los Angeles skyline whizzing past them on the left. "On Grand Avenue, between Fifth and Sixth. It's a good hotel, and it's close to work."

"Fine. Call my office as soon as you know," Tanner said.

Except for Devin giving directions, the two made the rest of the drive to the PT factory in silence. Tanner punched Devin's PIN number into the keypad mounted at the entrance, and the double iron gates swung open. He wheeled the big sedan into the parking lot and nosed into her spot, then walked around to open the door for her.

"You can run along," Devin said, as he helped her out of the car. "I'll be fine."

Tanner hesitated, his hand still on her arm. "But you're shaking," he said. "I'll walk in with you."

Devin felt a surge of gratitude. She hadn't been to the factory since the night before last, when Marva was brutally murdered in her office. She leaned on Tanner for support as they walked quickly down the same hall where she'd heard the shot, then past the spot where one of the guards had pounced on her.

The yellow police tape that Billy Hilgarde had told her was blocking the door to the executive suite was gone now. Devin led the attorney into the outer office, where Alex Anson sat at her desk. The two women hadn't spoken yet today, and Alex looked startled to see Devin come through the door. And Devin did a double take when she saw her assistant's face.

"My God, what's wrong with you?" Devin asked. The usually pert and pretty Alex Anson looked dreadful. She was puffy, red-eyed, and obviously distraught. Flinching under her boss's scrutiny, the younger woman looked away, but Devin could see that she'd been crying.

"What's wrong, Alex?" Devin repeated.

"I have to talk to you," Alex managed.

"Alright," Devin said. Turning to Tanner, she thanked him, and told him she'd call him later.

"Wait a minute," Tanner stopped her. Addressing Alex, his advocate instincts clearly kicking in, he said, "I'm John Tanner, Mrs. Bradshaw's attorney—is this something I should hear?"

Alex hesitated, then squeaked, "I think so . . ."

Devin was mystified. "Let's go into my office," she said, steeling herself against the picture that flooded her mind of Marva sprawled across the big desk, blood streaming from her head and running onto the glossy, sensuous pictures.

Once inside, the women on a sofa, Tanner in a chair

facing them, Alex broke down completely. Between choking sobs, she confessed to Devin that she'd lied to the detectives, told them that Paul wanted a divorce, even implied that Devin might have killed her husband to keep him from leaving her, to keep her inheritance intact. While her attorney silently studied Alex, Devin was stunned, not so much by the woman's betrayal as by the turnaround implicit in her teary confession.

"Why are you telling me this?" she finally asked.

"Because Sam said you're going to the gas chamber," Alex moaned. Devin felt faint.

"He said it didn't matter if you killed Paul, or Marva, or anybody," Alex wailed. "He said you were as good as convicted. He said the prosecutor would ask for capital punishment. I've done some terrible things, but I couldn't live with that . . ."

Feeling her head swim, Devin closed her eyes to keep the room from spinning.

"Oh, I'm sure whatever happened to Paul will come out," she heard Alex going on, as if from some great distance. "And this divorce business probably won't even matter, will probably turn out to mean nothing in the end, but I'd always know what I did if you . . . if you . . ."

Devin opened her eyes, making a herculean effort to regain control. She found herself actually trying to comfort the agitated woman.

"God, I've been asking myself all morning what the hell kind of person am I? What did you ever do to me, really?" she sobbed to Devin. "You met Paul, and he fell in love with you and married you. How could I hold that against you? And what does it even matter now? I've compromised all my principles, my father would be devastated—"

Tanner interrupted her. "Have you called the detectives to tell them this?" he asked her coldly.

"No . . ."

"Well, let's do that, shall we?" he said, a little more kindly then. "Don't worry," he added, "you've remedied your . . . *mistake,* before there was any real harm done."

Tanner got up and reached for the phone on the table by the sofa. Pulling a card out of his pocket, he dialed the number for the homicide detail at Parker Center.

"This is John Tanner," he barked into the phone. "I need Detective Ryan or Furrino, please."

After a pause, he said, "Dick, I've got Alexandra Anson here; she has something she wants to tell you." He pushed on the speaker button, and told Alex to go ahead.

Hesitantly, Alex doled out her story, while a stern Richard Ryan asked questions, prompting the narrative. When it was over, she sank back into the sofa cushions and sobbed.

"Just a minute, Miss Anson," Ryan's voice boomed over the speaker. "Do you realize the seriousness of perjuring yourself, and possibly implicating another person in murder?" Alex looked up at Tanner, panic etched on her features.

"Dick," Tanner said in the direction of the phone. "I don't think we're talking about lying to implicate a person in a murder here. I think we're talking about lying to implicate a person in a divorce. Can you and I and Furrino talk about this in private later this afternoon?"

Ryan's audible sigh emanated from the phone. "Fine," he said. "But one of us will have to come out there and take a formal statement." There was a pause, then they heard, "Three o'clock. Wanna beat the downtown rush hour."

"Three o'clock okay with you?" Tanner asked Alex.

"Yes," Alex sniffed. Tanner took the phone off the speaker then, said a few words to Detective Ryan, and hung up. Alex started crying uncontrollably again. Devin instinctively put an arm around her.

"Shh, shh, shh," she hushed, "it's over now. It's okay . . ."

"*Sam Bradshaw raped me!*" Alex blurted out then.

"What?" Devin and Tanner asked at the same time.

With that, Alex spilled out an ugly story of Sam forcing himself on her in his office in Santa Monica the night before. "He's evil through and through," she wailed. Devin and Tanner listened in astonishment.

"You'll have to report it," Devin said when she was finished.

"I can't," Alex whimpered. "I asked for it."

"Oh, Alex, that's ridiculous," Devin said. "All rape victims feel that way to some degree, but you're intelligent enough to know that's absurd."

"No, I *did* ask for it," Alex insisted. "I played Sam. I led him on. Besides, I need my job." Alex started weeping again.

"That's another reason women are often afraid to report rape," Devin put in. "Don't worry about your job. You're protected. You work for me—"

Tanner stopped her. "It has to be Alex's choice," he said pointedly to Devin.

"Well, don't you think—?" Devin started, before Tanner cut her off again.

"Listen, I have to go," he said. "Alex, don't forget, you have an appointment with the officers at three. Devin, walk out with me, will you? There are a couple of things I need to talk to you about."

"Sure," she said, more than a little puzzled. "Alex, I'll be back in a minute, okay? Meantime, pull yourself together. Go rustle me up a company car, I have to use one for a couple of days. Work is the best therapy."

"Okay," Alex said, wiping away the tears. Looking gratefully at Devin, she got up and walked into her own office.

Devin and Tanner followed, and the two continued out the door and down the hall. When they reached Tanner's car, he took out a card and scribbled his home number on it.

"Okay, three things," he said then, handing her the card. "One, get yourself out of that house tonight. Two, call and let me know where you are. And three, leave the rape business with Alex alone."

"I don't understand," Devin said, looking genuinely bewildered.

"Then let me explain. It's apparent that something has gone on between Alex Anson and Sam Bradshaw that might interest a court of law," Tanner said soberly. "If Alex is involved in a rape trial at the same time as we are pursuing your case, if indeed there is a case, her subpoenaed testimony might be seen to be prejudiced. If she doesn't want to press rape charges right now, I'd rather you didn't push her. Do you understand?"

"Not completely," Devin said.

"Okay, think about this," Tanner urged. "There has to be a reason why Sam Bradshaw wants you nailed for these crimes.

"That's easy," Devin said, turning both palms up and shrugging. "He wants me out of the company. And out of his pockets."

"Devin," Tanner said, looking at her intently. "There's something I haven't asked you yet."

"Yes?" she prompted, when Tanner paused.

"Did you kill your husband?"

"No," she said, shock registering on her face.

"Did you kill Marva Modine?"

"Of course not! How could you think that?" she demanded.

"Devin, I'm a criminal attorney. How could I *not* think that? Did you kill anybody? Ever?"

"No," Devin said quietly, slumping against the silver BMW.

"Well," said her barrister, "maybe Sam Bradshaw did."

75

Back in her office, Alex felt that a great weight had been lifted from her heart and soul. Picking up the phone, she arranged for a company vehicle for Devin. The transportation department promised to send the keys right up. Devin bustled back in the door then, a little breathless from seeing her attorney off.

"Okay, let's talk, shall we?" Devin smiled, beckoning Alex to accompany her.

Alex followed her boss into the inner office, and the two women ensconced themselves on the same sofa they'd only recently vacated. In the short time that had ensued, they both realized, the dynamic of their relationship had changed forever.

"I never want to see Sam Bradshaw again," Alex started without preliminaries. "How can I possibly manage that and still work for this company?"

"I can't much stand to see the man, either," Devin chuckled. "We'll just keep him over on his side of town as much as we can."

Alex went on at length then about how Sam had enlisted her in a campaign of dirty tricks against Devin and confessed that she had readily agreed to it. And that he had reinstated her old level of pay for doing it.

"I can't justify anything I did," Alex said soberly, "or how badly I treated you over the last four years. I can only explain it. It was because I was in love with Paul."

"Men!" Devin exclaimed. "Or I should say, *that* man!"

Feeling like members of a very exclusive club, the two women shared insights into the late Paul Bradshaw then— his weaknesses, his strengths, what attracted them to him and what repelled them, his abundant charm, his defective moral compass, his energy, his good looks, and the shabby way he treated women.

They talked about Marva and the horror of the last two days. Alex looked anxiously at Devin, who had tears in her eyes. The two women found themselves truly communicating for the first time.

"What about the rape?" Devin asked at one point, despite Tanner's urging to leave it alone. Her conscience wouldn't allow her to do that.

"I'm going to get tested for AIDS and for pregnancy," Alex said with amazing calm. "Beyond that, I'm going to put it out of my mind."

"Why on earth. . . ?"

"Because I'm just as culpable as he is," Alex said gravely. "Even if a judge didn't see it that way, I always would."

They confided that each felt this was the beginning of a new relationship between the two of them, and the end of their separate relationships with Paul Bradshaw and his control over their lives.

After Devin had left for home in a PT van, Alex sat at her own desk and lifted her purse out of the lower cabinet. She took out her makeup kit. From one of the drawers she removed a small hand mirror on a base and stood it atop her desk. The detectives were due in twenty minutes. She realized that she was not dreading her meeting with them. She would simply tell the truth. How easy. She marveled at the concept. Lying was hard. Living a life of cheating with another woman's husband, and all the strategies, the scurvy schemes, the subterfuge and fabrication—that was hard. For years, that behavior had poisoned her system and drained her spirits. Dabbing on blush, she realized she felt like a brand-new person.

Suddenly she stopped, hit by a terrible flash. "Oh my God," she wailed, and went running out of her office and down the hall to the central bank of elevators. Frantically, she pushed buttons, and headed for the production area.

"Puce!" she fairly screamed at herself. "Gotta stop the fucking *puce* deluge!"

76

Billy Hilgarde smiled as he watched Devin pulling into the massive iron gates of her Benedict Canyon manse. She looked like a high rider, wheeling a big company van that had the neon lime and hot-pink PT logo painted on both sides. Working down and dirty in the heart of South-Central has really humanized the golden girl, Billy mused. On second thought, he'd bet money that Devin had always been down-to-earth. Despite the glossy patina, the woman was loaded with soul.

She apparently hadn't noticed Billy's black Trans Am parked across the street, half a block away. He waited a few moments, then drove up to the east gate of the mansion and pushed the bell. Devin's voice acknowledged him.

"Billy, is that you?" she asked, obviously making his Trans Am on the security monitor.

"Yo! Gotta see you," he said in the general direction of the steel box. She buzzed him in.

They hugged briefly at the front door. "How you holding up?" he asked as she led him down the wide central hall into the oak-paneled game room.

"Not great, but I'm trying to keep a grip on my sanity," she said. "I had a morning date with the good cop–bad cop team at Parker Center. Those guys watch too much television," she sighed, going around behind the sunken bar that stretched across the east end of the room.

"Drink, Billy?" she asked.

"Got a beer?"

"Of course."

She pulled out a frosty Corona and slid it across the polished granite surface. She knew Billy liked to drink his beer out of the bottle. She took a small bowl of lime wedges from the fridge and set it up on the bar, then poured herself a glass of Evian.

"The detectives told my lawyer what happened to you last night," Devin said then, facing Billy across the bar.

"Scared the shit outta me—I've gotta get out of town, Devin."

His gaze wandered past the magnificent leaded French doors to the lush lawns and gardens that rolled down to the pool and the twin tennis courts beyond.

"This joint is like getting outta town *in* town," Billy remarked absently.

"Not really," Devin said. "I'm leaving too. Tonight."

Billy raised his eyebrows. "Smart," he said. "Those eyes are bearing down on us, Devin. On you and me."

"Tell me what happened last night."

"I was pulling up at Vanna's house, right after work, broad daylight, when some cowboy shoots a hole right through my back window and out the front windshield," Billy said, trying not to sound as agitated as he felt. "Missed me by that much," he added, holding his hands about a foot apart.

"Did you see anyone, anything?"

"Nothing! Y'know, if I'd been coming home to my digs in South-Central, the drive-by shooting capital of the universe, thank you, I'd figure it was just some Eight-Tray Crips road dog on a tear, and thank God he missed me. But this was the friggin' *Valley,* Devin!"

"How's Vanna taking it?"

"She's freaking! She has a three-year-old!"

"So you're leaving town?"

"Have to," he said. "That's why I came over here, to tell you that. I've got vacation time coming, and Vanna does too, so we're going to take Tiffany and get out of here. I had the glass in the car replaced in a raging rush this morning. If the case hasn't broken in a couple of weeks I'll send Vanna back, but *I'm* going to *stay* gone till it's over. Without pay is fine. I'm scared, Devin, and now I'm putting Vanna and the baby in harm's way."

"Of course, go," Devin told him. "And of course you'll draw your pay. I want you safe, Billy, and Vanna too."

He could see that she had tears in her eyes. For Marva, he knew.

"Jesus, what a mess," he said quietly. "Am I leaving you high and dry?"

"Not at all," she said. "The ad campaign is dead. I'm just going to scrap the whole thing."

"No," Billy said, "you have to use those ads, for Marva. She was an outrageous exhibitionist. She loved having people enjoy looking at her, you know that."

"Maybe you're right," Devin smiled sadly, her emerald green eyes still brimming with tears. "I'll have to think about that. Anyway, the ads are the least of my concerns right now."

Billy's leave of absence agreed upon, he found himself tap-dancing around those concerns of hers. He still didn't know what had gone on up on Mulholland the day all the trouble started, or what Devin had to do with it, if anything, and he wasn't about to ask. Nor would he ask where she was going or tell her where he and Vanna and the baby would be. The troubling fact of the matter was that Billy wasn't absolutely positive that Devin wasn't behind the near miss he took last night. He watched her now, sipping her Evian, an ice goddess with tears in her eyes.

And to be fair, he considered, maybe Devin wasn't really sure that he, Billy, didn't put on the hit that was meant for her but killed Marva instead. What they both knew for sure was that the other one was up there that day. And what neither of them knew for sure was whether the other one did it, or saw the deed go down.

It was obvious that the same thoughts were on both their minds, these two people who worked together, who had genuine affection for each other, but who couldn't totally trust each other, and with good reason. The stakes were too high. There was murder involved, and both of them had become targets.

Now they'd come to a turning point. They both felt it, Billy knew. He was going up north indefinitely, and Devin said she was moving out of her house tonight. He wanted detente with Devin, an understanding that involved no innuendo, no subtleties, no unspoken thoughts or fears, only the truth between them. While he was thinking about it, pulling on his Corona, watching a hummingbird buzz around the crimson bougainvillaea that hung from the beams outside the French doors, Devin surprised him by putting her toe in the water first.

"Billy," she said, "I know we've been circumspect with each other, we've respected each other's precarious position in all of this—but I want you to know that I 'saw no evil' up there on Mulholland Drive. Nothing. And that's the truth."

"You didn't see him get shot?" Billy asked, picking up her cue. "*You* didn't see him go over? You didn't—?"

"Shoot him? No, I didn't."

"But you talked to him. You fought with him. I heard it on the news on my way over here."

"That's what I told the detectives this morning," she said, "and *you* know how they work. They must have leaked it already, put my statement out to the press, to insinuate subliminally to the jury pool that I'm guilty. I've seen enough of those movies, too."

"But you had a big fight with the man right on the spot where he bought it, and *you* didn't see what happened?" Billy asked again, not able to disguise his incredulity.

"No, I didn't see what happened. We fought, and I left."

"You're saying whatever happened went down after you split?"

"After I was gone," she confirmed.

All of a sudden he knew why she was telling him this. She wanted to convince him that even though she was up there, she never saw what happened afterward. On the outside chance that Billy Hilgarde actually was the guy who killed Paul Bradshaw, she wanted him to know that nobody could prove it by her. That told him something. It told him for sure that she wasn't the killer, but she wasn't sure if he was.

Her candor prompted Billy to tell *his* story. How Scud Joe Jones, stoned out of his gourd, was so jazzed behind the wheel of his powerful Trans Am that day that he got into racing the Ferrari. It became some kind of crazy game with that "menso," Billy told her, and at one point up on Mulholland he just zoomed past Bradshaw on one of the dead-man's curves. Then, when he slowed down and waited for the man, laughing like a base-head crazo, the Ferrari just never caught up with them.

"So you never saw what happened either?" Devin asked.

"No," he told her. "If I did I'd have told the cops and got my own black ass out of a sling."

"You saw nothing. . . ?"

"Well, I saw *you*. Standing in the rain. Couldn't miss you out there."

Truth time, Billy thought. He told Devin exactly how it played out with Scud Joe then. How when the cops had first come down on him, he needed to talk to Joe about it, get their stories straight, so he went looking for him in the 'hood. And he couldn't find him, so he nailed Tonio to tell Joe to meet him at Maurice's. Then, driving down Pico coming up on the restaurant just before seven, how he saw Joe get hit right in front of his eyes. And much as he had loved the slob since grade school, Billy said, he sure as hell wasn't going to get mixed up in this killing, so he kept his head down and kept right on driving, ducked around the next corner, went home, put his car in the underground garage, locked himself in his apartment, and cried all night.

The next day, he told Devin, he called a couple of home-boys he could trust and told them to find out who the hell did Scud Joe. Told them to start with Tonio, find out what went on there. And they came back with a pretty wild rap: "Tonio told them right after I asked him to get the message to Joe, somebody rolled up to him, guy in a beat-up white truck, and asked him what Billy Hilgarde wanted. Tonio told him to fuck off. The guy peeled out a hundred-dollar bill, and Tonio told him Billy just wanted him to tell a friend to meet him for dinner. What friend? the guy asks, and peels off another hundred. Tonio says a guy they call Scud Joe Jones. Dinner where? the cat wanted to know. What time? And what's this Scud guy look like? A third hundred. Tonio gave the man what he paid for. Even told him Joe would probably be wearing his old purple-and-gold Lakers jacket, which he usually did," Billy said.

Devin was digesting all of it. "And who was the guy in the truck?" she asked.

"None of the homies knew him," he said. "White guy, young, dark hair, in jeans and a warm-up jacket."

Devin and Billy talked on for a while, looking at each other hard at times. Still testing.

"So where are you going?" Devin asked him finally. The ultimate test, since his life was on the line here. He hesitated for just a moment, then he told her.

"Northern California. Big Sur, the Ventana Inn."

"A honeymoon spot," she smiled.

"Don't scare me," Billy grinned. "I'm scared enough already. Let's not talk marriage."

"I won't. What I know about marriage we can put in an eggcup."

"And you?" he asked. "Where are you going?"

"Nowhere exotic like you," she answered. "I'm moving into a suite at Checkers downtown. You know the hotel?"

"Sure, I know it," he said. "Nice place."

"No one can know where I am," she said.

"No kidding. No one can know where either of us are." Spontaneously, the two shook hands on that pact. And finally, each completely trusted the other.

"Okay," Billy said then, "let's figure this damn thing out."

It was clear to him now that someone else was up on Mulholland Drive that day. Somebody who saw Devin up there and saw Billy and Scud Joe up there and believed that one or all of them might have seen what happened. That was the person who whacked Paul Bradshaw, and that was the person who did Scud Joe Jones, and that was the person who tried to nail Devin and who shot at Billy last night. And would surely try again.

"Devin, what did you see?" he asked her then. "While you were up there, did you see anything, anyone who looked out of place?" She looked blank.

"Was there any traffic at all?" he asked. "Think!"

Devin closed her eyes. "I don't know," she said dismally. "I was so focused on what was going on between Paul and me that the Trojan Marching Band could have gone past and I wouldn't have noticed."

"Okay, then let's think about *who*," he said. "Who had reason to get rid of Paul Bradshaw? You could say Billy Hilgarde, of course, a black guy who had a serious beef with the man and had a fight with him that morning. Or Scud Joe Jones, a stoned-out nutcase who'd do anybody for money, drugs, or just the sport.

"Or you could say Devin Bradshaw," he went on, "who would have been cut off with just a prenuptial settlement when she left him, but instead came up very, very rich. Have I got that right?" She nodded gloomily.

"Okay, who else had reason?" he demanded.

"God, lots of people," Devin said. "People who hated Paul, people he'd hurt, people I don't even know about, I'm sure."

"But it had to be someone who knew where he was going to be that day, knew where he was headed and knew his route."

"That's a lot of people," Devin threw back.

"What about that assistant of yours, Alex Anson?" he asked. "It was all over the pipeline that she was his lover for years, then he dumped her for you. Would she have known where he was going?"

"Of course," Devin told him. "Alex was his personal assistant. She scheduled his calendar."

"Well, where was *she* that afternoon?"

Devin thought for a minute. "I seem to remember someone saying Alex stayed out of work with a headache that day—"

"Hah!" Billy cut her off. "So what *about* her?"

"No," Devin said. "Not Alex."

"Why *not* Alex?" he demanded.

"Because I've gotten to know Alex," Devin said, "and I know she couldn't do something like that."

"Oh, give me a break, Devin," Billy scoffed. "That one has 'World-Class Bitch' scrawled across her forehead!"

"Hey, we've had our problems," Devin told him. "We hated each other, for God's sake. But that's because she thought I took Paul away from her, and maybe I did. But murder? No," she said with finality.

"What makes you so sure?"

"Yesterday, I might have thought differently," Devin told him. "But I happen to know Alex well enough today to know that she doesn't have the soul of a criminal."

Not entirely convinced, Billy pressed on. "Who else?" he asked. "Who else had a reason, or stood to gain, and knew where the man would be? Think, Devin."

"His brother," Devin said quietly. "My lawyer thinks it was his brother."

"Who's your lawyer?"

"John Tanner," Devin told him. Billy's eyes widened.

"Whoa! John Tanner gets murderers off," he said.

"Oh, thanks a lot for that vote of confidence," she tossed at him with not a little chagrin.

"So let's talk about the brother," Billy urged. "I've seen

the cat around the plant. Looks like a major league sleaze
to me."

"Sam Bradshaw stood to gain big, more than anyone."
Devin said. "And he's a pig, yes, but a murderer? Of his
own brother? Still, he did get it all," she reflected. "Total
control of the company, the money, the power . . ."

"So what about Sam Bradshaw?" Billy asked. "Does *he*
have the soul of a criminal?"

Devin pondered that for a bit. "I can't stand the man,
and he hates me," she said finally, "so it's hard for me to
be objective. But in my dealings with Sam from day one,
I'd say he's cut from the exact same cloth as his brother,
only more so, and less so."

"Explain," Billy said.

"He's got more of Paul's ruthlessness, his callousness,
but less of Paul's business genius and vision. Could he be
a killer? I don't know."

"So where was Sam Bradshaw on the day in question?"

"He went to his mother's house for the family luncheon, too."

"And did he know where Paul was?"

"Certainly," she said. "He knew that Paul was en route
from the PT plant to Regina's house. They were supposed
to meet there."

The more they explored it, the more sense it made to
Billy. Sam had keys to the Pulled Together factory, of
course, and could have been aware that Devin would be
working late the night Marva was killed—might have
known that she would have to approve the sales samples
for next-day shipping. Sam would have realized that besides
the guards, Devin would be alone in the plant for a while
after closing time.

There was something else to consider, Billy told her. Julius Jackson had turned up dead in the company limo, in
what the cops had dismissed as a run-of-the-mill South-
Central robbery, but as they'd discussed before, Billy had
never believed that. He'd always felt that maybe Julius
knew something. Sam easily could have had Julius hit, he
said now. Sam Bradshaw controlled the limo and Julius.

"And what about Scud Joe?" Billy went on. "Who
killed Joe?"

"You said it was a *young* white guy nosing around, laying
out money for information," Devin reminded him.

"Shit," Billy said, "guy like Sam Bradshaw is not gonna go knocking off some black dude in South-Central, are you kidding? He'd hire it done."

"Look," Devin said then, "Sam Bradshaw's a big, puffed-up, arrogant, sexist, not very talented egomaniac, but I just can't believe he would kill people."

"Well, you'd better believe *somebody* damn well killed people here," Billy said soberly, " 'cuz people definitely got killed, and it's looking like that same somebody who killed them is now gunning for you and me."

Devin shivered. "But murder? Sam?" she said, still incredulous.

"Why *not* Sam?" Billy demanded. "Give me a couple of good reasons why *not* Sam Bradshaw."

"Well, Sam is . . . so Beverly Hills!" she threw out.

"Oh, you mean it's just us black OG's from South-Central who chill folks? Wake up and smell the big money, woman," Billy hurled back.

Devin's phone rang. She picked it up. It was John Tanner.

"Bad news, Devin," he said in clipped tones. "Very bad news. They've done the tests on your Jaguar at the crime lab, and the paint matches the black paint transfer on your husband's Ferrari."

"My God," Devin gasped. "But how could that be?"

"You tell *me,* Devin," the attorney said tersely.

"I . . . I don't know."

"It means the front of your car came in contact with the back of his car. They found the bruise on your Jaguar."

Devin felt like all the oxygen had been sucked out of the room. "I didn't do it . . . ," she managed in a raspy voice.

"This looks very bad, Devin," Tanner persisted. "Your car hit your husband's car, and the tests show it happened within twenty-four hours of the time when he was killed."

After a few moments' pause, Devin squealed, "Oh! Of course! My car *did* hit his car!"

"Tell me," Tanner said dryly.

"I was going into the garage on the day of our big dinner party," she raced her words, "and I bumped into the back of the Ferrari. I'd forgotten about it."

"Really?" Tanner asked skeptically.

"Yes, of course, really," Devin insisted. "It was pouring rain, and I'd fractured my wrist . . ."

Billy listened with interest, his eyes narrowed, as Devin continued to explain how she'd run into the back of her husband's Ferrari on the day *before* he was killed, and how she'd inspected it at the time and couldn't see any damage. He heard her answer Tanner's questions several times over. What time? What were the circumstances? Who else knew about it? No one knew about it; she didn't tell anyone; it wasn't a problem; she forgot about it, she said. When Devin got off the phone, she was ashen.

"Tanner says I'm in worse trouble," she breathed. "He says the paint on my car matched—"

"I know, I heard," Billy interrupted. "Listen, I just got an idea. Tell me, what kind of car does Sam Bradshaw drive?"

Devin thought for a moment, trying to pull herself together. "I don't know. I never noticed," she offered weakly.

Billy picked up the phone then and called Bo Whitley, the head of security at Pulled Together. Bo was a black guy, a friend of his. Billy knew that the security department had a list of all the cars belonging to people who had company PIN numbers and designated spots in the PT parking lot. He asked Bo what kind of car Sam Bradshaw drove.

"Let's see," Whitley said. "Here it is—Samuel Bradshaw, *the Second*, it sez here, is listed as driving a 1993 black Cadillac de Ville."

"Bingo!" Billy said. "Catch you later, bro!" He put the phone down and looked at Devin, his wheels turning.

"The shop that services all the company trucks and cars, the one the company owns, Bradshaw Automotive," he said, "do they take care of the family vehicles too?"

"Yes," she replied. "Sam's son runs it. Paul always sent our cars there."

"Well, if Sam's Caddy was the lethal weapon, he'd sure as hell have had it fixed by now. And they'd have records there," Billy said, thinking out loud.

"The shop is right around the corner from L.A. Garb."

"Come on, Devin, let's go pay a visit, see what we can see!" Billy grabbed her impulsively.

"Are you crazy? What can we possibly see?"

"Probably nothing," Billy said, "but you never know."

He picked up the phone again and checked information for the number and address of Bradshaw Automotive in Santa Monica. And even as she was protesting, he managed to shuffle Devin out the door and into his Trans Am.

77

"This is nuts," Devin repeated. They were heading west on Sunset Boulevard, and Billy was explaining that she should distract whoever was there so he could take a look around the place.

"Tell them you need to buy some kind of truck or van for work, that you don't want to be driving your high-profile Jag into South-Central every day," he told her.

"But it's not a car dealership," Devin reminded him. "It's an auto-repair shop."

"I know, but tell 'em being that they're in the business, and being family and all, you figured they could give you some advice. Ask if they happen to have a good used vehicle for sale, or if they have any customers who are looking to sell one."

"You think they'll go for that?"

"Sure," Billy said. "Most mechanics know where to find a few good buys. Customers they know want to unload some wheels. Or ask them to tell you the best place to go, recommend a reputable dealer. Say you don't want anything new or fancy, just something that won't attract attention and that'll be reliable."

"Actually," Devin said, "that happens to be a good idea. Maybe I *should* get myself a nondescript car and just blend in."

"You bet it's a good idea, Devin," Billy said. "This is the nineties, and the carjacker is king. The trick nowadays is to be rich but look poor."

"Okay, so I should tell them I need some kind of clunker . . ."

"Just schmooze 'em, talk to them," Billy said, "so I can snoop around."

"And what exactly are you going to be looking for while I'm shopping for a used van?"

"I don't know—top of my wish list would be a black

Cadillac with the right front bashed in and the headlight busted, and some Ferrari-red paint stains on it."

"Oh sure," Devin smirked.

"If I really get lucky, maybe I can grab a look through some paperwork, see an invoice on a recent fix of a front end, like on a '93 black Caddy."

"Would they actually write it up?" she asked.

"Why not? Do you think Sam Bradshaw would tell the mechanics, 'Don't do any paperwork on this car—I just killed my brother with it'?"

Devin winced. "Maybe we've *both* seen too many movies," she said.

Billy pulled to a stop in front of the place, a standard-looking auto-service shop on Lincoln Boulevard in Santa Monica. The words BRADSHAW AUTOMOTIVE were lettered in black on a two-foot-high corrugated tin sign above the entrance. Inside they found Myles Bradshaw, in dirty jeans and an oily T-shirt, working on a vintage Fiat. Parked here and there were a few of the familiar yellow-and-orange panel trucks that said L.A. GARB on their sides, and one big van bearing the neon-hued Pulled Together logo.

"Myles, hi!" Devin said, flashing him a dazzling smile that would melt a glacier. "It's me, Devin."

"Oh, hello," Myles returned, unpleasantly, she thought, without stopping what he was doing.

Devin pointedly did not introduce Billy Hilgarde, but Myles didn't seem to care or even notice. While he kept his head buried under the hood of the Fiat, she delivered her prepared rap. Myles never stopped his tinkering to look at her. He's a Bradshaw, Devin reminded herself. Doesn't like me and isn't bothering to keep it a secret. The young man was abrupt, bordering on surly.

"Can't help you," he said when she was finished. "We don't sell cars. We fix 'em."

"Myles, you look like you've been working out," Devin said then, tossing him yet another brilliant smile. He continued to ignore her.

Devin couldn't remember a time in her life when she'd made such a considered effort to melt someone, trying to charm this sullen, churlish stepnephew of hers. Meantime, Billy Hilgarde was wandering around the place. After a time, Billy ambled over and asked Myles about a dirty oversized white Chevy Blazer that was parked against the far wall.

"Is that one for sale?" he queried.

"I told you," Myles spat, not looking up at Billy either, "nothing's for sale. I can't help you. Try some of the used-car lots around the corner."

"Good idea," Billy said. "Let's go, Devin. Santa Monica Boulevard is used-car row, we'll find something."

"You think?" Devin asked.

"I think," Billy grinned. "Thanks, man," he shot back at the head under the hood. Myles ignored them.

Billy helped Devin into his Trans Am, walked around to the driver's side, jumped in and closed the door, and immediately fished a card out of his wallet. He started the car, wheeled it out into traffic, then read a number off the card and punched it up on his car phone. Detective Furrino wasn't there, but Billy got his voice mail.

"Hi," he said into the speakerphone, "this is Billy Hilgarde. I'm calling to tell you that I really don't love getting shot at, so I'm leaving town. I'm outta here tonight," he told the machine, "going up the coast for a while. You can find me if you need me, at the Ventana Inn in Big Sur. It's listed, just ask for me. Call me if you have any problems with that.

"Also," he continued in a monotone, "I'd appreciate it if you didn't tell anybody where I am. With the people you and Ryan are interrogating, you might be telling the shooter."

He was about to sign off, then added a postscript. "Oh, and by the way, I suggest you guys take a good look at the dead man's brother, Sam Bradshaw—I hear he had about six reasons to want his brother dead, and the deceased's widow tells me the man is mean enough to've got it done. See ya. Over and out."

"Reporting in to Frick and Frack, huh?" Devin said.

"More like Beavis and Butt-head," Billy laughed. "If I don't tell them I'm leaving town, they'll probably decide I'm on the lam and put out an APB on me."

"So, how did you like my charming nephew?" Devin served up then, a mischievous grin lighting up her face.

"Yup, family's crazy about you, all right," Billy chuckled. "Must make you feel all warm and fuzzy."

"What did we learn, anything?"

"I don't know," Billy said. "I zeroed in on that beat-up white Blazer just because it fit the bill for the kind of junker you were supposed to be shopping for. But there was something about that old truck that bothered me."

"I'm sure it's because the mystery man who was dealing hundred-dollar bills in South-Central was reportedly in a beat-up white truck," Devin said.

"No, no, light-colored trucks are a dime a dozen," Billy countered, negotiating the Trans Am eastbound onto the Santa Monica Freeway. "But when I asked the kid about it, he jumped down my throat."

"That's because you were with me, the wicked, gold-digging stepaunt," she told him.

"Still," Billy said thoughtfully, "there was something about that truck . . ."

78

Devin poured herself an inch of Grand Marnier from the bar in Paul's study and sank gratefully into one of the plush leather chairs. Billy had left to pack up his car, collect Vanna and her toddler, and hit the Coast highway for higher ground. This was the first chance she'd had to read Tanner's letter. Picking up the gold letter opener set with cabochon-cut rubies that she'd gifted Paul with on their first Valentine's Day, she slit the top of the envelope. Reaching inside, she slid out a lone page typewritten on Brigant, Hale, Tanner & Lowe letterhead.

Glancing at the bottom of the sheet, she saw no secretary's notation—good, the missive was private, she hoped. She felt a surge of heat flush through her body at the sight of Tanner's bold signature. Making an effort to stop her hands from trembling, she read the letter.

Dear Devin,
  I have no idea what happened to make you so angry

with me, but I've been calling you every day, as you know,
because I want to set the record straight. I never betrayed
you, never would hurt you, never even told anyone that I
knew you until you retained my father as your legal coun-
sel. Since I am part of the firm, I was then obligated to tell
him about our professional relationship and what ended it,
because it relates to your case.

Devin read that paragraph three times. "... obligated to
tell him about our *professional* relationship ..." The subtext, she determined, was that he did not tell his father
about their *sexual* relationship. Thank God for small things,
she sighed.

Tanner went on to explain that even if he were subpoenaed or deposed as a witness against her, he could not be
compelled to divulge any of her confidences, because he's
a lawyer, and anything they spoke about was privileged.
The fact that they conducted their consults in the gym, he
noted, had no relevancy to their legal exchange. Lawyers
do business in gyms, in steam baths, on handball courts, in
restaurants, on the phone, anywhere, he noted. Brilliant,
she thought.

Most important, she believed wholeheartedly now that
he had not betrayed her. Picking up the phone, she dialed
the number that was etched in her memory. Tanner's number. When she heard his recorded voice on the answering
machine, her heart did an involuntary flip. The beep jolted
her back to reality.

"John, this is Devin," she said into the phone, and she
could hear the jitters in her own voice. "Umm ... I just
read your note," she began. "I know now that it wasn't
you who told Sam Bradshaw or anyone else that I had
intended to divorce my husband. I'm sorry I doubted you."

She paused for a beat. Had she used up her time, or was
this one of those machines that would let her go on at
length? She didn't know; all the previous messages she'd
left for him had been brief. No beep yet. Oh Lord, she
agonized, why was this so hard?

"I'm moving out of the Benedict house tonight, and you
left some of your things in the gym. The rack with your
own set of weights, several pairs of wrist and ankle rings,
some gym clothes, other items. I'm packing. I'll be here for

another few hours, and you're welcome to come by and pick up your things."

Still no cutoff beep. She thought for half a second, then added: "Remember I told you that the house does not belong to me, it's owned by the estate? Well, the sale is being handled by Paul's brother and a slew of lawyers, so after tonight I can't promise that you'll be able to get in and remove your things without wading through some legal red tape. To collect your stuff, I mean . . ."

She made a face as she babbled on into Tanner's machine. She fervently wished that she could erase the whole damn thing and start over. Make it shorter, simpler, more businesslike. Because she knew she hadn't even vaguely disguised the subtext of her message, which was, of course, "I want to see you."

She hung up the phone and sat very still for a minute, listening to the resounding thump of her racing heart. She realized she was still clutching Tanner's letter tightly in her hand, and in fact she'd managed to smudge his signature with her sweaty fingers. Get a grip, Devin Yorke, she scolded herself. His letter was quite impersonal; there was not a hint that he had any desire to pick up where their fiery but brief fling had left off. He could have loads of women, she was sure—why would he want one who'd already given him so much grief? Not to mention one with a monumental load of personal baggage, including a possible imminent arrest on murder charges. Who knows, maybe he believed she really did murder her husband. Closing her eyes, she willed her heartbeat to slow down. She could feel her system quickly returning to its normally low resting pulse rate. At least Tanner would be proud of that, she smiled ruefully.

She placed the letter in a visible spot on top of Paul's desk, so she wouldn't forget to take it with her. Then, on impulse, she put the gold and ruby letter opener from Cartier on top of it. She'd always loved that piece. It would probably end up being hawked at some auction house somewhere. Might as well take it with her too, for luck.

Her eyes fell upon the bulging accordion-file container that Essie Jackson had given her after Julius's funeral two days ago. Since she'd brought the tightly bound bundle of documents home, it had remained untouched on the desk. In the headlong rush and confusion of ensuing events, she'd forgotten about it. Running her hand over the smooth, terra-cotta-colored file folder, she supposed it contained trip logs, repair orders, and other papers related to the company limousine, carefully saved for more than thirty years by Paul's loyal chauffeur. She felt another twinge of sadness for the man, and for his wife and family.

Lifting a pair of scissors out of a desk drawer, she cut the twine that was wrapped around it. She decided to glance quickly through the file's contents to see if there was anything pertaining to Julius that Essie should have. Otherwise, she would leave the folder to be packed and stored with her personal things, and deal with it later when she was settled.

Devin eased the huge bunch of documents halfway out of the container. There had to be hundreds of them. Suddenly, she let out a gasp as she saw the title page of the file on the top of the stack: L.A. GARB, and under the name of the company, in small, discreet print, "Bragg, Schlemmer & Schultz." *The report!* Somehow, for some reason, Julius had a copy of the report!

She quickly pulled the inch-thick file out of the container. Scanning the first few single-spaced pages, her eyes widened as she caught the words "mismanagement" ... "fraud" ... "kickbacks" ... "rampant theft." At one point she spotted the underlined heading, "Rogue Deliveries." She fanned to the end of the report—it was 226 pages long.

Whatever these pages contained was what Sam Bradshaw didn't want her to know about. Devin felt sure that this elusive B.S.&S. report was going to provide some answers. She tucked it back inside the file container and slid the bulky package next to Tanner's letter and the jeweled opener. She would study the report carefully as soon as she got to the hotel. Right now she had a full agenda and not much time.

She did not look forward to the task of packing up her life tonight. Well, not her life. Just a few things that she wanted to take out of this palace of excess, with which she would start anew.

Which reminded her, better make a reservation. She picked up the phone and called Checkers to see if they had rooms available. Waiting for the reservations desk to pick up, she remembered reading that the infamous Charles Keating had stayed at Checkers during his lengthy federal trial on the Lincoln Savings and Loan fraud. Oh well, she thought with chagrin, if she was indicted for murder, Checkers was right around the corner from the courthouse.

She reserved a suite with a kitchenette for herself, and an adjoining room for Maria. She didn't want Maria staying in the big house alone. Sam could hire a crew to come in and clean. If there was anything to be learned from Marva's murder, it was that Devin could not take the chance, no matter how remote, that there could be yet another hapless victim of mistaken identity, someone a killer might think was Devin.

She picked up the phone again and rang for Maria. Before she and Billy had rushed out to Santa Monica, she'd told Maria that the two of them would be moving out of the house that night. In their brief exchange, she gave her housekeeper advice that she needed to heed herself: don't think of this as a big-deal move, think of it as a trip downtown and a few nights in a hotel. She was determined to keep her tension level down and to keep Maria from being overwhelmed as well. Thank God she didn't have a dog, she thought. Or *kids*!

Devin heaved a wistful sigh. She would so love to have a sweet little girl, a rambunctious little boy. *And* a dog. Would she ever have the family she dreamed of? Maybe that thunderous beat she'd heard earlier wasn't the sound of her heart after all, she grimaced. Maybe it was the just the raucous ticking of her biological clock.

"Yes, Mrs. Bradshaw?" Maria's refined voice came on the line.

"Maria, meet me in the kitchen, will you?" she asked. "We'll decide what we want to take to the hotel."

By the time Devin got down to the kitchen, Maria had already started gathering things. "We'll need the blender so I can make your fresh juice and fiber shakes—we'll have a little kitchen, yes?"

"Yes," Devin smiled. What would she do without Maria? Wonderful Maria was not thinking about the gas chamber, she was thinking about fresh squeezed carrot juice.

The two women compiled a hasty list. Devin would leave Maria to assemble, pack, and load the things, along with her own suitcases, into the station wagon. She carefully wrote out the name of the hotel and directions to it, so Maria could go on ahead and get their rooms settled. They would go separately because each woman would need her own car, Devin explained. Then she remembered that in place of her Jaguar there was a big PT van in the garage. Good, she thought, it's got more room to pack stuff.

"Don't you worry about anything, Mrs. Bradshaw," Maria comforted her now. "I'll warm up our little quarters before you get there."

"Thanks, Maria," Devin breathed. "I should be just an hour or so behind you."

"Can I help you with your packing?"

"No," Devin said. "I don't intend to bring much, or be too late tonight. I'm really tired. Anything we need later, we'll come back for."

Devin looked a little sadly around the gleaming, refulgent, double kitchen that *Architectural Digest* had labeled "a master chef's personal dream of paradise."

"All the flowers will die," she murmured absently, her eyes wandering to several of the lush arrangements that Mark Janssen filled the house with every week.

"I'll bring them," Maria pronounced.

"Oh, no . . ."

"Certainly, Mrs. Bradshaw," Maria protested. "We'll have fresh flowers in every cranny at the Checkerboard Hotel."

"Checkers," Devin laughed.

"Checkers," Maria echoed cheerfully. "I'll see you there soon."

As Maria launched into her packing chores, Devin stopped in the study to pick up the things she'd left on Paul's desk, then hurried upstairs to the master suite. She dropped the items she was carrying on a bench in her dressing room, then stepped into the bathroom. She really needed to relax for a few minutes to ease the tension that was building behind her eyes. Running hot water into the Jacuzzi tub, she shook some bath oils under the steaming tap and flipped on the jets.

She stepped out of her clothes and tossed them down the laundry chute. Easing into the bath, she sank her shoulders beneath the surface and closed her eyes, savoring the bubbling, swirling waters. She would try to clear her mind of the vortex of insanity and danger in which she found herself inexorably spinning. She refused to think about any of it; she would take this short respite to meditate.

When she climbed out of the tub she felt decidedly refreshed. The hot Jacuzzi was a good idea. Quickly, she
dried off, then pulled on a pair of jeans and a T-shirt. She
hauled four Louis Vuitton cases out of her dressing-room
cabinets, the same bags she'd started to fill the day her
husband was killed. Opening each of the suitcases and lining them up on the sofa, she wondered for a minute if she
should make a list. No, she decided, just throw some things
together and get on with it. It was already after seven. The
first items she packed were Essie Jackson's file, the Cartier
letter opener, and Tanner's letter.

A buzz sounded on the intercom, breaking her concen-
tration. It was Maria, reporting that she'd put everything
she thought they would need for now in the wagon, and
she was about to leave for the hotel.

"Call me when you're in our rooms," Devin told her.

"And you be sure to call me when you're ready to leave
the house," Maria returned. "I'll have tea waiting."

Devin put down the phone and turned to the task of
packing up a small slice of her life for what would be a
smaller life, but certainly more tranquil, more manageable,
and much more fulfilling, she hoped. She would not miss
her old life. Or this house. She was ready to leave it all.

Suddenly it hit her that for the first time ever, she was
completely alone on the huge estate. It was not a comfortable feeling. She hurried now, quickly opening closets and
drawers and tossing things into bags.

79

The key fit. He knew it would. Slowly, he turned it in
the lock until he heard the muffled *thump.* Easy. A
door within a gate, he shrugged. Silly concept. He pushed
inward on the fancy iron bars, carefully, noiselessly opening
the door. Not a creak. Why would there be? It was
nearly new.

Before closing it behind him, he made sure to press the

flip button that retracted the self-locking latch. If he left the door ajar, it would look suspicious from the street. This way it was closed, but not locked. He wouldn't have to use the key if he had to get the hell out of here in a hurry.

He knew there was no dog to worry about. Paul was stupid not to have kept a dog or two on these massive grounds. He used to say dogs fuck up your rugs, fuck up your furniture, fuck up your gardens, fuck up your peace and quiet. He'd tried to tell Paul that you needed dogs for the noise factor alone on an estate like this, in case you ever had intruders. After all, he was the practical one in the family. But Paul had just laughed, condescending as usual.

He padded across the spongy grass, still damp from yesterday's rain. Halfway down the west side of the house he encountered another gate, one he hadn't figured on. One he'd never noticed before, but that wasn't surprising. It was not as if he were a regular guest here. This side gate was definitely not in the house plans—it must have been a later addition. It was a fancy iron gate that matched the rest of the ornate ironwork, but this one didn't have the sophisticated dead latch. It was secured with just a laminated metal padlock.

He was in no mood for climbing, nor was he in great shape for this kind of caper, but he'd have to go over the eight-foot-high gate. He had no idea how to trip the lock, and he didn't have the tools to break it. Lifting the glinty padlock in his gloved right hand, he stooped to examine it. Hallelujah! The shackle was lined up in position with the hole, but it wasn't clamped down. The damn thing wasn't even locked! A lazy gardener's trick, he reflected. Don't bother locking the side gates so you could freely push them open and shut, get from the back to the front of the property without the nuisance of having to use a key every time.

He removed the padlock and dropped it in the grass, then pushed the big gate open. Quietly, he walked the length to the end of the house. Rounding the corner at the back of the lot, he scanned the expansive rear grounds for signs of activity. His gaze tracked over the gleaming, night-lit Olympic-sized swimming pool and the tennis courts beyond, and out past the rolling slopes that marked the property line. Nobody. Nothing.

The back of the house was shrouded with dense foliage. Funny, he'd never noticed that before. The house was practically new; how did it grow so fast? They must have brought in mature trees and plants. He'd have to get under the overhang and count the doors to the drop-room, which housed the entire central control system for the sprawling estate. At least that's what he was counting on.

He reached into an inside pocket and pulled out some tightly folded house plans. Not the entire set of plans; he'd have needed a suitcase to carry them. Crouching next to a low stone wall, he spread the few sheets out on the ground so they'd be illuminated, albeit dimly, by one of the low nightscape lights that dotted the property. Leafing through the cumbersome architectural renderings, he came upon the section he needed. The rear elevations. Fourteen doors, all of them the same dimensions. The outside entrance to the drop-room was supposed to be the sixth door from the west side of the house. Also foolish. There never should have been an outside door.

He'd have to find it by feel in the dark. He purposely hadn't brought a flashlight. If a light was seen moving across the grounds, somebody inside might immediately push one of the panic buttons and all hell would break loose. Pressing close to the back wall, he traversed the rear of the mansion and counted the doors. Three . . . four . . . five . . . six. This should be the one.

Again, the key fit. The same key! More foolish planning. For someone who'd never done this before, he couldn't believe how easy it was. For a man to whom this prowling business was totally alien, who was so nervous he could have a heart attack, for God's sake, he was astounded at what a piece of cake it was. In fact, it was a huge lesson to him in effective security.

He opened the door and peered inside, at dozens of glowing lights and digital readouts blinking in the dark. Locating a light switch, he pulled the door shut behind him and turned on the overhead lights. This was it! His eyes quickly scanned the sophisticated utility installation from one side to the other, across rows and rows of burnished black-and-chrome hi-tech equipment. It was all there. The main electrical power drop; the complex alarm-system hookup; TELCO, the drop for the phone lines; CATV, the cable-TV distribution system; the central vacuum system; the timing mechanisms for the irrigation works over the spacious grounds, and more.

He knew exactly what he had to do.

80

Devin held up a nude, ultrasheer teddy made of delicate, handmade Alençon lace, the bodice and hem interwoven with strands of the narrowest ivory-and-champagne-colored satin ribbons. She tossed it back into the drawer. Why bother? The way her life was going, she probably wouldn't be having sex again in this century. Packing was taking longer than she'd anticipated. It had turned into a bigger chore than just tossing a few things together. She needed to pull several weeks of outfits for work, complete with the right shoes, jewelry, and accessories, or she'd have to keep running back here, and she knew that would be a drain on her time and hard on her psyche.

It didn't help that her energy was completely sapped tonight, between the strain of events and her almost total lack of sleep over the past forty-eight hours. The thought of crawling into bed with a magazine and a cup of tea in a safe, cozy hotel suite kept her going. She made a mental note to call John Tanner Senior before it got too late, to let him know she'd be at Checkers. Tomorrow she'd cancel the newspapers, the mail, the flowers and the phones, keeping just one line in service to operate the gates. She scooped up some exercise clothes and pitched them into a suitcase. She was going to miss her fabulous gym. The workout room at the hotel was limited, so she planned to join a public gym until the Bel Air house was ready. She started sorting through drawers of lingerie and hose in her meticulously organized dressing area, when suddenly the lights in her bedroom suite went out. All of them.

Damn, great time for a power blowout! she fumed. Even the usually blinking digitals on TV monitors, VCRs, and clocks were dark. It was probably a circuit breaker. She was no good when it came to most mechanical failures, but she did know where the main circuit-breaker box was in the garage. It was a huge house, and this had happened before, the electric circuitry for some reason jamming on overload, temporarily blacking out entire wings of the mansion. In the past, though, someone had always been around to handle it. She would have to go downstairs and flip the breakers herself.

Groping her way in the dark through her dressing room, then out through the bedroom, she managed to find the double doors to the adjoining sitting room. From there, she headed toward the doors to the outside hall. But midway across the carpeted floor in the pitch black, she heard a noise. Stopping in her tracks, a chill gripping her body, she cocked her head and listened. And heard it again, downstairs. Someone was in the house!

Had Maria come back for something? Should she call out? Her instincts told her to be quiet. Noiselessly, except for the racket her heart was making, she moved the rest of the way to the high double doors of the master suite and secured the deadbolt lock. Then she felt her way over to one of the sofas in the sitting room, where she knew there was a telephone on the table at the far end. The way the electrical system was designed in the house, when the power went out, the phones did not. She would dial 911.

Eerily, there wasn't even the usual illumination filtering in through the windows. The extensive outside lighting throughout the grounds seemed also to be totally dark, and even the moon was shrouded by the heavy overcast trailing yesterday's storm. Devin stumbled across the sofa she'd been feeling for along the back wall and found the phone. She picked up the receiver, and quickly punched in the digits by touch, nine on the third row, right side of the grid, two ones at the top left—then she put the receiver to her ear. Nothing. *The line was dead.*

She dropped the phone and froze. Now she could hear the unmistakable sound of footsteps coming up the stairs, then along the hall, the tap-tapping on the limestone floors echoing in the stillness, amplified by the emptiness of the enormous house. For seconds that seemed an eternity, Devin was paralyzed.

Forcing herself to snap out of it, she rallied and made her way back through the glass doors of the sitting room and into the master bedroom. Stumbling hastily in the dark, she knocked into a table, sending a porcelain lamp crashing to the floor. Doggedly, she groped her way to the low chiffonnier by the side of the king-sized bed, where she kept the Smith & Wesson .38 that Irv Chapman had reverted to her name. It was loaded.

The detectives had returned that gun just a couple of weeks ago, and Devin knew exactly where to put her hands on it. Feeling around in the top drawer for a few seconds, she managed to get her fingers around the cold metal handle just as she heard a key turning in the lock in the next room. Someone was actually using a house key and coming into her bedroom suite!

Who had a key? Devin thought wildly as she cocked the pistol with expertise, even though her hand was shaking badly. All the doors in the house were keyed the same—one key would get you in any door, including the front door. Maria had a key. The rest of the help had turned in their keys before leaving her employ, but that wouldn't have stopped a devious soul from making a duplicate before doing so, Devin knew.

Tanner had a key! She'd given him a house key so he could come in through the door in the west gate in the early mornings without waking up the household. He would let himself into the gym, which was not on the alarm system, and where she would usually find him doing his warm-up stretches at six o'clock. When she fired him, she hadn't thought to ask that he return her key. Could this be Tanner coming to pick up his things, as she had invited him to tonight? No—if it were Tanner, he wouldn't be creeping into her locked bedroom suite in the dark.

All this flashed through her mind in seconds, while she listened in terror to somebody opening the locked door to the sitting room next door. Quickly, she scrambled toward the master bath. The immense bathroom door was made of oak-faced reinforced steel and had double deadbolts that locked from the inside. That door could *not* be opened from the outside with a key. It had been designed as a safe-room. There was a phone in there, although that line could be dead too, she knew. But at least if she could lock herself inside that room, nobody could get to her.

In the pitch black, she stumbled toward the door of the safe haven, clutching the gun so tightly that her hand hurt. Suddenly, she heard the etched-glass double doors from the sitting room open. The intruder was in the bedroom with her!

She dropped behind a settee and crouched noiselessly in the dark. She could feel the person moving stealthily about the room, could hear sharp intakes of breath. Her heart was pounding thunderously in her chest. She was about forty feet away from the safe-room. If she could make it to that refuge and double-bolt the impenetrable steel door, she could wait it out.

Maria was smart. When Devin didn't show up at the hotel, and when she couldn't reach her here at home, she would call out the troops. Even though Devin had never discussed the case or its attendant horrors with her, the woman had to be aware. She knew how devastated Devin was by Marva's murder, and Julius's too. She knew that they were leaving this house tonight for security reasons; she didn't need to be told. Why else would Devin insist on moving out just weeks before their new house in Bel Air was ready? In an hour or two, not much longer, when Maria couldn't find her, she would call the police and they'd begin a search. Meanwhile, Devin would be safe behind that steel-reinforced door, one that the intruder couldn't possibly penetrate.

Noiselessly, she moved on her hands and knees from out behind the French settee and crept across the floor toward her dressing room and the master bath beyond, the safe-room. Picking up her pace, she unwittingly brushed up against a large basket of orchids she'd forgotten was standing on the floor near the settee. She stopped. Had the intruder heard her? The plants were rustling from the impact. As she remained frozen in place, suddenly a shot ripped through the silence, and Devin actually felt the *whoosh* of a bullet blaze past her ears. She let out an involuntary yelp.

"Did I get you?" a man's jeering voice shattered the silence. Devin said nothing. She turned in the direction of the voice, and she thought she saw movement. She raised the .38 and squeezed the trigger.

"Hey!" the man wailed, then took two fast shots in her direction. She could hear the bullets thud into the wall behind her.

She moved, fast. He heard her and took another shot, and she could sense that this one was closer. She fired off two rounds into the darkness and prayed.

"You bitch, you're dead!" the man roared, and Devin

recognized the voice, even though he was obviously trying
to disguise it. It was Sam Bradshaw!

"Sam, don't. You're ruining your life," she uttered trem-
ulously, wedging herself down behind a wide club chair.
She had to fight to keep herself from passing out from fear.

"You're going to die, so what do you care?" he taunted
her, and Devin knew that she had to pull herself together
and try to talk him out of this. He had gone over the edge,
had crossed over into insanity.

"You killed Paul, didn't you, Sam?" she put out there
in the dark. "Tell me why."

"Because of the report," he said simply, and with that,
he took another shot. Five shots. It was impossible to know
how many he had in his gun, and probably he had more
rounds with him. There were just three shots left in her .38.

"Sam, did you kill Marva?" she whispered, sensing him
moving closer.

That summoned another shot, and Devin heard the bullet
thunk into the down upholstery of the heavy, overstuffed
chair that shielded her. While the noise still hung on the
air, she deftly moved from the shelter of the chair to behind
its mate a few feet away.

"It was supposed to be you," he breathed.

"Where did you find my gun?" Devin asked, trying to
sound conversational, trying to distract him so she could
make a break for her dressing room and the safe-room
beyond.

"In the desk drawer where Paul put it, where do you
think?" he threw back with disdain, and he took another
shot. She saw the blazing streak slash the air a foot from
where she was cowering behind the oversized club chair.
From the bullet's trajectory, she could tell that he was just
a few feet away from her on the other side of the chair.
Suddenly, she was fueled by adrenaline, made of steel now.

"Did you kill Julius, too?" she yelled, then quickly
moved from behind the chair to the side of a tall Edwar-
dian armoire, just a few yards away from the door to the
dressing room and safety beyond.

"Of course I killed Julius," he sneered, and with that, he
got off a shot that hit its mark. At first it felt like just a
gentle touch on the wrist, then a hot blast of pain seared
through her left hand and up her arm. Shit, he got me!

she inwardly raged, her terror turning to fury. In the *other wrist,* goddammit!

She cradled her bleeding hand between her midsection and her right elbow, as she wielded the .38 in her right hand. She wasn't about to let the bastard know he'd winged her. Peering out from around the side of the armoire, her eyes fully adjusted to the darkness now, she thought she saw a shadow moving across the room toward her. She shot at it. It kept moving. She shot again. She was enraged. She was shooting like a man now, shooting to save herself, shooting to kill.

She couldn't actually see him, but she could hear him, she could sense him, she could smell him. He was changing positions, crouching low, ducking behind furniture, just as she was doing. Her arm was vibrating with pain, and she could feel a stream of warm blood draining from the wound, saturating her thin T-shirt.

"You've got Paul's old .38," Sam almost sang out then. "That means you have one shot left, lady!"

She fired the shot directly at the spot his voice was coming from, and he let out a howl. She'd nailed him!

"You just nicked me!" he cried out. "And you're done. Six shots and you're out! Give it up, you're dead," he cackled. My God, the man was truly mad, Devin realized, as his voice grew higher-pitched, thinner, more desperate, crazy.

Suddenly, the peal of a telephone shrieked through the dark. After two rings there was a click, then Devin was stunned to hear the resonant voice of the dead Paul Bradshaw: "We can't take your call right now . . ." It took her a moment to realize what she was hearing . . .

It was the alarm system's emergency backup line, on a battery-powered cellular phone. She had forgotten about that isolated phone line. In the event the sophisticated burglar alarm in the mansion was tripped during a power outage or phone-system malfunction, its purpose was to automatically generate a call to the alarm system's monitoring station so the police would be alerted. *God help me,* she thought, *it's working! If it does what it's supposed to do, the police will come!* Devin said a silent prayer.

That backup system was also meant to function as a working outside phone line, which could be a lifeline in such an emergency. There was an answering machine hooked up to it for incoming messages, powered by the same battery pack. The engineer who'd designed the system had suggested that this critical backup phone be kept within convenient reach, so Paul had it installed inside the antique French commode by the bed.

The beep sounded, loud and piercing, followed by the familiar voice of Billy Hilgarde. Devin remembered then that the emergency number was listed in the computer records at the Pulled Together plant. Billy Hilgarde had several numbers for Devin in his book, including that one. Both people in the pitch black room could hear him talking now.

". . . and we're in the car, heading up the coast. I'm calling on this line because your other numbers just keep ringing, no answer, no machine picking up . . ." Of course not, Devin wanted to scream out, the lines have been cut! But Sam had not known about that lone backup line, which by design was separate and away from the main system installation.

"Pick up, Devin," Billy was calling to her on the machine now, "pick up if you're there. . .

"Okay," he went on, "maybe you've left for the hotel. I'll try Checkers, but if you get this, call me in the car . . . you have the number . . . I have some skinny that'll blow your mind! Remember I told the cops to check out Sam Bradshaw? Well, they actually returned my call . . ."

Both Devin and the man in her blackened bedroom were dead still, listening, as Billy's voice went on.

"They told me Sam's mother had a stroke on Monday, a mild one, probably triggered by all the shit going down in the family, but they said Sam has been with her almost constantly ever since. And he was definitely there on Monday night when the hit on Marva went down—Mrs. Bradshaw's housekeeper confirmed that.

"Also," Billy's amplified voice continued from the direction of the bed, "the detectives told me that Sam was not driving his black Caddy on the day his brother was killed— his Cadillac was in the shop. He was driving his weekend wheels, a Jeep Cherokee Wagoneer. And it's not black, it's maroon. This rules him out as the killer. I still think he hired the jobs done . . ."

Billy kept talking, and Devin had no way of letting him know that *Sam Bradshaw was in this room with her now, with a loaded gun in his hand and murder on his mind!*

Sam wasn't moving. And Devin couldn't move. They both knew that she was out of bullets.

"Also," Billy's voice droned on, "I finally figured out what was bothering me about that beat-up white truck we saw in the shop today. It was old, filthy, looked like it never got washed . . . it was dented and banged up . . . the paint was all chipped and scratched . . . but around the front end I noticed uniform strips of fairly clean, perfect white paint. It hit me later that there must have been some kind of grill, or brush guard—hardware of some sort bolted on the front end of that truck that'd been taken off fairly recently. Maybe it was something *black,* huh?" Billy queried pointedly. "Maybe all of the black paint transfer on the back of your husband's Ferrari wasn't from your Jag . . . maybe some of it came off a big white truck with a big black cowcatcher on it . . . an old, beat-up truck that was hanging around the company's auto shop that Sam had the killer use to knock his brother's car over the cliff. Then, when the news broke that the cops found black paint on the Ferrari, he had the brush guard removed. What do you think of that theory, Devin?" She thought it was a good one.

"So call me," Billy was saying now. "We've had dinner, and Tiffany is sleeping, so we're gonna drive straight through. We'll be in the car for the next four, five hours, then at the Ventana Inn, as I told you, in Big Sur . . ."

Oh no, Billy, don't say where you'll be! Devin wailed inwardly. Now Sam knows exactly where to find you! If he kills me, he'll send his shooter up the coast to finish the job!

". . . doesn't matter how late it is," Billy went on, "I need to talk to you, so call as soon as you get this, okay? 'Bye now . . . and you be careful."

Devin heard the answering machine click off. As she crouched down beside the armoire, suddenly it hit her. It was not some hired killer who worked for Sam Bradshaw, who used an old truck Sam provided from Bradshaw Automotive. Paul himself had told the world who his murderer was! *"My eyes . . . my eyes . . ."* he kept saying. In his last words before he died, Paul Bradshaw was giving the paramedics a vital clue. He was not complaining about his injured eyes. Paul was trying to tell them that . . . *It was Myles!*

Devin was completely taken aback. Of course, Myles was

the killer, not Sam's hired gun. Myles Bradshaw, Sam and Lizbeth's second child, the quiet antisocial one, the surly underachiever who worked in the auto shop. It was not Sam Bradshaw in this room trying to kill her, it was someone with a voice almost identical to Sam's . . . his son.

Why did he do it? The report, he'd said. Devin thought about the copy of the report packed at the bottom of one of her suitcases. She fervently wished she'd stumbled on it before tonight.

She would have to risk running out in the open for about fifteen feet in the darkness to get to the safe-room. Taking a deep breath, she bolted out from behind the armoire toward the open door to her dressing room.

Another shot cracked through the darkness, and she was hit again! Somewhere in the abdomen. She cried out in pain and doubled over, dropping her gun. In the instant before she lost consciousness, she was peripherally aware of what seemed like a bright, blinding light. Maybe it was the heavenly light you were supposed to see just as you die, her brain registered.

Then it was lights out for her.

81

"**P**atient is *in extremis*," the lead paramedic said crisply. "Let's snatch and run."

He and his partner applied a tight wrap to stop the effusive bleeding from the gunshot wound, then deftly bundled up and jostled the victim onto a gurney and into the ambulance idling on the motor court at the Bradshaw mansion. The injuries were massive; the prognosis wasn't good. Just as the medics were about to close up and take off, two LAPD detectives, flashing badges, jumped into the back of the cab with the patient.

"Hey! One man only, you know that! You can't both go," the medics were protesting in unison.

"Have to. Let's move," John Furrino urged.

"The patient is severely compromised—if this patient dies—"

"Yeah, well our case is severely fucked if this patient dies," Dick Ryan shot back.

It was standard operating procedure in the city of Los Angeles that only one law enforcement officer ride to the hospital with a crime victim, to leave as much room as possible in the limited space for the paramedics to minister to the patient. Still, the two medics knew that taking precious time to argue with the officers could impact badly on them if they lost the patient because of it. They were also aware that the victim was one of the prominent Bradshaws, a name that had the clout of powerful attorneys behind it. The lead paramedic leaped inside the back of the ambulance with the officers and the patient, while the other slammed the rear doors shut and sprinted around to the passenger seat, then signaled the EMT at the wheel to blast off, Code 3, red lights and siren blaring.

The patient seemed to be weaving in and out of consciousness, mumbling gibberish that was intermittently comprehensible. The paramedic started ventilating, administering oxygen through a canula, then treating for fluid challenge with two large-bore IVs, one in each arm. Moving around the medic, Furrino leaned in close to the critically injured victim's ear.

"Did you kill Paul Bradshaw?"

"Killed Paul Bradshaw," the patient mumbled.

"Why?" Furrino breathed.

"Money." That word was loud and clear.

"Delirious?" Furrino asked. Both detectives were bent low over the victim now, and Ryan had a tape recorder going.

"I don't think so," Ryan whispered. "What we have here is the dying looking for redemption."

The officers had seen and heard it many times before, a person near death with a surge of adrenaline and a need to talk, and they both knew that a deathbed statement, called a "dying declaration," was an admissible exception to the hearsay rule and did stand up in court. That's why they'd raced out of the squad room and bolted for the car when they heard the ADW call on the radio, assault with a deadly weapon at the Benedict Canyon Drive address that both detectives knew so well.

They arrived at the mansion minutes after the paramedics and got a preliminary briefing from the blues who were already there.

Leaving beat cops to secure the crime scene and call in the lab technicians, they had resolved to stay with the victim, and it was paying off with information that they hadn't been able to nail down in the three months since they'd been on the case.

Together they'd decided to flout the rules and both jam into the back of the ambulance with the shooting victim, even at the risk of impinging on the work of the paramedics in the cramped space. They'd forced the issue because they knew it would probably take both of them to untangle and interpret the victim's story. What one man couldn't understand, maybe the other would.

They also knew that each would probably have to back up his partner in court—the two would be asked to characterize the expressions on the victim's face, verify what they heard him say, and testify as to what they thought it meant. While the lead paramedic crouched on one side of the gurney monitoring vital signs, the officers huddled on the narrow bench that ran along the panel on the other side.

"Tell me how you did it," Furrino asked now, bending low and speaking clearly into the patient's ear. "Tell me how you killed Paul Bradshaw," he repeated.

In the course of the fourteen-minute drive from the Benedict manse to UCLA Medical Center in Westwood, Myles Bradshaw told his tale in fits and starts. Ryan and Furrino, later going back and forth over the tape, were able to piece together his scenario of what had transpired over the course of two successive stormy days up on Mulholland Drive.

First of all, his motive. Deciphering what Myles had babbled, they learned it was because of an efficiency report that Paul Bradshaw was going to act on at the luncheon meeting the following day. And as Detective Richard Ryan interpolated, it was because Myles Bradshaw would be busted, humiliated, and off the gravy train. On the afternoon of the big dinner party, when his father told him about the report, and what exactly was going to happen to him the following day at lunch, Myles stewed and fumed about it until he decided he wouldn't let it happen.

Later, the grand jury heard exactly how he did it, according to the dying declaration of Myles Benton Bradshaw, taped by LAPD detectives first class John Furrino and Richard Ryan, and witnessed by LAFD lead paramedic Steven Schpiel. Prompted by the detectives' questions, Myles Bradshaw had told how he knew that his uncle Paul would have to come across Mulholland Drive sometime close to one o'clock the next afternoon to get to his mother's house for the luncheon meeting. After the Bradshaw dinner party that night, Myles dropped off his date, then rode his Harley up onto Mulholland to do some scouting.

As is almost always the case with heavy rains up on Mulholland Drive, there were washouts—stretches where part of the blacktop had broken up and washed over the cliff on the valley side. Myles staked out two such washouts, complete with barricades, roadway signs and flashers, one on either side of his grandmother's house in Mulholland Estates.

Cut to the next day—meeting day. Murder day. Just before he left the shop, Myles called his uncle Paul on the pretext of confirming the time for lunch. His father's assistant, Geneen Landers, told him Paul was down at the South-Central plant, but lunch was at one o'clock. That told him what he needed to know. His uncle would be coming across Mulholland from the east. Myles left Bradshaw Automotive then, which was near the L.A. Garb headquarters in Santa Monica, where his father would be coming from. The last person he wanted to bump into was his father, so in order to avoid any possible chance of running into Sam Bradshaw en route, Myles went around the long way—east across Olympic Boulevard, then up through Beverly Hills and over Coldwater Canyon to Mulholland.

As he was driving across Mulholland, headed west, he spotted a woman up ahead—a slender woman in a raincoat standing out on the roadway in the pouring rain. Very unusual on rugged Mulholland, even in good weather. Must be car trouble, Myles had thought. As he got closer, he saw that it looked like *Devin Yorke*! Could that be? he'd wondered. Then he saw her car. The black Jag. Myles knew Devin's car; he'd worked on it many times. He figured it must have broken down on her way to the lunch at his grandmother's house. British cars were unreliable pieces of crap, Myles had mumbled into Ryan's tape recorder.

Of course he hated Devin He got a little rush of pleasure seeing her out there all cold and wet and muddy, he said.

She could freeze, she could drown, for all he cared. But if she saw him, she could ruin everything.

Abruptly, he pulled over to the side of the road. He needed to figure out how to get past Devin without being seen. She was staring his way, but she seemed intent on watching the road, probably for the Auto Club truck, Myles figured. Then, before he could decide how to handle the situation, the damnedest thing happened: his uncle Paul's red Ferrari—he knew that car intimately, too—went roaring past him, and Devin flagged it down. He watched in amazement the scene that went down in front of him: the two of them, Devin and Paul Bradshaw, slapping and slipping in the mud and duking it out. Then he saw his uncle clutching his eye and staggering, while Devin ran to her own car, got in, and screeched off down Benedict Canyon.

Seizing the moment, he roared forward in the old truck, one of a few utility vehicles he kept at the shop, a big beat-up white Chevy Blazer with a *jet black, wraparound brush bar attached to the front end,* Ryan later added with emphasis at that point in his testimony. Myles floored the Blazer and blasted past his uncle, who was limping back toward the Ferrari now, his back to the road. He raced around the next curve to the selected mud slide, parked the truck, put on his rain gear, and waited. The westbound lane was closed off at that spot, partially washed away. The few motorists who came through saw warning signs, city-posted flashers, wooden-horse barricades, and a highway worker in a yellow slicker and wide-brimmed hat, directing traffic around the slide.

As Ryan and Furrino testified to the grand jury, the city did have flashers and barricades and warning signs out, but it had no officer at the site. The city doesn't have that kind of manpower. But when Paul Bradshaw approached the washout, he was signaled to stop by this "highway worker" as he directed a car coming in the other direction through the one open lane.

When the lane was clear, and with no other traffic in sight, the man went over to Paul Bradshaw's car. Bradshaw was astounded to recognize his nephew, and even more astonished to see that he had a gun. Myles jumped into the Ferrari on the passenger side and held the gun on Bradshaw. He quickly pulled back his uncle's jacket and shot him point-blank in the ribs, aiming for his heart.

Myles then got out of the car, reached for the hand brake between the front seats, released it, and threw the Ferrari into gear. Shoving on the door frame and the steering wheel with his gloved hands, he tried to push the car toward the cliff, but one of its wheels was mired in mud, and the roadster wouldn't budge. So he darted across the road to where he'd parked the Blazer, got in, did a quick U-turn, and pulled it up behind his uncle's little sports car. One hard slam, at just the right angle. The right front end of the heavy truck glanced a blow to the left rear end of the smaller, lighter car, jolting it sharply to the right, where it catapulted over the cliff. Easy. Fast. There was no one in sight on the deserted road. And Myles Bradshaw kept on going—over the hill to grandmother's house.

He'd had one moment of panic, he said—when his mother approached the washout on her way across Mulholland from Trousdale. His plan was to step into the bushes if any of the family happened through on the way to lunch, but he didn't have time. Heart pounding, he pulled his hat down, averted his head, and looked the other way as he signaled Lizbeth Bradshaw through. She didn't recognize him. He supposed the last person she would expect to see directing city traffic in the pouring rain was her own son, so it turned out to be easy, he told the detectives. And he wasn't afraid that she'd recognize the truck. He was always tooling around in some odd vehicle or another, sometimes cars from outside that he was working on or testing.

No other Bradshaws had driven through the washout. His father had come from Santa Monica, and the rest of the family came from the other direction as well, Brentwood and Bel Air. But later, he heard on the news about the two black workers at the factory downtown, he said. They had followed his uncle; they were up there. They easily could have seen the whole thing. He had to take care of them, he told the detectives matter-of-factly, as if it would make perfect sense to them.

Myles's voice had grown increasingly weaker as he exerted himself to tell the tale. He finished by saying how surprised he was, how amazed that his uncle had actually survived it all, the gunshot and the brutal crash, even for a little while. "Tough old bird," Myles muttered. "Didn't matter," he murmured, with the barest hint of a smile flickering at the corners of his dried, cracked lips, his shithead uncle Paul had croaked without giving him up. "My luck held," Myles whispered.

The detectives could see that the young man's face was visibly bluer. The ambulance raced through the medical center gates on the UCLA campus.

"His vitals are deteriorating," the lead paramedic said. "Blood pressure's down, heart rate's up, he's in shock . . ."

"What about Julius?" Furrino demanded. "What about the model?"

"My luck held," Myles repeated softly, slurring the words as his eyes fluttered closed and his head rolled back on the long board.

"Too late, John," Ryan told his partner. In much the same circumstance as his uncle Paul before him, Myles Bradshaw succumbed just as the ambulance screeched to a halt in the hospital's emergency bay.

Looking down at the corpse, Furrino muttered, "Your luck just ran out, pal."

82

On the sixth floor of the same hospital that had received Myles Bradshaw, another patient lay comatose, clinging to life. It had been three days and nights since twin ALS dispatch teams had been sent to pick up the two shooting victims at the Bradshaw mansion. Mrs. Devin Bradshaw had been transported by advanced life support ambulance to UCLA Medical Center, arriving just minutes after her stepnephew. It was now late Saturday morning. Tanner had been in Devin's hospital room most of the time since that deadly night, taking up his vigil in a lone chair in a corner, alternately scanning newspapers, watching the news on television, trying with little success to concentrate on work he'd brought with him, and occasionally dozing off.

Devin had not regained consciousness. The doctors were saying it could go either way. They'd done extensive sur-

gery to repair her liver and spleen and to stop the massive
internal vascular hemorrhaging from a gunshot that had
ripped through her abdomen. In her fall, she'd hit her head
on a marble tabletop, sustaining a closed head injury that
had caused dangerous internal swelling. Her left forearm
was in a cast, mending from another bullet that had ripped
through her wrist. Devin lay unconscious with her head
raised, motionless, on life support, hooked up to a tangle
of wires and tubes, looking very pale and very small—and
it broke John Tanner's heart.

His father was coming over to see her this morning and
to drag his son out to lunch, he'd said. Tanner Senior had
found some information that was central to the Paul Bradshaw murder case, and he wanted to share it with his son
and law partner. He appreciated his father's industry, but
all of his own energies were focused on the woman lying
helpless in the hospital bed in front of him, and he found
it very difficult to care about the case.

His mind flashed back, as it often had over the past few
days, to that last, terrifying night in the Benedict Canyon
mansion. Tanner had accessed Devin's message inviting
him to come by and pick up his gym equipment because
she was moving out of the house that night. Of course, he
very much wanted to do that. To hell with the gym equipment—he was aching to see Devin, to talk to her, to be
with her.

He'd called her as soon as he got her message, but the
line just kept ringing. There was no answer, and no answering machine picking up. He continued trying the line for
awhile, but kept getting just the constant ringing. Since
Devin had said she'd only be there for a short time while
she packed, he didn't want to chance missing her, so he
jumped into his Range Rover and drove over to the Benedict house.

Arriving at the mansion, Tanner had come upon an eerie
sight. The estate was in total darkness. There was not one
light in any of the windows. The extensive outside lighting
that came on automatically at dusk was completely dark.
This was definitely not right. Even if Devin had already
moved out, it didn't make sense that she would leave the
estate in total darkness.

Grabbing a light that he kept in the utility box of his
Rover, Tanner let himself in the wrought-iron door within

the west-side gate, his usual entry route. He used the key to Devin's house that he hadn't gotten around to returning, or more likely that he'd kept as a talisman, a tie to Devin, in hopes that she would eventually see the truth. Once on the grounds, Tanner let himself in the front door with the same key. Groping, he located a bank of switches on the wall to the right, and tried flicking on some lights. Nothing. No power.

Almost immediately, before he'd moved from the entryway, Tanner heard the sound of a gunshot reverberating from the floor above. Then another. Lighting his way with the flashlight, he bounded up the curved central staircase. He heard screams then, Devin's screams. Following the sounds, he pushed into the sitting room of the master suite and burst through the glass double doors into the bedroom. His light illumined a man with a gun. Tanner sprang into the air and landed on him from behind with the full weight of his body, bringing him to the floor with a crash. The man came down hard on the barrel of his own gun, triggering the weapon to go off. An oddball gun, they'd said it was. An old Army service revolver from the fifties. And a bullet tore through Myles Bradshaw's chest.

The rest of that night was a blur for Tanner. Trying to call 911 but finding the phones dead. Wrapping Devin tightly in sheets to staunch the flow of great quantities of blood, not knowing if she were alive or dead. Running down the stairs to call for help on his car phone, then getting the heavy iron gates opened manually so the ambulances could come onto the grounds to the motor court. Then leaping back upstairs and cradling Devin's head in his lap, talking to her, soothing her while he waited for the paramedics.

In the midst of all the activity and confusion, when they'd managed in darkness to get Myles Bradshaw and Devin onto gurneys, down the staircase, and out of the house, Tanner jumped into his Range Rover and followed the ambulance transporting Devin to UCLA Medical Center, where he had been waiting almost constantly ever since. Waiting, hoping, and praying for Devin to open her eyes.

Tanner's father had steered him into the Ristorante Positano, a quiet eatery in Westwood near the UCLA campus.

Seated in a booth across from his son, he was startled to see how drawn and tired the younger man looked.

"The doctors say they just don't know, John. You need to get home and get some rest. Get back to work. Get your mind off it. This constant watch isn't doing either of you any good."

"I think it is, Dad," Tanner said quietly. "I talk to her. I think sometimes she hears me."

"Well, you're going to do what you're going to do," his father shrugged. "Just take care of your health, John."

"I am," his son returned. "I did a few laps around campus this morning, got my blood going, even had breakfast in the student cafeteria. Lumpy oatmeal. Not bad," he grinned. Tanner was very proud of his son and of the close bond the two men had.

"By the way, they scoured the Bradshaw kid's truck," he said. "They didn't come up with the brush guard, it's probably long gone to some dump somewhere, but they found a pair of work gloves with powder burns on them in the glove compartment."

"Are you going to stay with the case, Dad?"

"Oh, yes. If Devin ... *when* my client recovers," he amended, "she'll have to testify."

"She's going to recover—she has to."

"Let's order," Tanner Senior said, attempting to get his son's mind off his worry over Devin for at least awhile. "Then I've got something to show you," he smiled, lifting a thick cardboard file container from his briefcase and setting it up on the table.

"What is it, Dad?"

"Something we found in Devin's luggage that she was packing the night she was shot. Something I'm sure she hadn't read yet, or she certainly would have alerted me. It's a key to her husband's murder."

The waitress came and took their orders, then immediately brought cold bottles of Pellegrino to the table. While the two waited for their broiled whitefish and vegetables, Tanner Senior untied the strings around the bulging file folder. He removed a thick unbound document and dropped it on the table.

"This is a copy of a comprehensive efficiency report on L.A. Garb that Paul Bradshaw had commissioned from B.S.&S.," he told his son.

"Oh, Devin found out about that report when she saw notations of payment for it on the company books. I told her she'd have a tough time getting a copy of it from the Braggs, but she got one, huh?"

"I don't think she got it from the Braggs," his father answered. "I found it inside this file container full of other sensitive material having to do with Bradshaw's company. I think Paul Bradshaw had stashed this stuff somewhere, and it recently fell into Devin's hands. It looks like she meant to go through it at the hotel."

"And this is the B.S.&S. report?" Tanner asked, indicating the pages fanned out on the table.

"Appears to be, and it's a bombshell! I stopped by to see the son of my old pal Sol Schlemmer. He runs the L.A. office of Bragg, Schlemmer & Schultz. You know how hard-nosed those fellas are, but since the news broke of the double shooting Wednesday night, and since I had this copy of the report in my hand, Sol Junior gave me a little background. He told me that Devin had been around to see him, trying to get a copy, but of course Bradshaw's report wasn't even extant in their computer files anymore. But he remembered it very well."

Leafing through the pages on the table, Tanner explained to his son that the report had found egregious pockets of theft and inefficiency at L.A. Garb. A blatant source was Sam Bradshaw's financial department. According to the findings, most of the money drain within the workings of the company traced back directly or indirectly to the operations of the chief financial officer.

"Lose the brother!" the venerable Augustus Bragg had directed Paul Bradshaw at their private meeting at the B.S.&S. offices in Los Angeles, Sol Junior said, and both Schlemmer and Schultz had nodded their agreement. "Money is leaking out the doors and flying out the windows," he'd told Bradshaw "The brother's golf crony gets a hundred and sixty thousand dollars a year, and he's nothing more than a yes-man to Sam. An inflated cadre of assistants and secretaries are dotting the i's and crossing the t's on work for a fiscal system that squanders the company's money. Sam himself gets seven hundred and fifty thousand dollars a year, but forget his salary, that's nothing. The man is hopelessly over his head as CFO for this firm, which years ago outgrew Mr. Samuel Bradshaw's skill at financial management. His systems of finance are outdated and arcane, and it's costing L.A. Garb needless millions every quarter," Gus Bragg had told a sobered Paul Bradshaw.

What was needed, said the collective Braggs, was a young, sharp, no-nonsense nineties hotshot controller who could operate with half the staff, at a third of the cost and ten times the efficiency, and who could pinch a penny so hard that you could hear the screams from Santa Monica to South-Central Los Angeles and on into the next county.

And the kid, Myles Bradshaw—his auto-shop operation fronts petty fraud and embezzlement and not-so-petty theft, they said. As manager of the company-owned automotive shop that was meant to service their own vehicles as well as make money by taking in outside work, Myles Bradshaw was on the payroll for $52,000 a year, but that was chump change compared to what this kid was taking out of there. According to the findings in the report, Myles Bradshaw was robbing the company. He was routinely overbilling L.A. Garb for what each of the forty-three company cars and trucks cost for service at any given time, and the same was true of the fleet of personal vehicles he serviced for the Bradshaw family.

The auto shop's accounting went through Sam's department, of course, and the clerks never questioned it, because the bills were signed by their boss's son. Besides, Bradshaw Automotive was a company-owned store, one junior accountant had told the auditors, so it was just a matter of taking money out of one pocket and putting it into another, after all. What no one knew was that by a system of creative bookkeeping, double invoicing and the like, Myles Bradshaw was pocketing the excess. The auditors also found that Myles systematically inflated the cost of parts. And he cut and cashed checks made payable to phantom mechanics, who "day-checked at the shop when they were extra busy." The worst of the abuses, the biggest dollar losses from what was stolen under the table by Myles Bradshaw, according to the B.S.&S. report, was a system that he'd been able to rig of "lost deliveries"—shipments of garments that he managed to rubber-stamp through his father's department, which he had rogue drivers sell on the streets, then split the cash proceeds with him.

"Sol said the Bragg trio strongly recommended that Paul Bradshaw bring in the authorities on his nephew," Tanner

Senior told his son. "They told him that the police could nail Myles Bradshaw on the evidence their study had turned up alone. Or, if Bradshaw wanted to keep this quiet, wash the family's own dirty laundry in house, as it were, B.S.&S. could track down the paper trail and find out where Myles had been stashing the money. This kid wasn't smart enough to hide it well, they'd told Paul."

The study had turned up other incidentals, Tanner pointed out, like the fact that Paul's personal assistant, Alexandra Anson, was overpaid by three or four times, given her inflated salary, the bonuses, the car, the furs, the paid-for vacations and other perks. And the report went on and on. It was very thorough.

"Paul Bradshaw got his three hundred and fifty thousand dollars' worth," Tanner Senior said. "And my guess is he was ready to roll with it. I think this is what he was going to tell the family all about at lunch that day. Somehow his brother and his nephew got wind of it, and they got him before he could get them."

"And how does Devin fit into this?" Tanner asked his father.

"She just got caught in the cross fire," he said.

83

"You've gotta help me, Irv," Sam begged dolefully. "I Didn't kill anybody."

Sam Bradshaw and Irving Chapman were sitting in the attorney room at the Mens' Central Jail in downtown Los Angeles, where Sam Bradshaw had been held for the past three weeks. He was awaiting trial on three counts of aiding and abetting the first-degree murders of Joseph Bernard Jones, Marva Modine, and Julius Jackson, each of which, exactly like murder one, carried a sentence of twenty-five years to life. In combination the prosecution could, and probably would, ask for the death penalty. He was also charged with one count of accessory after the fact in the murder of his brother, Paul Bradshaw, in which the liability was derivative from aiding in a cover-up after the crime was committed and carried a maximum sentence of three years in prison.

The critically injured Myles Bradshaw, perhaps looking for some redemption from the authorities in case he survived, or from a higher authority if he died, had hung on just long enough to spill to the investigating detectives a plethora of incriminating information about his father's involvement in the murders. Chapman had just informed Sam that Myles's statement on tape would be admissible evidence, and in fact, the courts usually gave great credence to deathbed testimony. He also had explained again that there simply was no bail on murder charges.

"Well, did you get me a good man, yet? Or woman?" Sam demanded. He had asked Irv to check out Leslie Abramson, who'd been doing a notable job defending one of the Menendez brothers.

Chapman had been interviewing criminal attorneys and had not been successful at convincing any of the top people to take the case. Johnnie Cochran said it wasn't for him. Howard Weitzman said he was too busy. He'd asked John Tanner, who was representing Devin, for a recommendation. Tanner turned him down flat. "You're on your own, Irv. The man can barely keep the poison in his soul from seeping out on his shirt," he had wryly observed.

"Not yet," Irving told Sam now. "All the top guns I've talked to have full plates right now."

"Irv, what am I doing here? I didn't kill anybody! Am I going to do hard time?"

"I've told you, Sam, I don't know. I'm not qualified in this area. I'm going to find you someone who is," Irving said, looking uncomfortably around the windowless walls in the dingy room.

"But I didn't kill anybody, Irv," Sam protested again.

"I know, Sam," the lawyer said, turning back to him. "Look, I'm sorry, but I have to go—I've got a meeting."

Chapman let himself out the door, and a guard approached to escort Sam back to his cell. Sitting on the filthy mattress on the cot attached to the wall, Sam Bradshaw traveled in his mind again, as he had a hundred times before, over the labyrinthine course of the nightmare that had got him into this dismal place. And how after all he'd done for his son, Myles, in his final act on earth the boy had sold his father up the river.

It had all started with that fateful, hateful lunch. The one with his brother at Michael's on the day before Paul was killed. Paul had read to him several damning passages from the B.S.&S. report, passages that concerned Sam and Myles Then his brother lowered the boom, broke it to him as gently as a guy like Paul Bradshaw could, he supposed. Sam was through at the company, but he was going to be okay. Paul said he knew he wasn't really dishonest, at least not big-time dishonest. He was just woefully behind the curve in the business world these days, and he probably had no idea what kind of shit was going on right under his nose.

"And hell, Sammy, you're sixty-two," Paul had said with a condescending smile. "That's retirement age, anyway. The company will announce your retirement. We'll throw you a big party. Golf every day of the week for you now, big brother. It'll be a good life for you and Lizbeth."

"What about Myles?" Sam had asked quietly.

"Jesus, Myles is a different story," Paul had shot back. "You wanted your son in the business. I'd have killed to have your Allena, smart lawyer like her, but you pushed Myles on me. And now the little bastard is stealing me blind."

"He's always been slow, Paul."

"Slow, my ass!" his brother roared. "He's got a fucking cottage industry going down there at the fucking shop, and he's getting fucking rich!"

"I'll pay it all back," Sam had begged. "I'll talk to him—"

"Forget about it, Sammy," Paul had stopped him. "We'll keep it in the family, no police, but this little son of a bitch has to be taught a lesson."

And Paul was going to bust Myles, in front of the whole family, at the meeting the next day. He had to, he said. By rights, Myles should do prison time, Paul told him, but they would keep it in the family. "But the kid is out, out, out!" he'd reiterated, pounding on the table. "And like the report recommends, the fucking shop gets shut down. From now on we send the company vehicles outside to be serviced, and everyone in the damn family can pay to get their own damn cars fixed. The in-house automotive shop was a good

idea, but your thief of a son fucked it up for everybody,"
Paul had bellowed, waving the humiliating report under
Sam's nose. Patrons at the exclusive restaurant were cran-
ing to see what the commotion was about.

But Sam didn't have to worry, Paul had tried to reassure
him that day. None of the family was ever going to have
to worry about money. Sam would be set up with the same
kind of trust fund their mother had, which would pay all
his bills and give him and Beth an ample stipend besides.

Myles was out, of course, he'd repeated to him more
than once. He could go find himself a fucking job. Paul
said he'd leave it up to Sam how he wanted to deal with
his own son. "But because you're my brother, Sammy, and
the kid is blood," he'd said, "and because, hopefully, he'll
learn his lesson, I'm not going to cut Myles out of his inheritance—he'll still get his share when I'm gone."

For Sam, it was devastating. Benched. Out of action. Put
to pasture. A lousy charity case, his bills paid by his god-
damned brother. But for Myles—it was the impetus to murder. Sam flashed back to the moment when he'd learned
about the course Myles had embarked upon. It was the
next afternoon, when most of the family were gathered at
Regina's house waiting for Paul to arrive for lunch. Myles
was edgy, bursting with his terrible secret. At some point
he took his father aside and whispered what he'd done.

If only Sam had never known about it, he thought now,
how different things would be today. But Myles had always
told him everything. He'd even considered telling his dad
about his plan right after he'd hatched it in the rain the
night before, he'd said, but he knew that if he let his father
in on it in advance, Sam would talk him out of it.

True, if Myles *had* told Sam about his plan beforehand,
Sam most certainly would never have let him do it. He'd
have saved Myles from himself, as he'd done so many times
all through his only son's less than stable life. As it was,
when Myles did whisper his shocking secret to his father
in the privacy of the quiet den at Regina's house, out of
earshot of the rest of the Bradshaws, Sam simply did not
believe him.

Myles had always been passive, remote, introspective,
slow to learn—*different,* all his life. He had frequent flights
of fancy. This was probably yet another elaborate fantasy;
certainly it couldn't be true, Sam had thought that day.

And once again it had crossed his mind that Myles really needed professional help. He'd whispered in his son's ear that he was not to tell a soul about this, not a soul, until they could talk. Alone. That night. Then Sam would convince Myles that he had to get into therapy.

Shortly afterward, of course, Sam had got the call about Paul's "accident" from Devin Incredibly, it was true! He talked to his son at length that night, and the next, and the next, in the guest cottage where Myles lived on his parents' property. Sam was faced with two choices. He could persuade his son to turn himself in, then stand by him through what would be a scandalous murder trial, ostracizing and disruptive to the family. He would see his own fortune, his respectability, his brand-new future as head of the company, everything he had wanted all his life go down in flames. It would kill Lizbeth, it would kill him, Myles would be finished, of course, and Allena would be scarred.

Or he could help Myles try to bull this through. And if they could pull it off, if they got away with it, Sam would have it all. He would have control of the company, he would preside over a vast fortune, he'd be one of the most important men in the country, the son he had always been committed to protect would not be hurt, and his family would be intact.

That's the choice he made.

Putting his plans for Myles in motion, he instructed him to tell the police, in the course of their repeated questioning of family members, that when he was driving across Mulholland to his grandmother's house that day, he thought— he couldn't swear to it, but he was pretty sure—that he saw Devin's black Jaguar up ahead, making a U-turn on Mulholland, then speeding south down Benedict Canyon. When they asked why he didn't mention that to the rest of the family at the lunch, especially when his uncle Paul never showed up, he was to say because even though he was in the habit of noticing cars, he wasn't a hundred percent sure that it was Devin's Jag. At one point, the cops had asked him how sure was he? Ninety percent, he'd answered.

And when the detectives had let Sam know that there were two other witnesses who might have seen what happened up on Mulholland Drive—Billy Hilgarde and his friend—Sam explained to Myles that all three were a grave danger to them. Especially Devin! *Devin must be destroyed* was the refrain that Sam had pounded repeatedly into the consciousness of his impressionable son. And somewhere on the dark journey of his own soul to the far side of hell, Sam had argued to himself that if Myles had killed one person, what would it matter if he killed two? Or three, or four? But Sam hadn't killed anybody.

He told Myles that Julius had been the keeper of the infamous B.S.&S. report for Paul. He'd explained to his son how for years, Julius had kept a file of secret documents for his uncle in a hidden compartment right inside the limousine. Julius had been Paul's only real confidante, Sam had told Myles The chauffeur probably knew about everything that was in the report and what Paul had intended to do about it, he'd said, and that made old Julius Jackson very dangerous indeed. He even gave Myles an interesting idea. And he'd told Myles about Paul's old service revolver, loaded and handy in the secret compartment in the limo.

And so it was that Myles Bradshaw, whose voice sounded exactly like his father's on the phone, had put in a call to Julius in the car, saying he was Sam calling from the health club. He then asked Julius to go down to the Pulled Together plant and pick up a client, a buyer from Dillard's who would be waiting in the lobby in fifteen minutes. As a company courtesy, Julius was to run the woman out to the airport. Sam had even told Myles that the route Julius always took to the PT factory was east on the Santa Monica Freeway, then down the Harbor Freeway into South-Central Los Angeles, and off at the Florence Avenue exit to San Pedro Street. Myles was around a corner in an alley off Main, watching and waiting for the big silver limo to come down the street. But Sam never killed anybody.

On another afternoon, he'd made it a point to let Myles know that Devin would be alone in the big Pulled Together factory in South-Central Los Angeles after hours that night, signing off on samples that had to be shipped the next day. Myles had keys to the PT factory, he reminded him—it had been his job to take vehicles in and out. And Sam told Myles about a little-used side door, keyed the same, for entry. And he gave Myles the gun he'd removed from the desk in the executive office at PT. On the Sunday before Devin took over as president of the division, Sam had driven down to South-Central and swept his brother's office. He'd picked up several things of Paul's-a Tiffany desk clock with a diamond face that had looked out of place in that shabby office anyway, a gold-plated putter that Frank Sinatra had given Paul for chairing a charity golf tournament, which his brother had casually tossed into a corner at his PT office. And the gun—the Smith & Wesson .38-caliber revolver. His brother had told him about it. "In case you ever run into trouble down in that hellhole, Sammy, I want you to know that it's there and it's loaded," he'd said. And he'd told Sam where the key to the locked drawer was taped, on the underside of his desk, above the kneehole. And Sam had given that gun to Myles But Sam never killed anybody.

It was a shame about the model, he thought now. Such a beautiful woman, and he had to admit that Devin's ad campaign had looked like it was going to be dynamite. Sam was genuinely sorry about the model. When Myles realized he'd got the wrong blonde, he'd stashed the gun there at the factory. Good thinking. It was registered to Devin Everything had come so close to working out.

That Scud fellow was easy for Myles to find. He'd missed seeing Hilgarde that night, and he'd missed getting him another night in front of his girlfriend's house, but he'd intended to catch up with him next, after he killed Devin

Devin should have been easy. As executor of his brother's estate, Sam had keys to the mansion, as well as a full set of plans. He'd given a key to Myles, explaining that the one key would open every door in the house, including the door to the drop-room. Late one night, back in Myles's cottage, Sam went over the house plans with Myles, showing him the location of the drop-room and the layout of the equipment inside. Myles knew how to cut the power and phone lines—he had always been good with technical details. But Sam didn't do anything, didn't kill anyone.

Now Sam Bradshaw's life was shattered. His son was dead, the boy who had always been the slow one, the one who'd needed him so much. And Allena, his beautiful daughter, Allena, the bright, successful lawyer, had distanced herself from her father. She'd come into town for Myles's funeral. He'd hoped he could talk to her about his defense, get some help. But right after her brother's funeral she went back to Europe, and Sam went back to jail.

And Sam's wife of many years, the long-suffering and

regal Lizbeth Allenwood Bradshaw, had let him know that she was shocked and horrified at the evil he was capable of. She'd filed for divorce and had already moved back to her family homestead in the posh Pacific Heights section of San Francisco.

Suddenly, everything went dark in the cell block. Ten o'clock sharp, lights out—no announcement, no by-your-leave, no reading lamp, nothing. And still he sat there, on the thin, bare, dirty mattress. Would he get used to this? Would he ever get out? Would he die here? And yet, he hadn't killed anybody.

84

"**D**evin, put that down!" Tanner said, in as stern a voice as he could muster.

"But this is *my good* arm, now," Devin laughed, holding up a five-pound chrome dumbbell in her right hand.

"Put it down, Dev, or we're out of the gym," he said even more firmly, although he had trouble keeping a smile from the corners of his mouth.

"Okay," she giggled. "But it feels so good!"

"It won't be long now," Tanner cajoled, giving her a loving but protective look. "But there's no way I'm going to let you rush it, any step of the way."

"Bummer!" Devin frowned. "By the time I start working out again, it'll be too late. I'll be totally frumped out."

Tanner rolled his eyes. "Right," he said, "there's a huge danger of that happening." He looked appreciatively from Devin's bare feet with Chinese red toenails up to her long lean frame, which even the loose-fitting, floor-length silk print dress she wore couldn't camouflage.

"Trust me, *I'm* in worse shape than you'll ever be," Tanner told her. "I haven't gone near a set of weights since you threw me out."

"Why don't I believe that?" Devin challenged, giving Tanner's tall, trim torso an approving glance.

"Believe it," he insisted "I said to myself, if Devin won't work out with me, I'll just deteriorate. That'll teach her."

Devin laughed happily It was her first day in her new gym in her new house behind copper green gates and lush foliage in the quiet community of Bel Air. Of course, she couldn't *do* anything in the gym. She was bandaged everywhere—her arm, her head, her midsection. Devin was nowhere near workout condition. She would be able to begin minimal exercise in a couple of months, her doctor said, then escalate gradually as she continued to heal.

It was lunchtime, and Tanner had come over ostensibly to design her start-up program for when the time came. Actually, Tanner was humoring her. Devin was so anxious to get back to normal that he'd suggested the gym session today, so he could study the equipment and work out her early routines, he said. In fact, he didn't have to study the equipment—he'd planned and supervised the outfitting of Devin's home exercise room weeks ago, soon after she'd made the move to the new house right from the hospital. But being in the gym, just being there, was therapy for Devin, Tanner knew, and he loved that she was glowing. He put a protective arm around her slight shoulders.

"Don't worry, we'll build you up to fighting form again," he said.

"I can't wait," Devin sighed, looking wistfully at the gleaming, still unused equipment. "It seems as if I've been ailing forever."

"Hardly, Dev—it's been less than two months."

"And considering I was sure I had died and gone to heaven. I saw the white light," she chuckled.

"Yeah, and it was only me with my trusty Brinkmann power lantern," he grimaced.

"Well, you were sent by God, there's no question about that," she said. Tanner tightened his grip around her shoulders.

"I am so proud of you," he said softly.

"Because I can lift five pounds?" Devin asked mischievously, looking up into his concerned eyes.

"Because you've come through hell, and you've survived, and because you're the strongest, most wonderful, most beautiful woman I have ever known."

"Hmmm," Devin furrowed her brow. "How many women have you known?"

Tanner started toting on his fingertips. "About seven thousand," he answered, "but I've never been in love."

"Whoa!" she jumped on him. "That's one of the big lies! Every woman has heard them all. *The check is in the mail—*"

"All right, all right," he stopped her. "I have never been in love ... until now.

"Well, if you've never been in love, how do you know what it feels like?" she teased.

Tanner took her in his arms, being careful not to squeeze her sore midriff, or her sore head or sore arm, and he kissed her. A long, loving, gentle, passionate, deep soul kiss. "That's what it feels like," he murmured, when he reluctantly released her.

Devin lingered in his arms. "I know," she whispered.

"It's a miracle we ever get anything done," Tanner laughed. "And it'll be even worse when you're completely mended. We'll work out in the mornings, then you won't be able to get me out of here. I'll never go to work again."

"You'd better go to work, or I'll have to answer to your father. I do not want John Senior mad at me!"

"Couldn't happen. He adores you," Tanner smiled.

"Speaking of work," Devin said, "I can't wait to get back to work. I get briefed every day, and I make decisions, and I sketch out numbers at home and fax them in to Alex, but I'm aching to get back in the middle of it all."

"You will, darling, soon enough. And also speaking of work, are you sure you're up for the dinner party tonight?"

"Oh, absolutely. I don't have to do a thing," Devin assured him. "I've got all my old help, my pals, coming in. Andres is cooking, Laguya is coming over to help Maria, even Bruno, my wonderful butler, will be here to tend bar and make sure everything goes smoothly."

"Still, I don't know why you want to entertain when you still have trouble getting up out of a chair," Tanner frowned.

"I need to," she said. "Tonight is my first, unofficial housewarming, with just a few very special people who have made it through all this with me. I'm looking forward to having them in my new home." Then, thoughtfully, she added, "I'm so happy, John."

"So am I. If this is all a dream, I hope I never wake up. And if it's not a dream, shall we get on with this?" Tanner smiled, turning to the weight rack. He picked up a set of the smallest weights, one pound each.

"We'll start with these babies," he grinned, cocking his head. "*When* we start, that is." Devin looked obliquely at the puny weights and groaned.

Tanner was back at seven. A fire was blazing in the living room, Kenny G was playing on the stereo system, the house smelled like a gourmet Parisian bistro, and Devin was breathtaking. Tanner held her at arms' length to admire her.

"You are heavenly," he pronounced. "What is that?"

"Oh ... this caftan is a Carole Little," she said, looking down at the bias-cut ivory chiffon confection with palest gold metallic inserts that swirled around her ankles to the floor. "Carole knows that I can't get clothes on over this suit of armor they've got me trussed up in, so she sent over a selection of these."

Carole Little was a hugely successful designer with a thriving factory in South-Central Los Angeles. The two had met when Devin ran Pieces.

"You know Carole Little?"

"She's a friend who's back in my life," Devin smiled. "She sent a bowl of tulips to the hospital when she heard on the news that I'd been shot, and we picked up from there."

Tanner smiled his approval. Devin was reaching out to old friends again and eager to make new ones. Her life with Paul Bradshaw had been insular, a closed club, and she'd lost touch with friends. Now she felt reborn. Though her lifestyle was certainly scaled down socially, on a different level it was broadening, encompassing more of the bright, creative, interesting people who lived and worked in the City of Angels. Despite her sore, achy body, Devin had never felt so alive.

"Oh," Tanner said then, turning toward a gigantic, beautifully wrapped box he'd left in the entry. "Let me get my housewarming present."

"John, I specifically told everyone *no gifts*. My idea of a housewarming is to have good friends warm my house."

"Well, this is actually a gym-warming gift. Come on, open it," he grinned, hefting the big box into the living room.

Despite her rule, Devin smiled with delight. She slid the huge, floppy crimson bow gently off the top, tore the wrapping paper from the box like a kid at Christmas, opened up the lid, and dove into a mountain of hot-pink and orange tissue paper. And came up with a soft, colorful, eccentric-looking life-sized Popeye the Sailor Man.

"The original pumped-up guy," Tanner explained, pointing out Popeye's bulging biceps.

"Oh, I love him!" Devin shrieked. "He's for the gym?"

"Of course he's for the gym," Tanner said. "If you ever get in there before I do in the morning and you don't feel like even being awake, Popeye will make you smile."

"Come on, let's take him in there," Devin beamed, her green eyes sparkling. "Where should we put him?"

"Everywhere," Tanner said. "He can sit on top of the weight rack, he'll want to do bench presses from time to time, he'll love doing his abdominals on the Nautilus machine . . ."

"Popeye's going to be happy in this house," Devin promised. "Just like me."

The doorbell rang. Tanner sat Popeye on the stationary bike, with his feet on the pedals and his hands on the handlebars, and he and Devin went to the front door. It was Alex, and with her was Martin Berman, who was weighed down by another large box.

"Alex, come in—but no gifts, I told you."

"This isn't a gift," Alex laughed. "We're going to drink it all tonight." Tanner took the box out of Berman's hands and hoisted it up onto the entry table.

"Heavy," he observed.

"Open it," Alex insisted. "I'm dying for Devin to see the card." The "card" was a sheet of Associated Press wire copy, with CONGRATULATIONS! scrawled across the page in neon yellow highlighter pen. The story, released two days before, led with an account of the appointment of Devin Yorke Bradshaw as the new chairperson and CEO of L.A. Garb, with full support of the stockholders and the board. Mrs. Bradshaw's first appointment in her new position, the copy read, was to install Alexandra Anson, her former personal assistant at the Pulled Together factory, to replace her as president of the South-Central Los Angeles division. The text went on:

Other new appointees under Devin Bradshaw's banner are Ruby Johnson, production assistant at Pulled Together

*since its founding early last year, transferring to the Santa
Monica headquarters as Mrs. Bradshaw's personal assistant, and Paul Bradshaw Junior, son of the late founder
and owner of L.A. Garb, who will also be moving from
the South-Central division to Santa Monica, to work in
production at the main plant. Bradshaw said he welcomes
the opportunity to continue his apprenticeship with the
company.*

*Mrs. Bradshaw says she has immediate plans for expan-
sion, including a full line of large-size womenswear and a
line of children's clothes, both boys' and girls; to go into
production for the fall market.*

"I *love* this 'card,' Alex," Devin squealed. "I'm going to
frame it and hang it in my office. And thank you, Martin—
it obviously came from the news wires."

"Wow, look what we have here!" Tanner trumpeted.
"An entire *case* of Domaine Ott Blanc de Blanc!"

"It's a great Provence white," Martin said.

"Great? It's brilliant!" Tanner exclaimed, admiring the
label on one of the bottles. "Where in hell did you find
this, buddy?"

"Oh, Martin is unbelievably resourceful," Alex smiled up
at her six-foot-four newsman. "I don't even *ask* anymore
where he finds the stuff he finds."

"The best thing I've ever found is you," Berman beamed
at Alex.

"Well, let's get a few of these iced down," Tanner said,
and he carried four bottles of the vintage wine back to
the bar.

The rest of the guests arrived in succession. Pauly, whose
progress Devin would continue to guide at the Santa Monica plant, with his new girlfriend, Melanie Blank, a young
reporter at Channel Six. Alex and Martin had introduced
them. Right behind them were Billy and Vanna, arm in
arm, obviously very much in love. After the hellish night
when Devin had come so close to death, after it was all
over and the killer was exposed, when there was nothing
more that Billy could do to help, and he himself was finally
out of danger, Billy Hilgarde and Vanna Brylock applied
for a license up at Big Sur and were married by a Baptist
minister in a grove of cypress trees on one of the rugged
beaches of Carmel. They'd returned to Los Angeles as a

family, daughter Tiffany in tow, all of them radiant. And they'd promised to let Devin give them a proper wedding reception when she was fully recovered. Billy and Vanna were back at work at PT, shooting new pictures for the ad campaign. Devin intended to mingle shots of just the two of them with the already existing photos and videos. The world knew what had happened to Marva Modine, and Devin had decided that Billy was right—releasing Marva's last, stunning pictures would be the company's tribute to her.

"Here's our housewarming present that is definitely not a present," Billy grinned, hauling in a bulky cardboard carton that was emitting great swells of steam.

"It's smoking!" Devin cried, backing away.

"That's dry ice," Billy laughed. "It's abalone."

"Excuse me?" Devin wrinkled her nose.

"Abalone," Billy repeated. "Ten gorgeous shells. Dinner for ten. Vanna and I dove for it at Big Sur."

"It's cleaned and frozen," Vanna quickly put in, seeing Devin's consternation. "And packed back in the original gorgeous pearly abalone shells," she said.

"Want to know the best part about this gift?" Billy asked.

"Please," Devin said, laughing now.

"I come with it. You store it, and when you're ready, Vanna and I will come over and I'll cook it. It has to be pounded, lightly seasoned and breaded, and sautéed exactly right. I do great abalone. You can't hardly get it anymore," he added. "It's just about farmed out in California."

Devin was warming to the whole idea. "Fabulous!" she said. "Let's do it next week—on Friday night again."

"You got it. Now where do you want it?" Billy demanded, flashing his wide magic grin, still clutching the unwieldy carton that was giving off billows of dry steam.

"In the kitchen," Devin laughed. "Tell Maria to put it in one of the Traulsens out back."

The last guest to arrive was Allena Bradshaw, strangely beautiful, as usual, and, as usual, alone. She was in town for a week and had called Devin to ask how she was doing, and Devin had persuaded her to come to dinner tonight. Devin welcomed her into her home, and into her arms for a gentle embrace. Gentle because everything still hurt, as she explained to Allena, but she assured her she had a bear hug coming when everything was healed.

"Lots of them, Allena," Devin told the woman, who looked characteristically gorgeous, mysterious, fascinating-and lost. When Devin released her, she thought she saw tears welling in Allena's misty gray eyes.

"I'm so sorry—" Allena started. It was the first time the two women had seen each other since Paul Bradshaw's funeral.

"*I'm* sorry," Devin stopped her. "You're the one who's lost so much—your brother, your uncle, your mother and father ..."

"I've always been so detached," Allena murmured. "It's hard. Mother's strong—she'll be fine. But let's not talk about it now."

"Of course not," Devin said gently, drawing the woman into the living room. Let's have some wine. And one day we *will* talk, Allena. I want you to be my friend."

"Oh Lord, you'll have me crying for sure," Allena whispered, looking up to check that no one else was listening. "About that wine ..."

"Coming up," Devin smiled, and she signaled to Bruno.

"I have a gift for you," Allena said then, removing a small gold box from her purse.

"Oh, no, Allena, I said no gifts."

"This is different—it's something I want you to have. Open it later," she said, and she slipped the little box into the pocket of Devin's caftan.

Bruno announced that dinner was served, and the guests moved into the intimate dining room, with its warm terracotta-tinted walls, its profusion of potted trees and flowers, and a blazing fire dancing in the corner fireplace. A dark cherrywood table was beautifully set for nine. When everyone was seated, Tanner offered a toast.

"On the occasion of this very special housewarming," he said, lifting his glass, "I propose we drink to the incredible woman who owns this house, and who also owns my heart." He leaned over and kissed Devin, and everyone applauded and toasted with Alex and Martin's splendid wine.

"I haven't given you my gift yet," Pauly said then.

"Oh no!" Devin protested. "I told you no ..."

"I know, I know, but it's not really a gift ... it's a part

of me." Pauly took a small black velvet box out of his jacket pocket and handed it to Devin.

"I had two of these made—my mother has the other one," he told Devin "She's the woman who saved my life, and you're the woman who saved my future."

Devin's thoughts flashed to Rosemary, who also very nearly got herself in trouble on that insane Friday on Mulholland. After it was all over, Rosemary and Alex had confided to Devin in a hospital visit that they, too, had made a mad drive to head off Paul Bradshaw with a personal agenda of their own that day. Rosemary was hell-bent on a mission to save Pauly. The two had apparently got up there too late, never saw Paul Bradshaw, but they'd lied to the detectives about it. Well, they didn't lie, exactly, Rosemary had pointed out. Alex *did* have a migraine headache, and Rosemary *did* drive her home. They simply neglected to mention their side trip to the crime scene. With a gun in her purse, Rosemary had divulged, rolling her eyes. Spunky woman, the first Mrs. Bradshaw, Devin smiled now, as she fingered Pauly's gift.

"Open it, Devin," Billy prodded, breaking her reverie. She lifted the lid, and took out an exact replica of the coin that Pauly was given at his commencement from rehab on the day of his symbolic rebirth. The medallion was cast in solid gold and hung on a thick gold-link chain.

"It's beautiful," Devin breathed.

"I always carry mine," Pauly said, pulling his own copper coin with the triangle symbol out of his pocket. "But I had Harry Winston cast yours and mom's in eighteen-carat gold, because you two are pure gold."

"You've come a long way, Pauly," Devin said quietly.

"And learned a lot," he countered. "I've even learned that I miss my dad. He wasn't all bad, was he, Devin?"

"No," she said, reaching across the table to take one of the young man's hands in hers. "Of course he wasn't all bad."

Devin handed the gold piece to Tanner then, and he fastened it around her neck. "Thank you, Pauly," was all she could manage, with a catch in her throat.

"No, thank *you*," Paul Junior said. "Thanks for helping me through some rough times in the joint, Devin, and for nudging me into PT. I love the rag business!"

"I'm glad," Devin told him, "because one day you'll run the whole company. It's your birthright."

"Oh? And what will you be doing then?" he inquired.

"Hopefully, bringing up babies."

"I'll drink to that," Tanner raised his glass.

Bruno had come into the dining room. "Madame," he ventured, "the sea bass, may we serve?"

"Yes, Bruno, do serve the sea bass," Devin smiled. "And please, pour more wine. We all definitely need more wine."

Dinner was superb, and Devin and her guests loosened up completely and chatted nonstop. Billy Hilgarde had seconds of everything. Even Allena Bradshaw seemed more than usually outgoing and relaxed. Between dinner and dessert, Devin excused herself, indicating to Bruno as she passed him to refill the wineglasses. She ran upstairs to her master suite. After the laughter and a few tears, she wanted to do a quick patch on her makeup.

Before tackling her smudgy eyeliner, Devin sank gratefully into one of the soft down couches in her small sitting room and closed her eyes for a few moments. She thought about Pauly, who tugged at her heart when he said he missed his dad. She missed Paul a little, too—missed the good things about him. Only Allena's presence tonight had kept her from responding to Pauly that no, Paul Bradshaw was not all bad . . . *unlike his brother.*

Allena! Devin thought. Allena's gift was still in one of the roomy pockets of her caftan. She fished out the neatly wrapped box and untied the narrow gold cord wound several times around it. Nestled within several layers of white tissue was a small, exquisitely carved jade box, with a lid of solid gold and four tiny gold feet. Chinese, Devin knew, and rare.

Gently, she lifted the hinged golden lid and opened up the box . . . and froze. Engraved on the inside of the lid were the words:

To Allie
. . . with all my love,

Marva

"Oh God!" Devin exclaimed aloud to the empty room. *Allena Bradshaw was Marva's lover!* Suddenly she understood. That explained Allena's detachment from the family.

That explained why she chose a life of travel, working mostly in Europe. That explained why she never came to family functions with a date, never had a relationship she would talk about. That explained her mystery, her remoteness. That explained Allena.

And Marva. Marva had tap-danced around her broken love affair, had let Devin know that she was hurting. Devin should have drawn her out. She should have been there for her, listened to her. But something in Devin had raised a red flag, made her put Marva off, even after they'd become friends. It was probably the leftover vestiges of Pasadena conservatism in her soul that made her protect herself from hearing about Marva's gay relationship.

She felt new tears well up behind her eyes. She regretted her missed opportunity, fervently wishing that she had another chance to comfort Marva. But the truth was, she simply wasn't completely comfortable dealing with lesbianism. Marva—wonderful, outgoing, free-spirited Marva—had no such binding inhibitions.

But obviously Allena did. Allena's way of dealing with the fact that she was gay was to run and hide. But tonight was a major turning point for Allena, Devin knew—she had reached out to unburden her secret, and with it, Devin hoped, some of her grief.

Devin placed the little box carefully on the polished pine table next to the couch and went into her bathroom. She looked into the mirror and gasped. Beyond repair, she decided. She quickly dipped a cotton ball into a tub of cleansing cream and removed the black eyeliner smudges and most of the rest of her makeup with it. Her bare face shone, her eyes were red from weeping, but she dabbed on some lip gloss and ran her fingers through her short blond hair. Her guests would understand. Most of them had been through an emotional minefield tonight, too.

As she rejoined the group at table, she caught Bruno's eye and nodded for him to begin serving dessert. Maria and Laguya brought in bowls of steaming poached pears and two beautiful tartes tartin. Bruno poured coffee, then served small snifters of Sambuca Romana, floated with vanilla coffee beans. It was a wonderful dinner, Devin thought with satisfaction. But far beyond that, it had been a remarkable night.

They all sat for a while over coffee and liqueur and affable conversation, then the guests began to make moves to leave. All were mindful that Devin was still quite frail, and no one wanted to overtax her on her first social evening since she'd been so gravely injured. She and Tanner drifted to the front door to see them off. Allena came to the entryway and said a warm good night as she, too, prepared to go.

"Oh, no you don't," Devin smiled and pulled her back. "You and I have to talk."

Devin waved good-bye to the last of the guests, asked Tanner to excuse her for a few minutes, then steered Allena down the broad hallway and into the small library, where Maria always kept a cozy fire going in the evenings. She closed the door behind them and led Allena to the sofa in front of the fireplace.

"You opened my gift," Allena guessed, when they'd settled.

"Yes," Devin said. "So please help me understand. Why did you two break off your relationship?"

"I ended it," Allena said. "It had been going on for almost three years, since Marva first started working for L.A. Garb and I met her at the company Christmas party that year. But it was all too close to home for my comfort level, especially after she'd slept with Paul—" Allena stopped herself abruptly, raising her hand to her mouth.

"It's okay, I knew about that," Devin reassured her. "Marva told me."

"That's just it," Allena said. "Marva Modine was the most uninhibited free spirit I have ever known. Maybe she inherited the French savoir faire from her mother. But I could never be that way. I'm an attorney and a businesswoman. Marva was a model, an actress—her life was a seamless work of wonderfully eccentric performance art. It couldn't work for us. I couldn't even be comfortable with my sexual preference in this *country,* let alone in this fishbowl of a city, with a woman who worked for the family business, and in such a high-profile capacity."

Devin listened, and when Allena paused, she asked, "Why did you give the jade box to me, Allena? You should keep it."

"I have a lot of beautiful things to remember Marva by, and beautiful memories. But I think you know why I gave you the box. Because you cared for Marva, too. Oh, not the way I did, but you loved her. She told me she felt that, and it was very important to her while we both adjusted to an extremely painful breakup."

"Yes," Devin said, and she found herself holding back yet another onslaught of tears. "I did love Marva. Do love her. I miss her terribly."

"So do I," Allena returned, and Devin saw her eyes moisten too. "You know," Allena offered then, "all my life I kept my secret and kept my distance because I didn't want to embarrass my family. What a joke!" she managed, shaking her head.

Now her tears flowed freely. Devin moved to put an arm around her. "What are you going to do now, Allena?"

"That's another big chunk of irony," Allena said huskily. "Now it would hardly matter to the family if I came home and made a life with Marva, would it? But now it's too late."

"But it's not too late for you to be true to yourself. To stop running and make a good life with someone, with your head held high."

"It's still hard," Allena returned. "I wouldn't be known as an accomplished attorney—I'd be called a lesbian lawyer."

"Allena, this is the nineties," Devin protested. "You work in the music business. Are Elton John, Melissa Ethridge, or k. d. lang going to care? I don't think *Frank Sinatra* would give a damn about your sexual preference, as long as you got him a good contract."

Allena smiled. "You are truly a friend," she said. "That's the other reason why I gave you the little jade box. To tell you about myself and to invite your friendship."

"You have my friendship," Devin told the woman. "I felt a connection to you from the first. Though we'd never really talked, Allena, I always had the feeling that you were the only Bradshaw with whom I could feel simpatico at all. Now, of course, there's Pauly and Rosemary."

"Yes, they're special," Allena said. "Maybe there's hope for rapprochement between myself and my family."

"Include me in your family," Devin smiled.

"I do. And now I'm going to leave you to my colleague, your very special John Tanner. I'm happy for you, Devin," she said, getting up from the sofa. Then she added, "And

I'm going to think about what you said. Who knows, maybe I *can* go home again."

Devin stood and gave Allena another hug. The two walked arm in arm out of the library, down the hall, and to the front door, where they said their good nights. Closing the door behind Allena, Devin turned to see Tanner standing in the living room, looking at her with eyes full of concern and love. *Her* Tanner!

"Oh, John," she said, moving toward him. "I am absolutely exhausted—mentally, physically, emotionally, and every other way conceivable. What a night!"

Tanner closed the distance between them in six giant steps and scooped her up gently in his arms.

"Darling Devin," he said, kissing her lightly on the cheek. "Mmm, salty," he smiled, tasting the new tears she'd just shed.

"Oh, I know," she apologized. "I am absolutely cried out, I promise."

Tanner started up the stairs with Devin cradled in his arms. "I'm putting you to bed, my lovely," he whispered.

"I have a better idea," Devin murmured, her head snuggled against his shoulder. "*Take* me to bed, darling."